Sorceline
Book 2

SYLVIA DOUYÉ

Illustrated by
PAOLA ANTISTA

Colors by
LOWENAEL AND MARINA DUCLOS

Translated by
TANYA GOLD

Andrews McMeel
PUBLISHING®

Andrews McMeel Publishing
a division of Andrews McMeel Universal
1130 Walnut Street, Kansas City, Missouri 64106

www.andrewsmcmeel.com

Published in French by Editions Glénat as two volumes:

Original Title: Sorceline – *Tome 04 : Rêve et cauchemort!*
Authors: Sylvia Douyé (Text) & Paola Antista (Artwork)
© Editions Glénat 2021 by Douyé & Antista – ALL RIGHTS RESERVED

Original Title: Sorceline – *Tome 05 : Le Saigneur de Vorn*
Authors: Sylvia Douyé (Text) & Paola Antista (Artwork)
© Editions Glénat 2022 by Douyé & Antista – ALL RIGHTS RESERVED

23 24 25 26 27 SDB 10 9 8 7 6 5 4 3 2 1

ISBN: 978-1-5248-8231-0

Library of Congress Control Number: 2021948437

Made by:
RR Donnelley (Guangdong) Printing Solutions Company Ltd.
Address and location of manufacturer:
No. 2, Minzhu Road, Daning, Humen Town,
Dongguan City, Guangdong Province, China 523930
1st Printing – 3/27/23

ATTENTION: SCHOOLS AND BUSINESSES
Andrews McMeel books are available at quantity discounts with bulk purchase for educational, business, or sales promotional use. For information, please e-mail the Andrews McMeel Publishing Special Sales Department: sales@amuniversal.com.

Part 1

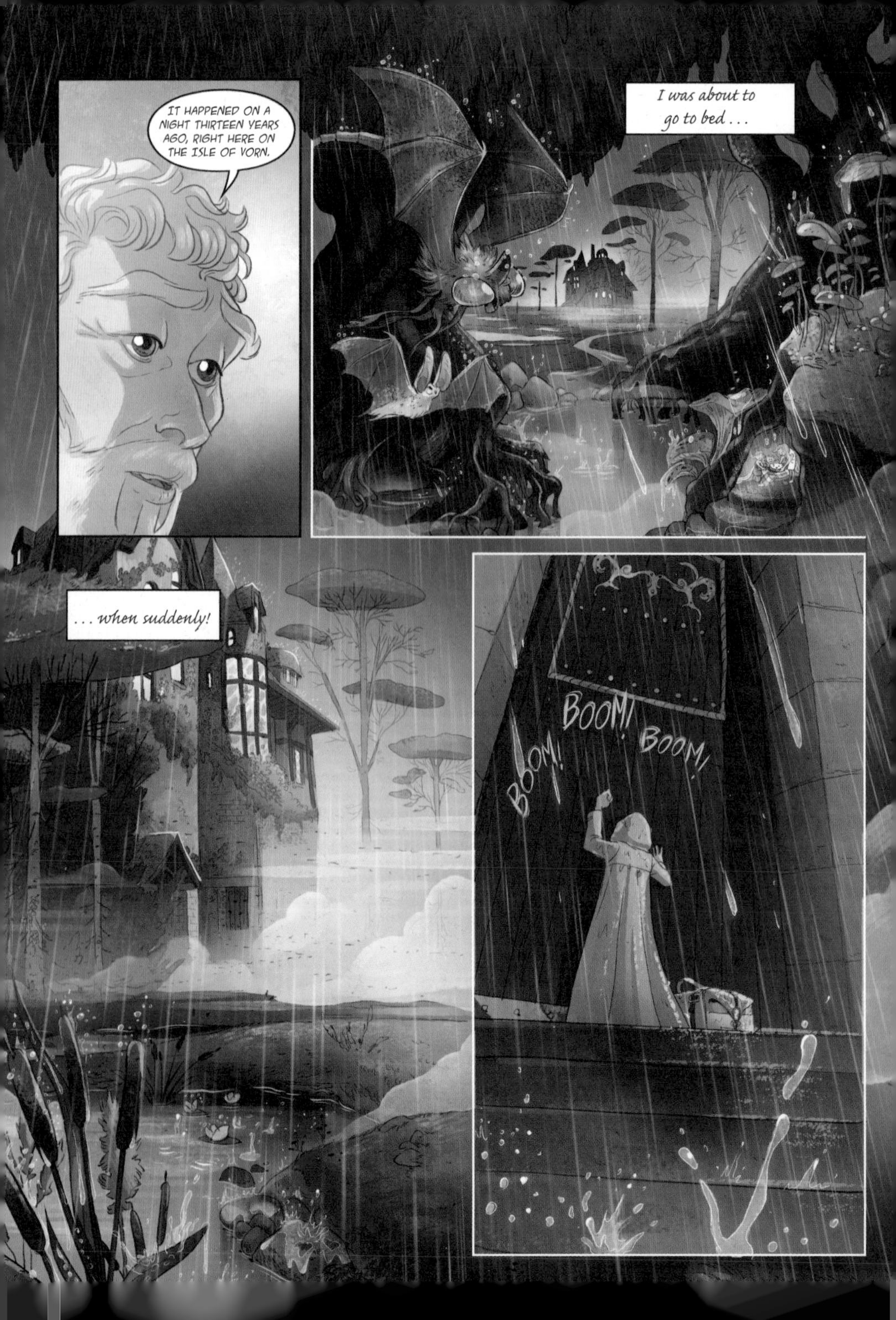
IT HAPPENED ON A NIGHT THIRTEEN YEARS AGO, RIGHT HERE ON THE ISLE OF VORN.
I was about to go to bed . . .
. . . when suddenly!
BOOM!
BOOM!
BOOM!

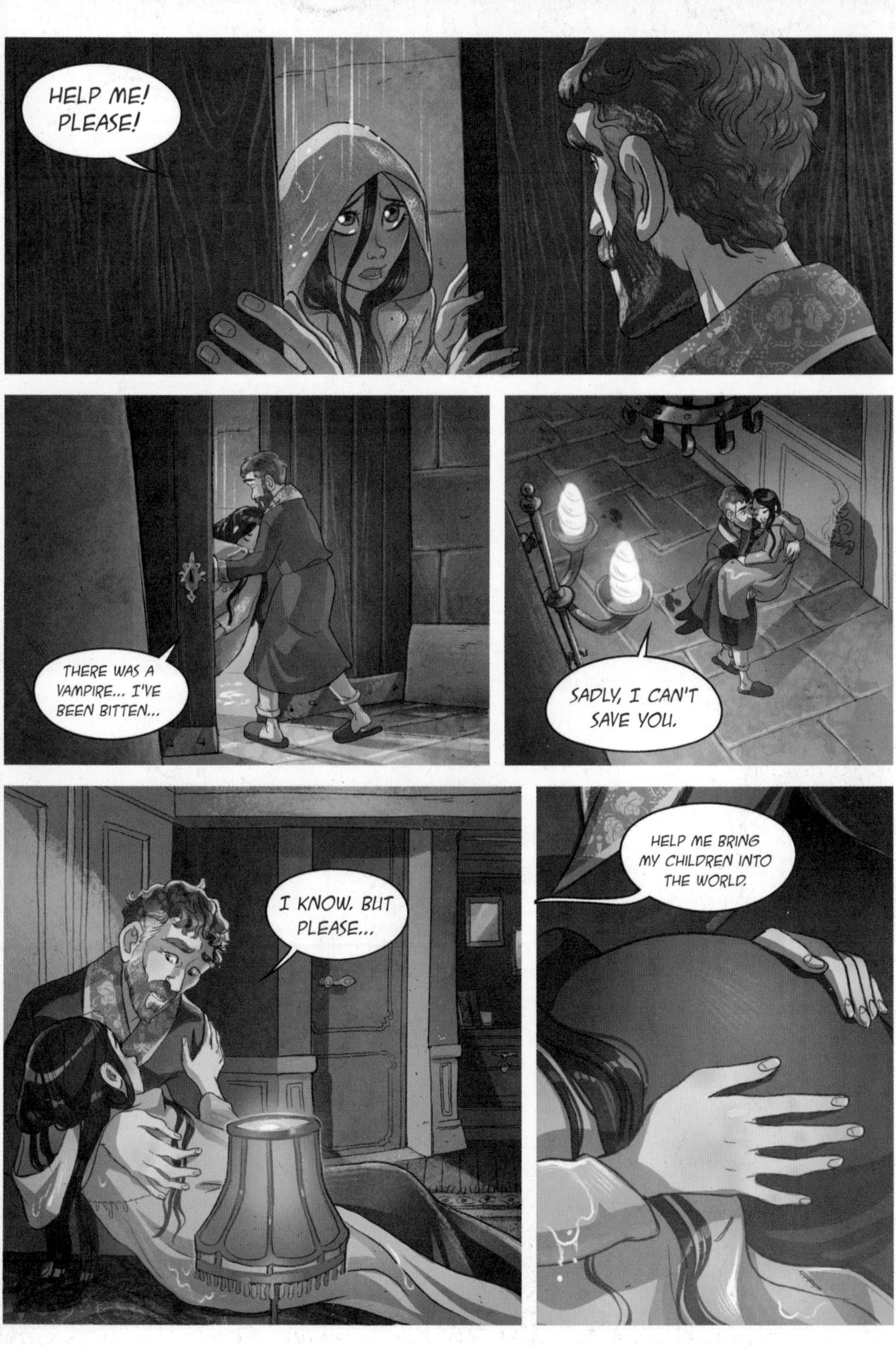
HELP ME! PLEASE!
THERE WAS A VAMPIRE... I'VE BEEN BITTEN...
SADLY, I CAN'T SAVE YOU.
I KNOW. BUT PLEASE...
HELP ME BRING MY CHILDREN INTO THE WORLD.

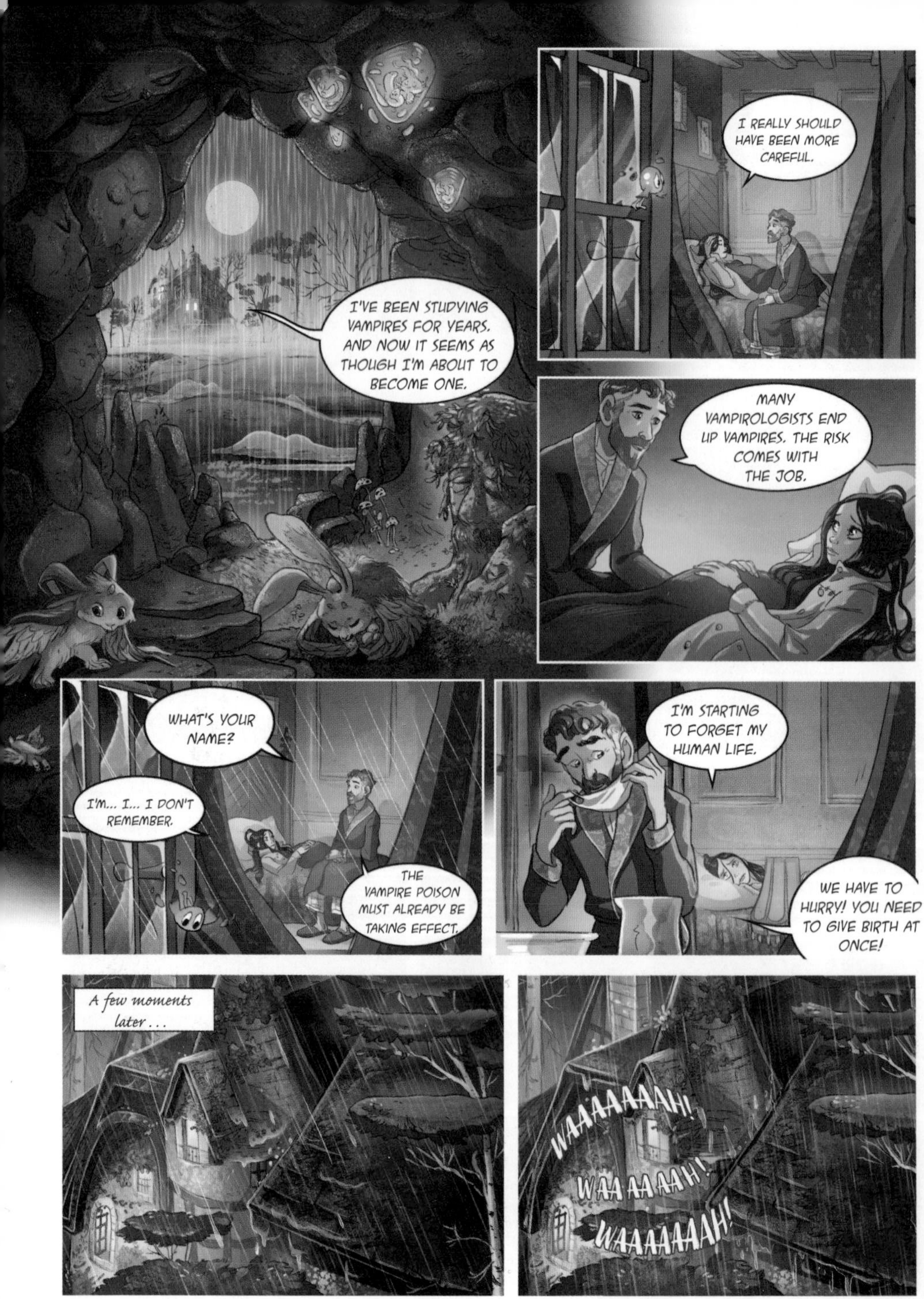
I'VE BEEN STUDYING VAMPIRES FOR YEARS. AND NOW IT SEEMS AS THOUGH I'M ABOUT TO BECOME ONE.
I REALLY SHOULD HAVE BEEN MORE CAREFUL.
MANY VAMPIROLOGISTS END UP VAMPIRES. THE RISK COMES WITH THE JOB.
WHAT'S YOUR NAME?
I'M... I... I DON'T REMEMBER.
THE VAMPIRE POISON MUST ALREADY BE TAKING EFFECT.
I'M STARTING TO FORGET MY HUMAN LIFE.
WE HAVE TO HURRY! YOU NEED TO GIVE BIRTH AT ONCE!
A few moments later . . .
WAAAAAAAH!
WAA AA AAH!
WAAAAAAAH!

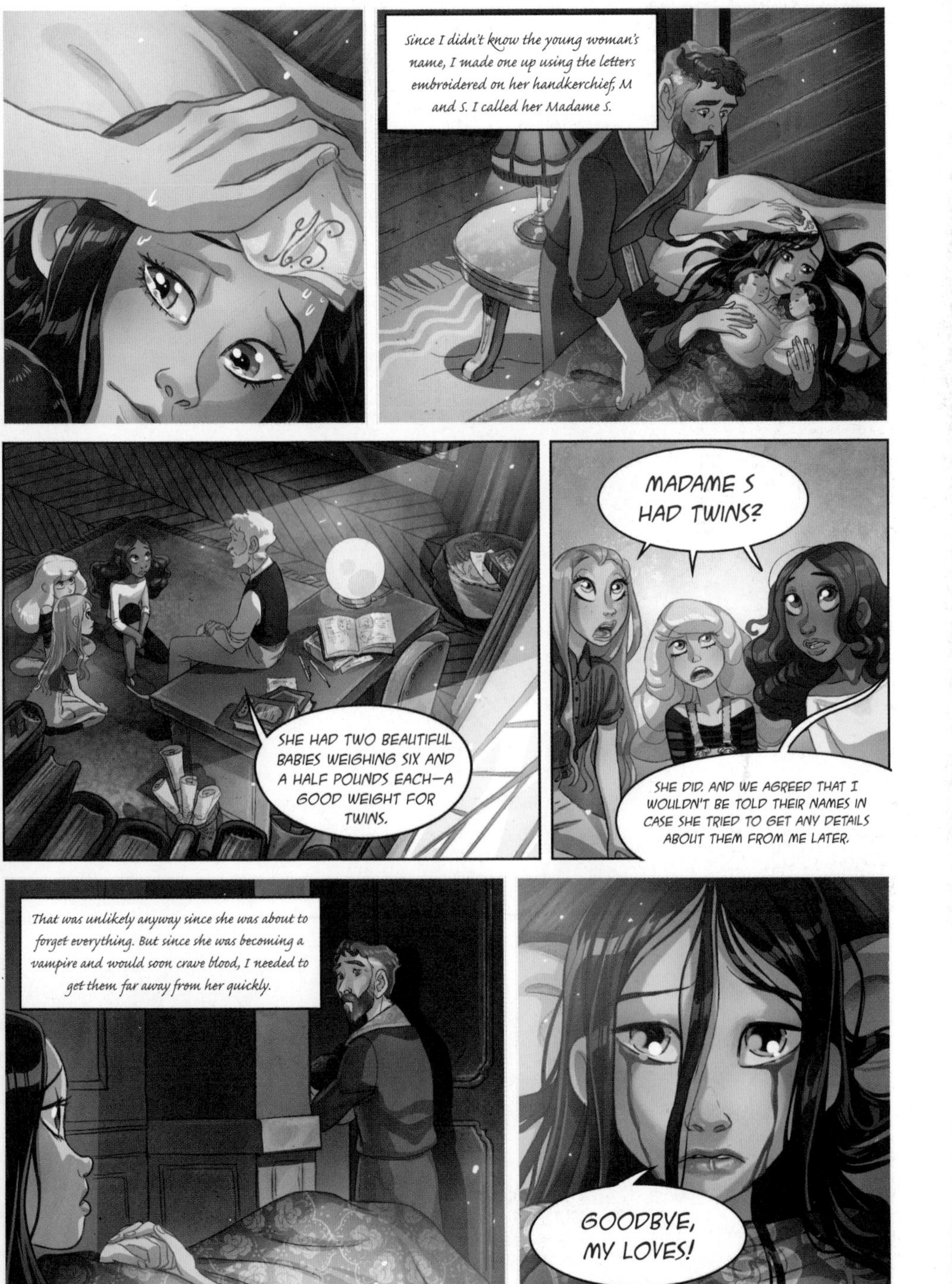

Since I didn't know the young woman's name, I made one up using the letters embroidered on her handkerchief, M and S. I called her Madame S.
SHE HAD TWO BEAUTIFUL BABIES WEIGHING SIX AND A HALF POUNDS EACH—A GOOD WEIGHT FOR TWINS.
MADAME S HAD TWINS?
SHE DID. AND WE AGREED THAT I WOULDN'T BE TOLD THEIR NAMES IN CASE SHE TRIED TO GET ANY DETAILS ABOUT THEM FROM ME LATER.
That was unlikely anyway since she was about to forget everything. But since she was becoming a vampire and would soon crave blood, I needed to get them far away from her quickly.
GOODBYE, MY LOVES!

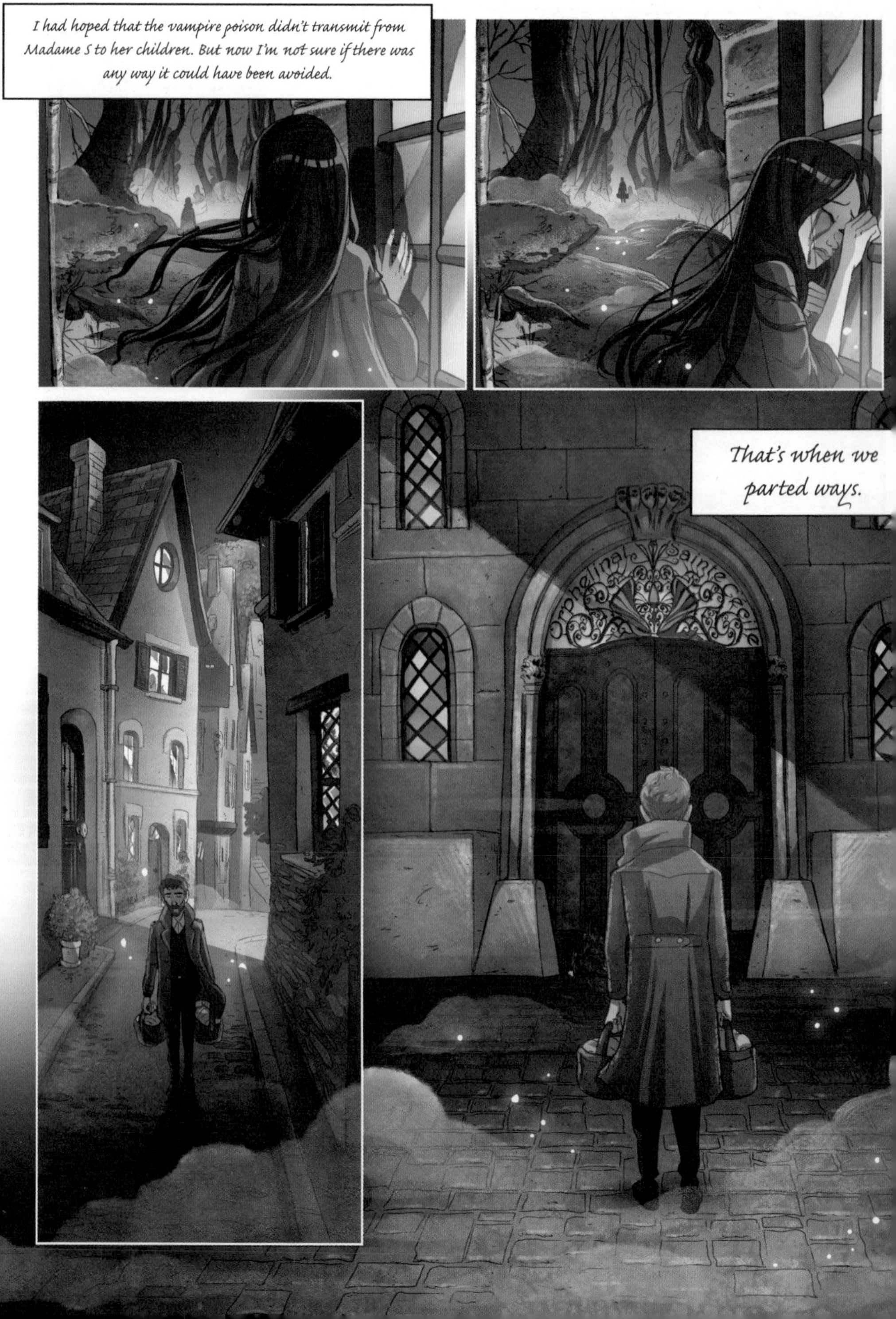
I had hoped that the vampire poison didn't transmit from Madame S to her children. But now I'm not sure if there was any way it could have been avoided.
That's when we parted ways.
Orphelinat Sainte Cécile

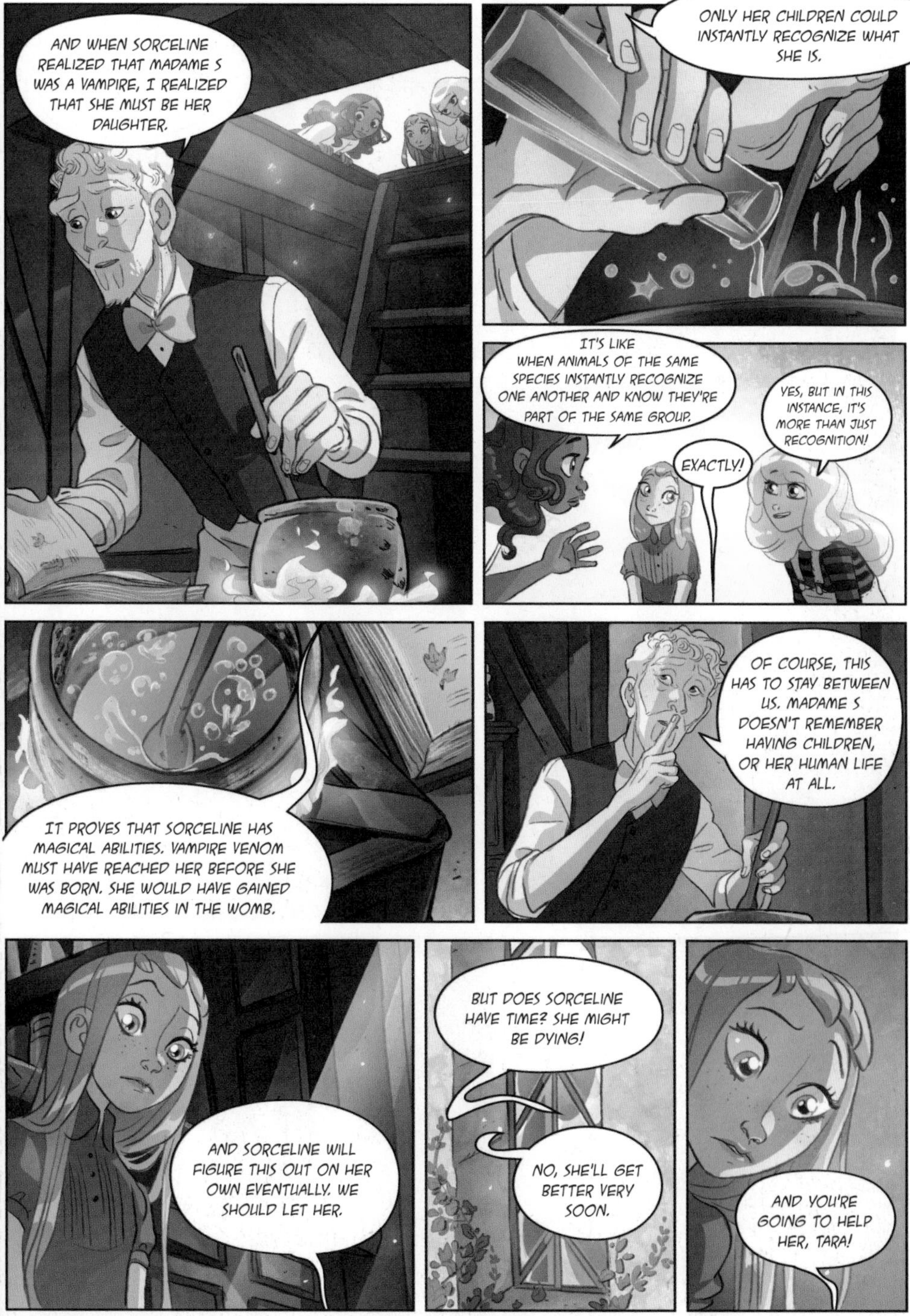

AND WHEN SORCELINE REALIZED THAT MADAME S WAS A VAMPIRE, I REALIZED THAT SHE MUST BE HER DAUGHTER.
ONLY HER CHILDREN COULD INSTANTLY RECOGNIZE WHAT SHE IS.
IT'S LIKE WHEN ANIMALS OF THE SAME SPECIES INSTANTLY RECOGNIZE ONE ANOTHER AND KNOW THEY'RE PART OF THE SAME GROUP.
EXACTLY!
YES, BUT IN THIS INSTANCE, IT'S MORE THAN JUST RECOGNITION!
IT PROVES THAT SORCELINE HAS MAGICAL ABILITIES. VAMPIRE VENOM MUST HAVE REACHED HER BEFORE SHE WAS BORN. SHE WOULD HAVE GAINED MAGICAL ABILITIES IN THE WOMB.
OF COURSE, THIS HAS TO STAY BETWEEN US. MADAME S DOESN'T REMEMBER HAVING CHILDREN, OR HER HUMAN LIFE AT ALL.
AND SORCELINE WILL FIGURE THIS OUT ON HER OWN EVENTUALLY. WE SHOULD LET HER.
BUT DOES SORCELINE HAVE TIME? SHE MIGHT BE DYING!
NO, SHE'LL GET BETTER VERY SOON.
AND YOU'RE GOING TO HELP HER, TARA!

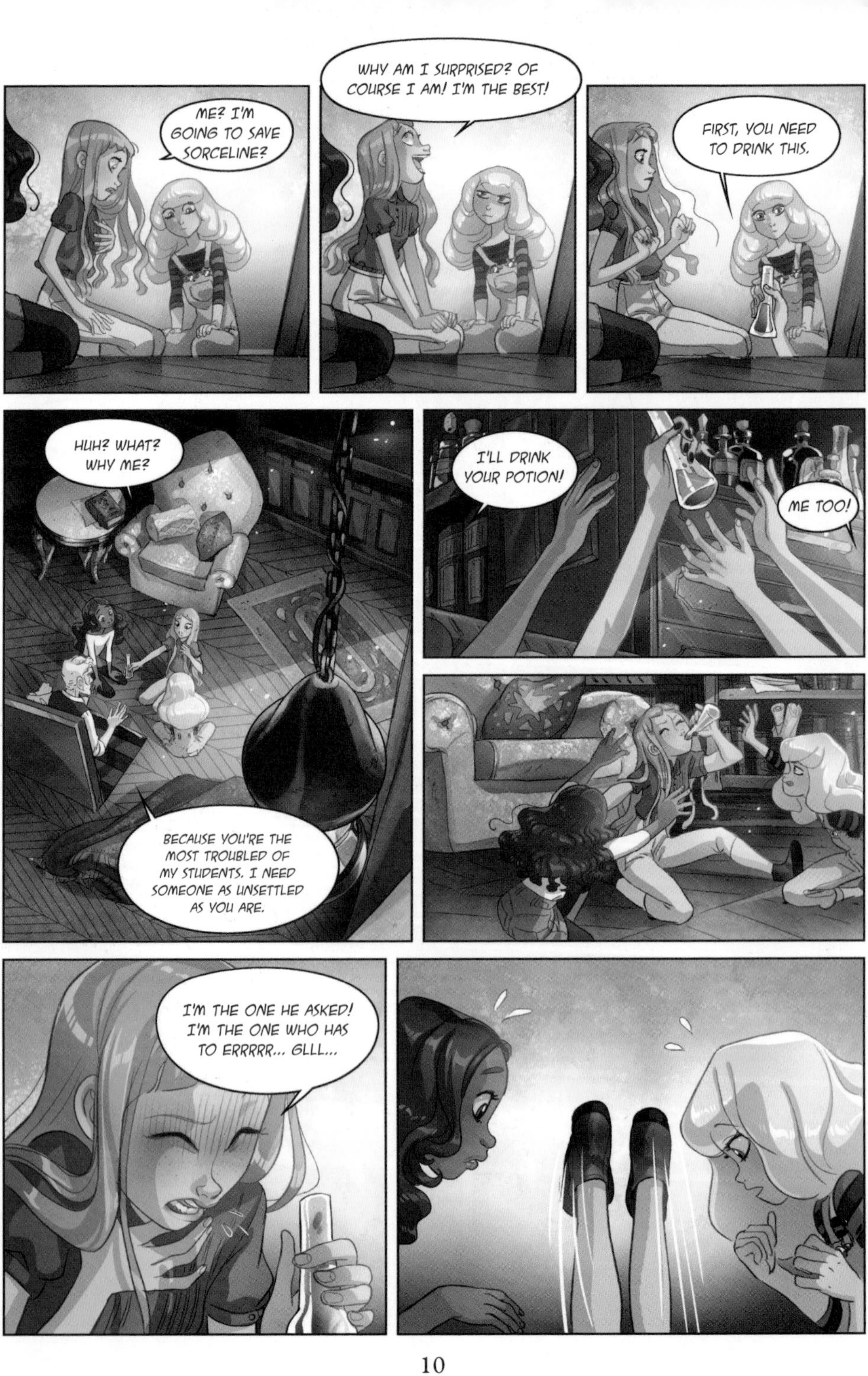
ME? I'M GOING TO SAVE SORCELINE?
WHY AM I SURPRISED? OF COURSE I AM! I'M THE BEST!
FIRST, YOU NEED TO DRINK THIS.
HUH? WHAT? WHY ME?
BECAUSE YOU'RE THE MOST TROUBLED OF MY STUDENTS. I NEED SOMEONE AS UNSETTLED AS YOU ARE.
I'LL DRINK YOUR POTION!
ME TOO!
I'M THE ONE HE ASKED! I'M THE ONE WHO HAS TO ERRRRR... GLLL...

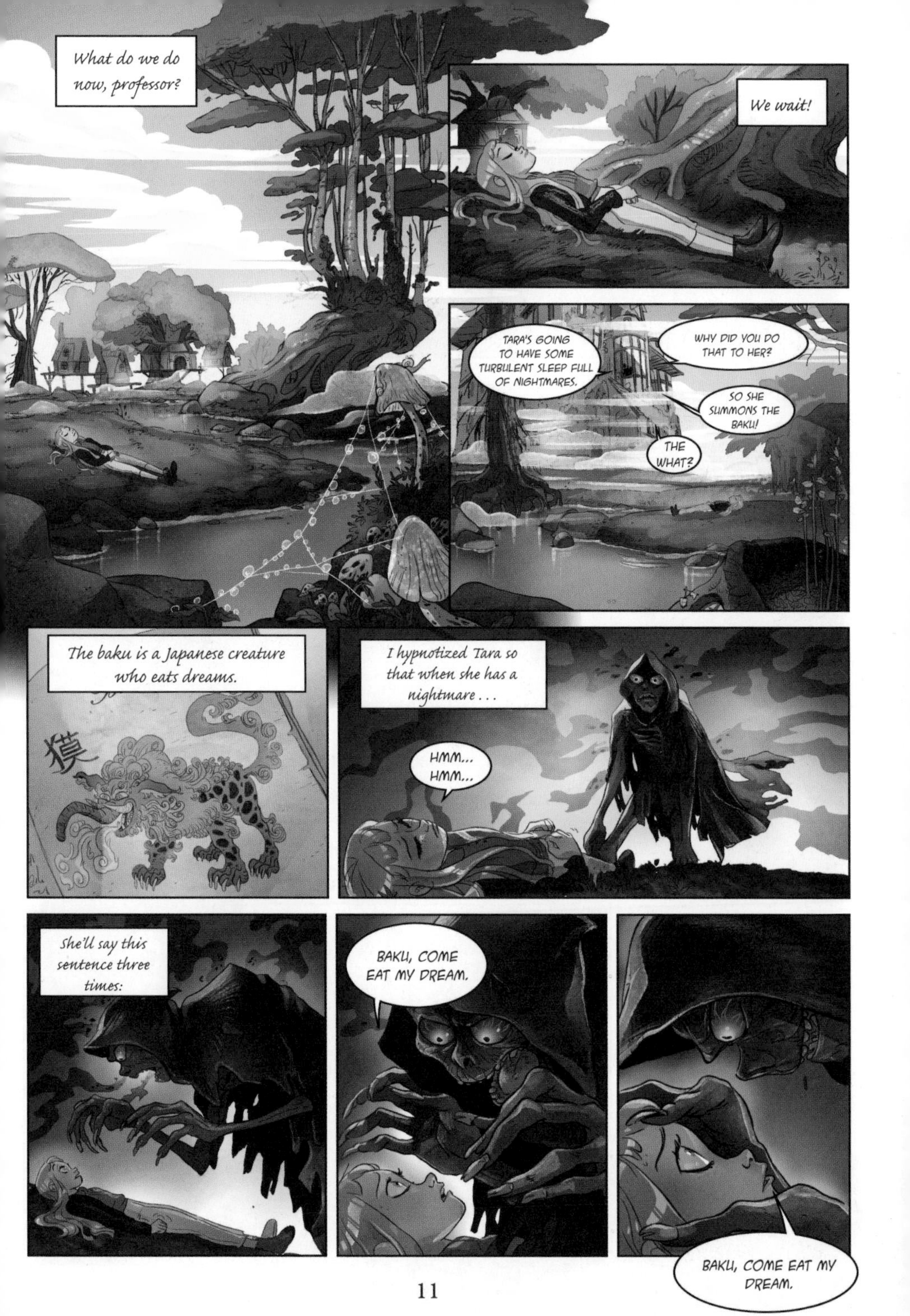
What do we do now, professor?
We wait!
TARA'S GOING TO HAVE SOME TURBULENT SLEEP FULL OF NIGHTMARES.
WHY DID YOU DO THAT TO HER?
SO SHE SUMMONS THE BAKU!
THE WHAT?
The baku is a Japanese creature who eats dreams.
獏
I hypnotized Tara so that when she has a nightmare . . .
HMM... HMM...
She'll say this sentence three times:
BAKU, COME EAT MY DREAM.
BAKU, COME EAT MY DREAM.

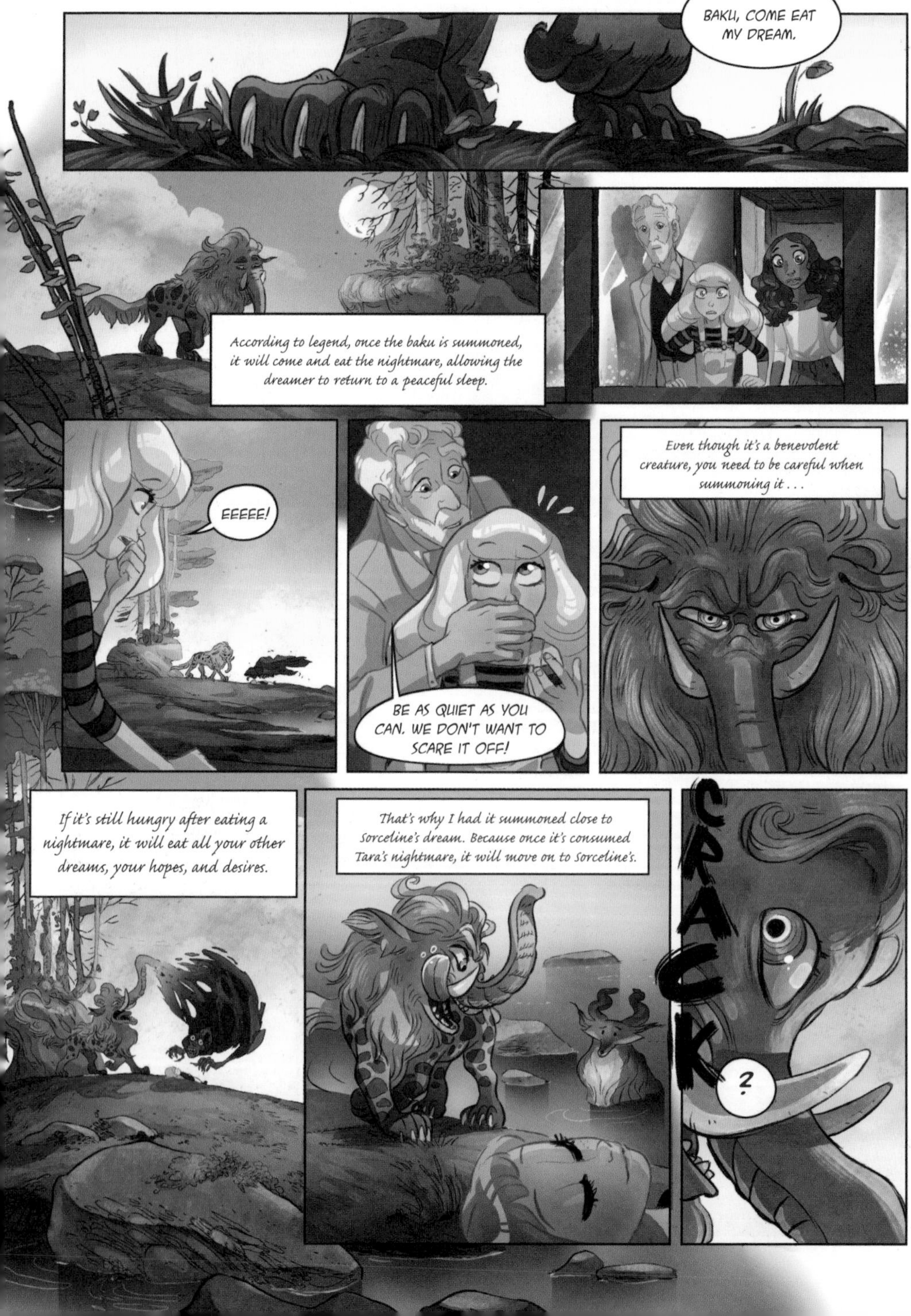

BAKU, COME EAT MY DREAM.
According to legend, once the baku is summoned, it will come and eat the nightmare, allowing the dreamer to return to a peaceful sleep.
EEEEE!
BE AS QUIET AS YOU CAN. WE DON'T WANT TO SCARE IT OFF!
Even though it's a benevolent creature, you need to be careful when summoning it . . .
If it's still hungry after eating a nightmare, it will eat all your other dreams, your hopes, and desires.
That's why I had it summoned close to Sorceline's dream. Because once it's consumed Tara's nightmare, it will move on to Sorceline's.
CRACK
?

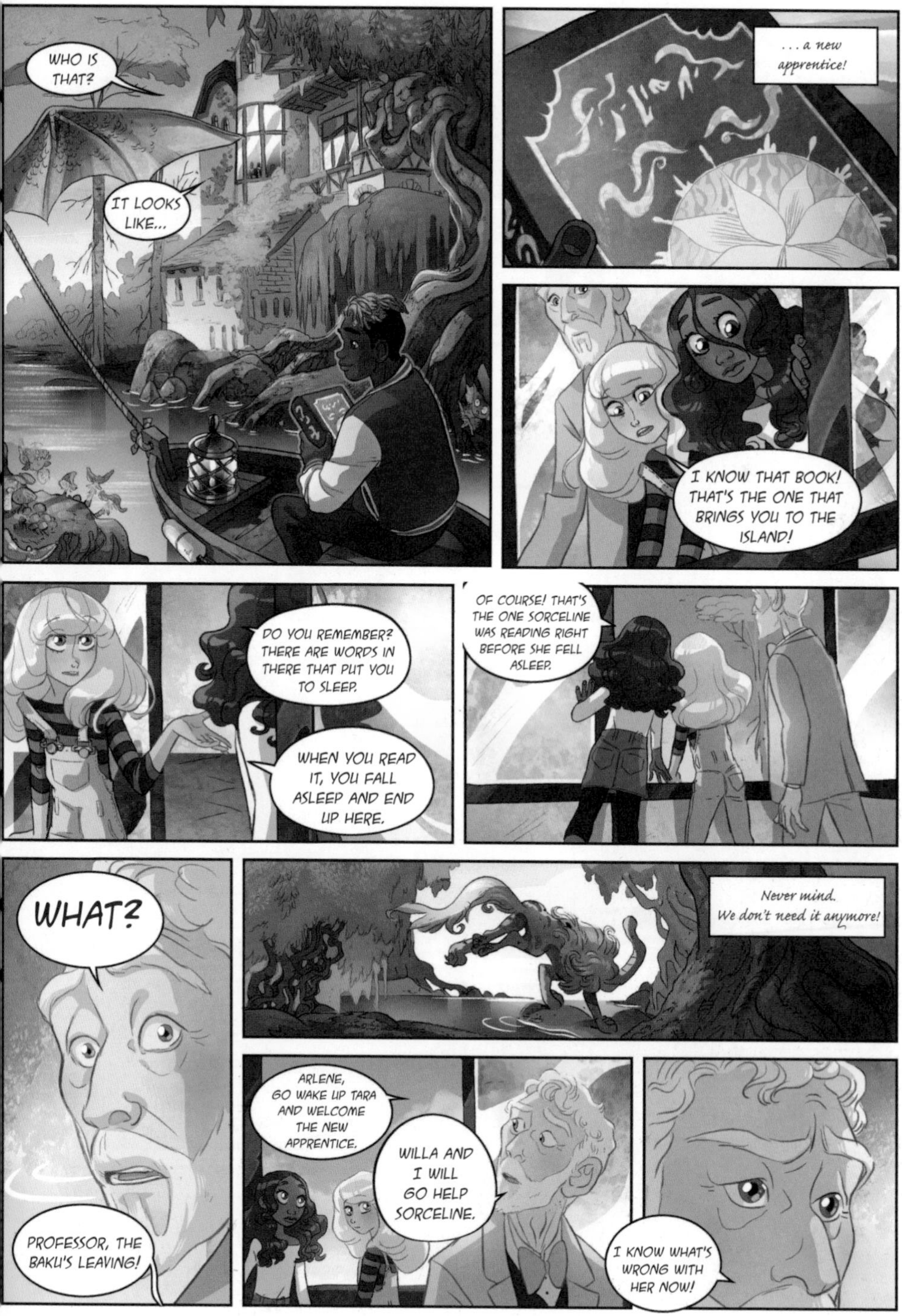
WHO IS THAT?
IT LOOKS LIKE...
. . . a new apprentice!
I KNOW THAT BOOK! THAT'S THE ONE THAT BRINGS YOU TO THE ISLAND!
DO YOU REMEMBER? THERE ARE WORDS IN THERE THAT PUT YOU TO SLEEP.
WHEN YOU READ IT, YOU FALL ASLEEP AND END UP HERE.
OF COURSE! THAT'S THE ONE SORCELINE WAS READING RIGHT BEFORE SHE FELL ASLEEP.
WHAT?
PROFESSOR, THE BAKU'S LEAVING!
Never mind. We don't need it anymore!
ARLENE, GO WAKE UP TARA AND WELCOME THE NEW APPRENTICE.
WILLA AND I WILL GO HELP SORCELINE.
I KNOW WHAT'S WRONG WITH HER NOW!

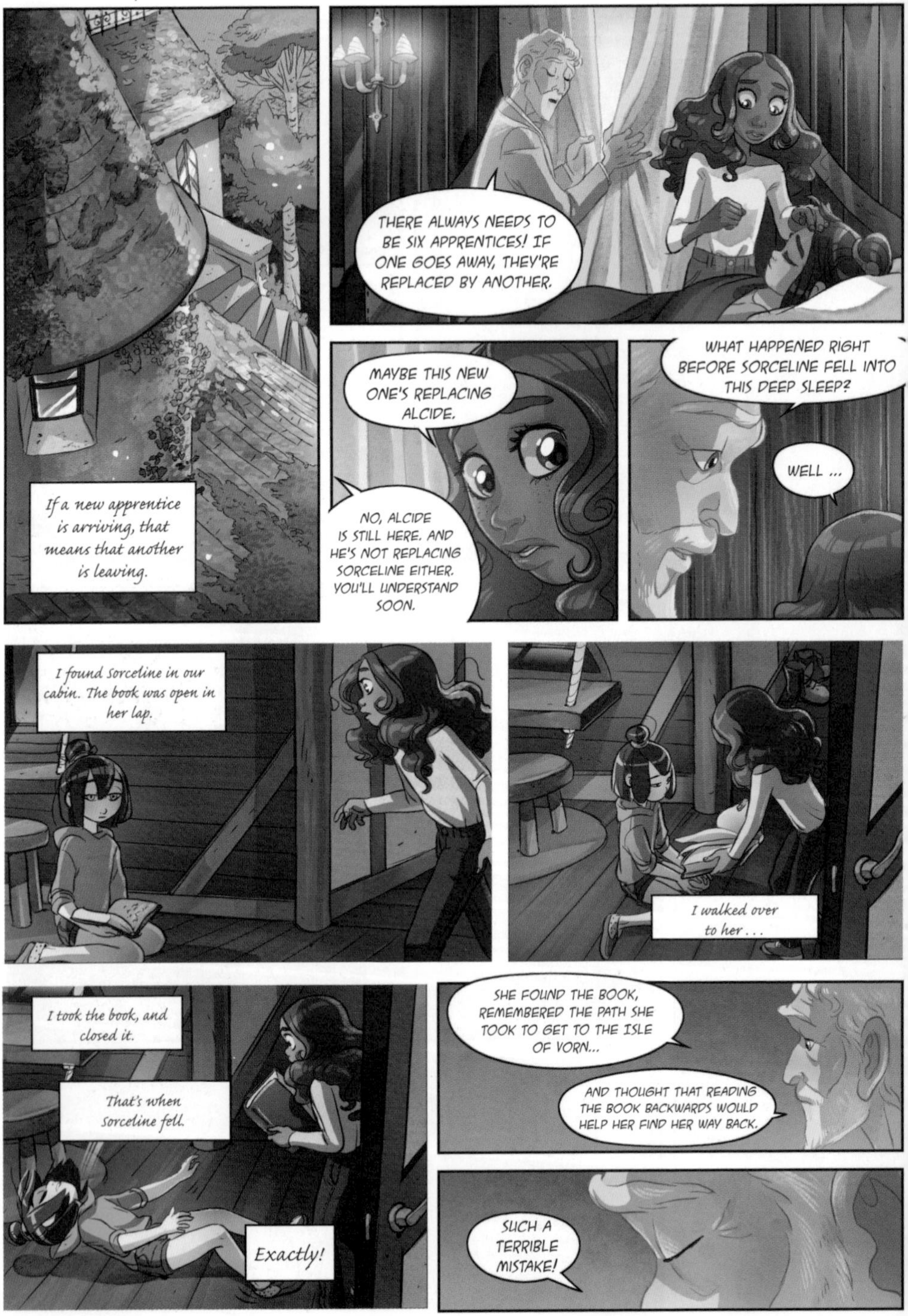
If a new apprentice is arriving, that means that another is leaving.
THERE ALWAYS NEEDS TO BE SIX APPRENTICES! IF ONE GOES AWAY, THEY'RE REPLACED BY ANOTHER.
MAYBE THIS NEW ONE'S REPLACING ALCIDE.
NO, ALCIDE IS STILL HERE. AND HE'S NOT REPLACING SORCELINE EITHER. YOU'LL UNDERSTAND SOON.
WHAT HAPPENED RIGHT BEFORE SORCELINE FELL INTO THIS DEEP SLEEP?
WELL ...
I found Sorceline in our cabin. The book was open in her lap.
I walked over to her . . .
I took the book, and closed it.
That's when Sorceline fell.
Exactly!
SHE FOUND THE BOOK, REMEMBERED THE PATH SHE TOOK TO GET TO THE ISLE OF VORN...
AND THOUGHT THAT READING THE BOOK BACKWARDS WOULD HELP HER FIND HER WAY BACK.
SUCH A TERRIBLE MISTAKE!

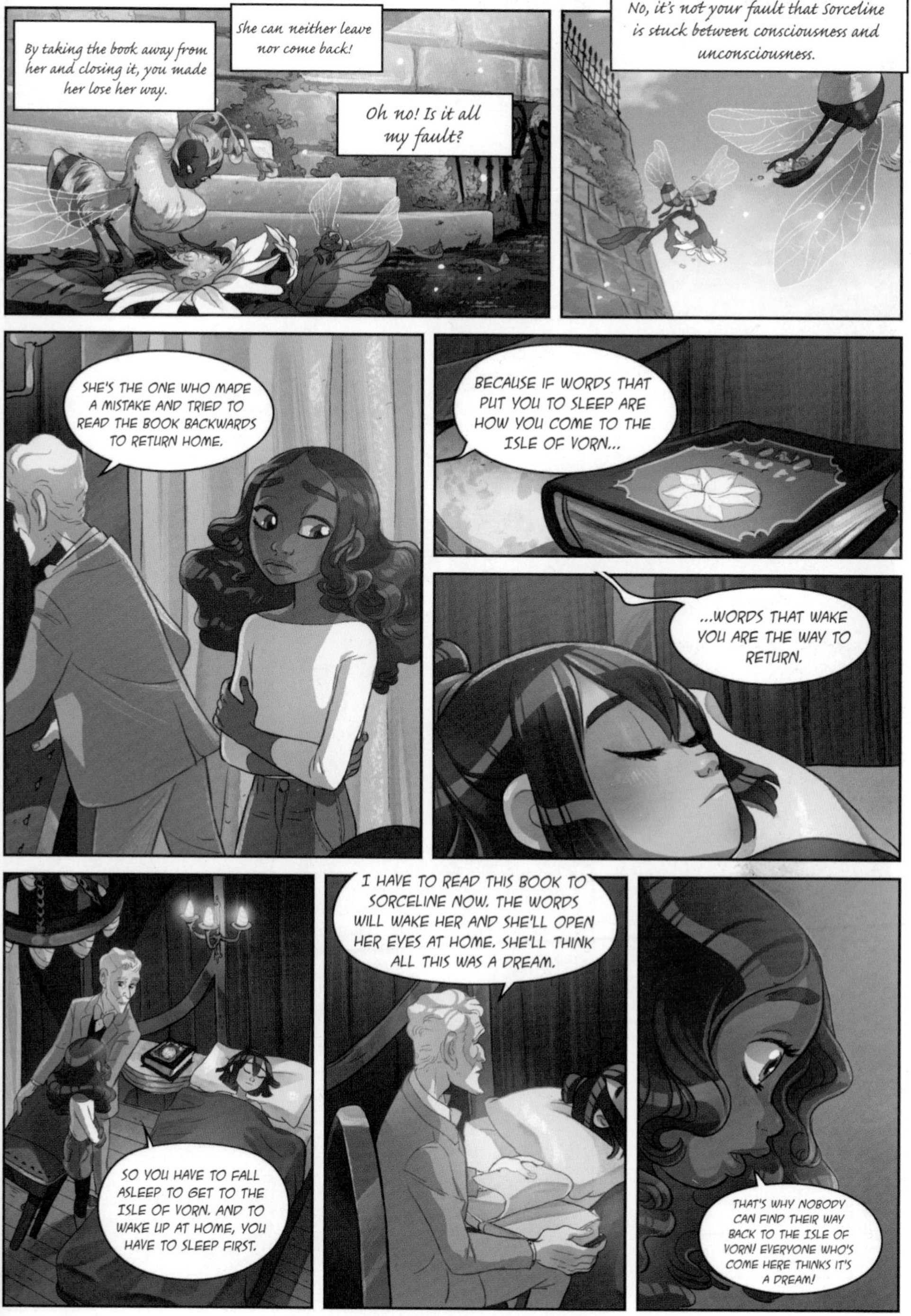
By taking the book away from her and closing it, you made her lose her way.
She can neither leave nor come back!
Oh no! Is it all my fault?
No, it's not your fault that Sorceline is stuck between consciousness and unconsciousness.
SHE'S THE ONE WHO MADE A MISTAKE AND TRIED TO READ THE BOOK BACKWARDS TO RETURN HOME.
BECAUSE IF WORDS THAT PUT YOU TO SLEEP ARE HOW YOU COME TO THE ISLE OF VORN...
...WORDS THAT WAKE YOU ARE THE WAY TO RETURN.
SO YOU HAVE TO FALL ASLEEP TO GET TO THE ISLE OF VORN. AND TO WAKE UP AT HOME, YOU HAVE TO SLEEP FIRST.
I HAVE TO READ THIS BOOK TO SORCELINE NOW. THE WORDS WILL WAKE HER AND SHE'LL OPEN HER EYES AT HOME. SHE'LL THINK ALL THIS WAS A DREAM.
THAT'S WHY NOBODY CAN FIND THEIR WAY BACK TO THE ISLE OF VORN! EVERYONE WHO'S COME HERE THINKS IT'S A DREAM!

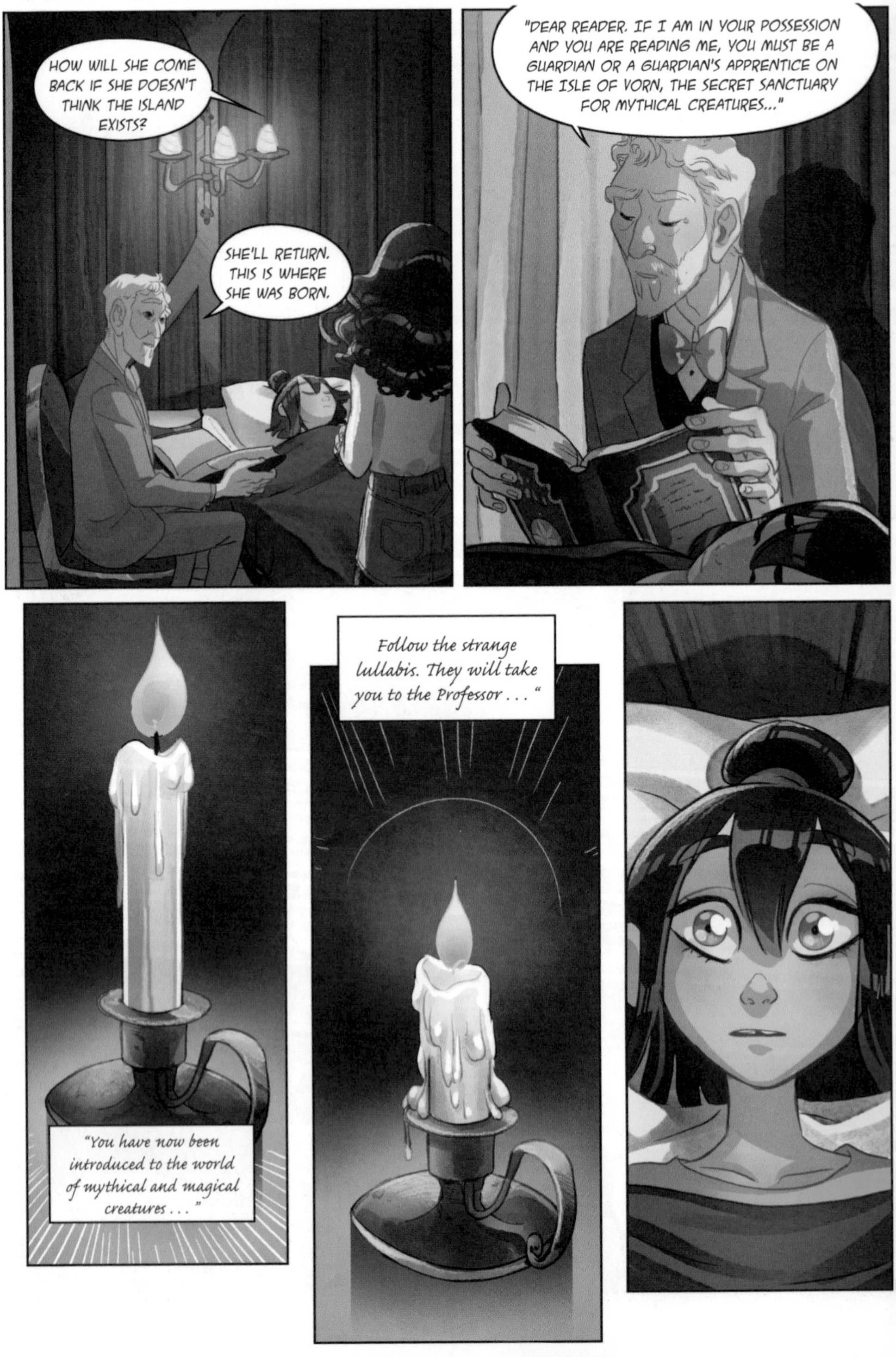

HOW WILL SHE COME BACK IF SHE DOESN'T THINK THE ISLAND EXISTS?
SHE'LL RETURN. THIS IS WHERE SHE WAS BORN.
"DEAR READER. IF I AM IN YOUR POSSESSION AND YOU ARE READING ME, YOU MUST BE A GUARDIAN OR A GUARDIAN'S APPRENTICE ON THE ISLE OF VORN, THE SECRET SANCTUARY FOR MYTHICAL CREATURES..."
"You have now been introduced to the world of mythical and magical creatures . . ."
Follow the strange lullabis. They will take you to the Professor . . . "

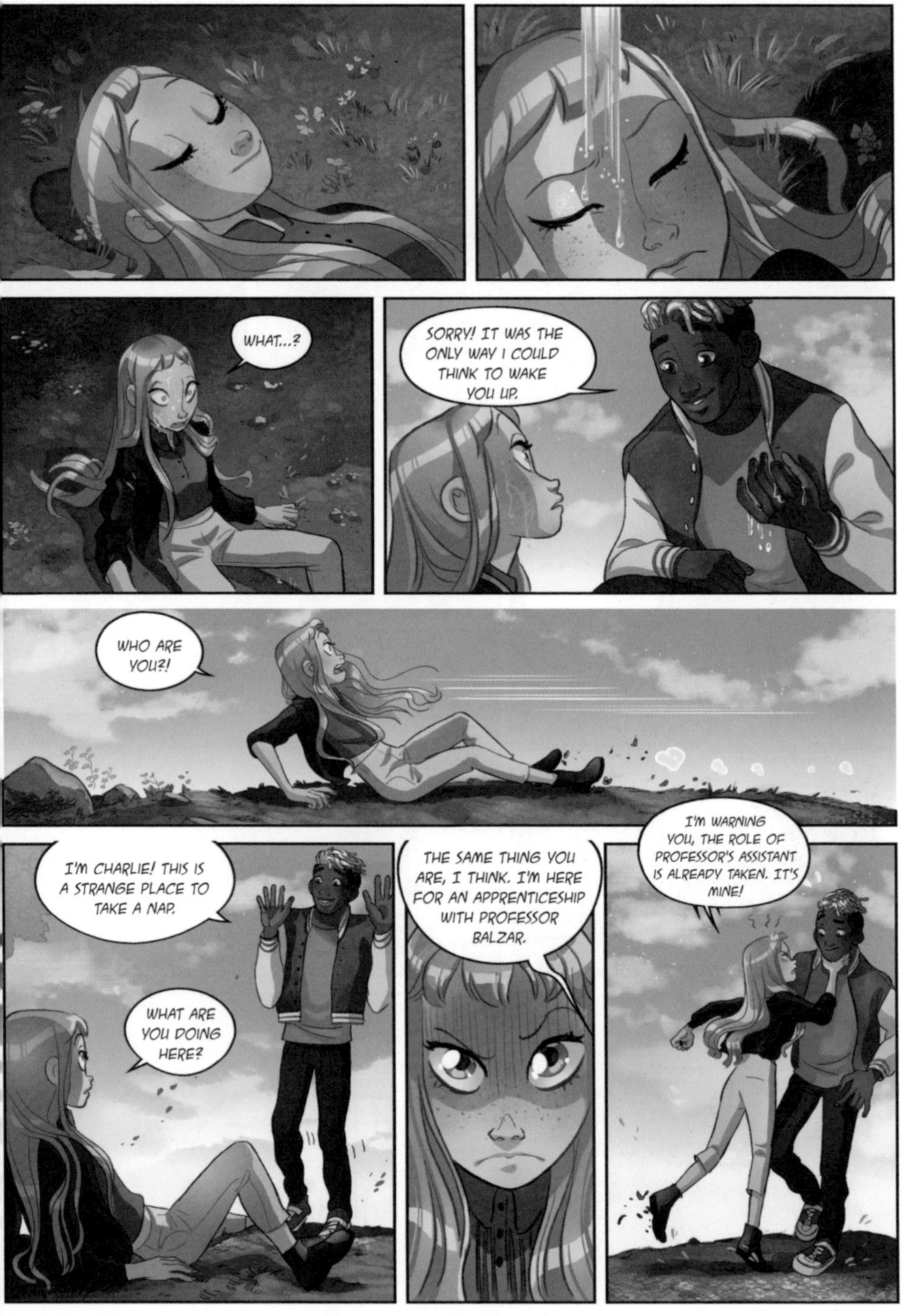
WHAT...?
SORRY! IT WAS THE ONLY WAY I COULD THINK TO WAKE YOU UP.
WHO ARE YOU?!
I'M CHARLIE! THIS IS A STRANGE PLACE TO TAKE A NAP.
WHAT ARE YOU DOING HERE?
THE SAME THING YOU ARE, I THINK. I'M HERE FOR AN APPRENTICESHIP WITH PROFESSOR BALZAR.
I'M WARNING YOU, THE ROLE OF PROFESSOR'S ASSISTANT IS ALREADY TAKEN. IT'S MINE!

TARA! THAT'S NO WAY TO WELCOME A NEW APPRENTICE!

WHAT ARE YOU CARRYING? A GNOME?

I FOUND HIM ON THE WAY HERE. HE'S DYING OF LAUGHTER. HE'LL END UP CHOKING.

YOU'RE RIGHT! LOOK, HE HAS A FEVER BLISTER!

HE MUST HAVE HILARIOUS HERPES! MAKING HIM LAU... UNCONTROLLABL...

DO YOU WANT TO HOLD HIM? HE COULD BE YOUR FIRST PATIENT.

LET'S BRING HIM TO THE MANOR.

WHAT ARE YOU TALKING ABOUT?

WHAT ARE YOU TALKING ABOUT?

OH NO! YOU CAN'T SEE MYTHICAL CREATURES?

I THOUGHT THAT ONCE I GOT TO THE ISLAND, I'D SOMEHOW BE ABLE TO SEE THEM.

DON'T WORRY. YOU MIGHT GET THERE.

THAT'S NOT TRUE! EITHER YOU SEE THEM OR YOU DON'T. IT'S LIKE ANIMALS THAT CAN SEE ULTRAVIOLET.

YOU HAVE THE ABILITY OR YOU DON'T. YOU CAN'T ACQUIRE IT.

SORRY...

...I DOUBT YOU'LL BE ABLE TO BECOME THE PROFESSOR'S ASSISTANT WITH THAT PROBLEM.

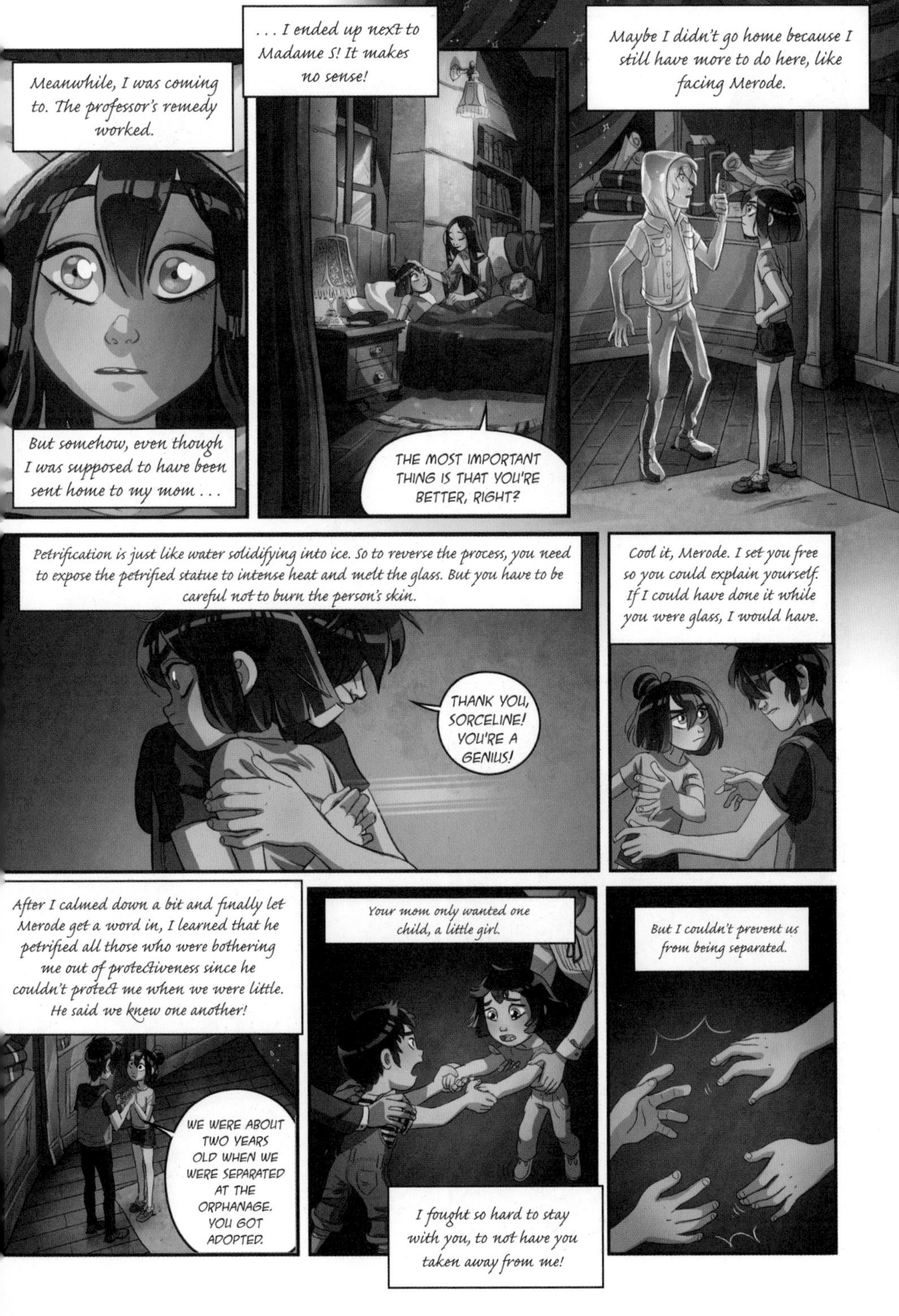

Meanwhile, I was coming to. The professor's remedy worked.
But somehow, even though I was supposed to have been sent home to my mom . . .
. . . I ended up next to Madame S! It makes no sense!
THE MOST IMPORTANT THING IS THAT YOU'RE BETTER, RIGHT?
Maybe I didn't go home because I still have more to do here, like facing Merode.
Petrification is just like water solidifying into ice. So to reverse the process, you need to expose the petrified statue to intense heat and melt the glass. But you have to be careful not to burn the person's skin.
THANK YOU, SORCELINE! YOU'RE A GENIUS!
Cool it, Merode. I set you free so you could explain yourself. If I could have done it while you were glass, I would have.
After I calmed down a bit and finally let Merode get a word in, I learned that he petrified all those who were bothering me out of protectiveness since he couldn't protect me when we were little. He said we knew one another!
WE WERE ABOUT TWO YEARS OLD WHEN WE WERE SEPARATED AT THE ORPHANAGE. YOU GOT ADOPTED.
Your mom only wanted one child, a little girl.
I fought so hard to stay with you, to not have you taken away from me!
But I couldn't prevent us from being separated.

I NEVER FORGOT THAT DAY. I NEVER FORGOT YOU. AND I KNEW YOU WERE THE SISTER I LOST AS SOON AS I SAW YOU ...

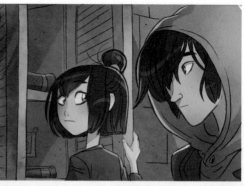

HOW DID YOU KNOW?

INSTINCT, AN ABILITY, I'M NOT REALLY SURE.

BUT I DIDN'T SAY ANYTHING.

WHY NOT?

DON'T YOU THINK IT'S A WEIRD COINCIDENCE THAT WE'RE BOTH HERE RIGHT NOW?

YOU'RE RIGHT. IT IS WEIRD!

IT'S DANGEROUS TOO!

WE SHOULD BE CAREFUL AND NOT TELL THE OTHERS ABOUT US.

GOOD IDEA!

IT'LL BE OUR SECRET!

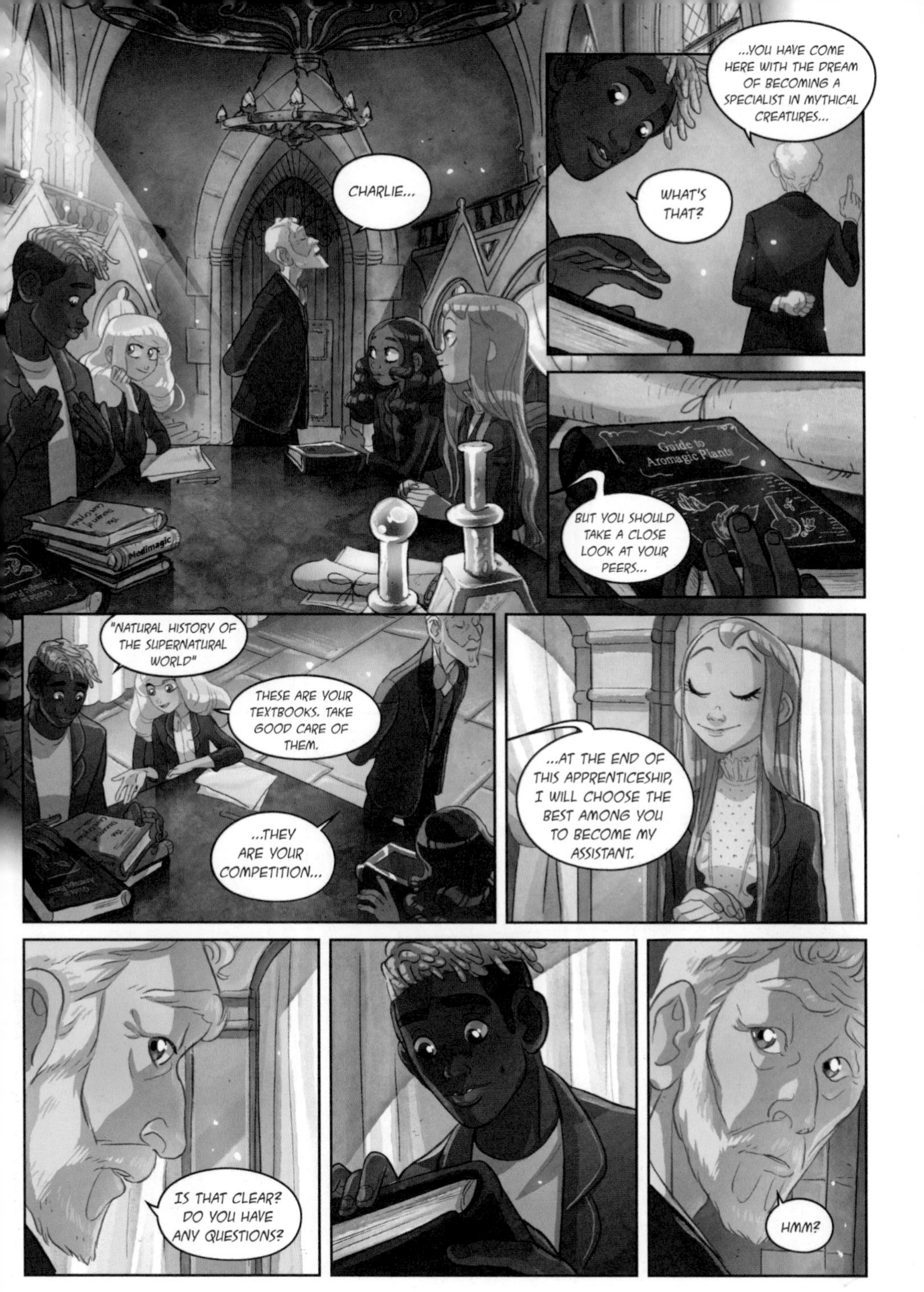
CHARLIE...
...YOU HAVE COME HERE WITH THE DREAM OF BECOMING A SPECIALIST IN MYTHICAL CREATURES...
WHAT'S THAT?
Guide to Aromagic Plants
BUT YOU SHOULD TAKE A CLOSE LOOK AT YOUR PEERS...
"NATURAL HISTORY OF THE SUPERNATURAL WORLD"
THESE ARE YOUR TEXTBOOKS. TAKE GOOD CARE OF THEM.
...THEY ARE YOUR COMPETITION...
...AT THE END OF THIS APPRENTICESHIP, I WILL CHOOSE THE BEST AMONG YOU TO BECOME MY ASSISTANT.
IS THAT CLEAR? DO YOU HAVE ANY QUESTIONS?
HMM?

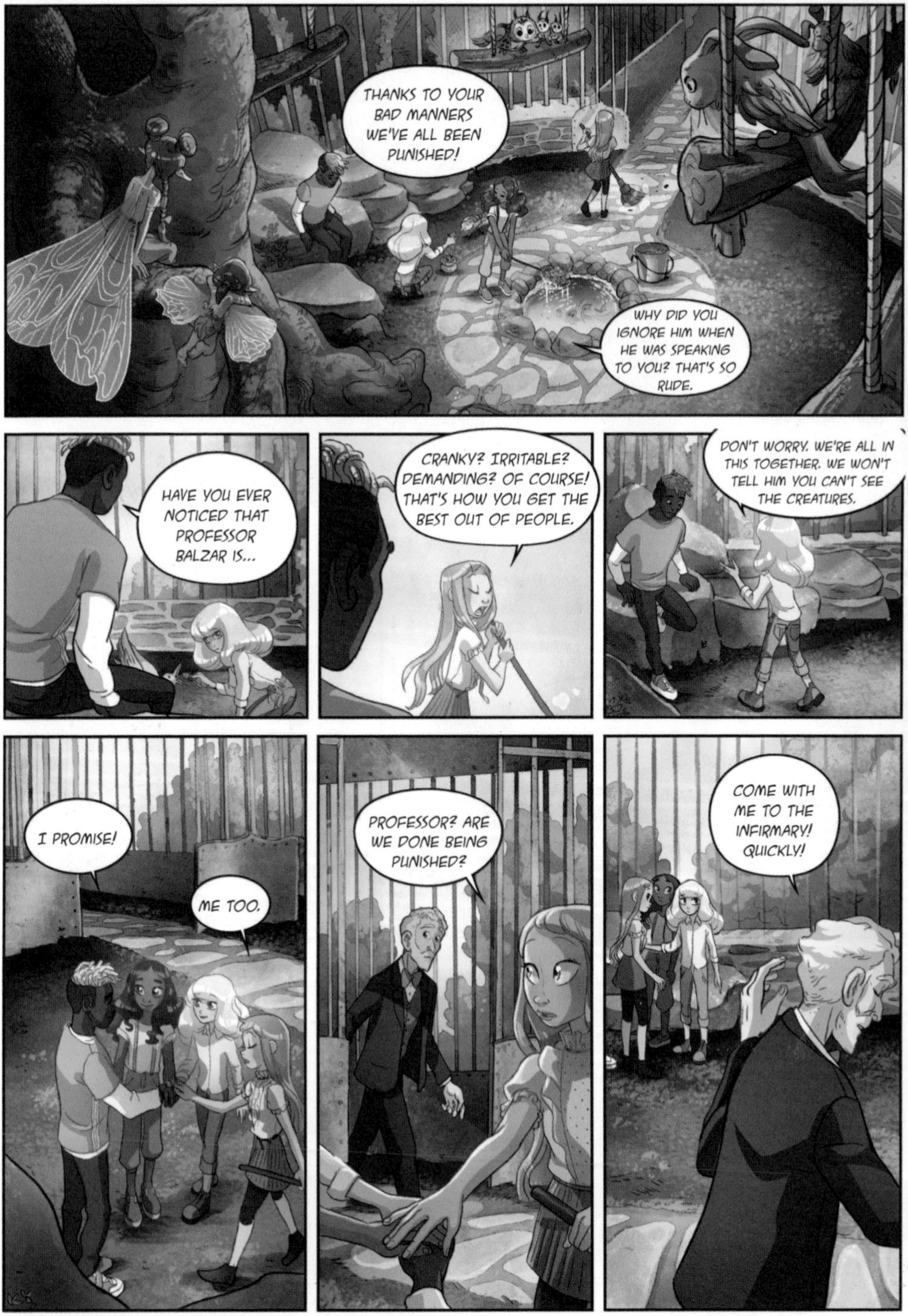
THANKS TO YOUR BAD MANNERS WE'VE ALL BEEN PUNISHED!
WHY DID YOU IGNORE HIM WHEN HE WAS SPEAKING TO YOU? THAT'S SO RUDE.
HAVE YOU EVER NOTICED THAT PROFESSOR BALZAR IS...
CRANKY? IRRITABLE? DEMANDING? OF COURSE! THAT'S HOW YOU GET THE BEST OUT OF PEOPLE.
DON'T WORRY. WE'RE ALL IN THIS TOGETHER. WE WON'T TELL HIM YOU CAN'T SEE THE CREATURES.
I PROMISE!
ME TOO.
PROFESSOR? ARE WE DONE BEING PUNISHED?
COME WITH ME TO THE INFIRMARY! QUICKLY!

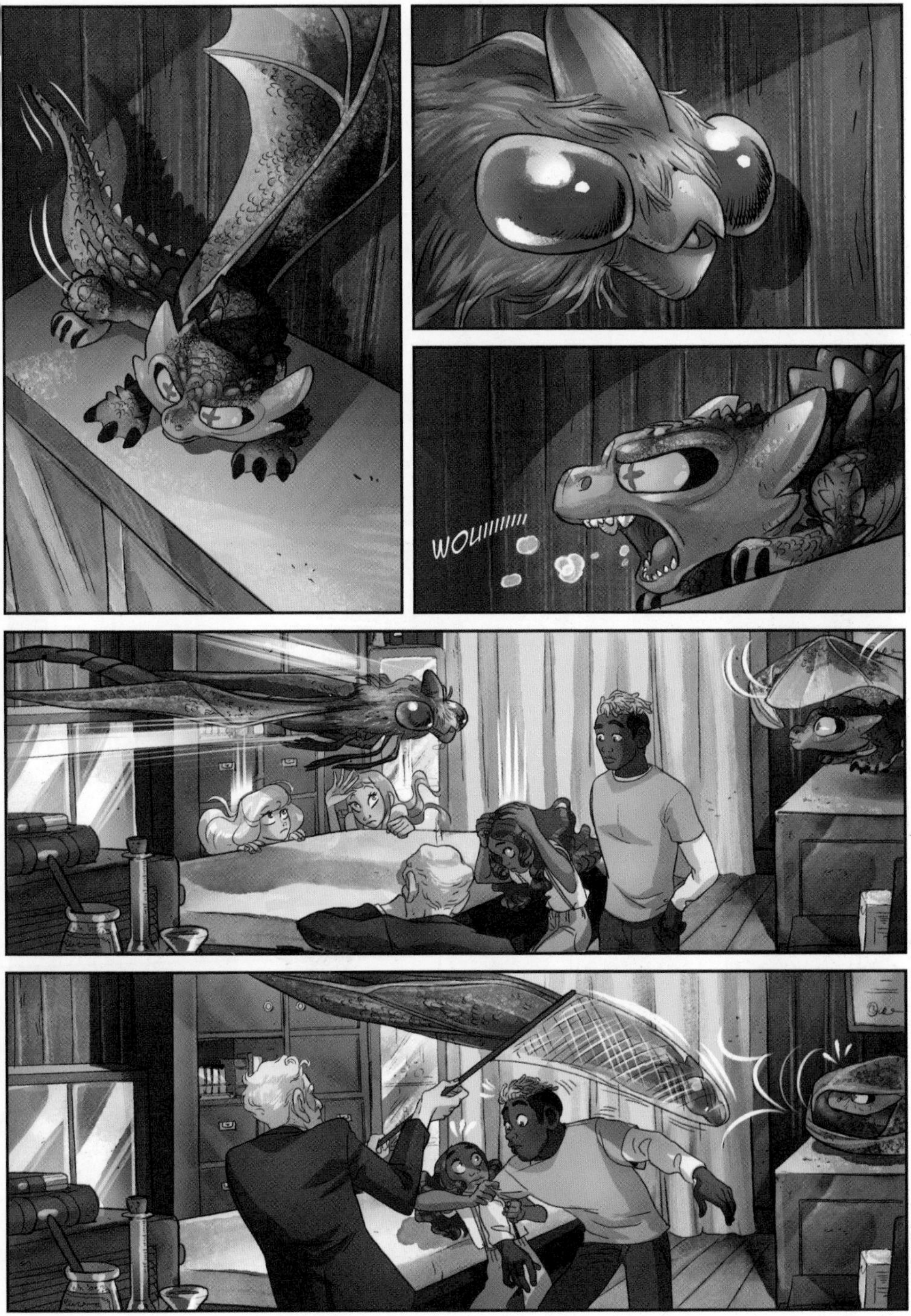
WOUIIIIIIII

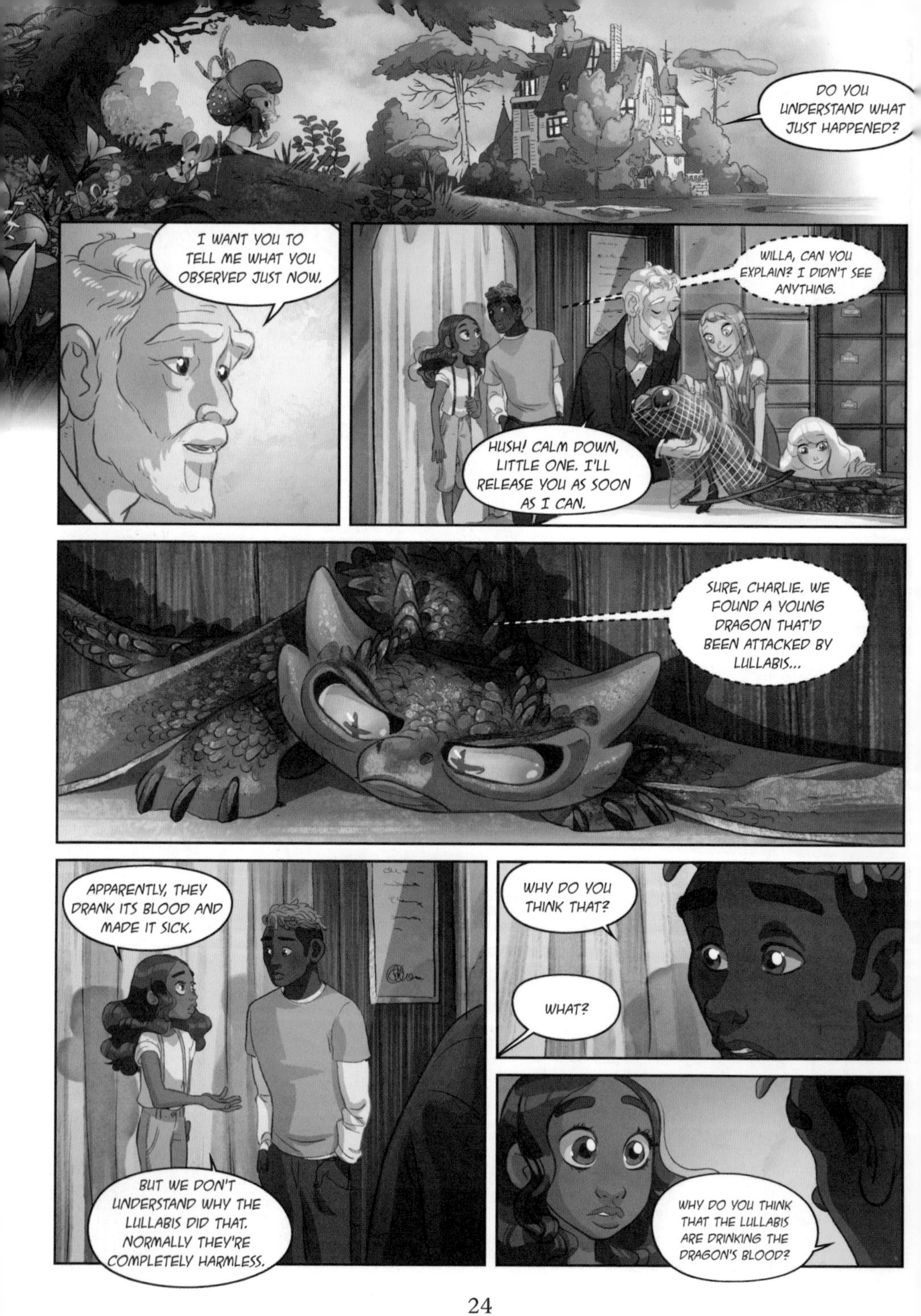

DO YOU UNDERSTAND WHAT JUST HAPPENED?
I WANT YOU TO TELL ME WHAT YOU OBSERVED JUST NOW.
WILLA, CAN YOU EXPLAIN? I DIDN'T SEE ANYTHING.
HUSH! CALM DOWN, LITTLE ONE. I'LL RELEASE YOU AS SOON AS I CAN.
SURE, CHARLIE. WE FOUND A YOUNG DRAGON THAT'D BEEN ATTACKED BY LULLABIS...
APPARENTLY, THEY DRANK ITS BLOOD AND MADE IT SICK.
BUT WE DON'T UNDERSTAND WHY THE LULLABIS DID THAT. NORMALLY THEY'RE COMPLETELY HARMLESS.
WHY DO YOU THINK THAT?
WHAT?
WHY DO YOU THINK THAT THE LULLABIS ARE DRINKING THE DRAGON'S BLOOD?

WE KNOW THAT THE DRAGON IS SICK BECAUSE ITS BLOOD IS PURPLE INSTEAD OF RED.

IT'S LIKE YOU ADDED BLUE TO IT.

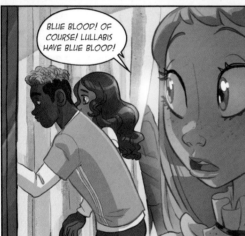

BLUE BLOOD! OF COURSE! LULLABIS HAVE BLUE BLOOD!

YES! IF YOU MIX THE LULLABIS' BLUE BLOOD WITH THE DRAGON'S RED BLOOD, YOU GET PURPLE BLOOD.

THAT MUST MEAN THAT IT'S NOT THE LULLABIS DRINKING DRAGON'S BLOOD, BUT THE OTHER WAY AROUND!

I SHOULD HAVE KNOWN! AND YOU EVEN POINTED ME IN THE RIGHT DIRECTION, ARLENE!

YOU KNEW THAT THE DRAGON'S MOTHER'S BLOOD MIXED WITH LULLABIS BLOOD WOULD TURN PURPLE?

PFFF! YOU DON'T NEED SPECIAL ABILITIES TO FIGURE OUT THAT BLUE + RED = PURPLE.

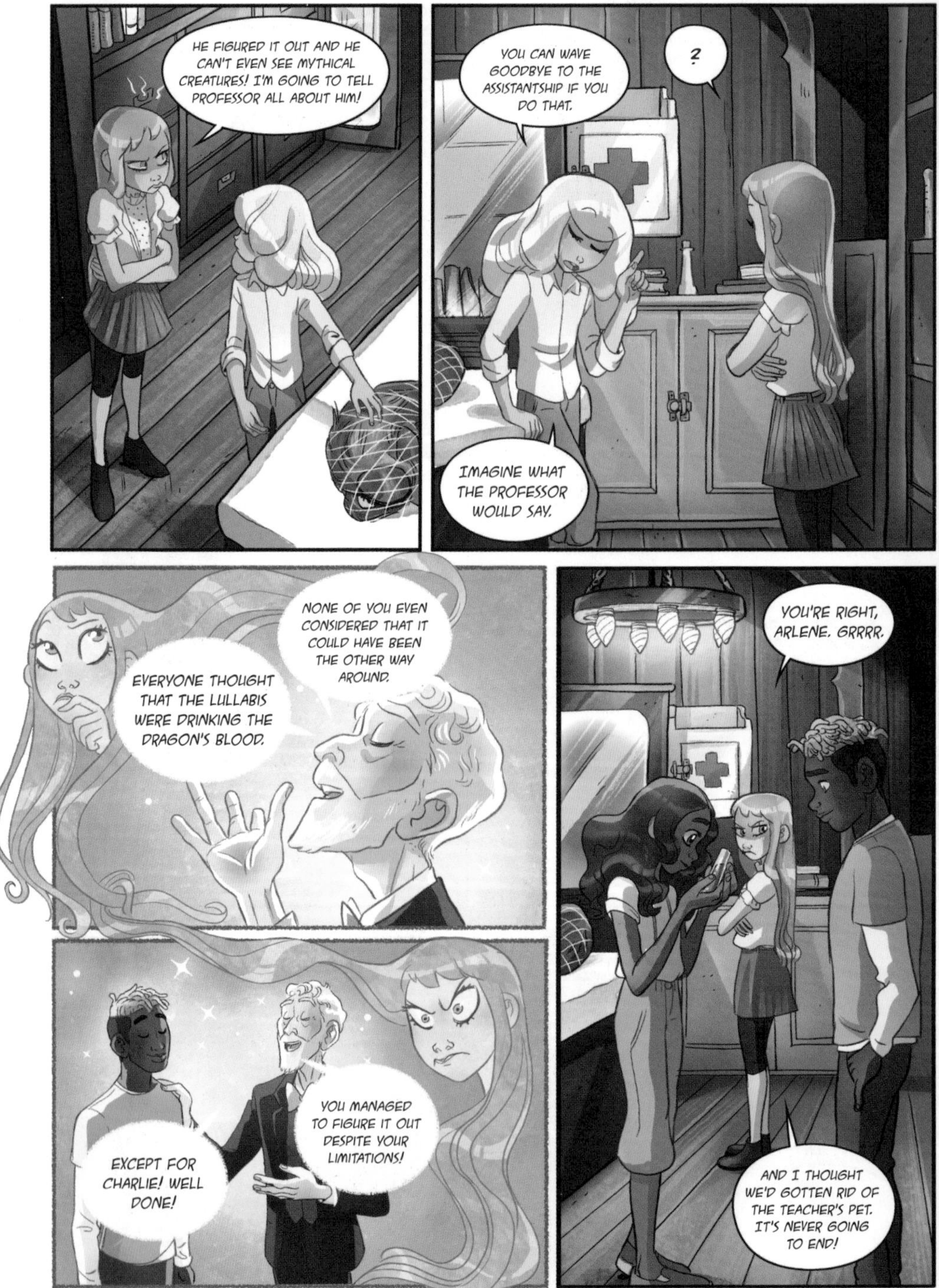
HE FIGURED IT OUT AND HE CAN'T EVEN SEE MYTHICAL CREATURES! I'M GOING TO TELL PROFESSOR ALL ABOUT HIM!
YOU CAN WAVE GOODBYE TO THE ASSISTANTSHIP IF YOU DO THAT.
?
IMAGINE WHAT THE PROFESSOR WOULD SAY.
EVERYONE THOUGHT THAT THE LULLABIS WERE DRINKING THE DRAGON'S BLOOD.
NONE OF YOU EVEN CONSIDERED THAT IT COULD HAVE BEEN THE OTHER WAY AROUND.
EXCEPT FOR CHARLIE! WELL DONE!
YOU MANAGED TO FIGURE IT OUT DESPITE YOUR LIMITATIONS!
YOU'RE RIGHT, ARLENE. GRRRR.
AND I THOUGHT WE'D GOTTEN RID OF THE TEACHER'S PET. IT'S NEVER GOING TO END!

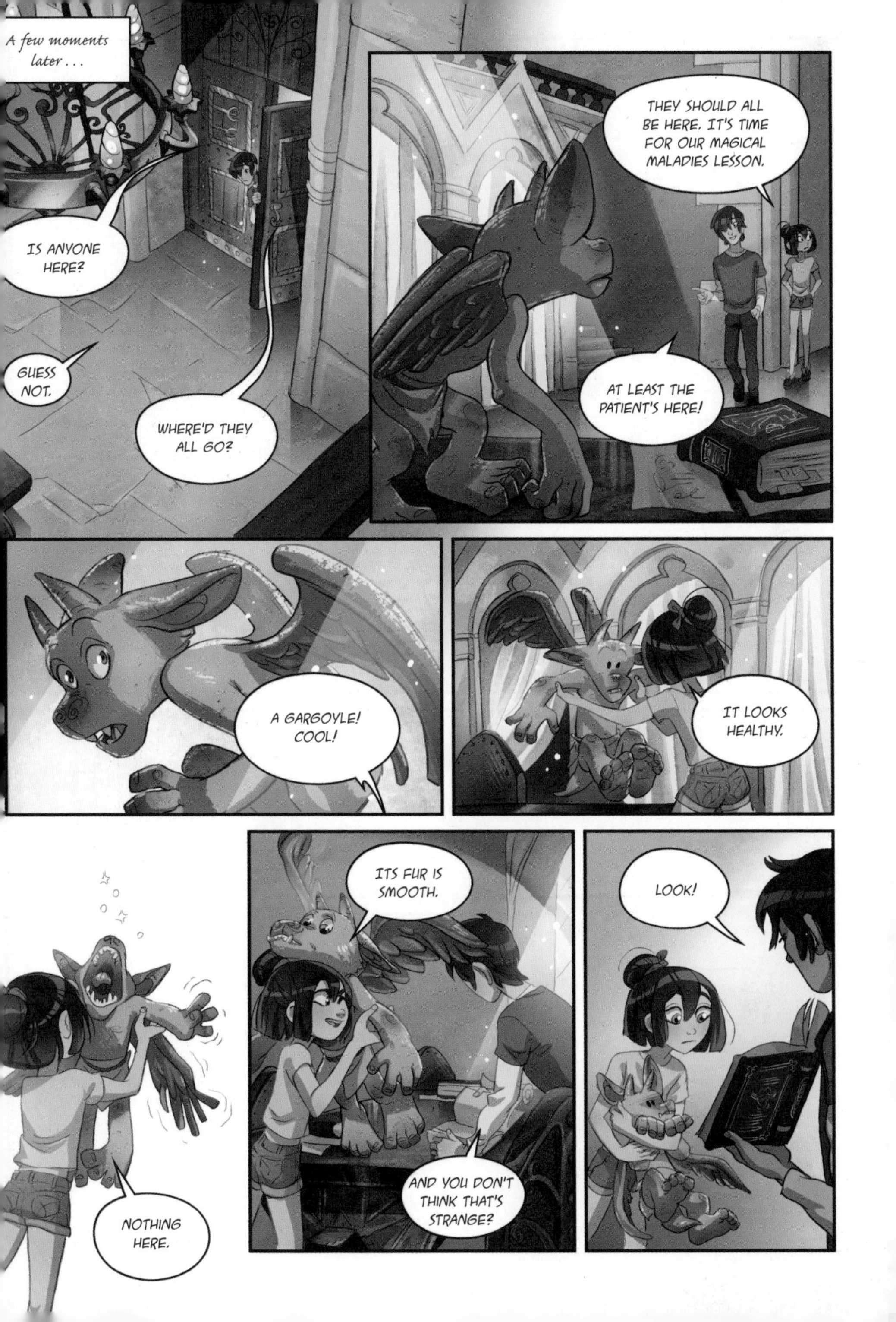

A few moments later . . .
IS ANYONE HERE?
GUESS NOT.
WHERE'D THEY ALL GO?
THEY SHOULD ALL BE HERE. IT'S TIME FOR OUR MAGICAL MALADIES LESSON.
AT LEAST THE PATIENT'S HERE!
A GARGOYLE! COOL!
IT LOOKS HEALTHY.
NOTHING HERE.
ITS FUR IS SMOOTH.
AND YOU DON'T THINK THAT'S STRANGE?
LOOK!

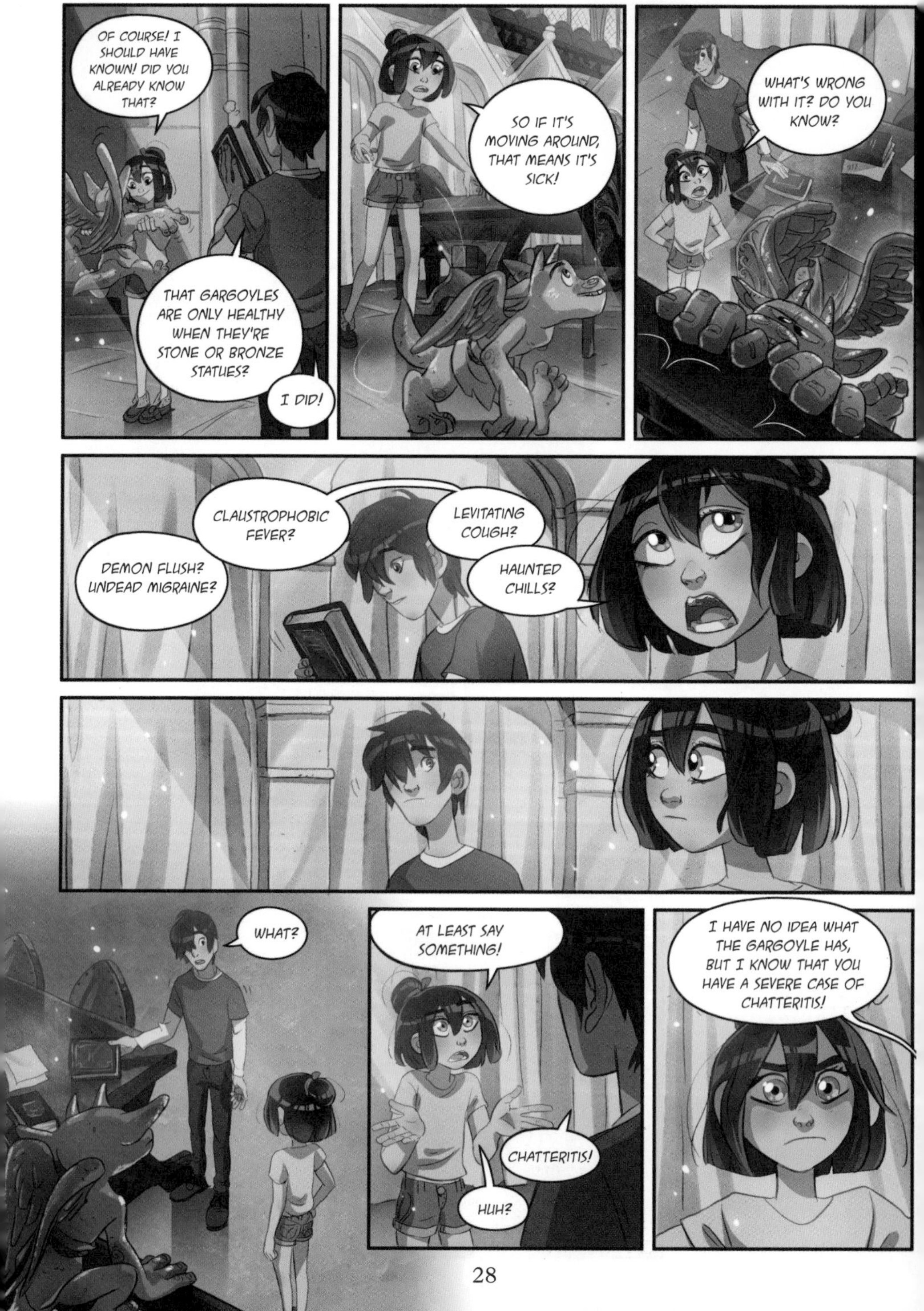
OF COURSE! I SHOULD HAVE KNOWN! DID YOU ALREADY KNOW THAT?
THAT GARGOYLES ARE ONLY HEALTHY WHEN THEY'RE STONE OR BRONZE STATUES?
I DID!
SO IF IT'S MOVING AROUND, THAT MEANS IT'S SICK!
WHAT'S WRONG WITH IT? DO YOU KNOW?
DEMON FLUSH? UNDEAD MIGRAINE?
CLAUSTROPHOBIC FEVER?
LEVITATING COUGH?
HAUNTED CHILLS?
WHAT?
AT LEAST SAY SOMETHING!
CHATTERITIS!
HUH?
I HAVE NO IDEA WHAT THE GARGOYLE HAS, BUT I KNOW THAT YOU HAVE A SEVERE CASE OF CHATTERITIS!

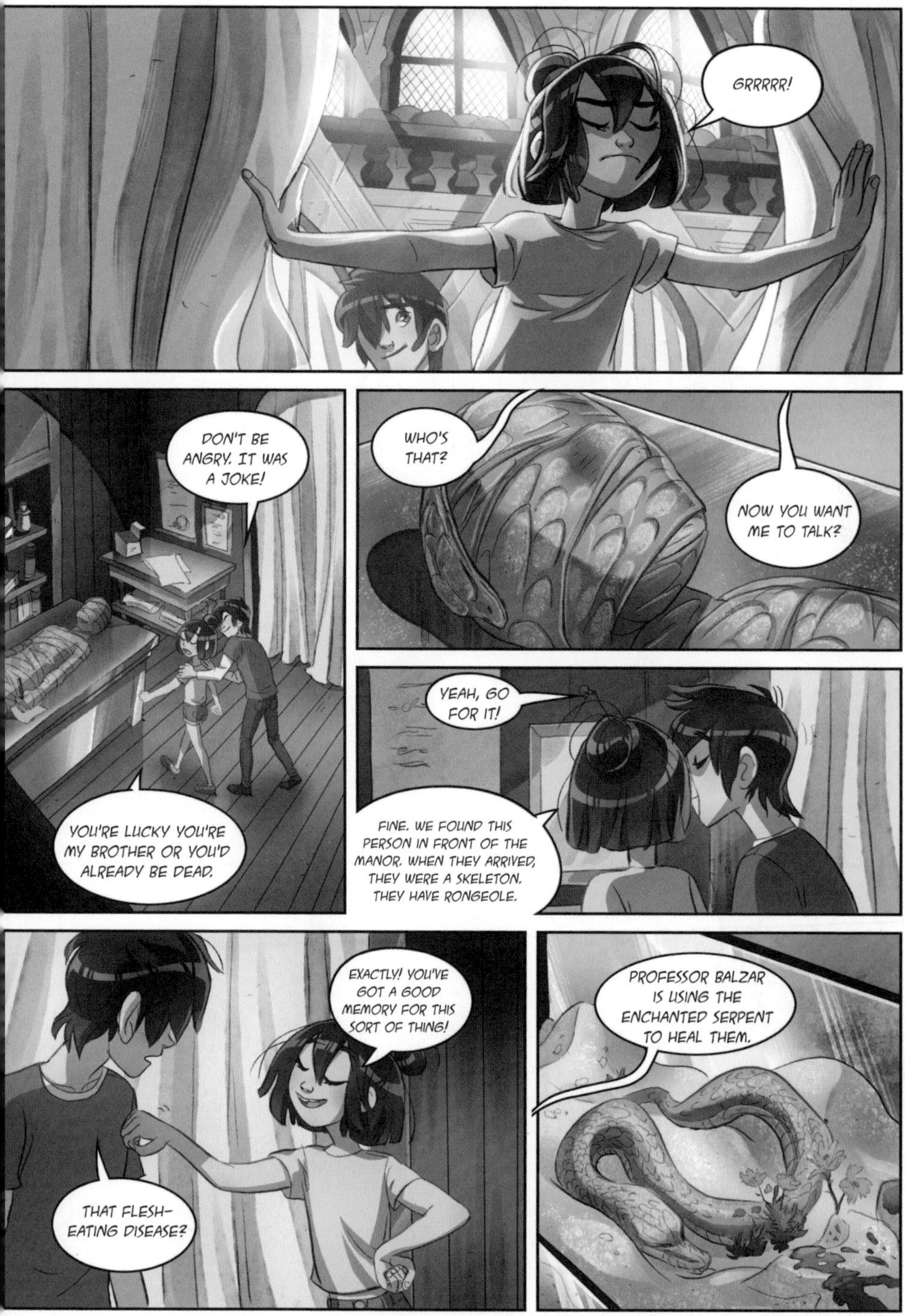
GRRRRR!
DON'T BE ANGRY. IT WAS A JOKE!
YOU'RE LUCKY YOU'RE MY BROTHER OR YOU'D ALREADY BE DEAD.
WHO'S THAT?
NOW YOU WANT ME TO TALK?
YEAH, GO FOR IT!
FINE. WE FOUND THIS PERSON IN FRONT OF THE MANOR. WHEN THEY ARRIVED, THEY WERE A SKELETON. THEY HAVE RONGEOLE.
THAT FLESH-EATING DISEASE?
EXACTLY! YOU'VE GOT A GOOD MEMORY FOR THIS SORT OF THING!
PROFESSOR BALZAR IS USING THE ENCHANTED SERPENT TO HEAL THEM.

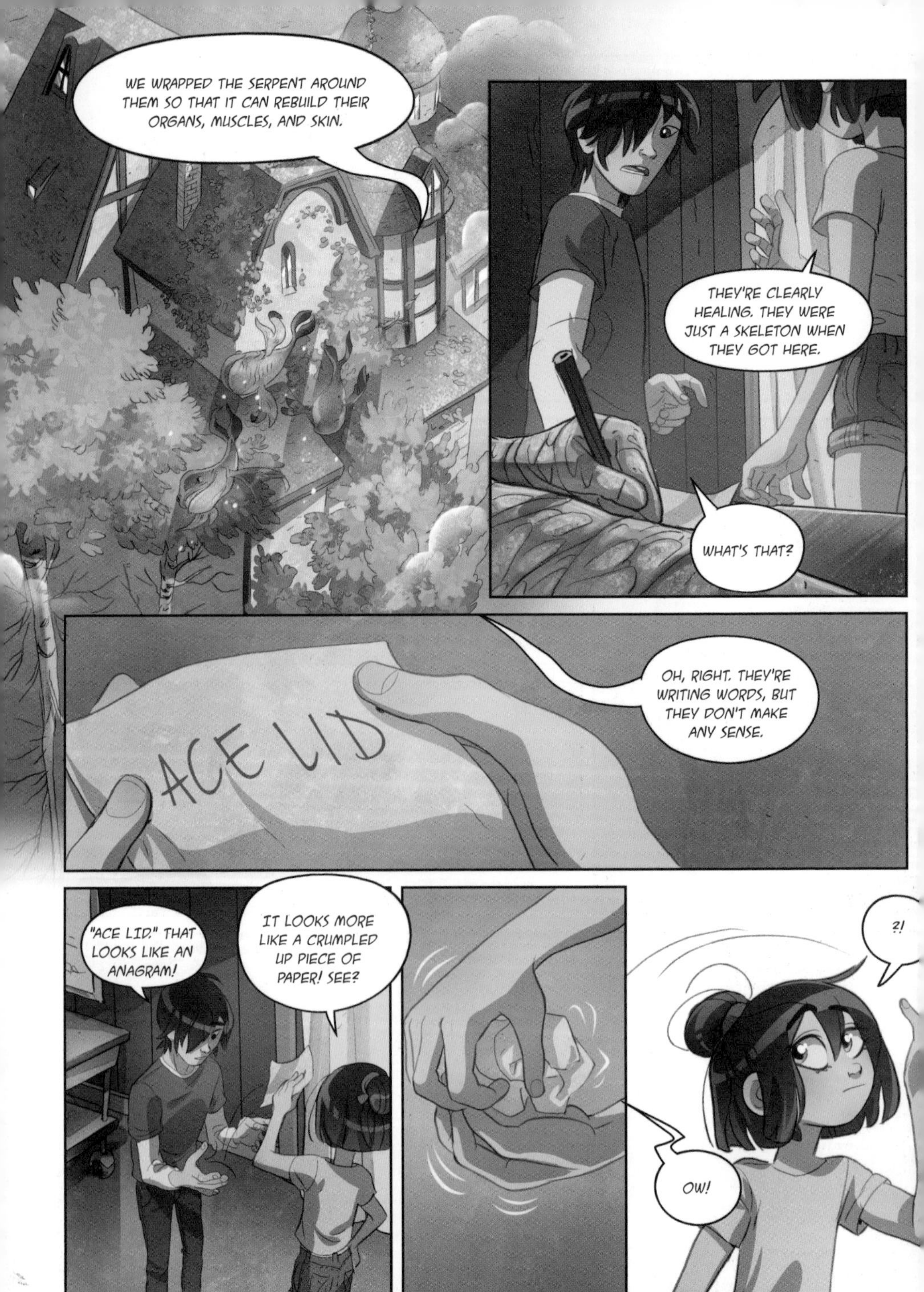
WE WRAPPED THE SERPENT AROUND THEM SO THAT IT CAN REBUILD THEIR ORGANS, MUSCLES, AND SKIN.
THEY'RE CLEARLY HEALING. THEY WERE JUST A SKELETON WHEN THEY GOT HERE.
WHAT'S THAT?
ACE LID
OH, RIGHT. THEY'RE WRITING WORDS, BUT THEY DON'T MAKE ANY SENSE.
"ACE LID." THAT LOOKS LIKE AN ANAGRAM!
IT LOOKS MORE LIKE A CRUMPLED UP PIECE OF PAPER! SEE?
OW!
?!

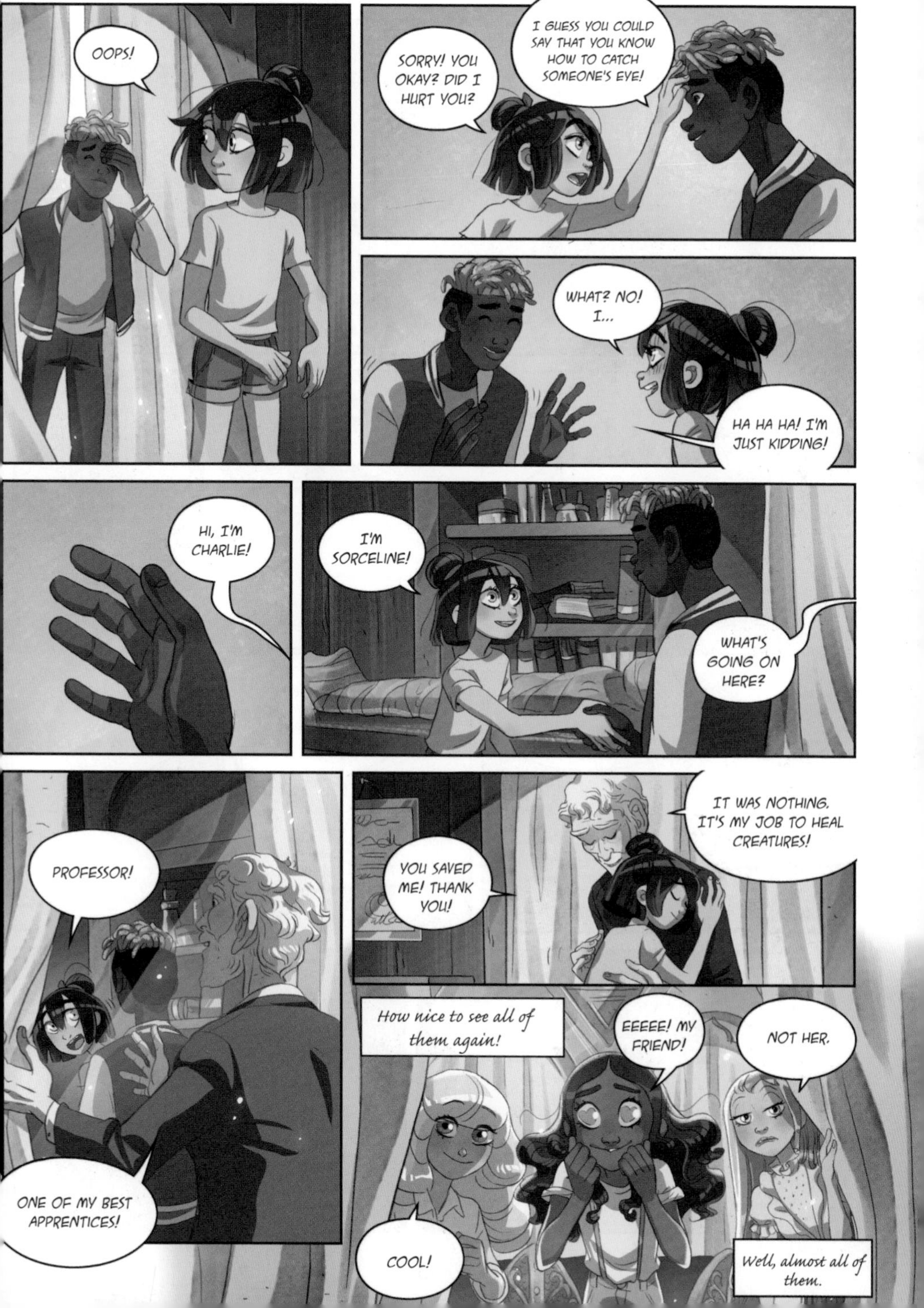
OOPS!
SORRY! YOU OKAY? DID I HURT YOU?
I GUESS YOU COULD SAY THAT YOU KNOW HOW TO CATCH SOMEONE'S EYE!
WHAT? NO! I...
HA HA HA! I'M JUST KIDDING!
HI, I'M CHARLIE!
I'M SORCELINE!
WHAT'S GOING ON HERE?
PROFESSOR!
ONE OF MY BEST APPRENTICES!
IT WAS NOTHING. IT'S MY JOB TO HEAL CREATURES!
YOU SAVED ME! THANK YOU!
How nice to see all of them again!
EEEEE! MY FRIEND!
NOT HER.
COOL!
Well, almost all of them.

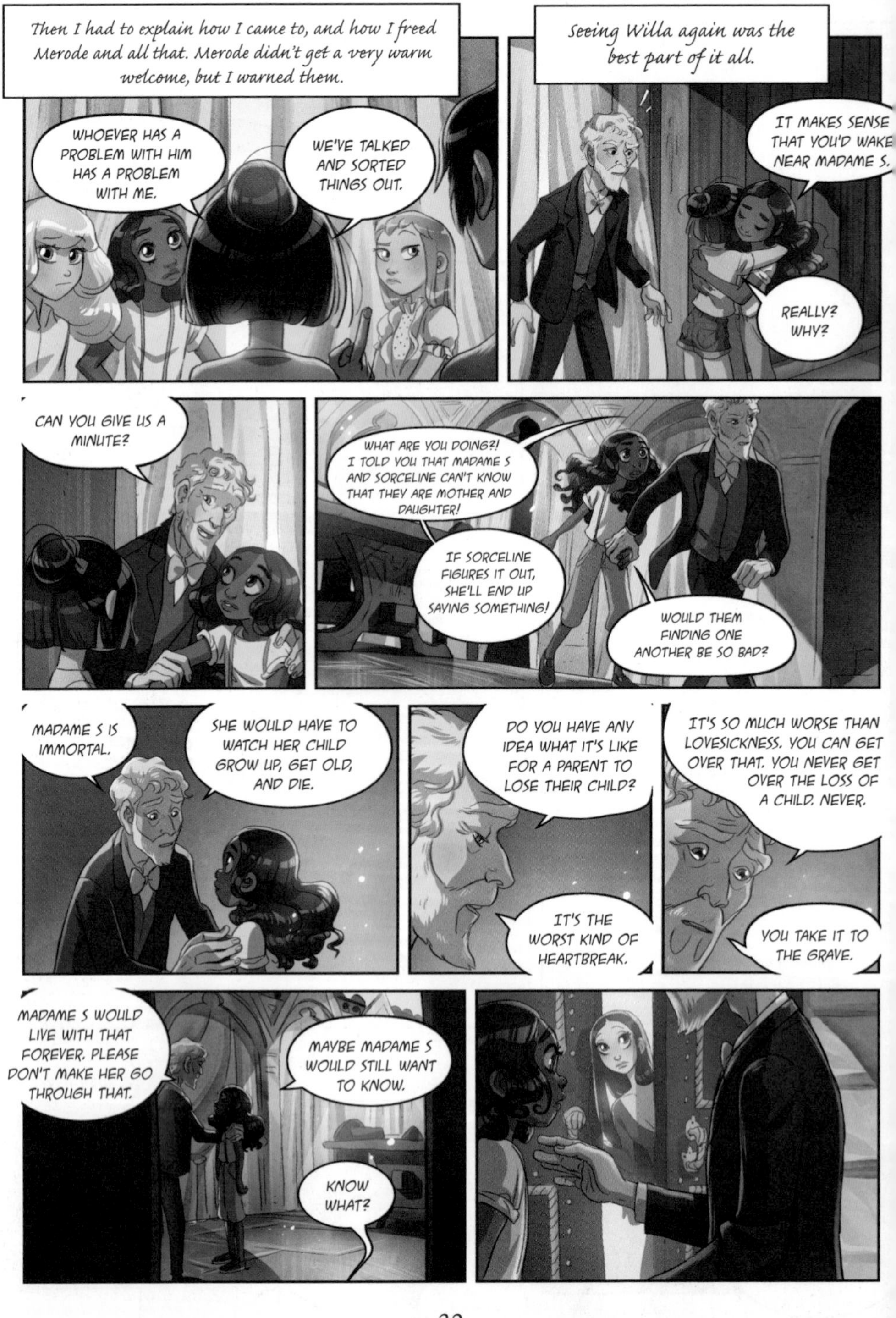

Then I had to explain how I came to, and how I freed Merode and all that. Merode didn't get a very warm welcome, but I warned them.
WHOEVER HAS A PROBLEM WITH HIM HAS A PROBLEM WITH ME.
WE'VE TALKED AND SORTED THINGS OUT.
Seeing Willa again was the best part of it all.
IT MAKES SENSE THAT YOU'D WAKE NEAR MADAME S.
REALLY? WHY?
CAN YOU GIVE US A MINUTE?
WHAT ARE YOU DOING?! I TOLD YOU THAT MADAME S AND SORCELINE CAN'T KNOW THAT THEY ARE MOTHER AND DAUGHTER!
IF SORCELINE FIGURES IT OUT, SHE'LL END UP SAYING SOMETHING!
WOULD THEM FINDING ONE ANOTHER BE SO BAD?
MADAME S IS IMMORTAL.
SHE WOULD HAVE TO WATCH HER CHILD GROW UP, GET OLD, AND DIE.
DO YOU HAVE ANY IDEA WHAT IT'S LIKE FOR A PARENT TO LOSE THEIR CHILD?
IT'S THE WORST KIND OF HEARTBREAK.
IT'S SO MUCH WORSE THAN LOVESICKNESS. YOU CAN GET OVER THAT. YOU NEVER GET OVER THE LOSS OF A CHILD. NEVER.
YOU TAKE IT TO THE GRAVE.
MADAME S WOULD LIVE WITH THAT FOREVER. PLEASE DON'T MAKE HER GO THROUGH THAT.
MAYBE MADAME S WOULD STILL WANT TO KNOW.
KNOW WHAT?

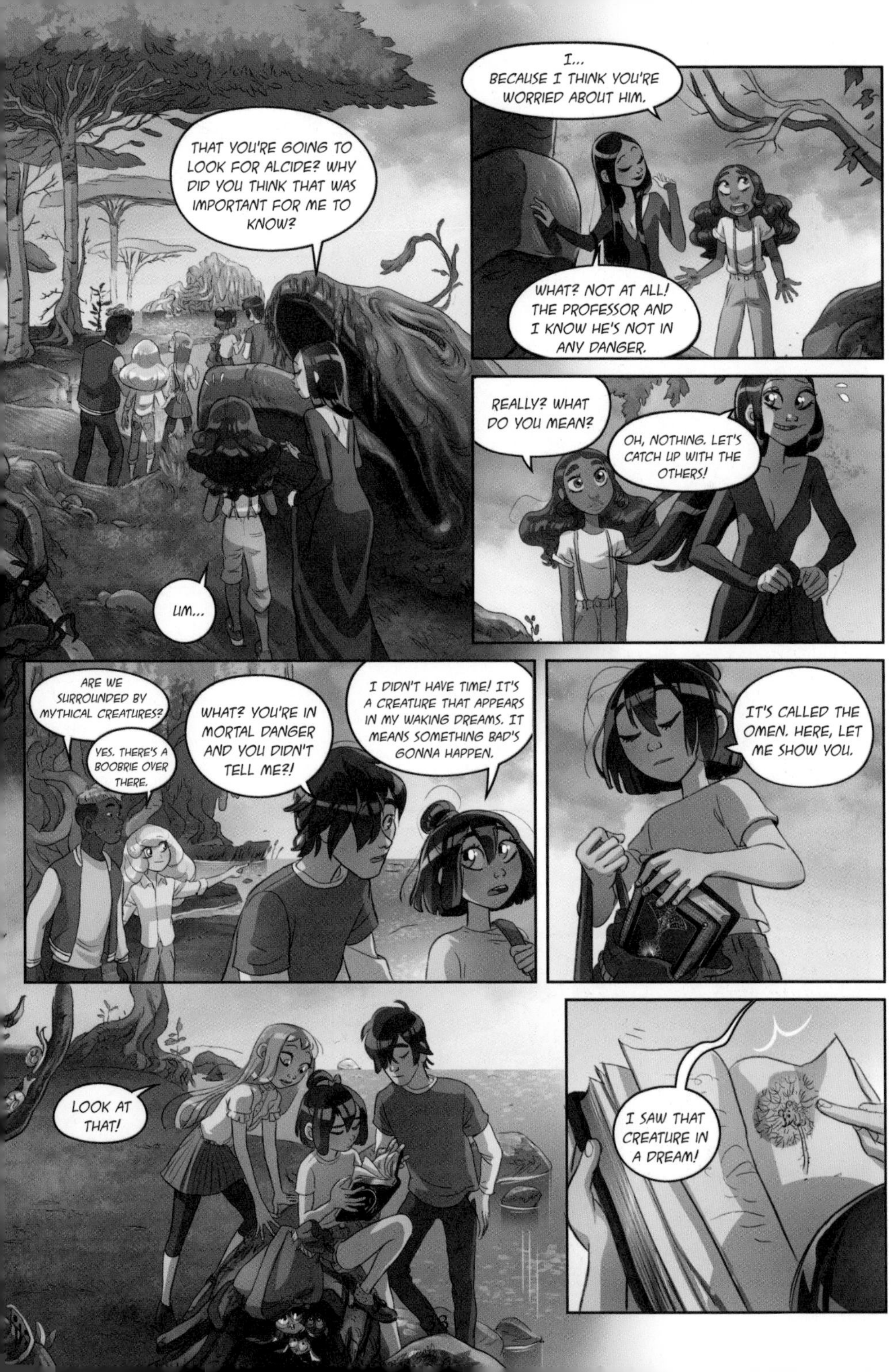
THAT YOU'RE GOING TO LOOK FOR ALCIDE? WHY DID YOU THINK THAT WAS IMPORTANT FOR ME TO KNOW?
UM...
I... BECAUSE I THINK YOU'RE WORRIED ABOUT HIM.
WHAT? NOT AT ALL! THE PROFESSOR AND I KNOW HE'S NOT IN ANY DANGER.
REALLY? WHAT DO YOU MEAN?
OH, NOTHING. LET'S CATCH UP WITH THE OTHERS!
ARE WE SURROUNDED BY MYTHICAL CREATURES?
YES. THERE'S A BOOBRIE OVER THERE.
WHAT? YOU'RE IN MORTAL DANGER AND YOU DIDN'T TELL ME?!
I DIDN'T HAVE TIME! IT'S A CREATURE THAT APPEARS IN MY WAKING DREAMS. IT MEANS SOMETHING BAD'S GONNA HAPPEN.
IT'S CALLED THE OMEN. HERE, LET ME SHOW YOU.
LOOK AT THAT!
I SAW THAT CREATURE IN A DREAM!

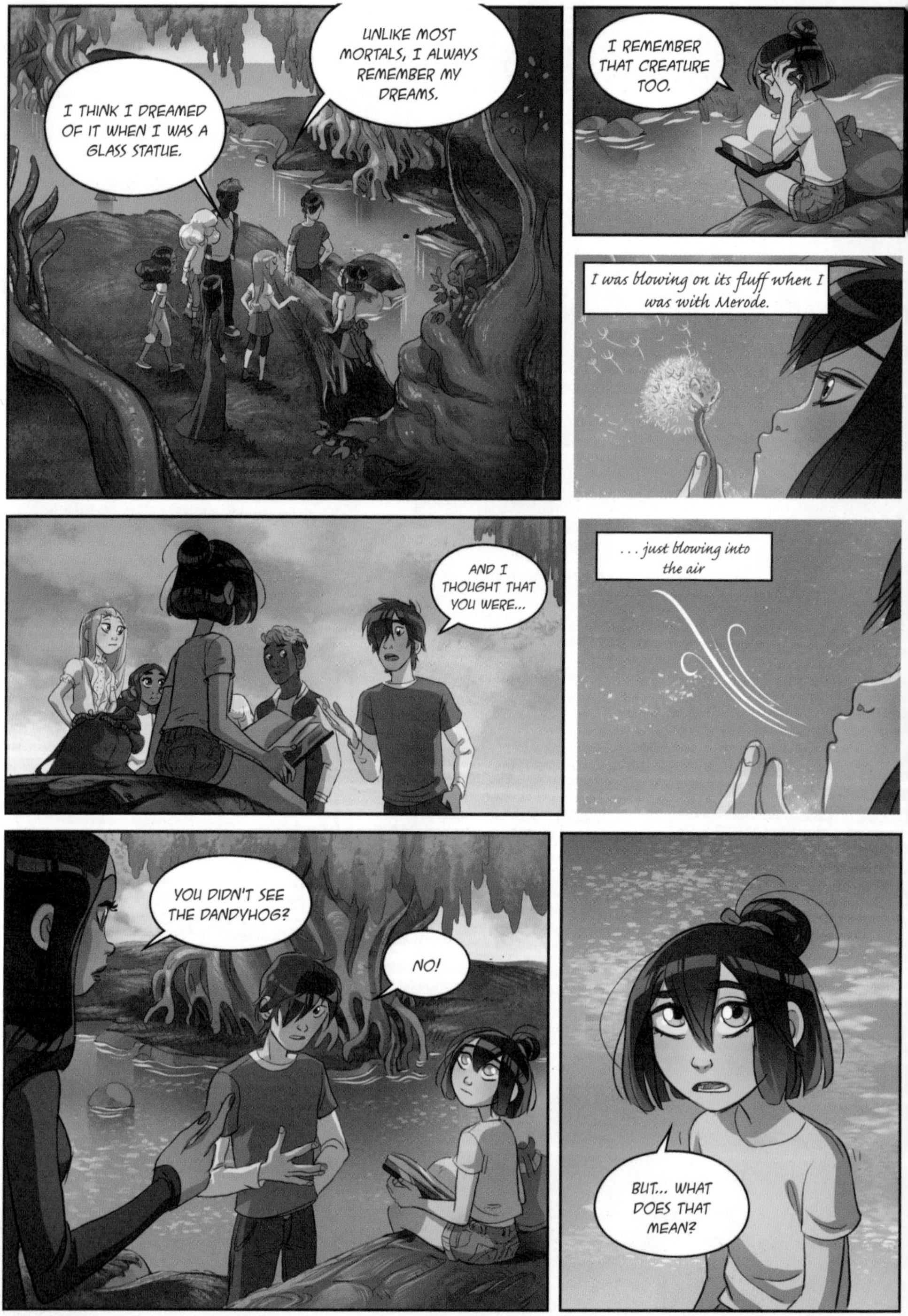
I THINK I DREAMED OF IT WHEN I WAS A GLASS STATUE.
UNLIKE MOST MORTALS, I ALWAYS REMEMBER MY DREAMS.
I REMEMBER THAT CREATURE TOO.
I was blowing on its fluff when I was with Merode.
AND I THOUGHT THAT YOU WERE...
. . . just blowing into the air
YOU DIDN'T SEE THE DANDYHOG?
NO!
BUT... WHAT DOES THAT MEAN?

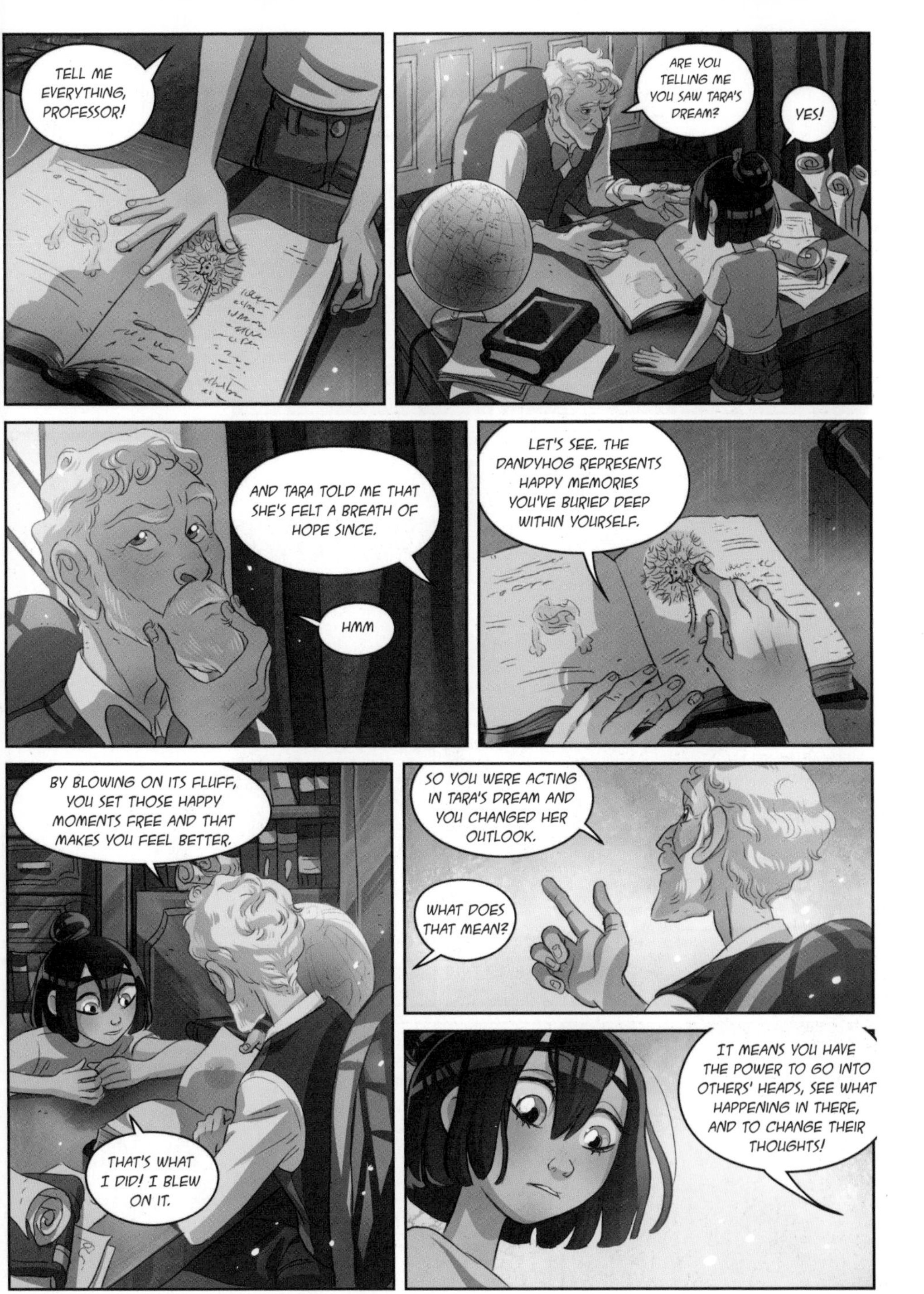
TELL ME EVERYTHING, PROFESSOR!
ARE YOU TELLING ME YOU SAW TARA'S DREAM?
YES!
AND TARA TOLD ME THAT SHE'S FELT A BREATH OF HOPE SINCE.
HMM
LET'S SEE. THE DANDYHOG REPRESENTS HAPPY MEMORIES YOU'VE BURIED DEEP WITHIN YOURSELF.
BY BLOWING ON ITS FLUFF, YOU SET THOSE HAPPY MOMENTS FREE AND THAT MAKES YOU FEEL BETTER.
THAT'S WHAT I DID! I BLEW ON IT.
SO YOU WERE ACTING IN TARA'S DREAM AND YOU CHANGED HER OUTLOOK.
WHAT DOES THAT MEAN?
IT MEANS YOU HAVE THE POWER TO GO INTO OTHERS' HEADS, SEE WHAT HAPPENING IN THERE, AND TO CHANGE THEIR THOUGHTS!

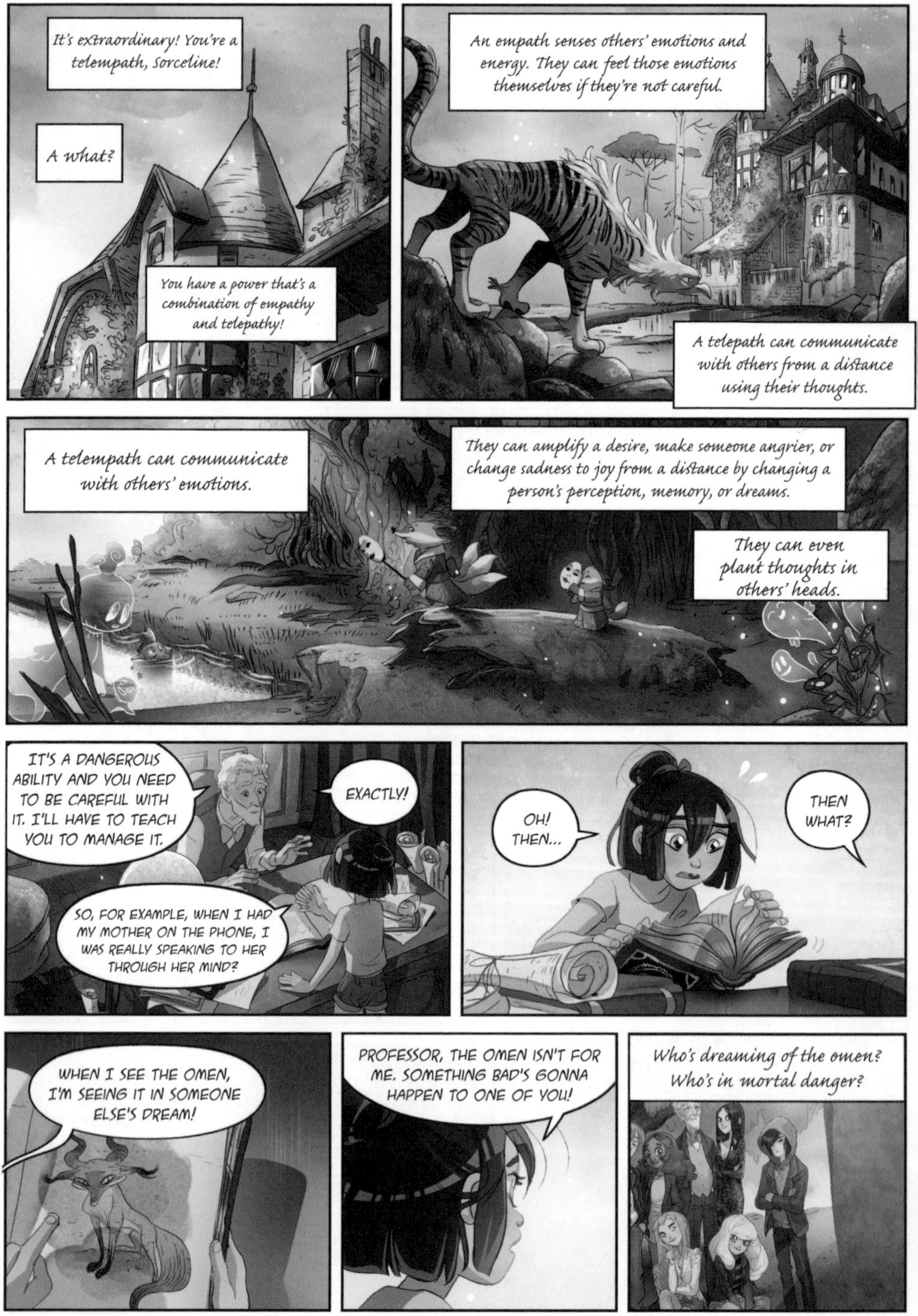
It's extraordinary! You're a telempath, Sorceline!
A what?
You have a power that's a combination of empathy and telepathy!
An empath senses others' emotions and energy. They can feel those emotions themselves if they're not careful.
A telepath can communicate with others from a distance using their thoughts.
A telempath can communicate with others' emotions.
They can amplify a desire, make someone angrier, or change sadness to joy from a distance by changing a person's perception, memory, or dreams.
They can even plant thoughts in others' heads.
IT'S A DANGEROUS ABILITY AND YOU NEED TO BE CAREFUL WITH IT. I'LL HAVE TO TEACH YOU TO MANAGE IT.
EXACTLY!
SO, FOR EXAMPLE, WHEN I HAD MY MOTHER ON THE PHONE, I WAS REALLY SPEAKING TO HER THROUGH HER MIND?
OH! THEN...
THEN WHAT?
WHEN I SEE THE OMEN, I'M SEEING IT IN SOMEONE ELSE'S DREAM!
PROFESSOR, THE OMEN ISN'T FOR ME. SOMETHING BAD'S GONNA HAPPEN TO ONE OF YOU!
Who's dreaming of the omen? Who's in mortal danger?

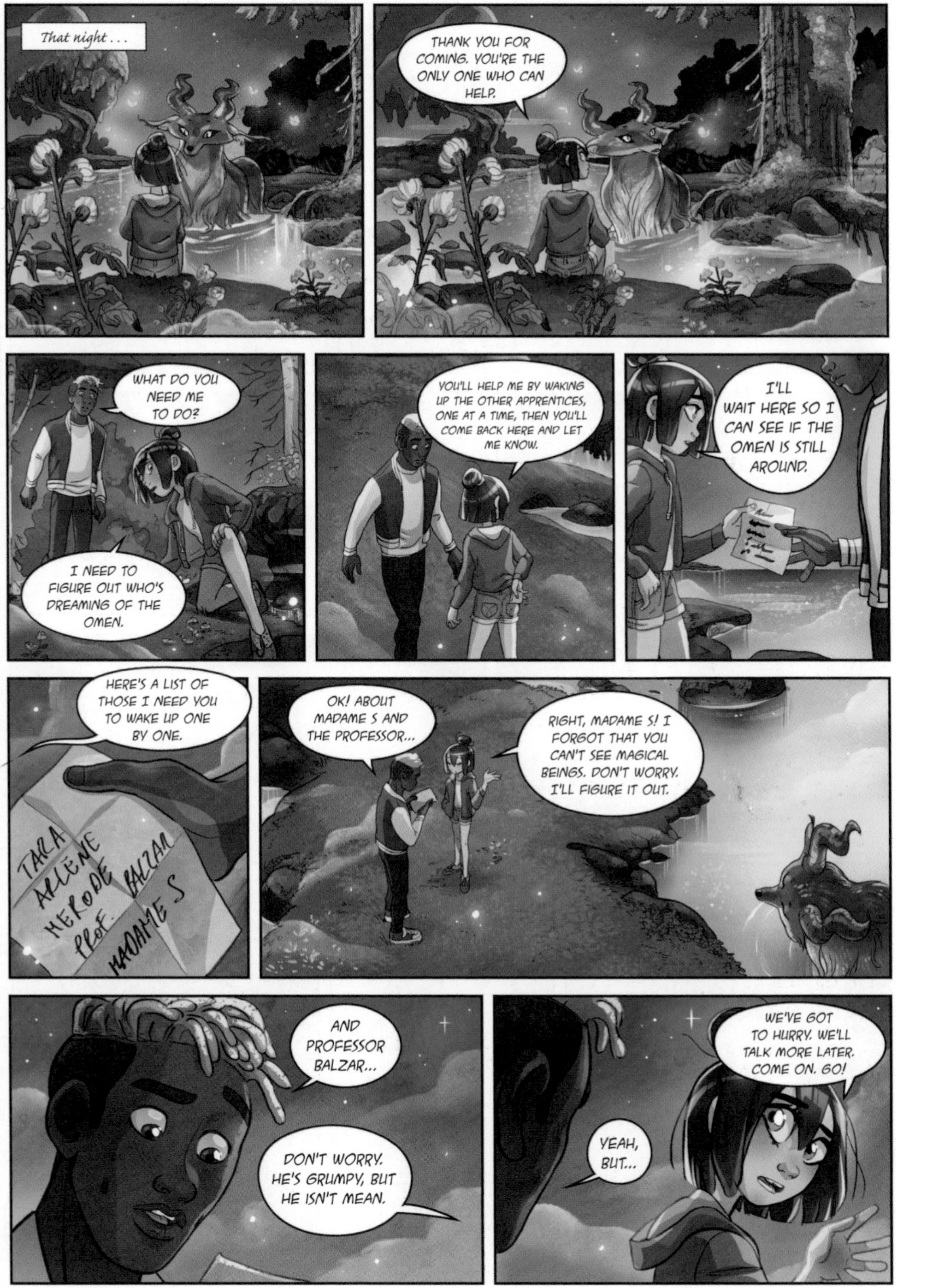
That night . . .
THANK YOU FOR COMING. YOU'RE THE ONLY ONE WHO CAN HELP.
WHAT DO YOU NEED ME TO DO?
I NEED TO FIGURE OUT WHO'S DREAMING OF THE OMEN.
YOU'LL HELP ME BY WAKING UP THE OTHER APPRENTICES, ONE AT A TIME, THEN YOU'LL COME BACK HERE AND LET ME KNOW.
I'LL WAIT HERE SO I CAN SEE IF THE OMEN IS STILL AROUND.
HERE'S A LIST OF THOSE I NEED YOU TO WAKE UP ONE BY ONE.
TARA
ALLENE
MERODE
PROF. BALZAR
MADAME S
OK! ABOUT MADAME S AND THE PROFESSOR...
RIGHT, MADAME S! I FORGOT THAT YOU CAN'T SEE MAGICAL BEINGS. DON'T WORRY. I'LL FIGURE IT OUT.
AND PROFESSOR BALZAR...
DON'T WORRY. HE'S GRUMPY, BUT HE ISN'T MEAN.
WE'VE GOT TO HURRY. WE'LL TALK MORE LATER. COME ON. GO!
YEAH, BUT...

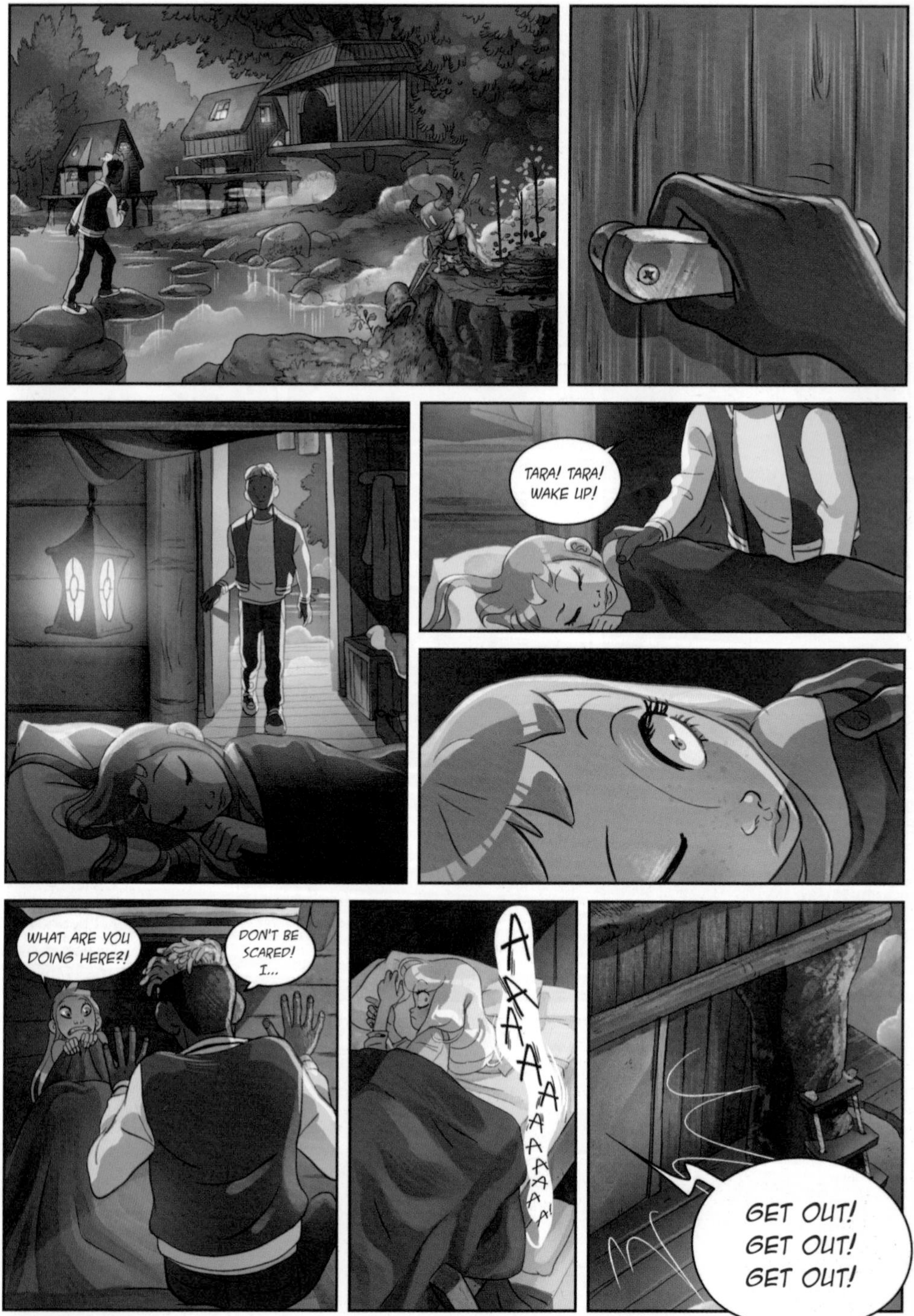
TARA! TARA! WAKE UP!
WHAT ARE YOU DOING HERE?!
DON'T BE SCARED! I...
AAAAAAAAAAAA!
GET OUT! GET OUT! GET OUT!

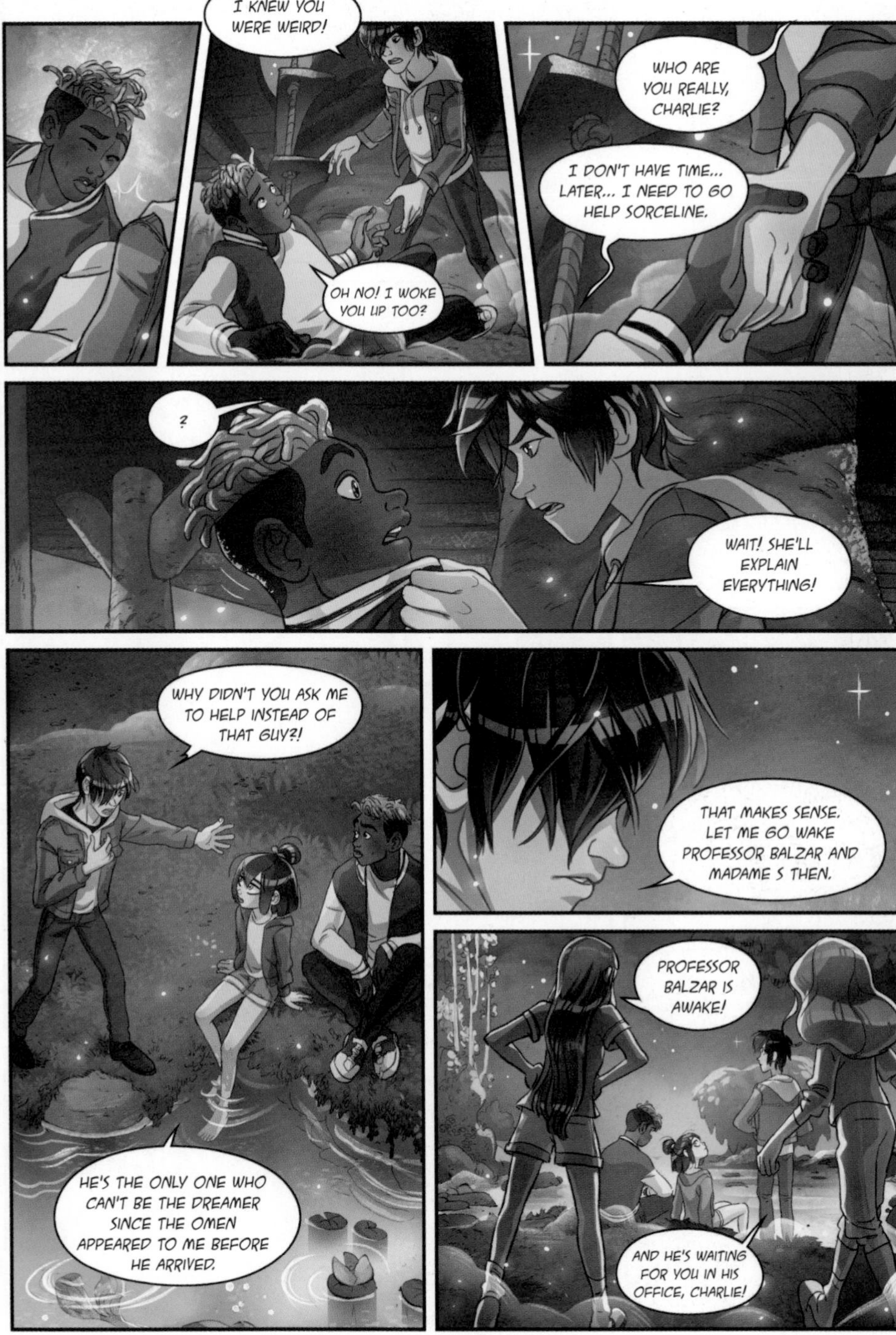
I KNEW YOU WERE WEIRD!
OH NO! I WOKE YOU UP TOO?
WHO ARE YOU REALLY, CHARLIE?
I DON'T HAVE TIME... LATER... I NEED TO GO HELP SORCELINE.
?
WAIT! SHE'LL EXPLAIN EVERYTHING!
WHY DIDN'T YOU ASK ME TO HELP INSTEAD OF THAT GUY?!
HE'S THE ONLY ONE WHO CAN'T BE THE DREAMER SINCE THE OMEN APPEARED TO ME BEFORE HE ARRIVED.
THAT MAKES SENSE. LET ME GO WAKE PROFESSOR BALZAR AND MADAME S THEN.
PROFESSOR BALZAR IS AWAKE!
AND HE'S WAITING FOR YOU IN HIS OFFICE, CHARLIE!

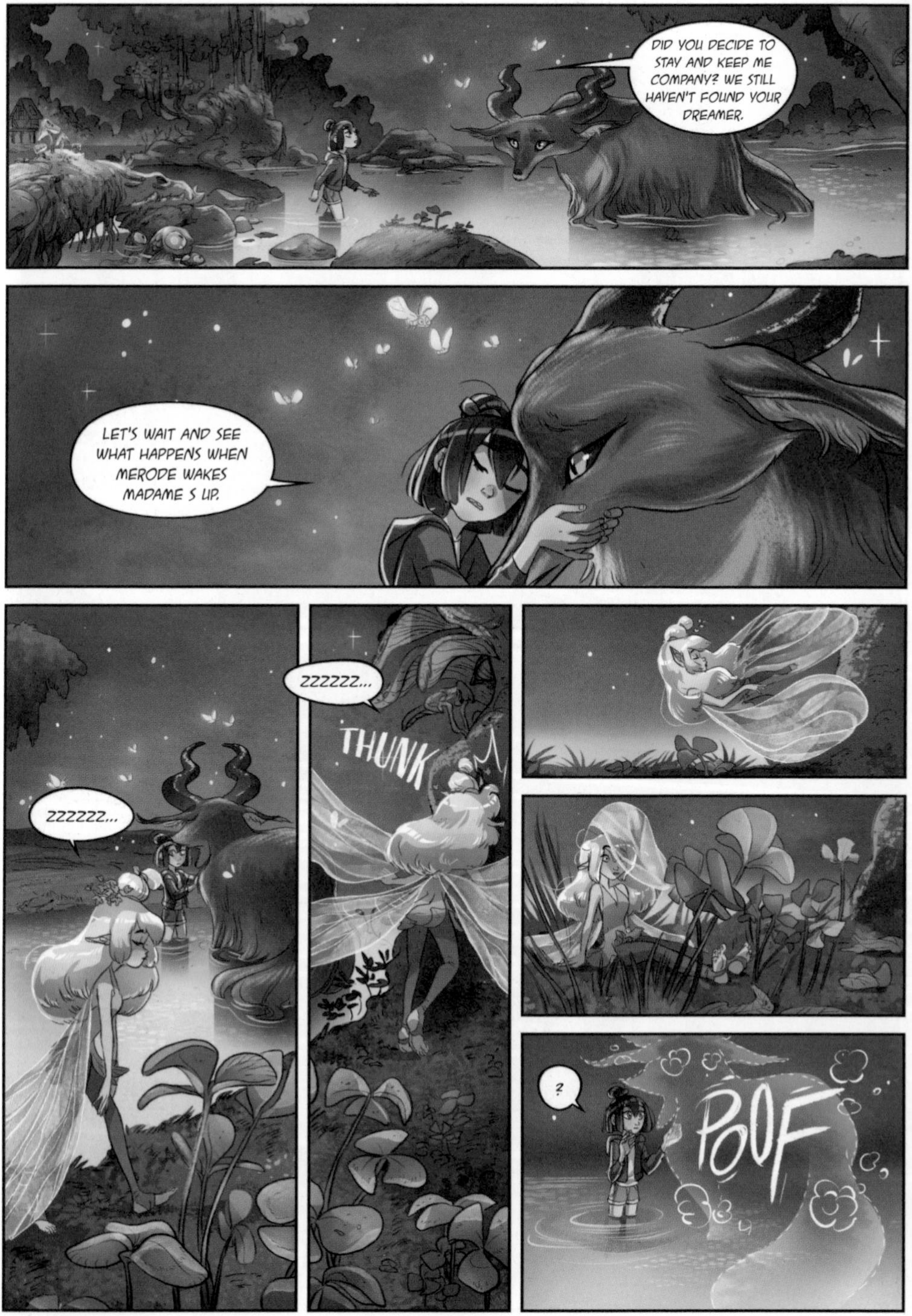
DID YOU DECIDE TO STAY AND KEEP ME COMPANY? WE STILL HAVEN'T FOUND YOUR DREAMER.
LET'S WAIT AND SEE WHAT HAPPENS WHEN MERODE WAKES MADAME S UP.
ZZZZZZ...
ZZZZZZ...
THUNK
?
POOF

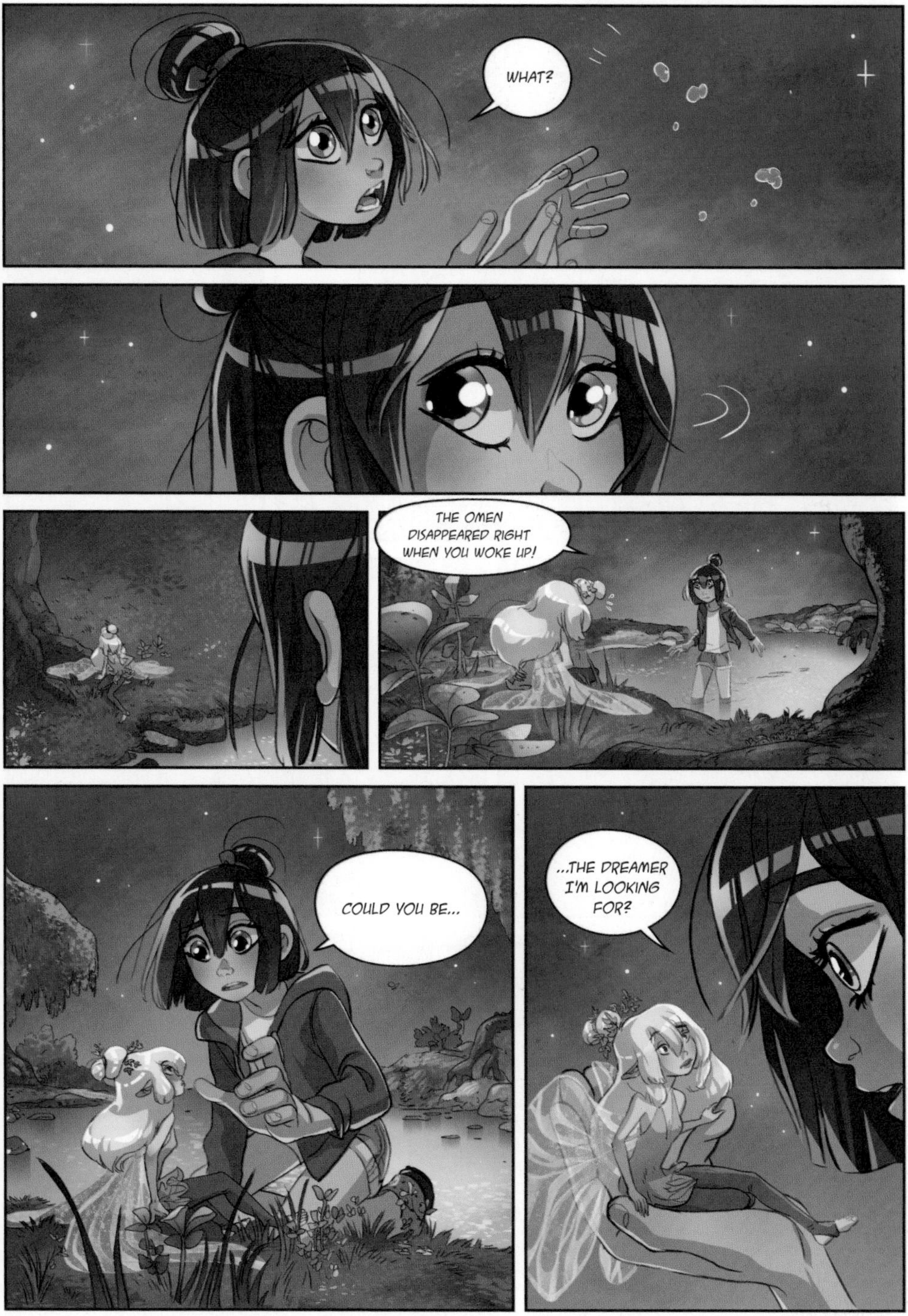
WHAT?
THE OMEN DISAPPEARED RIGHT WHEN YOU WOKE UP!
COULD YOU BE...
...THE DREAMER I'M LOOKING FOR?

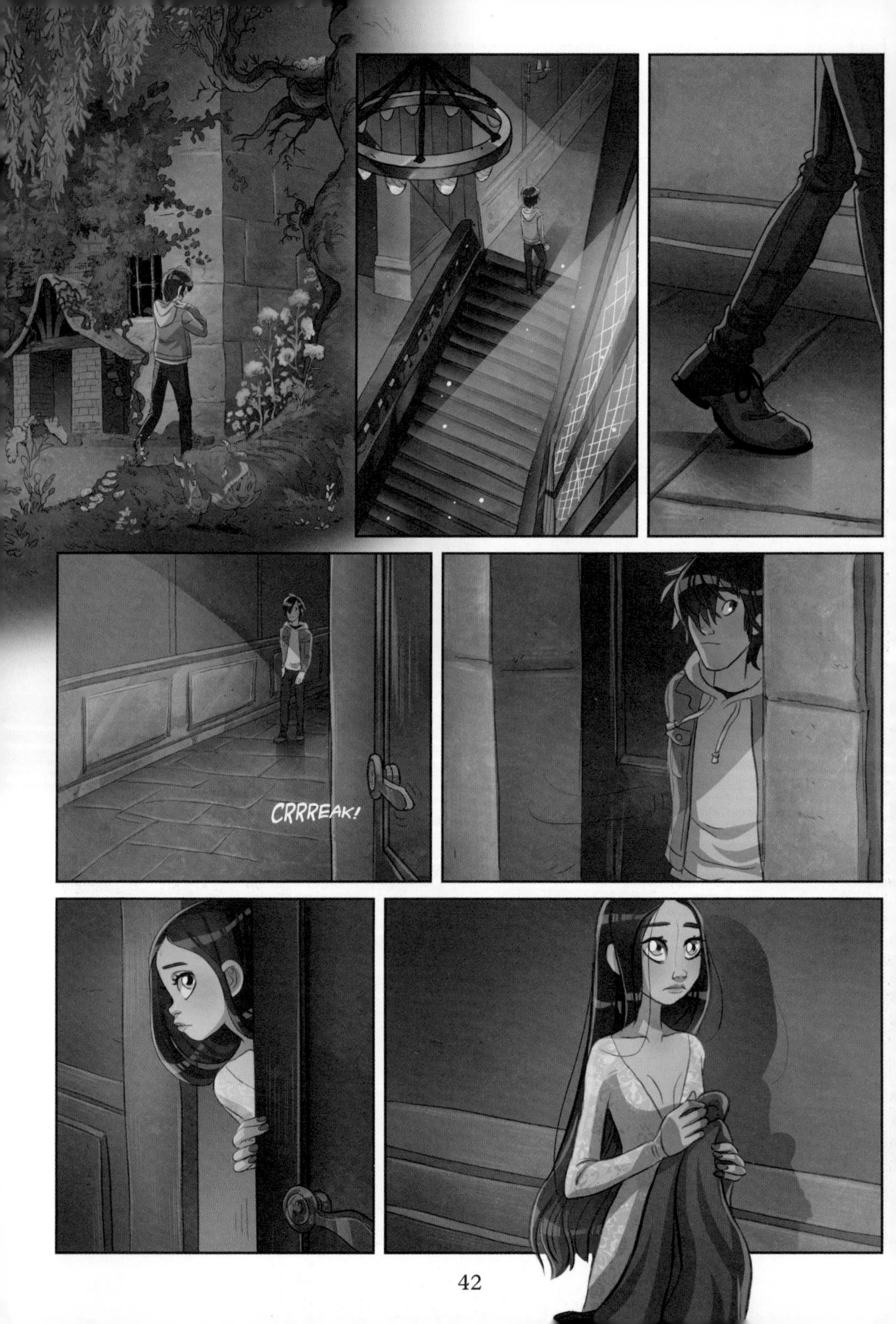
CRRREAK!

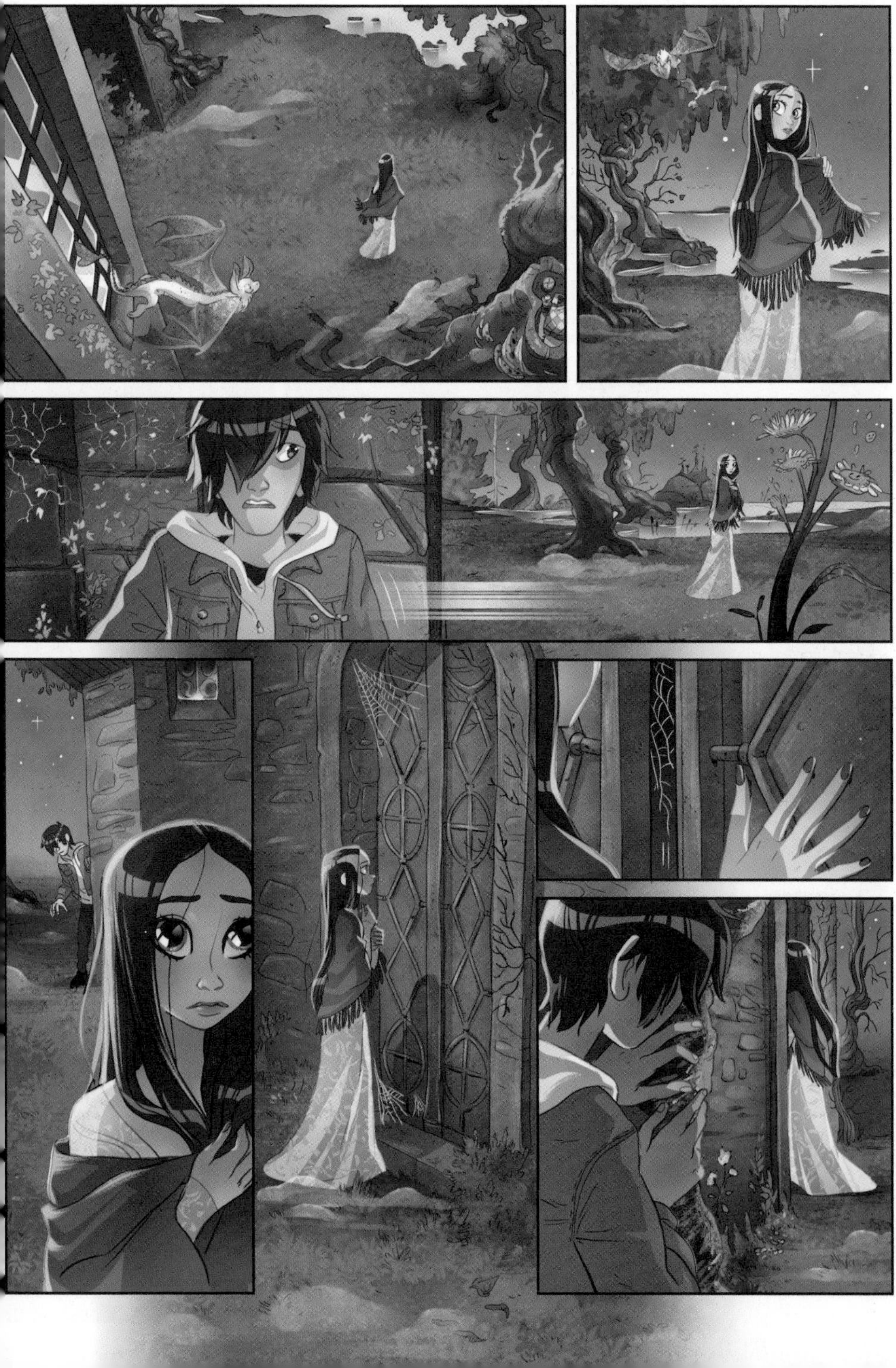

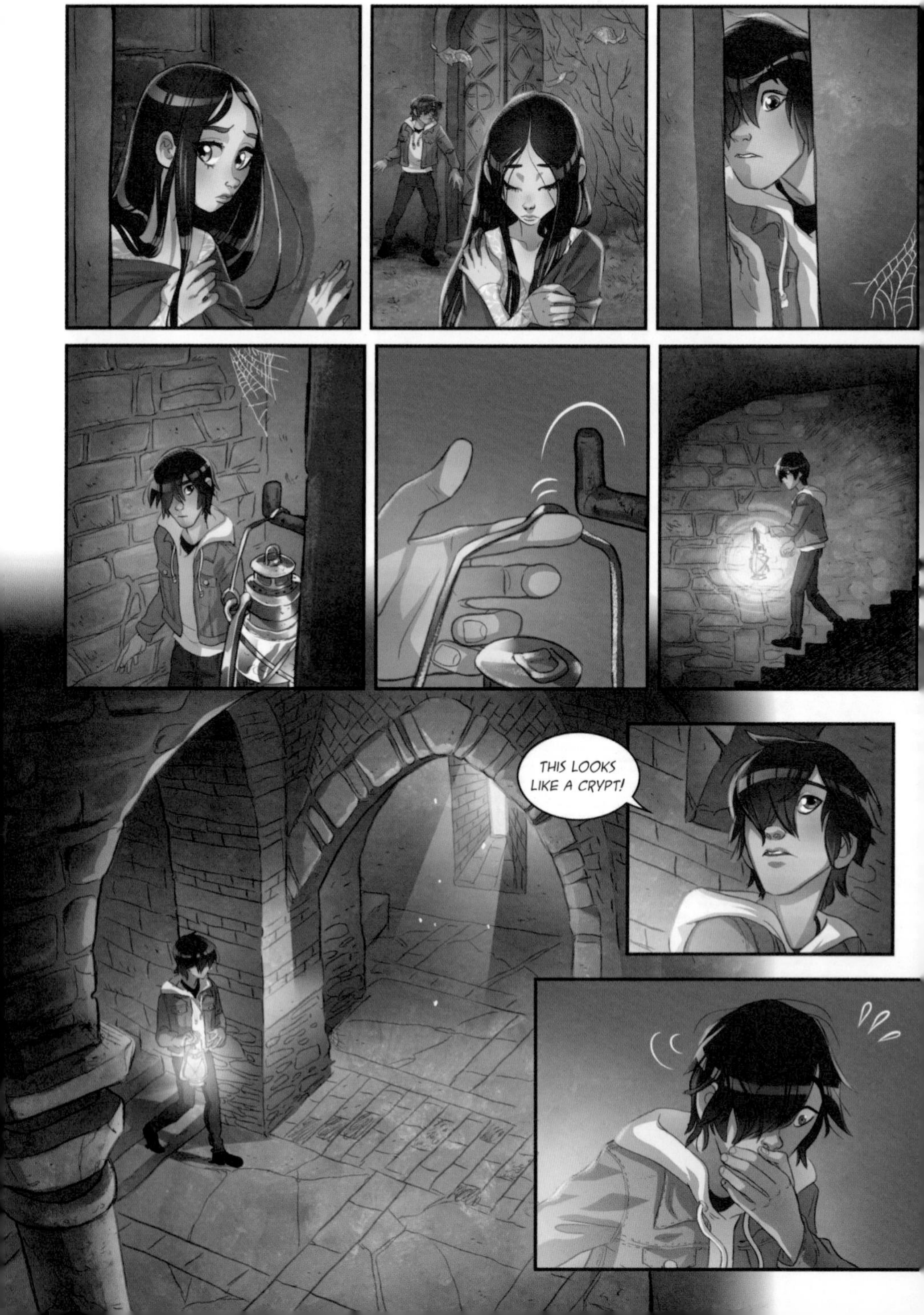
THIS LOOKS LIKE A CRYPT!

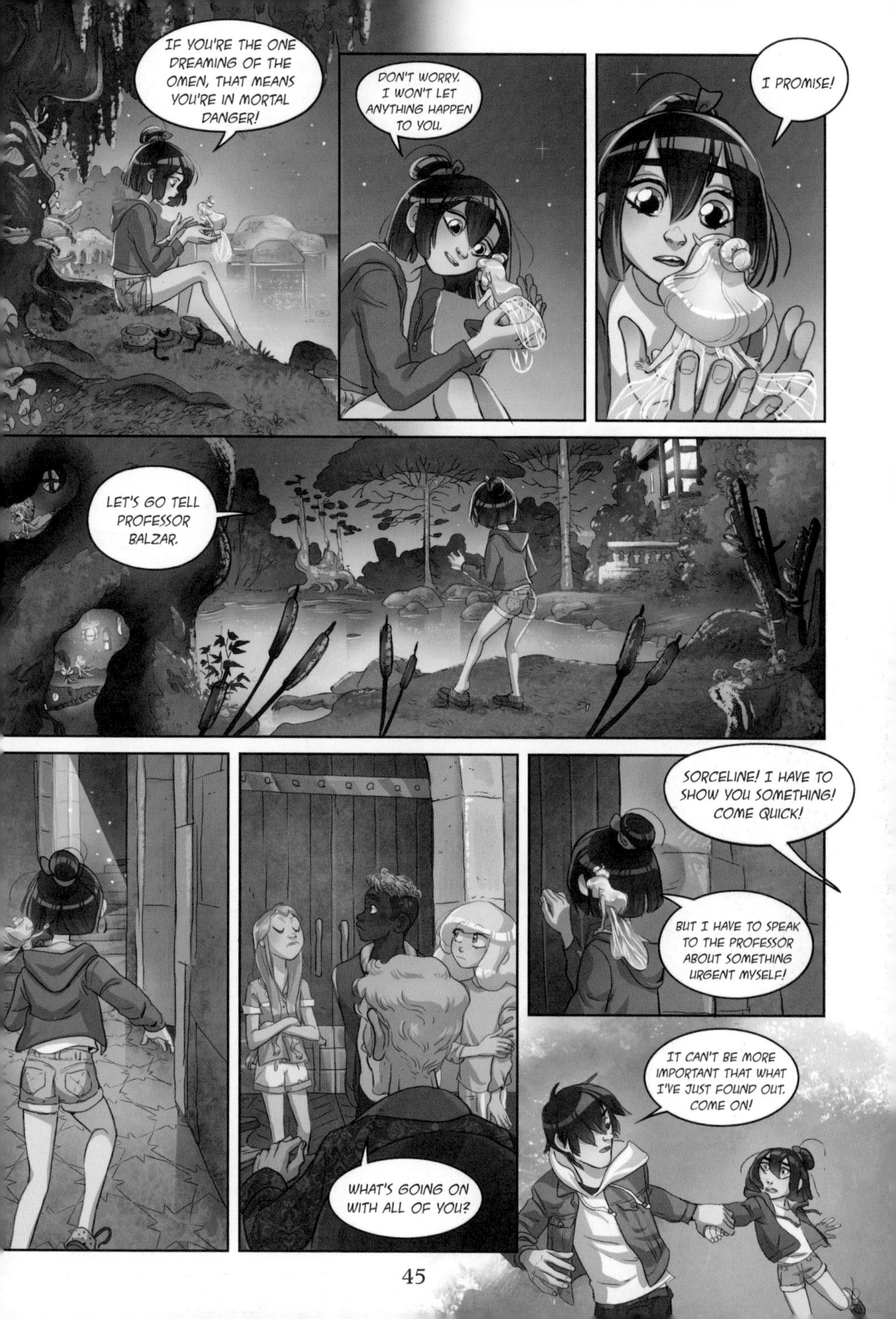
IF YOU'RE THE ONE DREAMING OF THE OMEN, THAT MEANS YOU'RE IN MORTAL DANGER!
DON'T WORRY. I WON'T LET ANYTHING HAPPEN TO YOU.
I PROMISE!
LET'S GO TELL PROFESSOR BALZAR.
WHAT'S GOING ON WITH ALL OF YOU?
SORCELINE! I HAVE TO SHOW YOU SOMETHING! COME QUICK!
BUT I HAVE TO SPEAK TO THE PROFESSOR ABOUT SOMETHING URGENT MYSELF!
IT CAN'T BE MORE IMPORTANT THAT WHAT I'VE JUST FOUND OUT. COME ON!

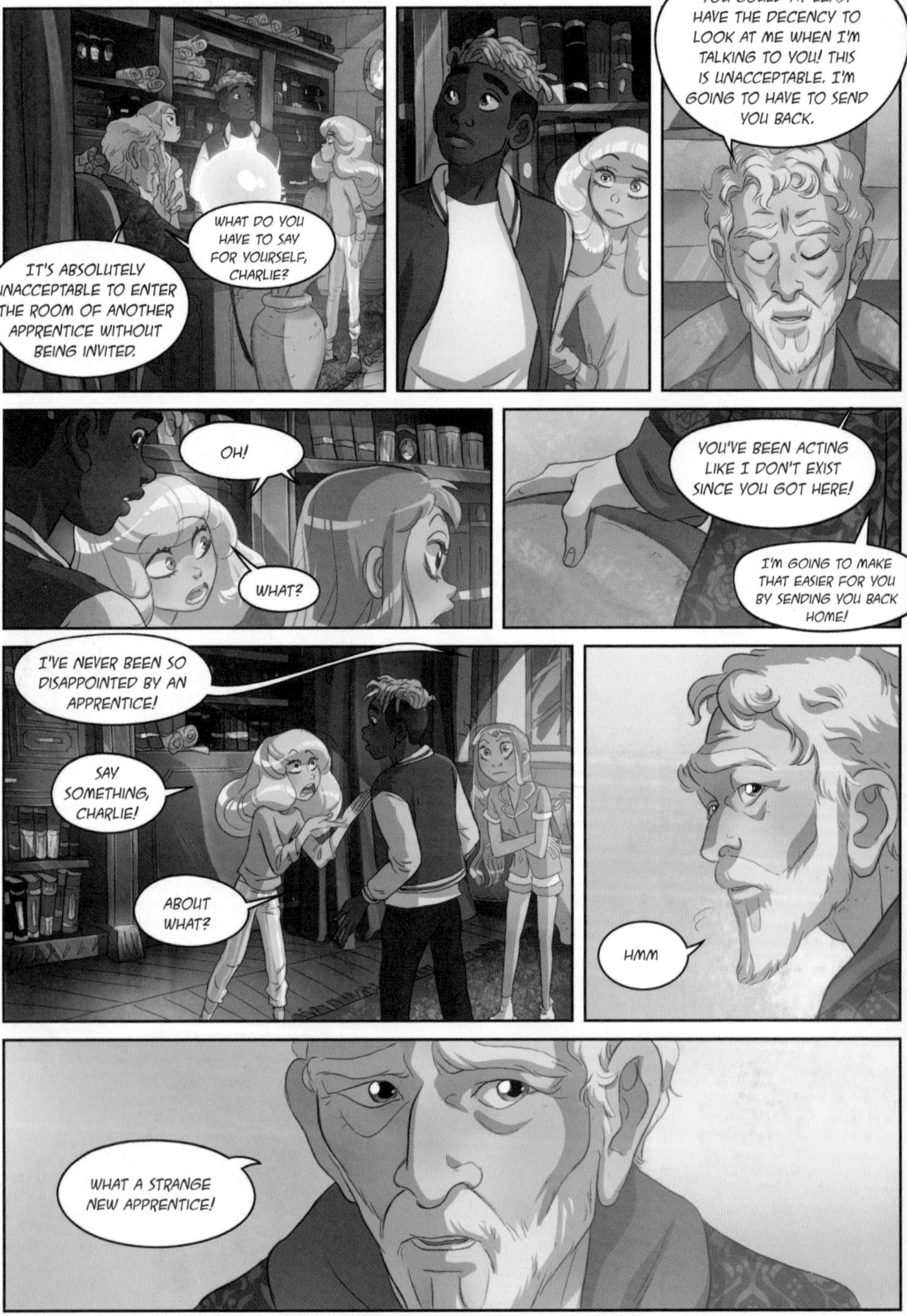
WHAT DO YOU HAVE TO SAY FOR YOURSELF, CHARLIE?
IT'S ABSOLUTELY UNACCEPTABLE TO ENTER THE ROOM OF ANOTHER APPRENTICE WITHOUT BEING INVITED.
YOU COULD AT LEAST HAVE THE DECENCY TO LOOK AT ME WHEN I'M TALKING TO YOU! THIS IS UNACCEPTABLE. I'M GOING TO HAVE TO SEND YOU BACK.
OH!
WHAT?
YOU'VE BEEN ACTING LIKE I DON'T EXIST SINCE YOU GOT HERE!
I'M GOING TO MAKE THAT EASIER FOR YOU BY SENDING YOU BACK HOME!
I'VE NEVER BEEN SO DISAPPOINTED BY AN APPRENTICE!
SAY SOMETHING, CHARLIE!
ABOUT WHAT?
HMM
WHAT A STRANGE NEW APPRENTICE!

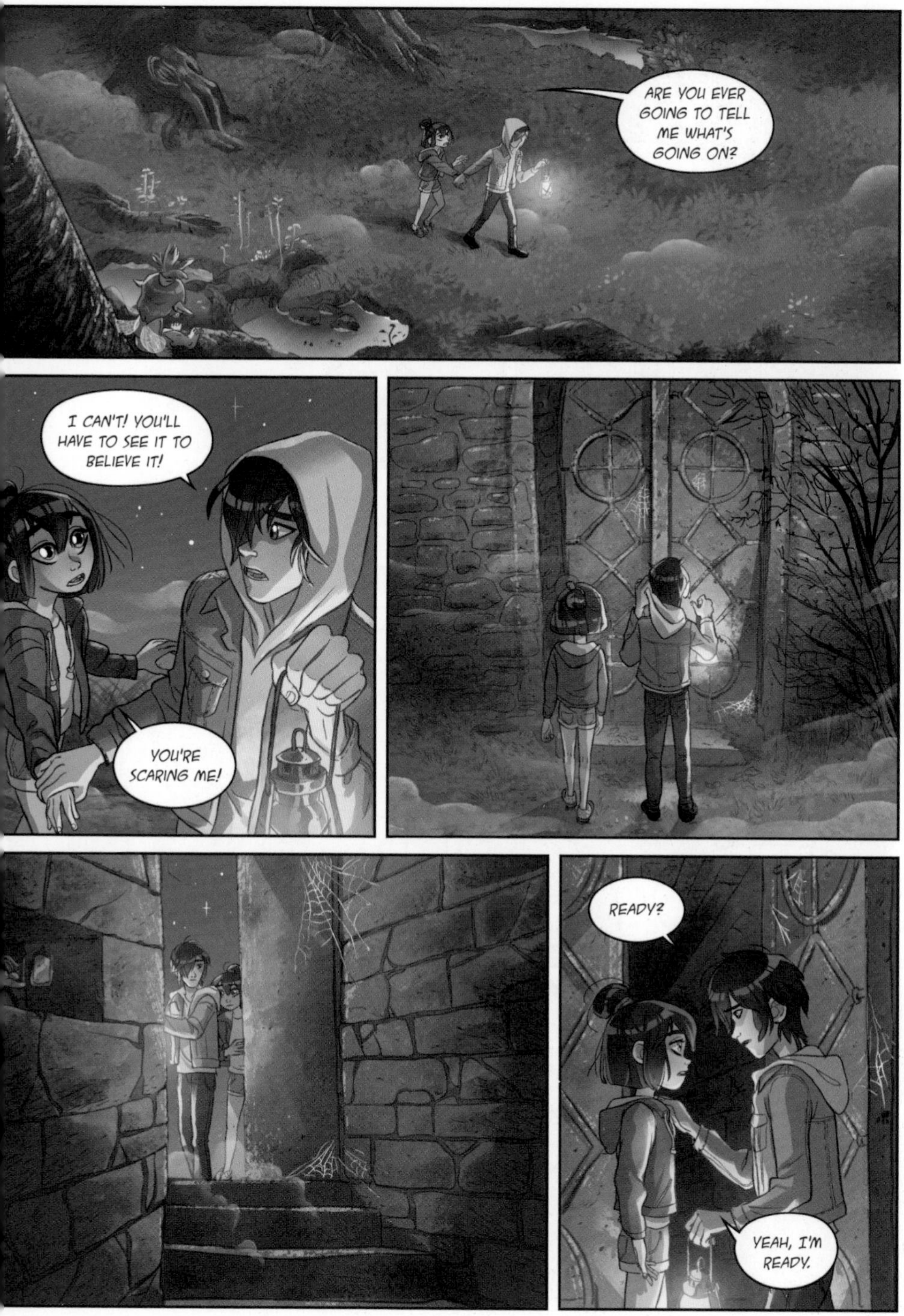
ARE YOU EVER GOING TO TELL ME WHAT'S GOING ON?
I CAN'T! YOU'LL HAVE TO SEE IT TO BELIEVE IT!
YOU'RE SCARING ME!
READY?
YEAH, I'M READY.

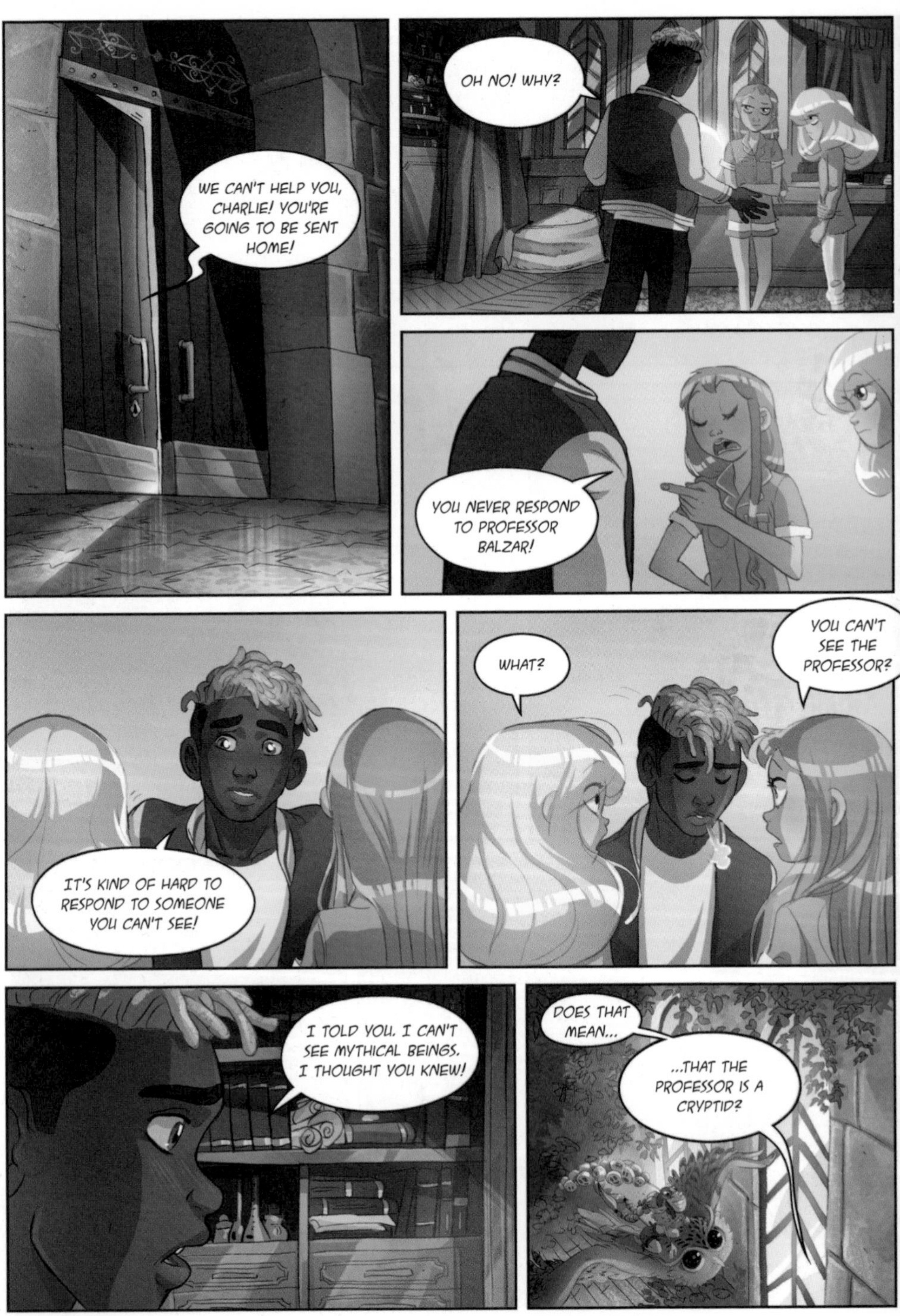
WE CAN'T HELP YOU, CHARLIE! YOU'RE GOING TO BE SENT HOME!
OH NO! WHY?
YOU NEVER RESPOND TO PROFESSOR BALZAR!
IT'S KIND OF HARD TO RESPOND TO SOMEONE YOU CAN'T SEE!
WHAT?
YOU CAN'T SEE THE PROFESSOR?
I TOLD YOU. I CAN'T SEE MYTHICAL BEINGS. I THOUGHT YOU KNEW!
DOES THAT MEAN...
...THAT THE PROFESSOR IS A CRYPTID?

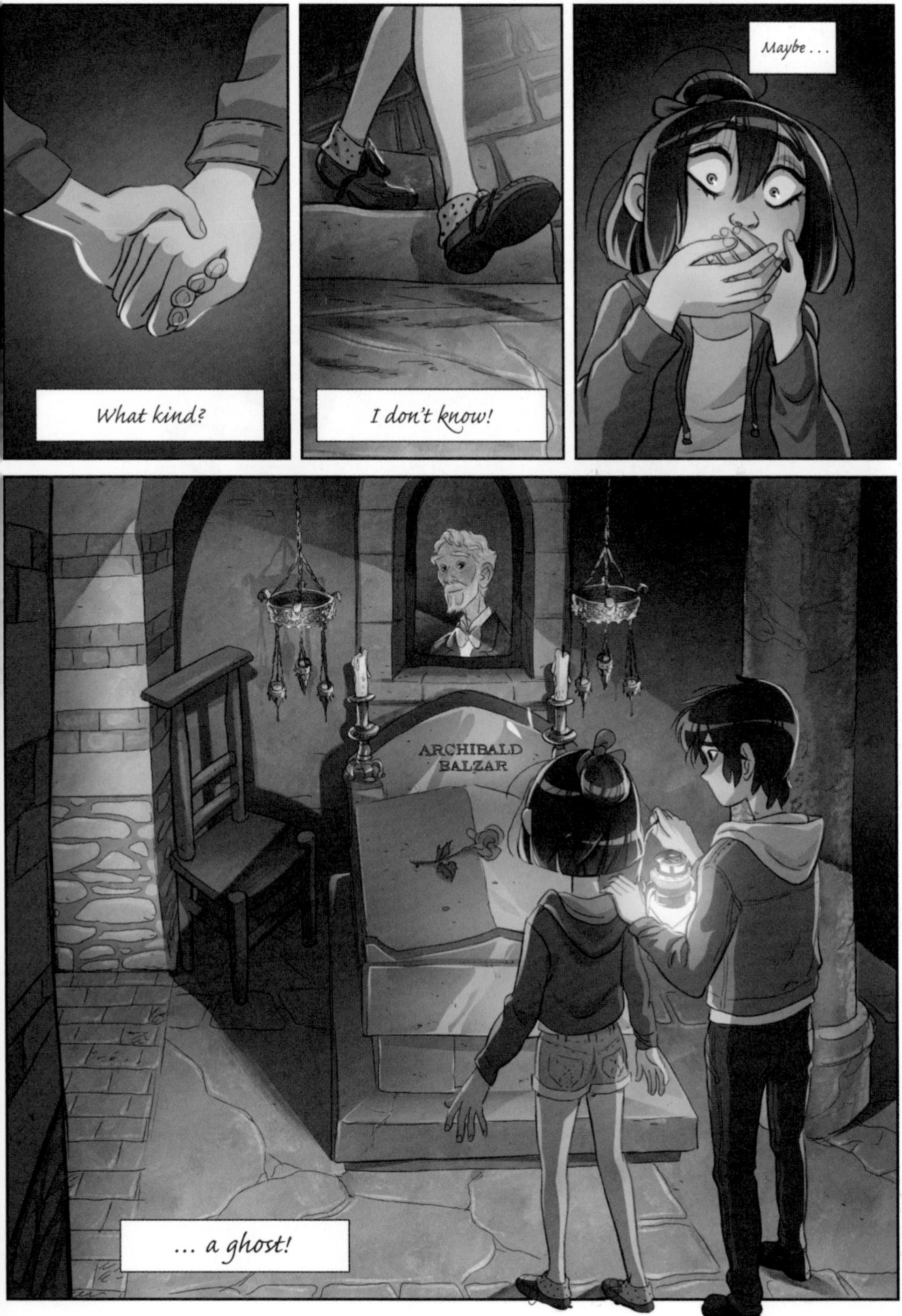
What kind?
I don't know!
Maybe . . .
ARCHIBALD BALZAR
... a ghost!

Part 2

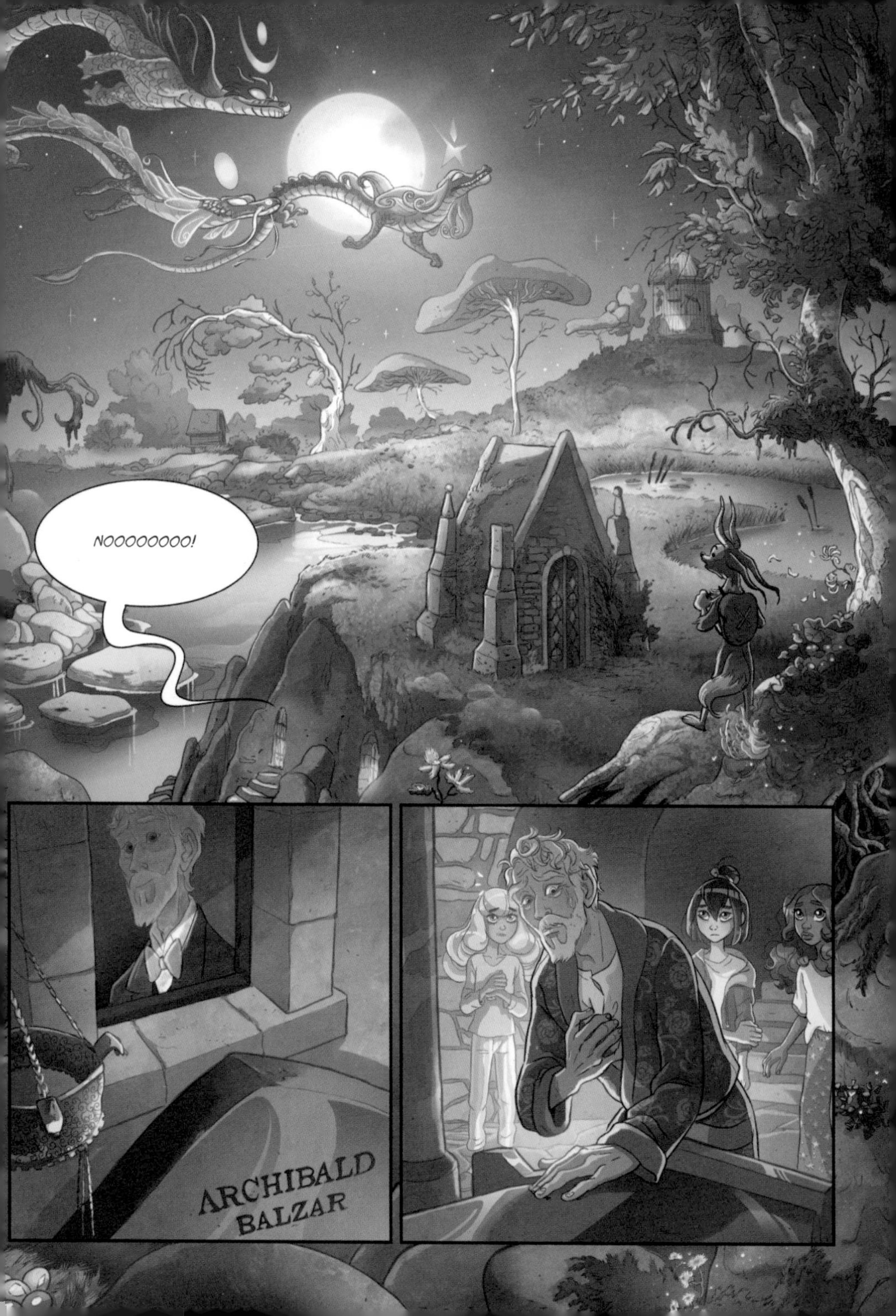
NOOOOOOOO!
ARCHIBALD
BALZAR

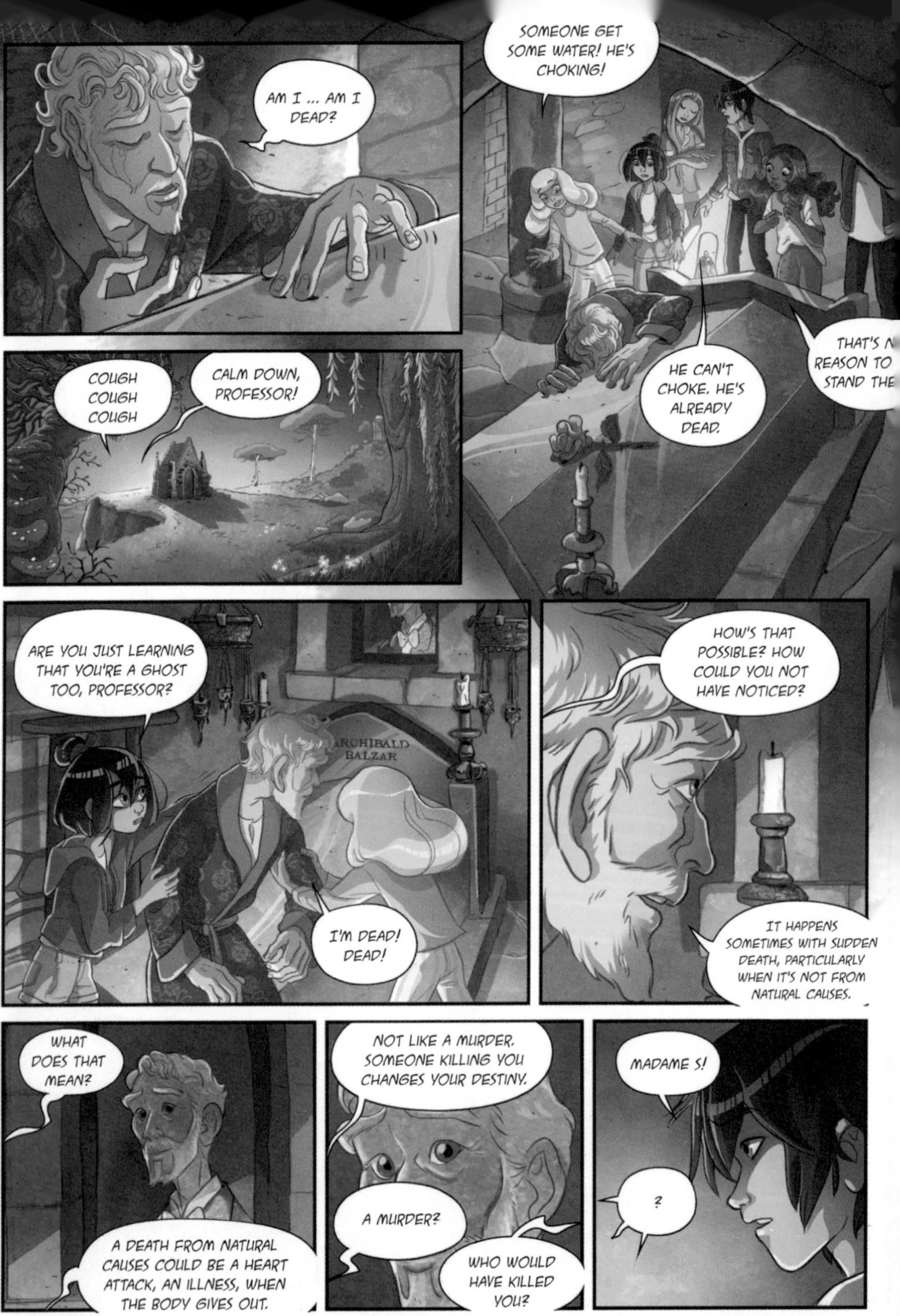
AM I ... AM I DEAD?
SOMEONE GET SOME WATER! HE'S CHOKING!
COUGH COUGH COUGH
CALM DOWN, PROFESSOR!
HE CAN'T CHOKE. HE'S ALREADY DEAD.
THAT'S N
REASON TO
STAND THE
ARE YOU JUST LEARNING THAT YOU'RE A GHOST TOO, PROFESSOR?
ARCHIBALD BALZAR
I'M DEAD! DEAD!
HOW'S THAT POSSIBLE? HOW COULD YOU NOT HAVE NOTICED?
IT HAPPENS SOMETIMES WITH SUDDEN DEATH, PARTICULARLY WHEN IT'S NOT FROM NATURAL CAUSES.
WHAT DOES THAT MEAN?
A DEATH FROM NATURAL CAUSES COULD BE A HEART ATTACK, AN ILLNESS, WHEN THE BODY GIVES OUT.
NOT LIKE A MURDER. SOMEONE KILLING YOU CHANGES YOUR DESTINY.
A MURDER?
WHO WOULD HAVE KILLED YOU?
MADAME S!
?

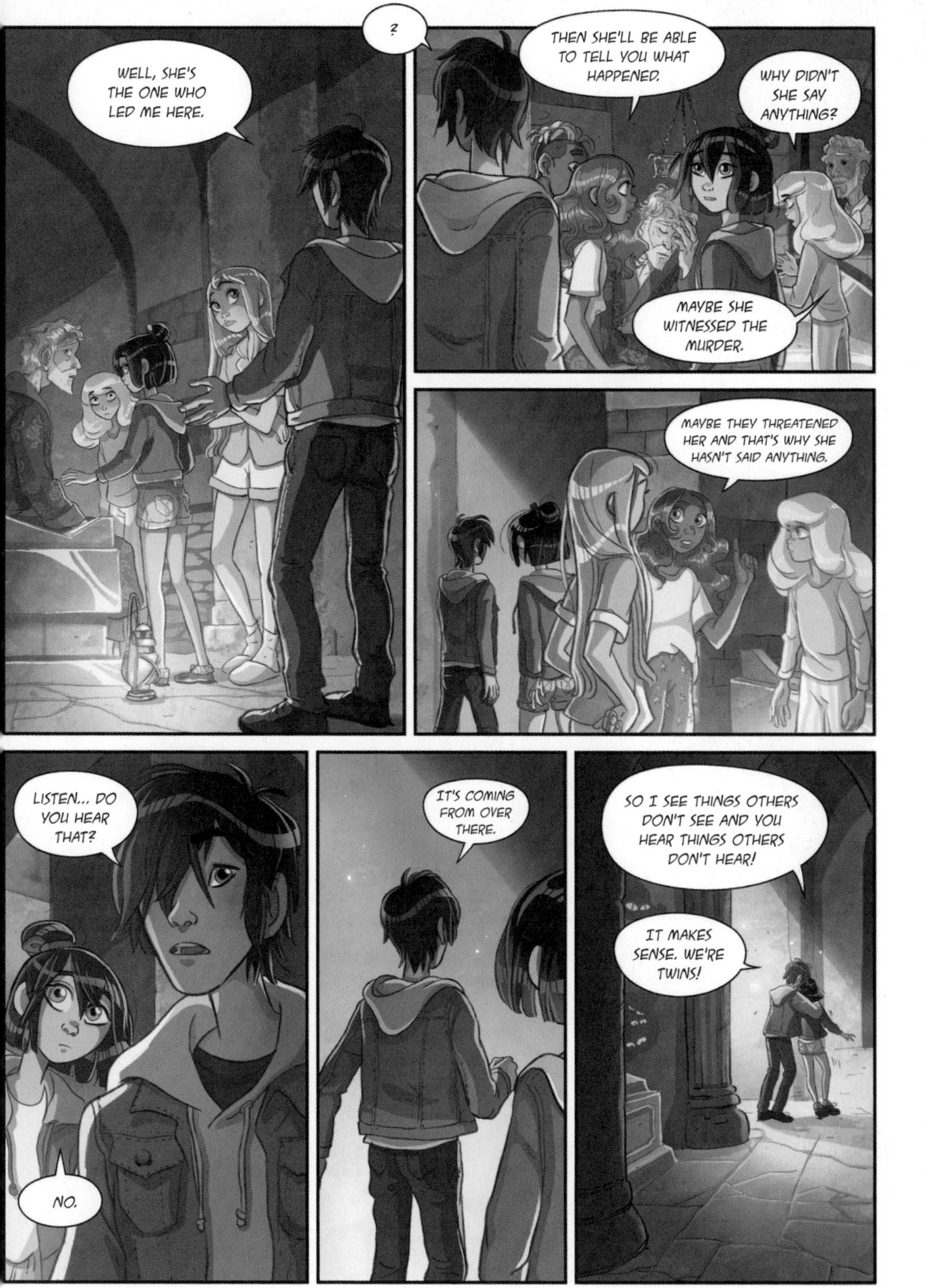
?
WELL, SHE'S THE ONE WHO LED ME HERE.
THEN SHE'LL BE ABLE TO TELL YOU WHAT HAPPENED.
WHY DIDN'T SHE SAY ANYTHING?
MAYBE SHE WITNESSED THE MURDER.
MAYBE THEY THREATENED HER AND THAT'S WHY SHE HASN'T SAID ANYTHING.
LISTEN... DO YOU HEAR THAT?
NO.
IT'S COMING FROM OVER THERE.
SO I SEE THINGS OTHERS DON'T SEE AND YOU HEAR THINGS OTHERS DON'T HEAR!
IT MAKES SENSE. WE'RE TWINS!

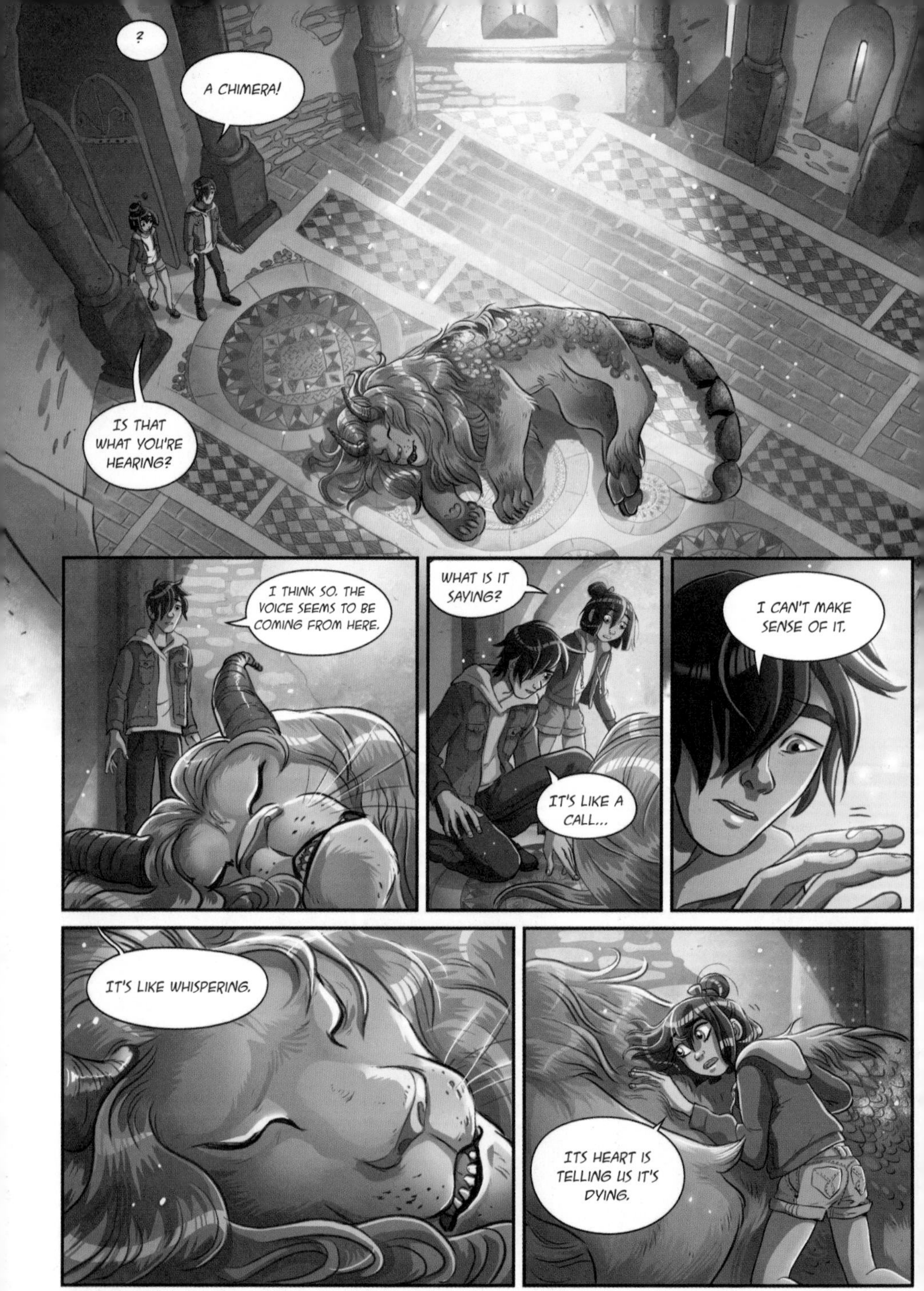
?
A CHIMERA!
IS THAT WHAT YOU'RE HEARING?
I THINK SO. THE VOICE SEEMS TO BE COMING FROM HERE.
WHAT IS IT SAYING?
IT'S LIKE A CALL...
I CAN'T MAKE SENSE OF IT.
IT'S LIKE WHISPERING.
ITS HEART IS TELLING US IT'S DYING.

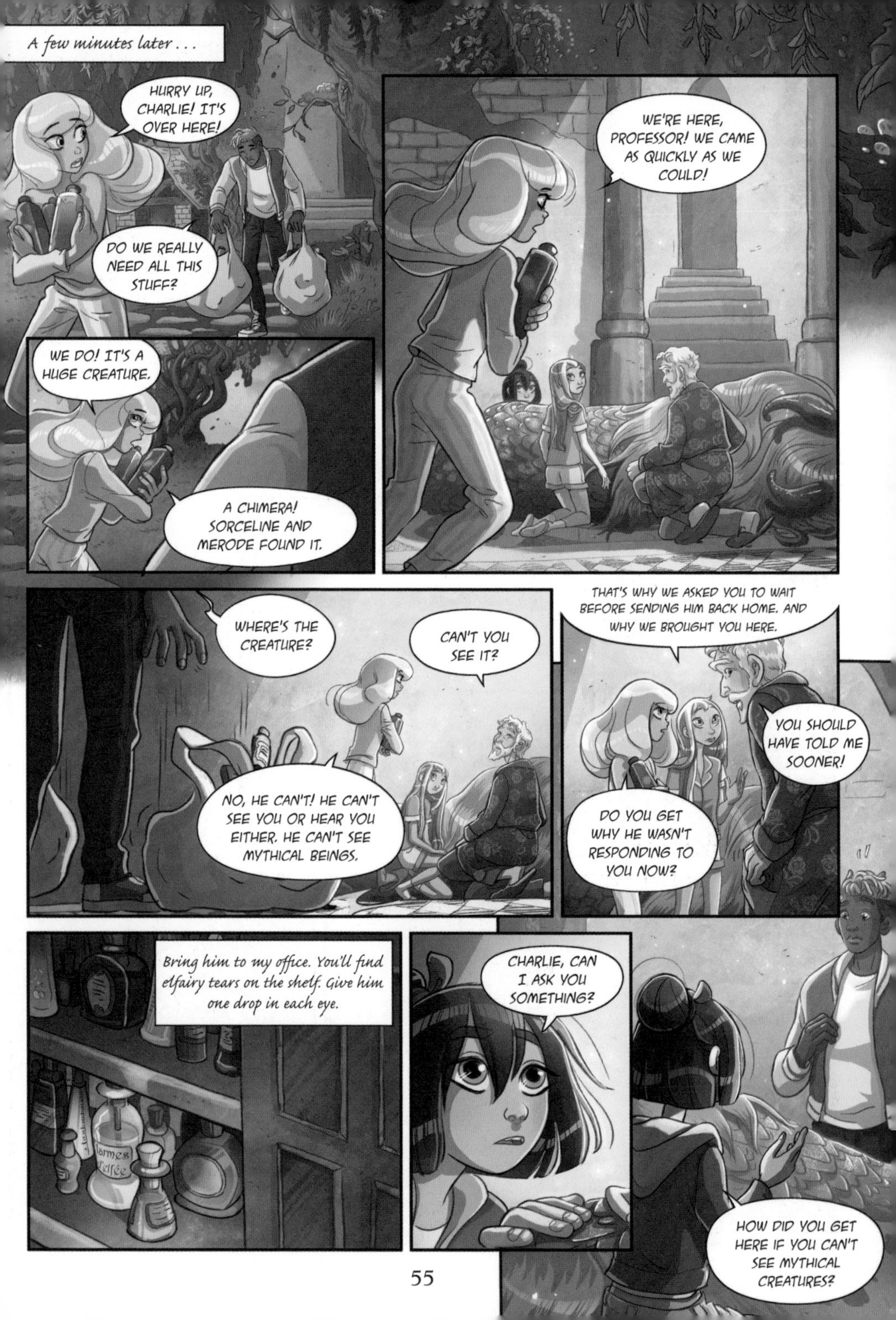
A few minutes later . . .
HURRY UP, CHARLIE! IT'S OVER HERE!
DO WE REALLY NEED ALL THIS STUFF?
WE DO! IT'S A HUGE CREATURE.
A CHIMERA! SORCELINE AND MERODE FOUND IT.
WE'RE HERE, PROFESSOR! WE CAME AS QUICKLY AS WE COULD!
WHERE'S THE CREATURE?
CAN'T YOU SEE IT?
NO, HE CAN'T! HE CAN'T SEE YOU OR HEAR YOU EITHER. HE CAN'T SEE MYTHICAL BEINGS.
THAT'S WHY WE ASKED YOU TO WAIT BEFORE SENDING HIM BACK HOME. AND WHY WE BROUGHT YOU HERE.
YOU SHOULD HAVE TOLD ME SOONER!
DO YOU GET WHY HE WASN'T RESPONDING TO YOU NOW?
Bring him to my office. You'll find elfairy tears on the shelf. Give him one drop in each eye.
larmes d'elfée
CHARLIE, CAN I ASK YOU SOMETHING?
HOW DID YOU GET HERE IF YOU CAN'T SEE MYTHICAL CREATURES?

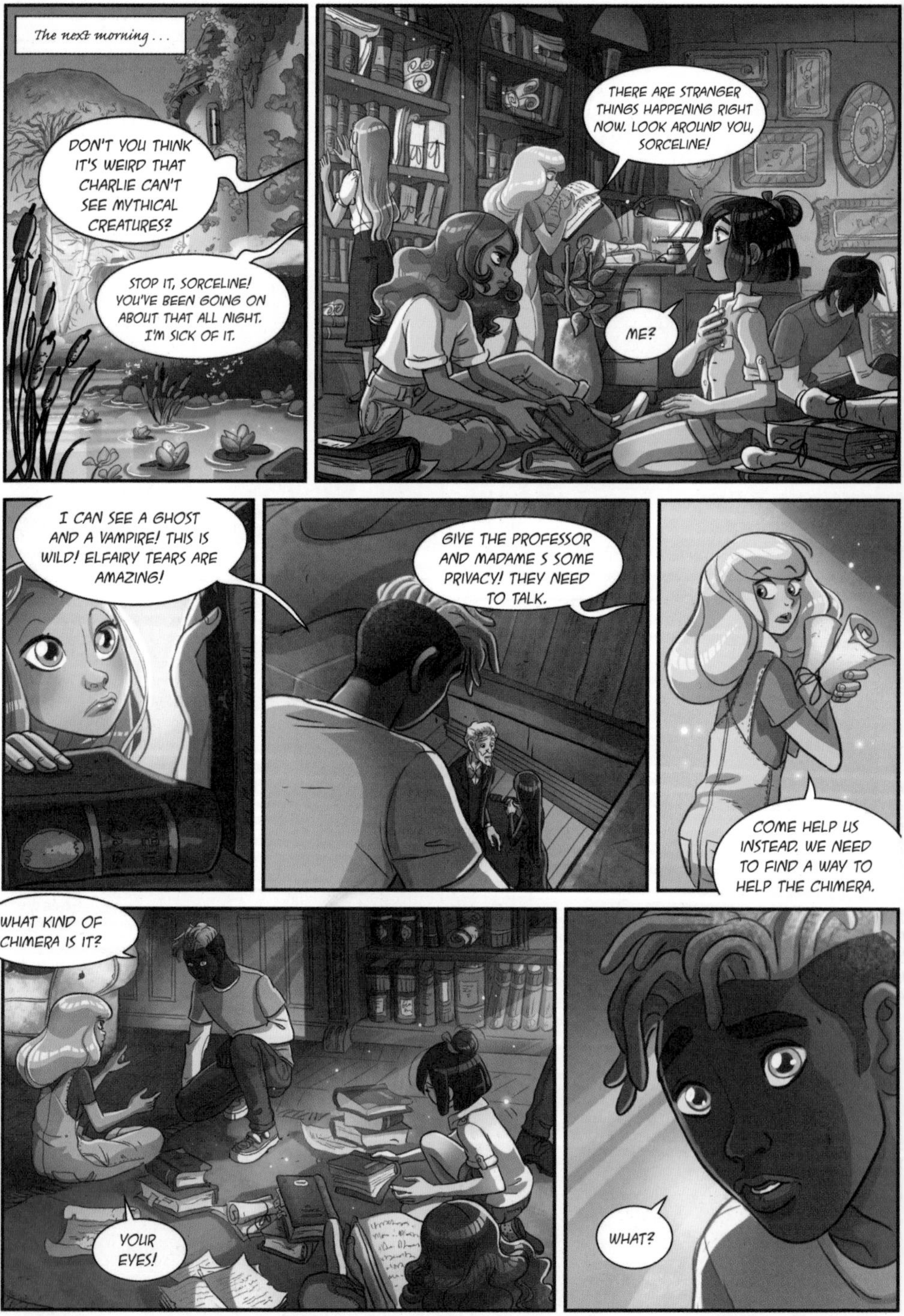
The next morning . . .
DON'T YOU THINK IT'S WEIRD THAT CHARLIE CAN'T SEE MYTHICAL CREATURES?
STOP IT, SORCELINE! YOU'VE BEEN GOING ON ABOUT THAT ALL NIGHT. I'M SICK OF IT.
THERE ARE STRANGER THINGS HAPPENING RIGHT NOW. LOOK AROUND YOU, SORCELINE!
ME?
I CAN SEE A GHOST AND A VAMPIRE! THIS IS WILD! ELFAIRY TEARS ARE AMAZING!
GIVE THE PROFESSOR AND MADAME S SOME PRIVACY! THEY NEED TO TALK.
COME HELP US INSTEAD. WE NEED TO FIND A WAY TO HELP THE CHIMERA.
WHAT KIND OF CHIMERA IS IT?
YOUR EYES!
WHAT?

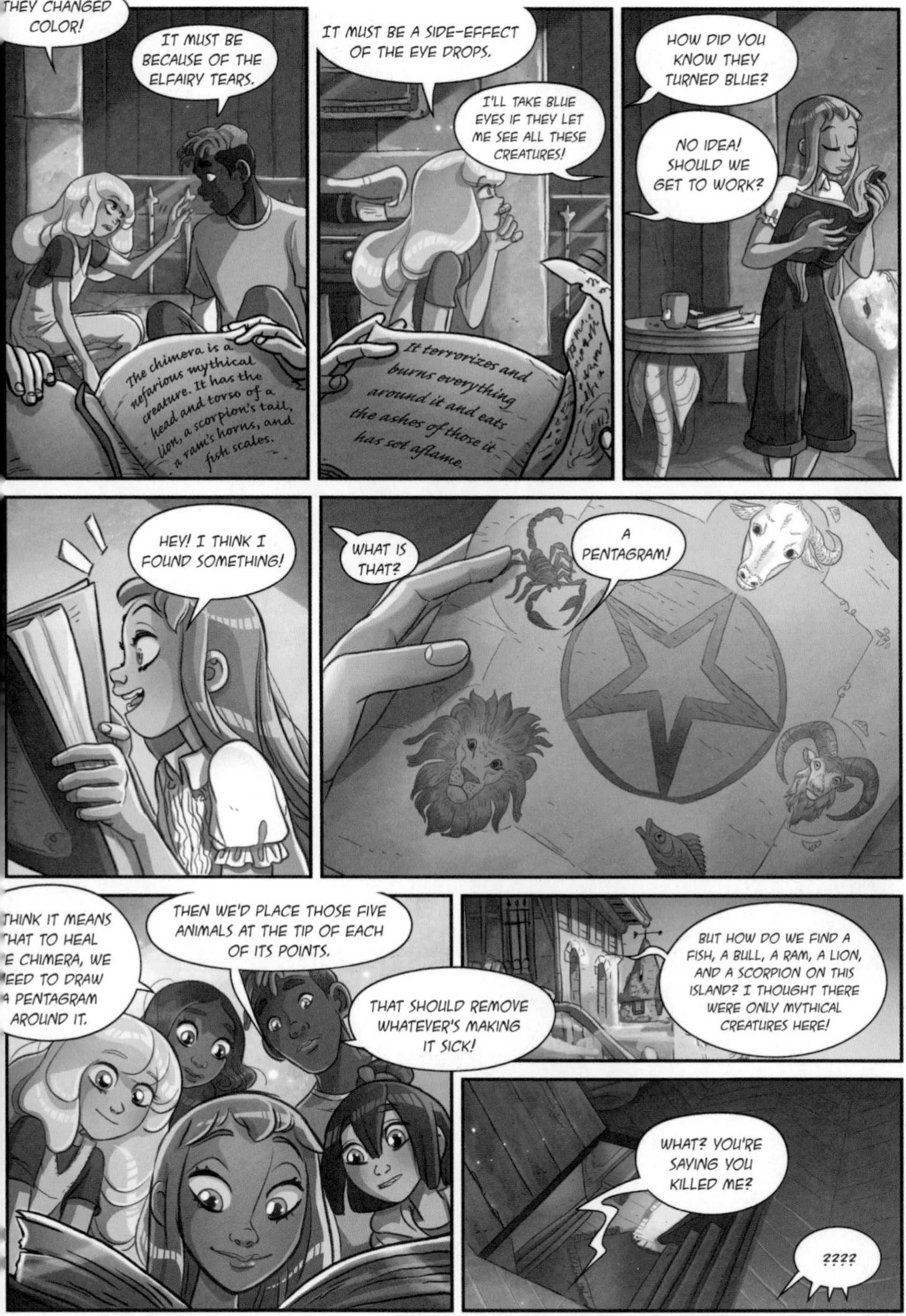

THEY CHANGED COLOR!
IT MUST BE BECAUSE OF THE ELFAIRY TEARS.
The chimera is a nefarious mythical creature. It has the head and torso of a lion, a scorpion's tail, a ram's horns, and fish scales.
IT MUST BE A SIDE-EFFECT OF THE EYE DROPS.
I'LL TAKE BLUE EYES IF THEY LET ME SEE ALL THESE CREATURES!
It terrorizes and burns everything around it and eats the ashes of those it has set aflame.
HOW DID YOU KNOW THEY TURNED BLUE?
NO IDEA! SHOULD WE GET TO WORK?
HEY! I THINK I FOUND SOMETHING!
WHAT IS THAT?
A PENTAGRAM!
THINK IT MEANS THAT TO HEAL E CHIMERA, WE EED TO DRAW A PENTAGRAM AROUND IT.
THEN WE'D PLACE THOSE FIVE ANIMALS AT THE TIP OF EACH OF ITS POINTS.
THAT SHOULD REMOVE WHATEVER'S MAKING IT SICK!
BUT HOW DO WE FIND A FISH, A BULL, A RAM, A LION, AND A SCORPION ON THIS ISLAND? I THOUGHT THERE WERE ONLY MYTHICAL CREATURES HERE!
WHAT? YOU'RE SAYING YOU KILLED ME?
????

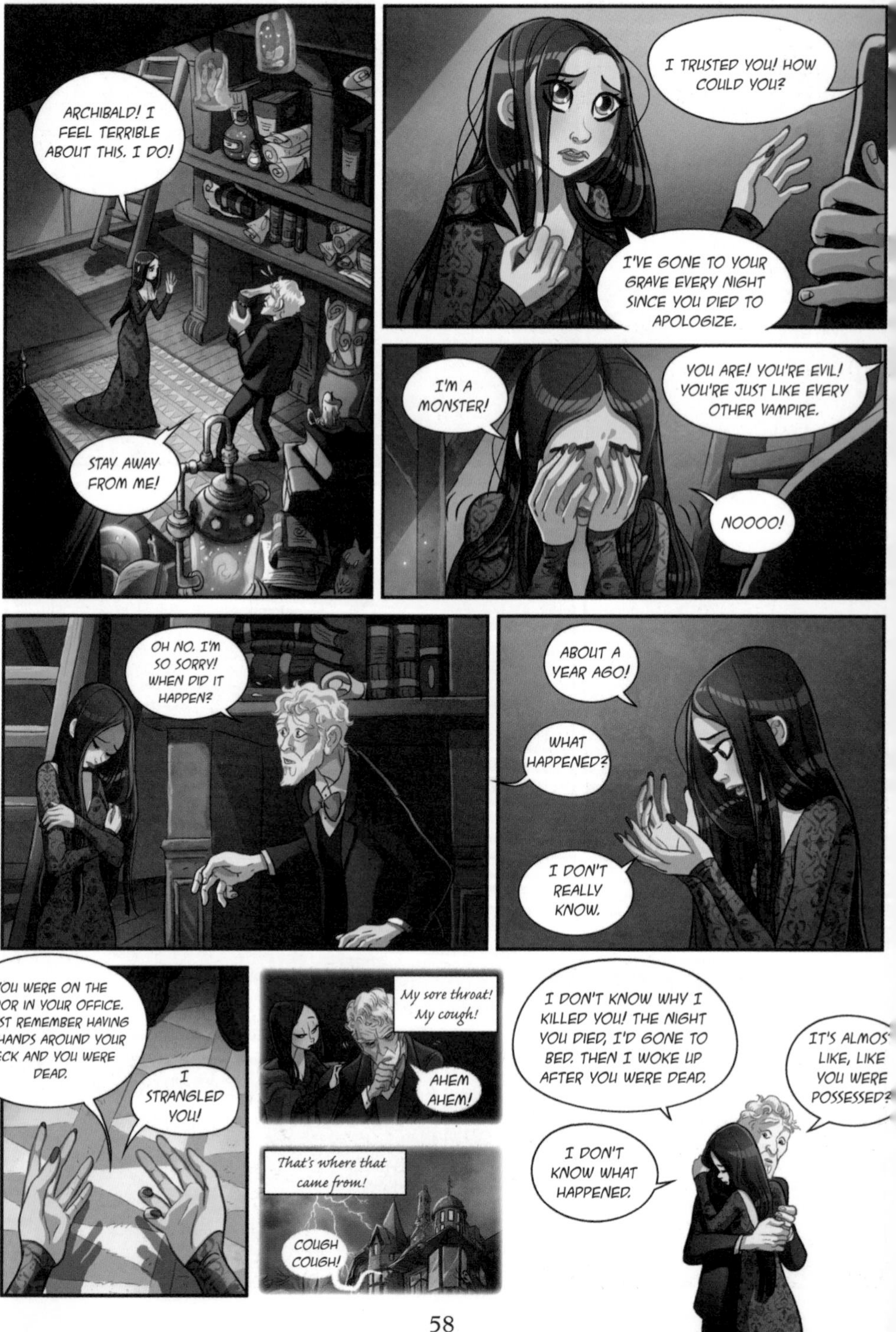
ARCHIBALD! I FEEL TERRIBLE ABOUT THIS. I DO!
STAY AWAY FROM ME!
I TRUSTED YOU! HOW COULD YOU?
I'VE GONE TO YOUR GRAVE EVERY NIGHT SINCE YOU DIED TO APOLOGIZE.
I'M A MONSTER!
YOU ARE! YOU'RE EVIL! YOU'RE JUST LIKE EVERY OTHER VAMPIRE.
NOOOO!
OH NO. I'M SO SORRY! WHEN DID IT HAPPEN?
ABOUT A YEAR AGO!
WHAT HAPPENED?
I DON'T REALLY KNOW.
YOU WERE ON THE FLOOR IN YOUR OFFICE. I JUST REMEMBER HAVING MY HANDS AROUND YOUR NECK AND YOU WERE DEAD.
I STRANGLED YOU!
My sore throat! My cough!
AHEM AHEM!
That's where that came from!
COUGH COUGH!
I DON'T KNOW WHY I KILLED YOU! THE NIGHT YOU DIED, I'D GONE TO BED. THEN I WOKE UP AFTER YOU WERE DEAD.
IT'S ALMOS LIKE, LIKE YOU WERE POSSESSED?
I DON'T KNOW WHAT HAPPENED.

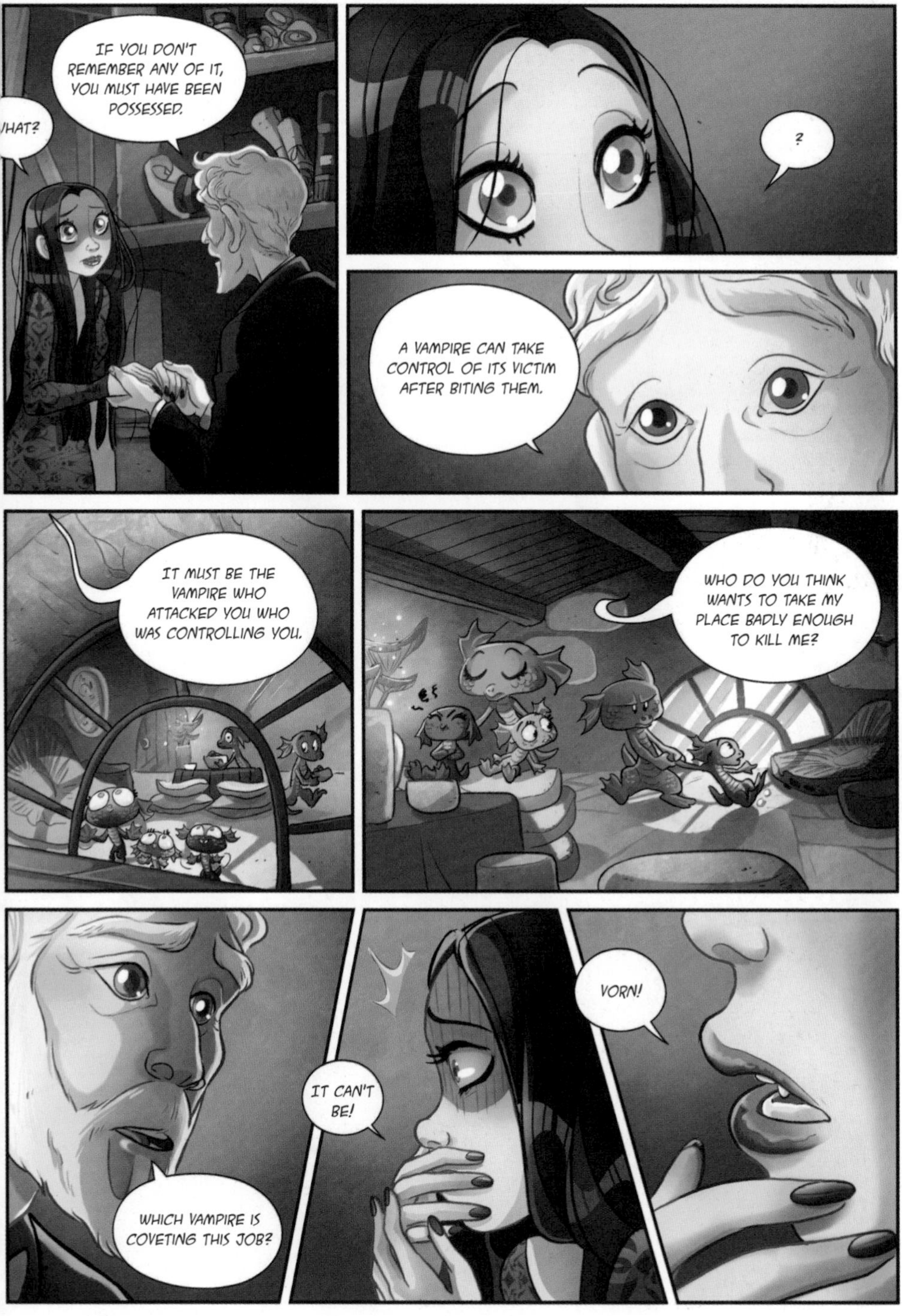
IF YOU DON'T REMEMBER ANY OF IT, YOU MUST HAVE BEEN POSSESSED.
WHAT?
?
A VAMPIRE CAN TAKE CONTROL OF ITS VICTIM AFTER BITING THEM.
IT MUST BE THE VAMPIRE WHO ATTACKED YOU WHO WAS CONTROLLING YOU.
WHO DO YOU THINK WANTS TO TAKE MY PLACE BADLY ENOUGH TO KILL ME?
WHICH VAMPIRE IS COVETING THIS JOB?
IT CAN'T BE!
VORN!

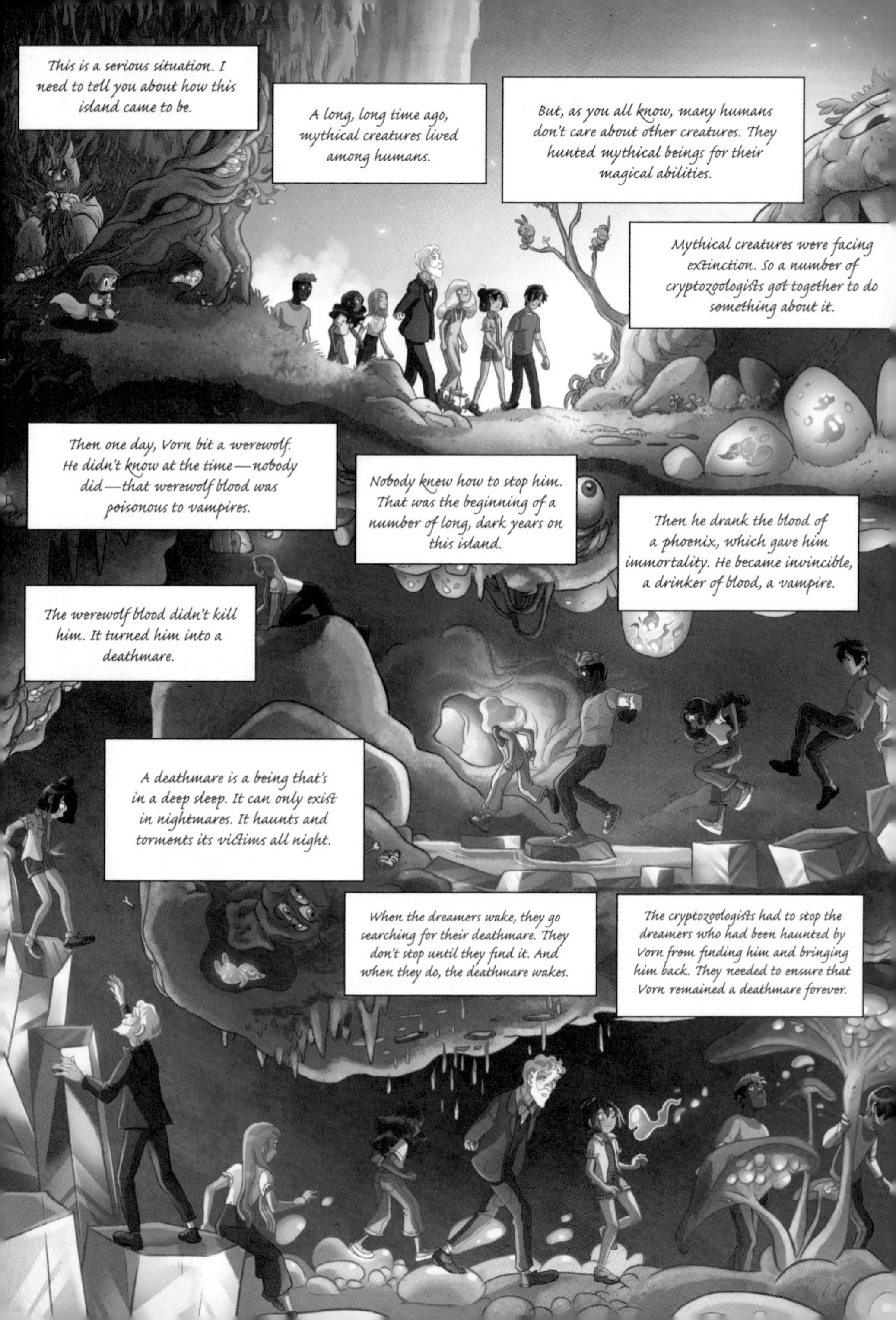
This is a serious situation. I need to tell you about how this island came to be.
A long, long time ago, mythical creatures lived among humans.
But, as you all know, many humans don't care about other creatures. They hunted mythical beings for their magical abilities.
Mythical creatures were facing extinction. So a number of cryptozoologists got together to do something about it.
Then one day, Vorn bit a werewolf. He didn't know at the time—nobody did—that werewolf blood was poisonous to vampires.
Nobody knew how to stop him. That was the beginning of a number of long, dark years on this island.
Then he drank the blood of a phoenix, which gave him immortality. He became invincible, a drinker of blood, a vampire.
The werewolf blood didn't kill him. It turned him into a deathmare.
A deathmare is a being that's in a deep sleep. It can only exist in nightmares. It haunts and torments its victims all night.
When the dreamers wake, they go searching for their deathmare. They don't stop until they find it. And when they do, the deathmare wakes.
The cryptozoologists had to stop the dreamers who had been haunted by Vorn from finding him and bringing him back. They needed to ensure that Vorn remained a deathmare forever.

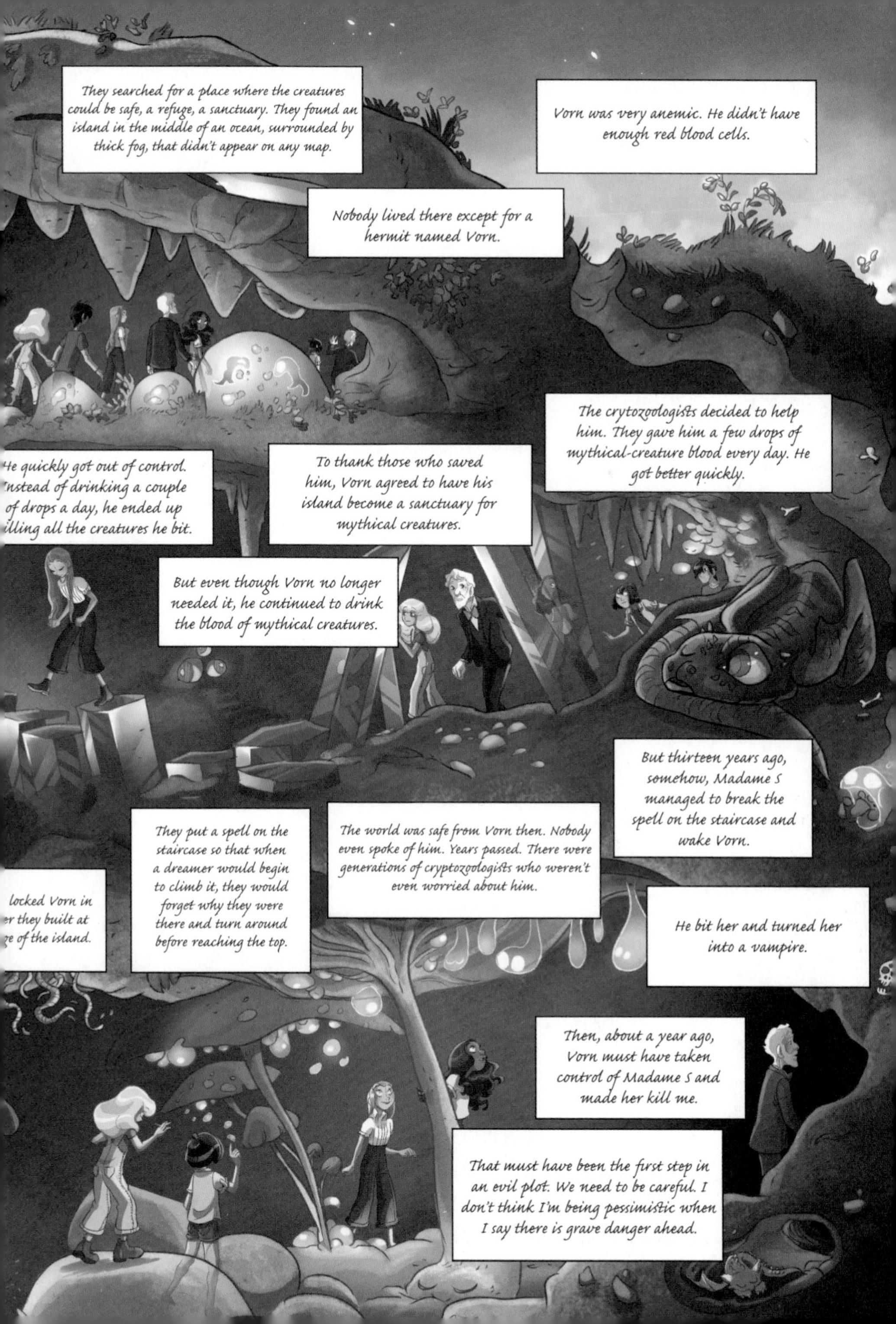
They searched for a place where the creatures could be safe, a refuge, a sanctuary. They found an island in the middle of an ocean, surrounded by thick fog, that didn't appear on any map.
Nobody lived there except for a hermit named Vorn.
Vorn was very anemic. He didn't have enough red blood cells.
The crytozoologists decided to help him. They gave him a few drops of mythical-creature blood every day. He got better quickly.
To thank those who saved him, Vorn agreed to have his island become a sanctuary for mythical creatures.
But even though Vorn no longer needed it, he continued to drink the blood of mythical creatures.
He quickly got out of control. nstead of drinking a couple of drops a day, he ended up illing all the creatures he bit.
locked Vorn in er they built at e of the island.
They put a spell on the staircase so that when a dreamer would begin to climb it, they would forget why they were there and turn around before reaching the top.
The world was safe from Vorn then. Nobody even spoke of him. Years passed. There were generations of cryptozoologists who weren't even worried about him.
But thirteen years ago, somehow, Madame S managed to break the spell on the staircase and wake Vorn.
He bit her and turned her into a vampire.
Then, about a year ago, Vorn must have taken control of Madame S and made her kill me.
That must have been the first step in an evil plot. We need to be careful. I don't think I'm being pessimistic when I say there is grave danger ahead.

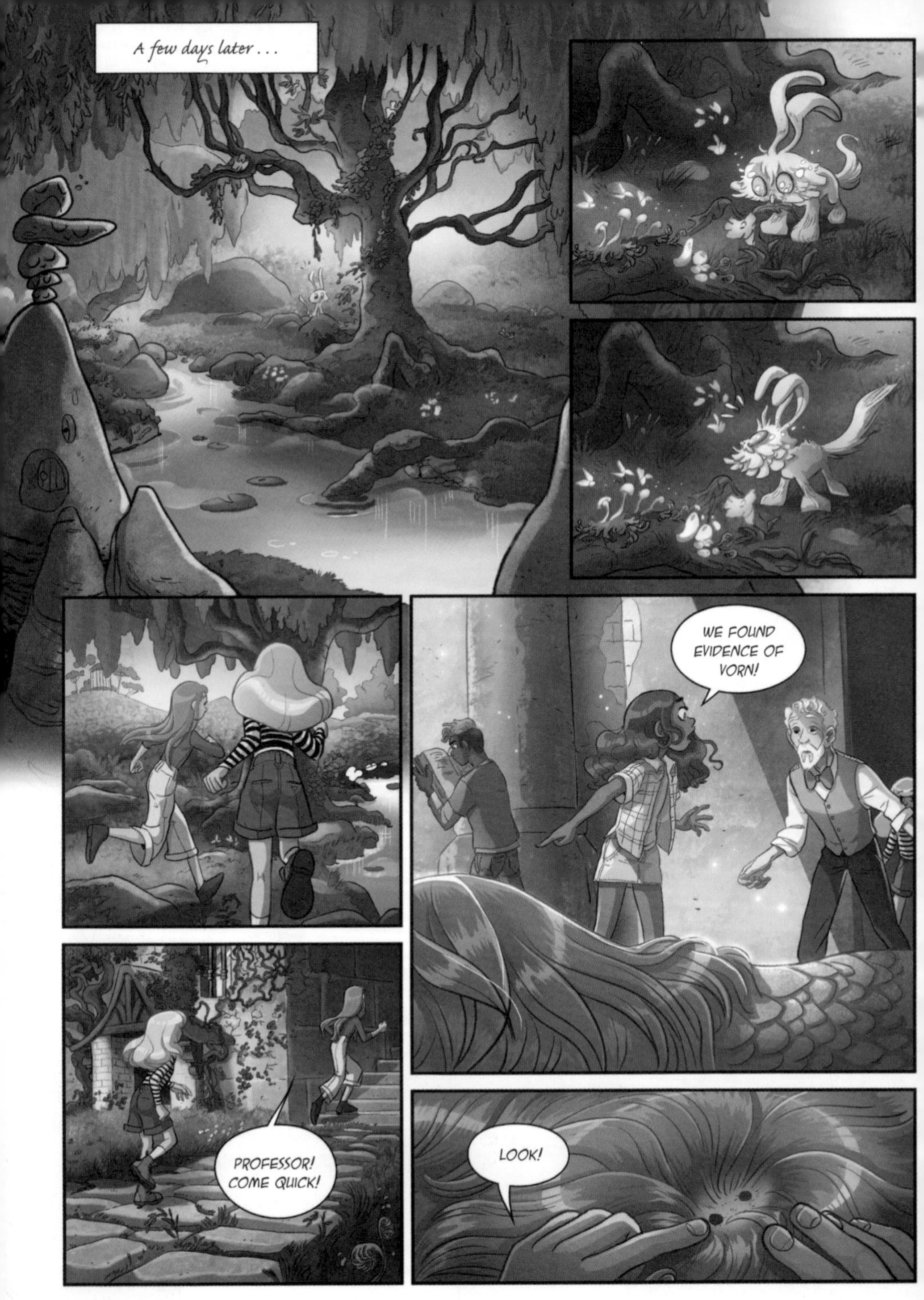
A few days later . . .
PROFESSOR! COME QUICK!
WE FOUND EVIDENCE OF VORN!
LOOK!

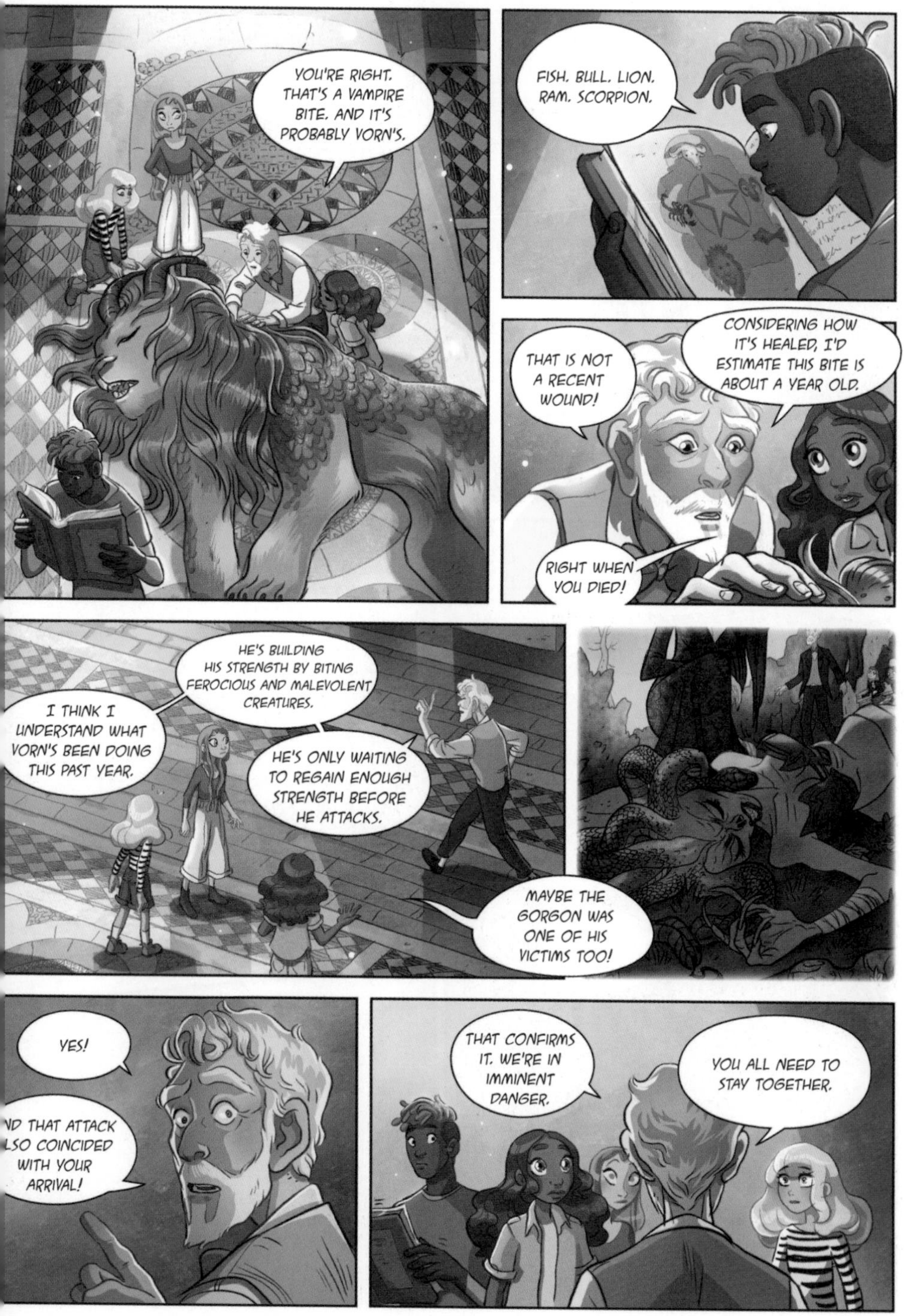
YOU'RE RIGHT. THAT'S A VAMPIRE BITE. AND IT'S PROBABLY VORN'S.
FISH. BULL. LION. RAM. SCORPION.
THAT IS NOT A RECENT WOUND!
CONSIDERING HOW IT'S HEALED, I'D ESTIMATE THIS BITE IS ABOUT A YEAR OLD.
RIGHT WHEN YOU DIED!
I THINK I UNDERSTAND WHAT VORN'S BEEN DOING THIS PAST YEAR.
HE'S BUILDING HIS STRENGTH BY BITING FEROCIOUS AND MALEVOLENT CREATURES.
HE'S ONLY WAITING TO REGAIN ENOUGH STRENGTH BEFORE HE ATTACKS.
MAYBE THE GORGON WAS ONE OF HIS VICTIMS TOO!
YES!
ND THAT ATTACK LSO COINCIDED WITH YOUR ARRIVAL!
THAT CONFIRMS IT. WE'RE IN IMMINENT DANGER.
YOU ALL NEED TO STAY TOGETHER.

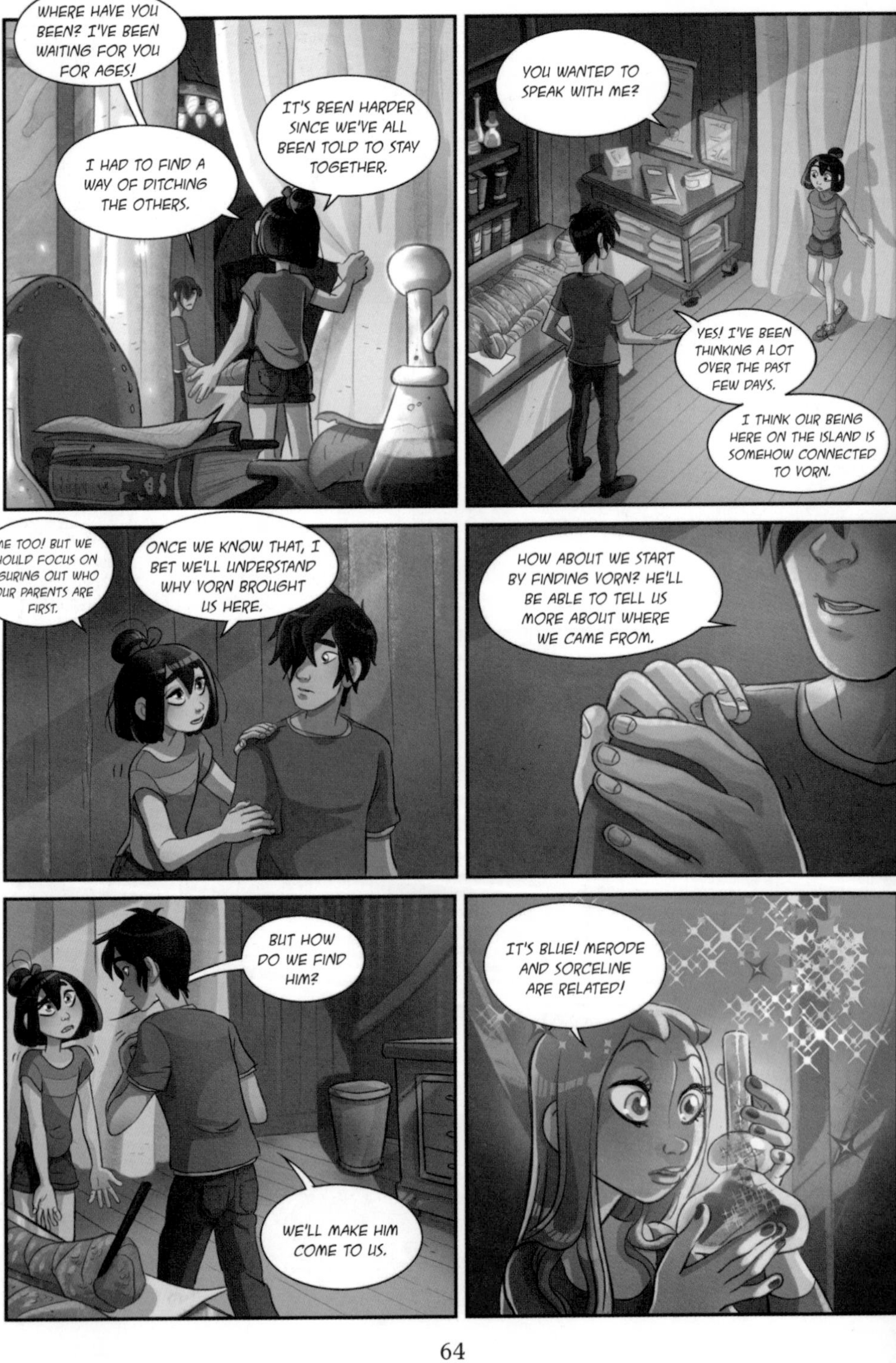
WHERE HAVE YOU BEEN? I'VE BEEN WAITING FOR YOU FOR AGES!
I HAD TO FIND A WAY OF DITCHING THE OTHERS.
IT'S BEEN HARDER SINCE WE'VE ALL BEEN TOLD TO STAY TOGETHER.
YOU WANTED TO SPEAK WITH ME?
YES! I'VE BEEN THINKING A LOT OVER THE PAST FEW DAYS.
I THINK OUR BEING HERE ON THE ISLAND IS SOMEHOW CONNECTED TO VORN.
ME TOO! BUT WE SHOULD FOCUS ON FIGURING OUT WHO OUR PARENTS ARE FIRST.
ONCE WE KNOW THAT, I BET WE'LL UNDERSTAND WHY VORN BROUGHT US HERE.
HOW ABOUT WE START BY FINDING VORN? HE'LL BE ABLE TO TELL US MORE ABOUT WHERE WE CAME FROM.
BUT HOW DO WE FIND HIM?
WE'LL MAKE HIM COME TO US.
IT'S BLUE! MERODE AND SORCELINE ARE RELATED!

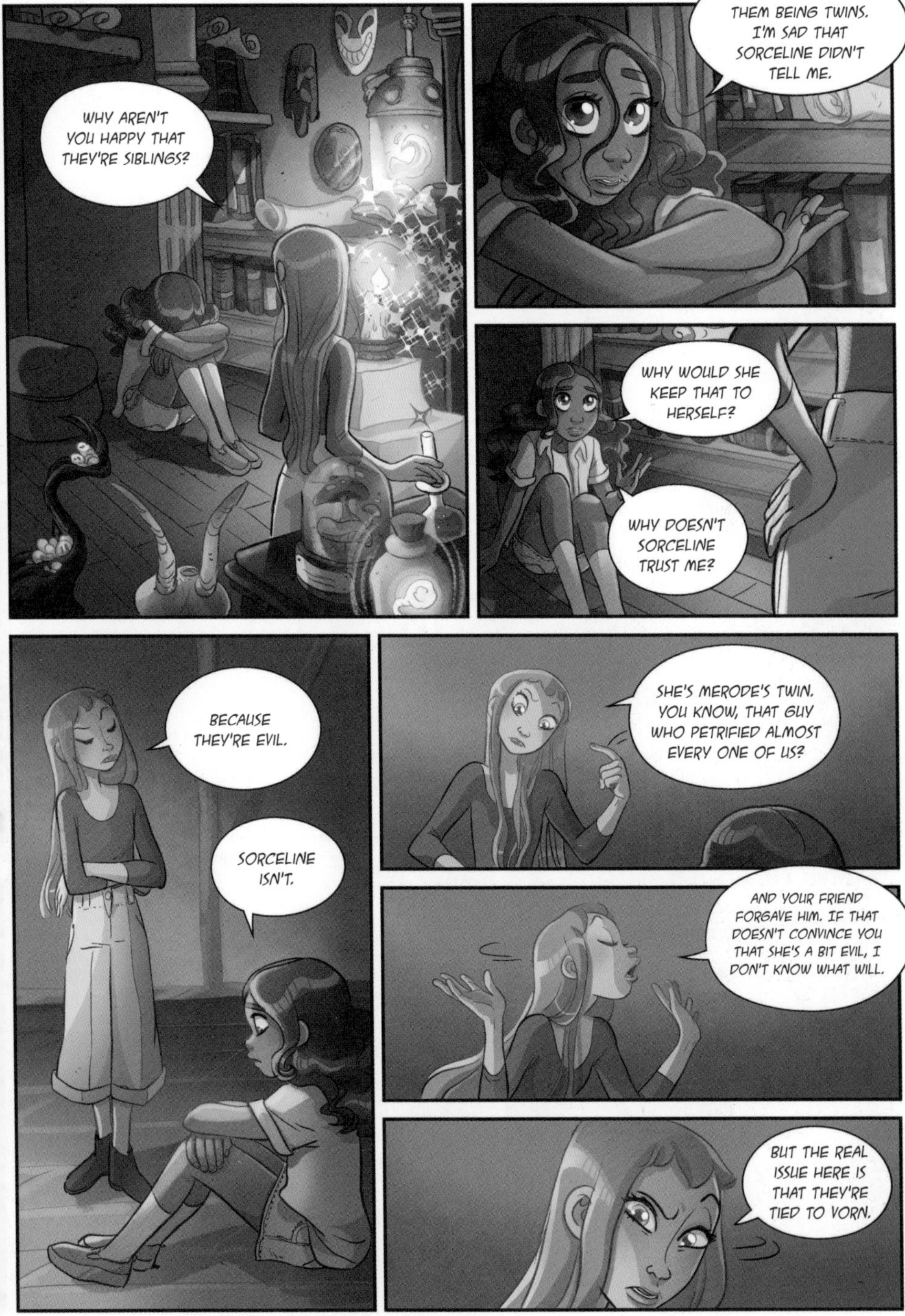
WHY AREN'T YOU HAPPY THAT THEY'RE SIBLINGS?
I'M NOT SAD ABOUT THEM BEING TWINS. I'M SAD THAT SORCELINE DIDN'T TELL ME.
WHY WOULD SHE KEEP THAT TO HERSELF?
WHY DOESN'T SORCELINE TRUST ME?
BECAUSE THEY'RE EVIL.
SORCELINE ISN'T.
SHE'S MERODE'S TWIN. YOU KNOW, THAT GUY WHO PETRIFIED ALMOST EVERY ONE OF US?
AND YOUR FRIEND FORGAVE HIM. IF THAT DOESN'T CONVINCE YOU THAT SHE'S A BIT EVIL, I DON'T KNOW WHAT WILL.
BUT THE REAL ISSUE HERE IS THAT THEY'RE TIED TO VORN.

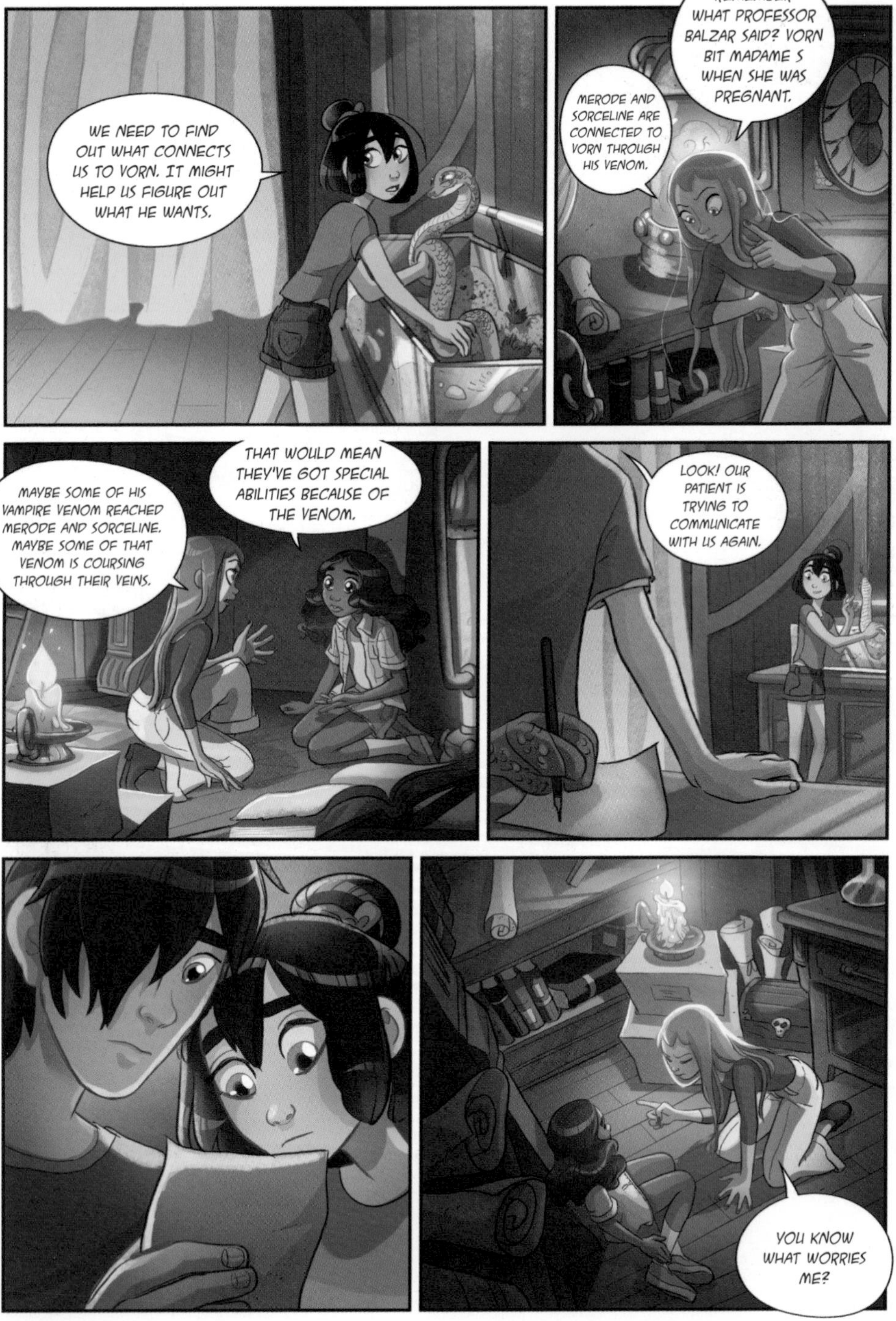
WE NEED TO FIND OUT WHAT CONNECTS US TO VORN. IT MIGHT HELP US FIGURE OUT WHAT HE WANTS.
REMEMBER WHAT PROFESSOR BALZAR SAID? VORN BIT MADAME S WHEN SHE WAS PREGNANT.
MERODE AND SORCELINE ARE CONNECTED TO VORN THROUGH HIS VENOM.
MAYBE SOME OF HIS VAMPIRE VENOM REACHED MERODE AND SORCELINE. MAYBE SOME OF THAT VENOM IS COURSING THROUGH THEIR VEINS.
THAT WOULD MEAN THEY'VE GOT SPECIAL ABILITIES BECAUSE OF THE VENOM.
LOOK! OUR PATIENT IS TRYING TO COMMUNICATE WITH US AGAIN.
YOU KNOW WHAT WORRIES ME?

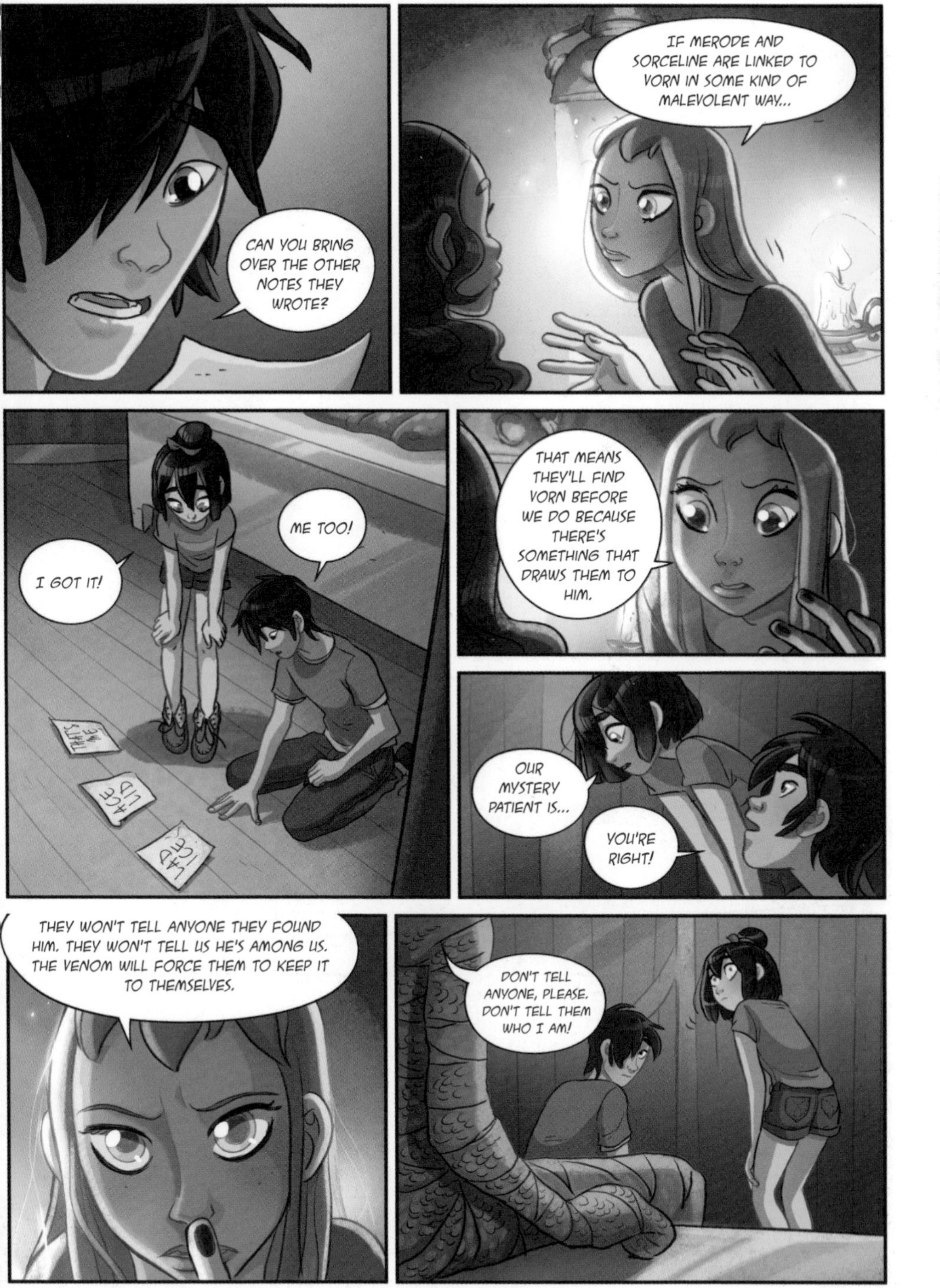
CAN YOU BRING OVER THE OTHER NOTES THEY WROTE?
IF MERODE AND SORCELINE ARE LINKED TO VORN IN SOME KIND OF MALEVOLENT WAY...
I GOT IT!
ME TOO!
THAT MEANS THEY'LL FIND VORN BEFORE WE DO BECAUSE THERE'S SOMETHING THAT DRAWS THEM TO HIM.
OUR MYSTERY PATIENT IS...
YOU'RE RIGHT!
THEY WON'T TELL ANYONE THEY FOUND HIM. THEY WON'T TELL US HE'S AMONG US. THE VENOM WILL FORCE THEM TO KEEP IT TO THEMSELVES.
DON'T TELL ANYONE, PLEASE. DON'T TELL THEM WHO I AM!

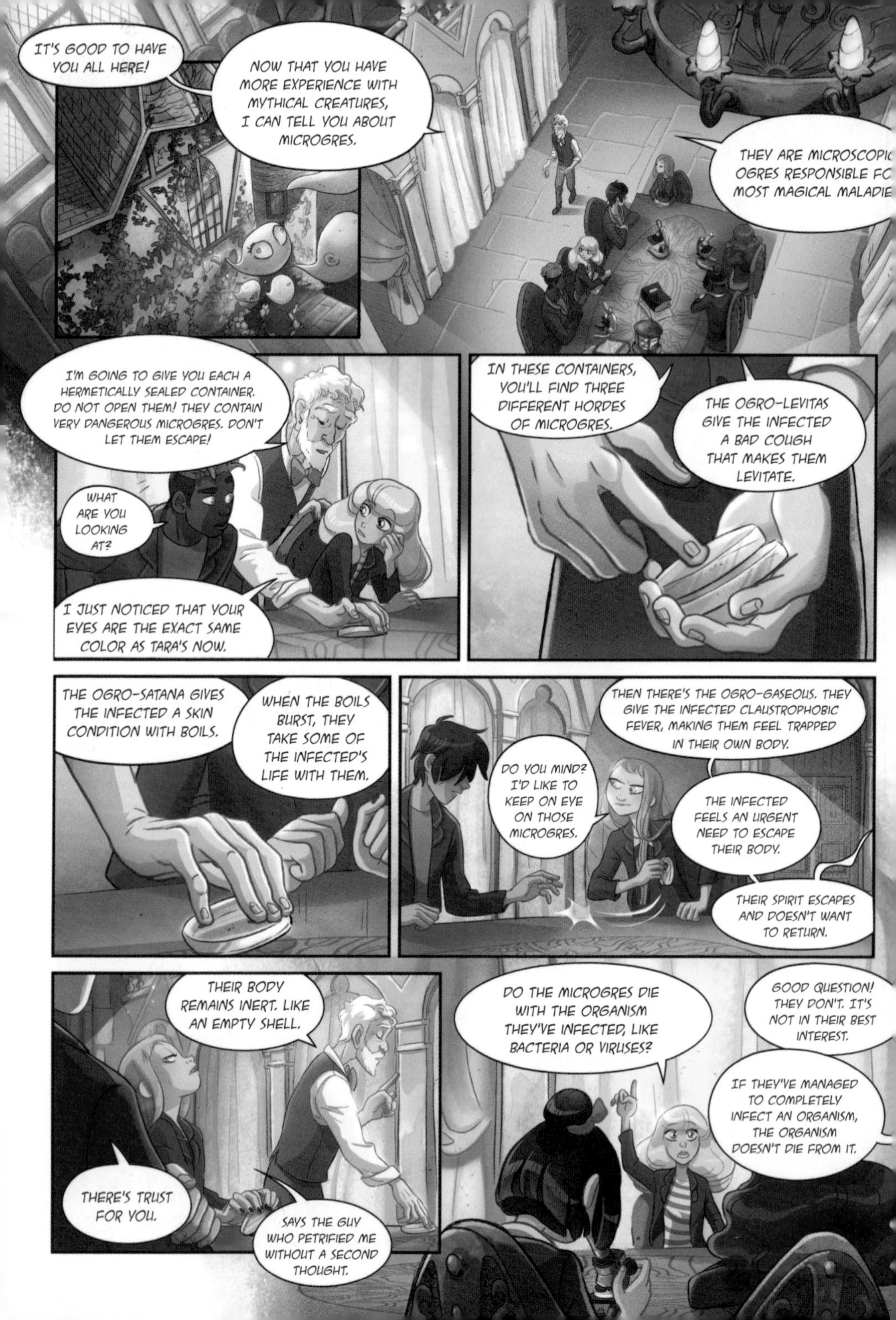
IT'S GOOD TO HAVE YOU ALL HERE!
NOW THAT YOU HAVE MORE EXPERIENCE WITH MYTHICAL CREATURES, I CAN TELL YOU ABOUT MICROGRES.
THEY ARE MICROSCOPIC OGRES RESPONSIBLE FO MOST MAGICAL MALADIE
I'M GOING TO GIVE YOU EACH A HERMETICALLY SEALED CONTAINER. DO NOT OPEN THEM! THEY CONTAIN VERY DANGEROUS MICROGRES. DON'T LET THEM ESCAPE!
WHAT ARE YOU LOOKING AT?
I JUST NOTICED THAT YOUR EYES ARE THE EXACT SAME COLOR AS TARA'S NOW.
IN THESE CONTAINERS, YOU'LL FIND THREE DIFFERENT HORDES OF MICROGRES.
THE OGRO-LEVITAS GIVE THE INFECTED A BAD COUGH THAT MAKES THEM LEVITATE.
THE OGRO-SATANA GIVES THE INFECTED A SKIN CONDITION WITH BOILS.
WHEN THE BOILS BURST, THEY TAKE SOME OF THE INFECTED'S LIFE WITH THEM.
THEN THERE'S THE OGRO-GASEOUS. THEY GIVE THE INFECTED CLAUSTROPHOBIC FEVER, MAKING THEM FEEL TRAPPED IN THEIR OWN BODY.
DO YOU MIND? I'D LIKE TO KEEP ON EYE ON THOSE MICROGRES.
THE INFECTED FEELS AN URGENT NEED TO ESCAPE THEIR BODY.
THEIR SPIRIT ESCAPES AND DOESN'T WANT TO RETURN.
THEIR BODY REMAINS INERT. LIKE AN EMPTY SHELL.
THERE'S TRUST FOR YOU.
SAYS THE GUY WHO PETRIFIED ME WITHOUT A SECOND THOUGHT.
DO THE MICROGRES DIE WITH THE ORGANISM THEY'VE INFECTED, LIKE BACTERIA OR VIRUSES?
GOOD QUESTION! THEY DON'T. IT'S NOT IN THEIR BEST INTEREST.
IF THEY'VE MANAGED TO COMPLETELY INFECT AN ORGANISM, THE ORGANISM DOESN'T DIE FROM IT.

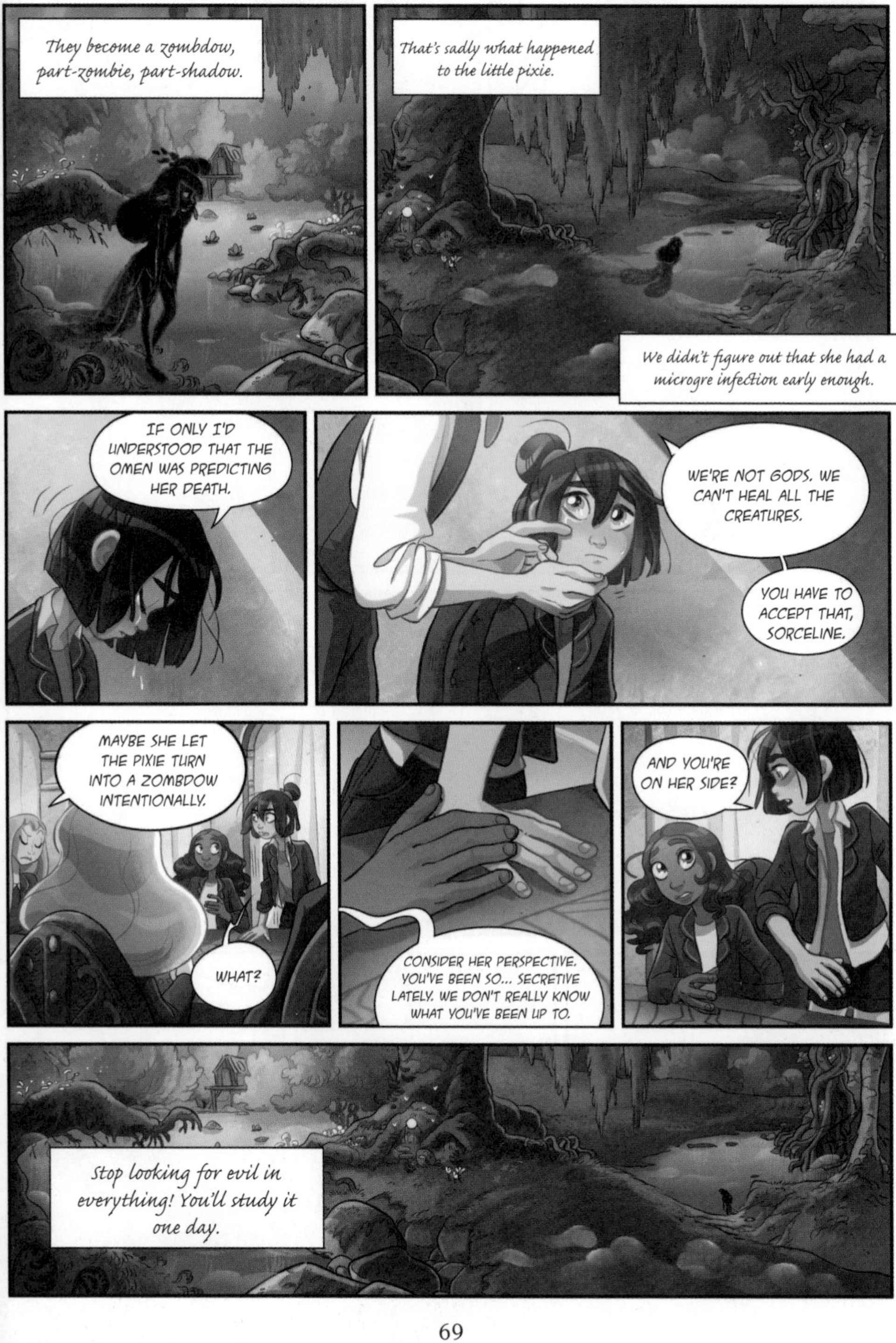
They become a zombdow, part-zombie, part-shadow.
That's sadly what happened to the little pixie.
We didn't figure out that she had a microgre infection early enough.
IF ONLY I'D UNDERSTOOD THAT THE OMEN WAS PREDICTING HER DEATH.
WE'RE NOT GODS. WE CAN'T HEAL ALL THE CREATURES.
YOU HAVE TO ACCEPT THAT, SORCELINE.
MAYBE SHE LET THE PIXIE TURN INTO A ZOMBDOW INTENTIONALLY.
WHAT?
CONSIDER HER PERSPECTIVE. YOU'VE BEEN SO... SECRETIVE LATELY. WE DON'T REALLY KNOW WHAT YOU'VE BEEN UP TO.
AND YOU'RE ON HER SIDE?
Stop looking for evil in everything! You'll study it one day.

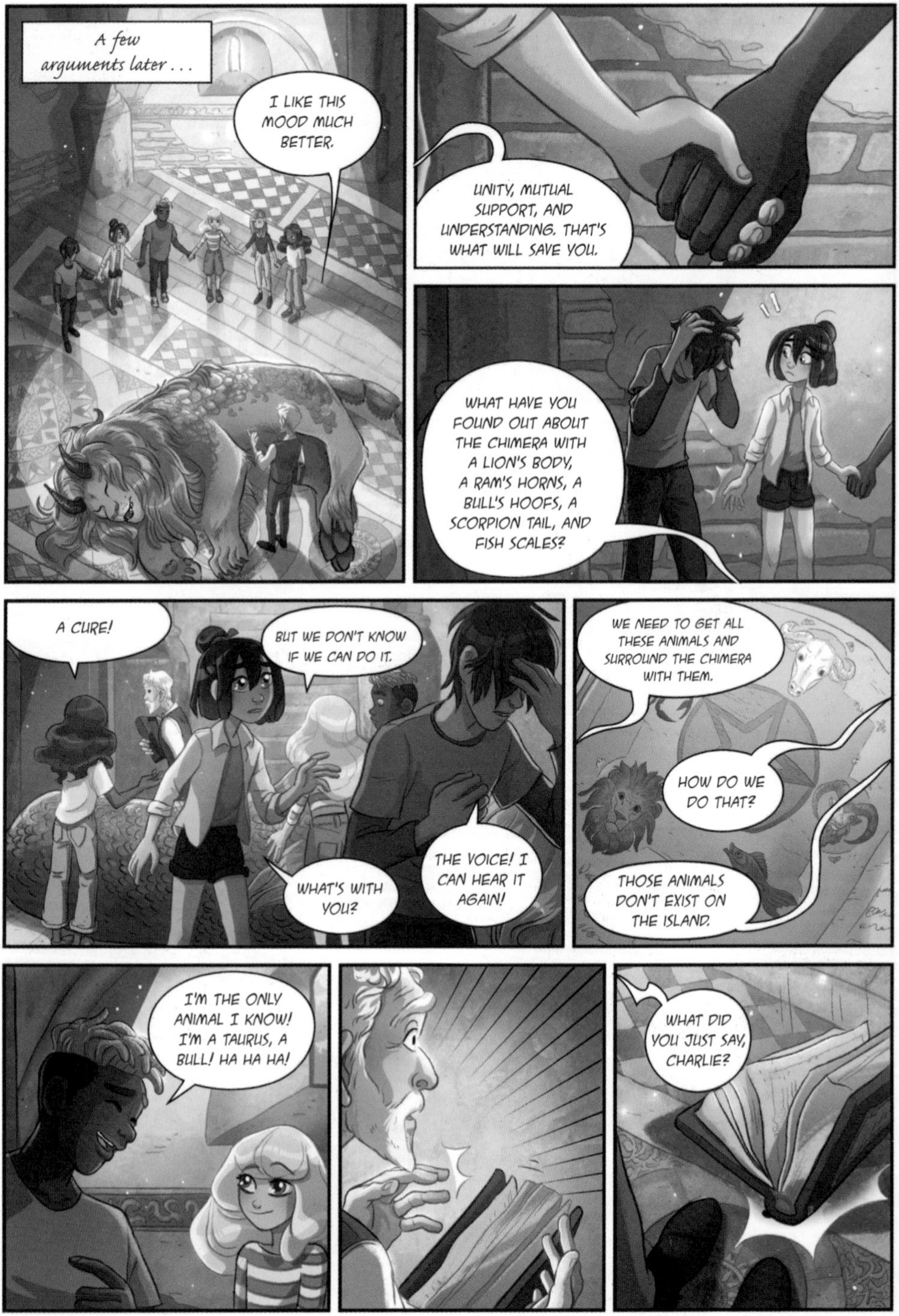
A few arguments later . . .
I LIKE THIS MOOD MUCH BETTER.
UNITY, MUTUAL SUPPORT, AND UNDERSTANDING. THAT'S WHAT WILL SAVE YOU.
WHAT HAVE YOU FOUND OUT ABOUT THE CHIMERA WITH A LION'S BODY, A RAM'S HORNS, A BULL'S HOOFS, A SCORPION TAIL, AND FISH SCALES?
A CURE!
BUT WE DON'T KNOW IF WE CAN DO IT.
WHAT'S WITH YOU?
THE VOICE! I CAN HEAR IT AGAIN!
WE NEED TO GET ALL THESE ANIMALS AND SURROUND THE CHIMERA WITH THEM.
HOW DO WE DO THAT?
THOSE ANIMALS DON'T EXIST ON THE ISLAND.
I'M THE ONLY ANIMAL I KNOW! I'M A TAURUS, A BULL! HA HA HA!
WHAT DID YOU JUST SAY, CHARLIE?

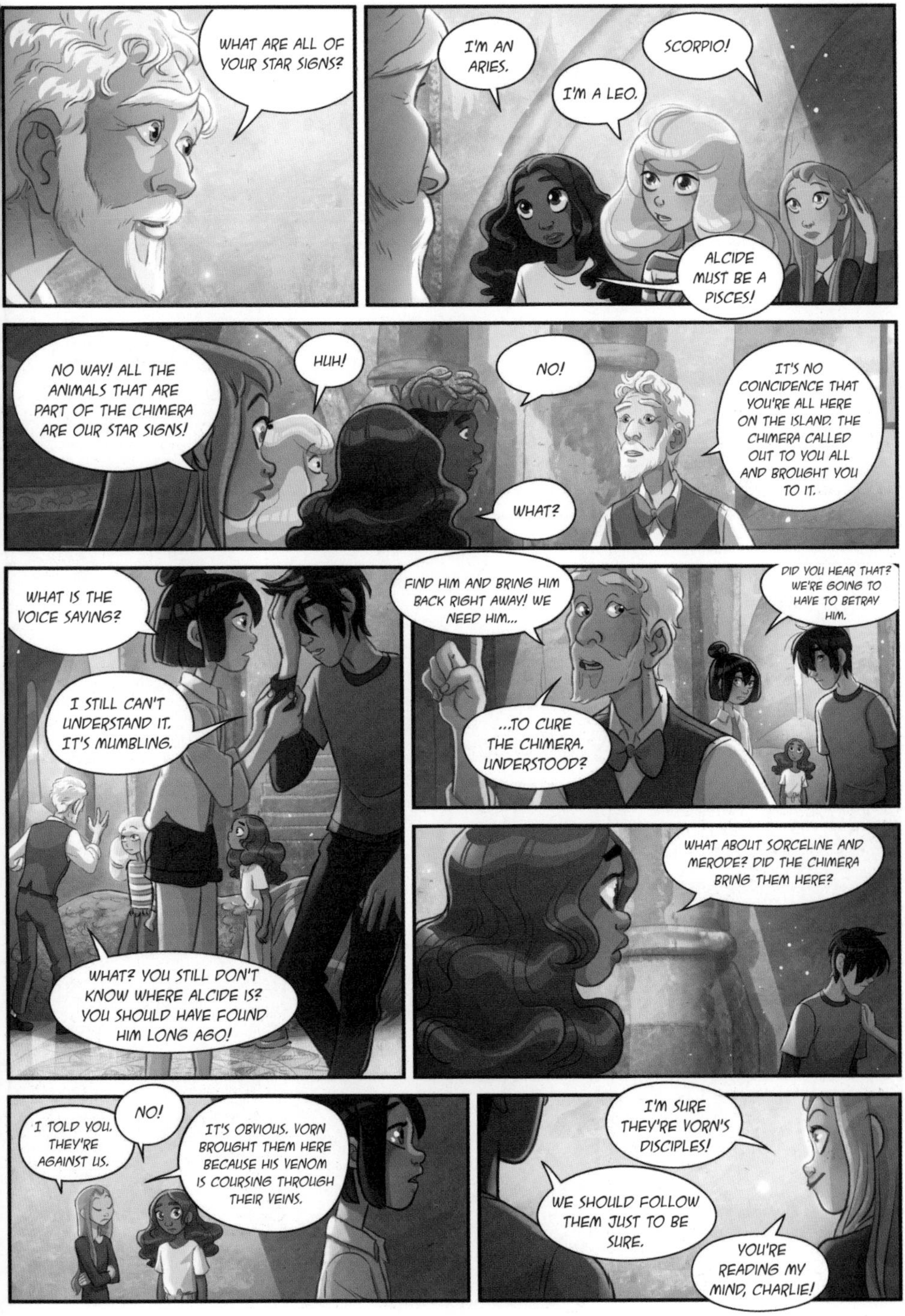

WHAT ARE ALL OF YOUR STAR SIGNS?
I'M AN ARIES.
I'M A LEO.
SCORPIO!
ALCIDE MUST BE A PISCES!
NO WAY! ALL THE ANIMALS THAT ARE PART OF THE CHIMERA ARE OUR STAR SIGNS!
HUH!
NO!
WHAT?
IT'S NO COINCIDENCE THAT YOU'RE ALL HERE ON THE ISLAND. THE CHIMERA CALLED OUT TO YOU ALL AND BROUGHT YOU TO IT.
WHAT IS THE VOICE SAYING?
I STILL CAN'T UNDERSTAND IT. IT'S MUMBLING.
WHAT? YOU STILL DON'T KNOW WHERE ALCIDE IS? YOU SHOULD HAVE FOUND HIM LONG AGO!
FIND HIM AND BRING HIM BACK RIGHT AWAY! WE NEED HIM...
...TO CURE THE CHIMERA. UNDERSTOOD?
DID YOU HEAR THAT? WE'RE GOING TO HAVE TO BETRAY HIM.
WHAT ABOUT SORCELINE AND MERODE? DID THE CHIMERA BRING THEM HERE?
I TOLD YOU. THEY'RE AGAINST US.
NO!
IT'S OBVIOUS. VORN BROUGHT THEM HERE BECAUSE HIS VENOM IS COURSING THROUGH THEIR VEINS.
I'M SURE THEY'RE VORN'S DISCIPLES!
WE SHOULD FOLLOW THEM JUST TO BE SURE.
YOU'RE READING MY MIND, CHARLIE!

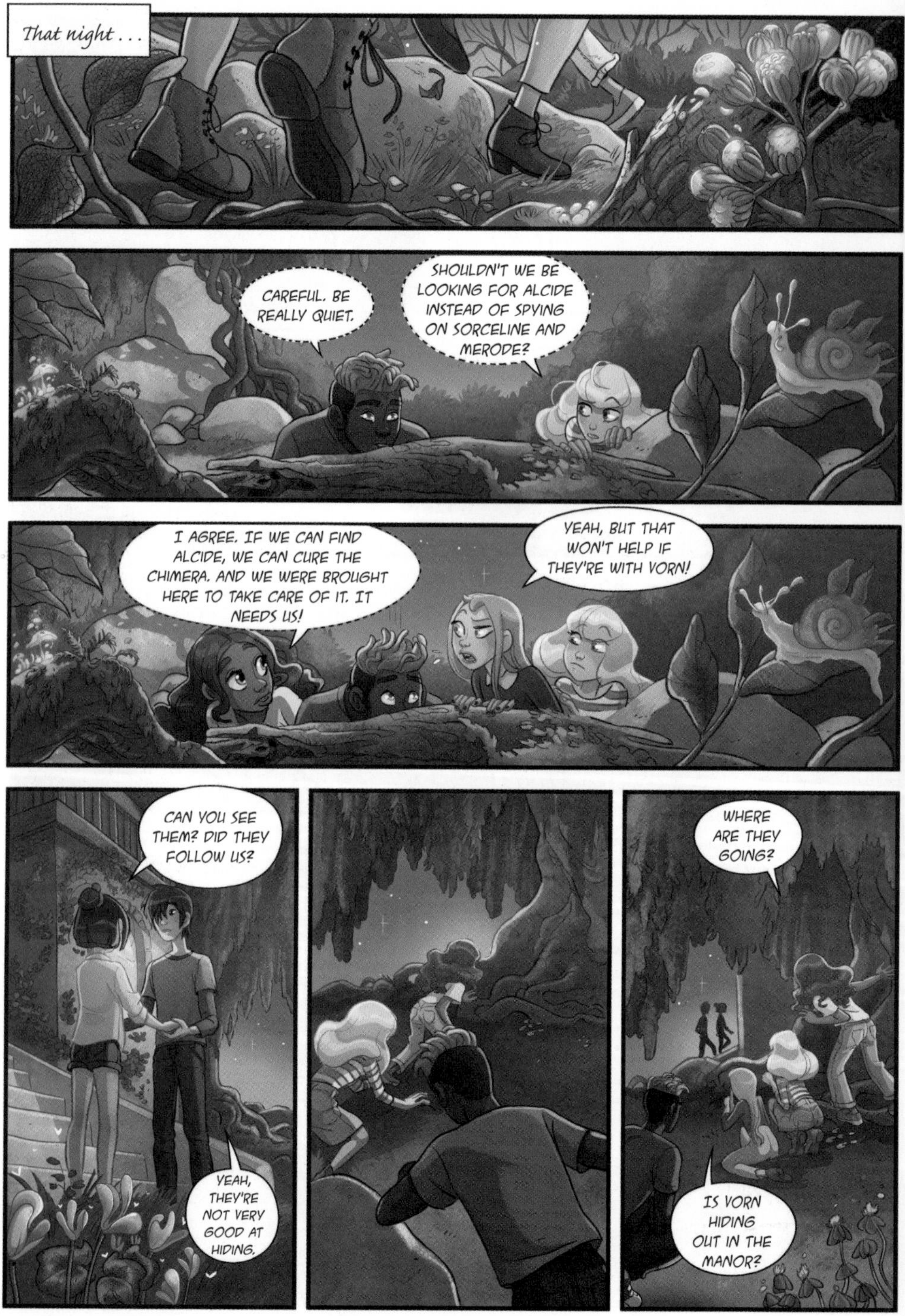
That night . . .
CAREFUL. BE REALLY QUIET.
SHOULDN'T WE BE LOOKING FOR ALCIDE INSTEAD OF SPYING ON SORCELINE AND MERODE?
I AGREE. IF WE CAN FIND ALCIDE, WE CAN CURE THE CHIMERA. AND WE WERE BROUGHT HERE TO TAKE CARE OF IT. IT NEEDS US!
YEAH, BUT THAT WON'T HELP IF THEY'RE WITH VORN!
CAN YOU SEE THEM? DID THEY FOLLOW US?
YEAH, THEY'RE NOT VERY GOOD AT HIDING.
WHERE ARE THEY GOING?
IS VORN HIDING OUT IN THE MANOR?

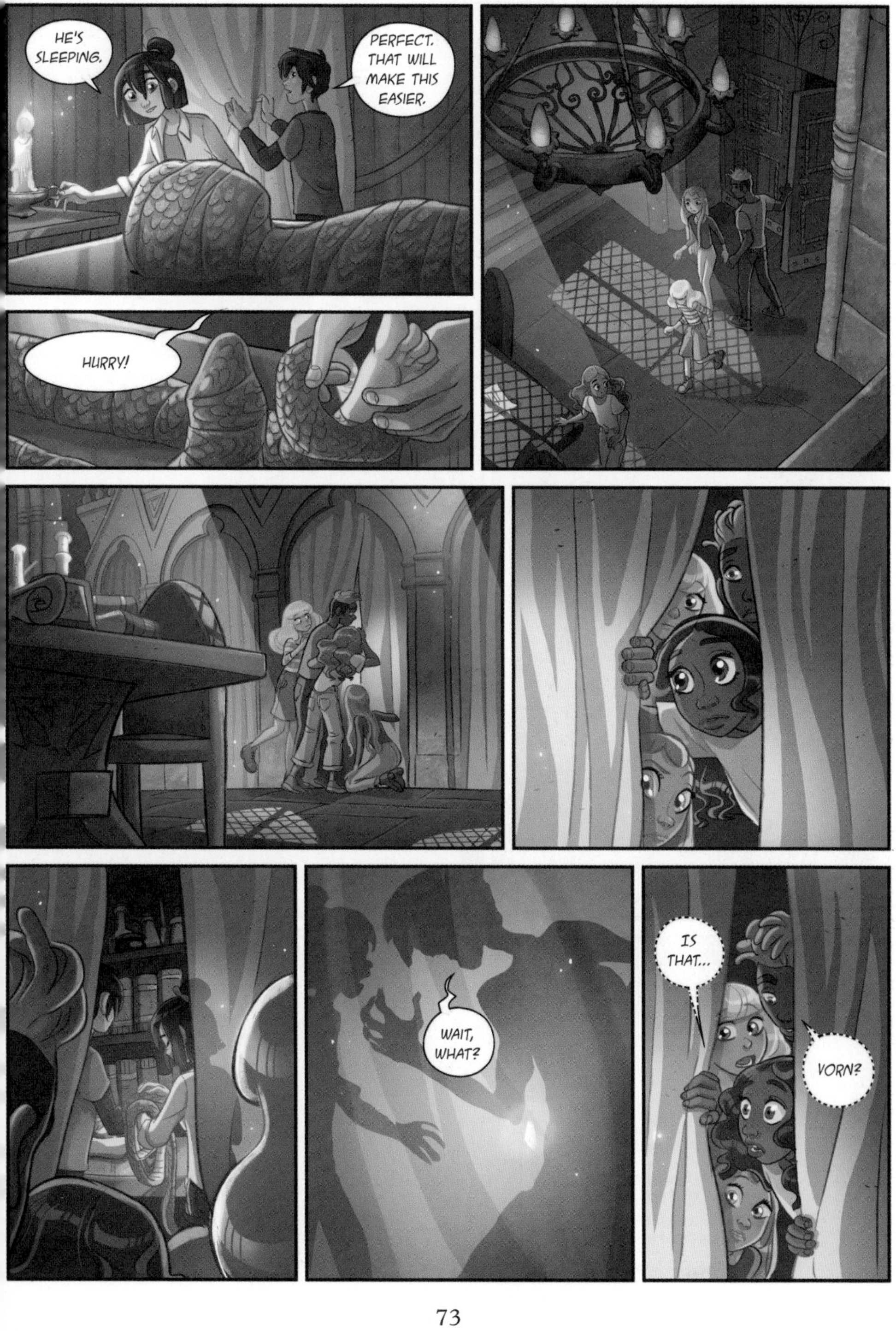
HE'S SLEEPING.
PERFECT. THAT WILL MAKE THIS EASIER.
HURRY!
WAIT, WHAT?
IS THAT...
VORN?

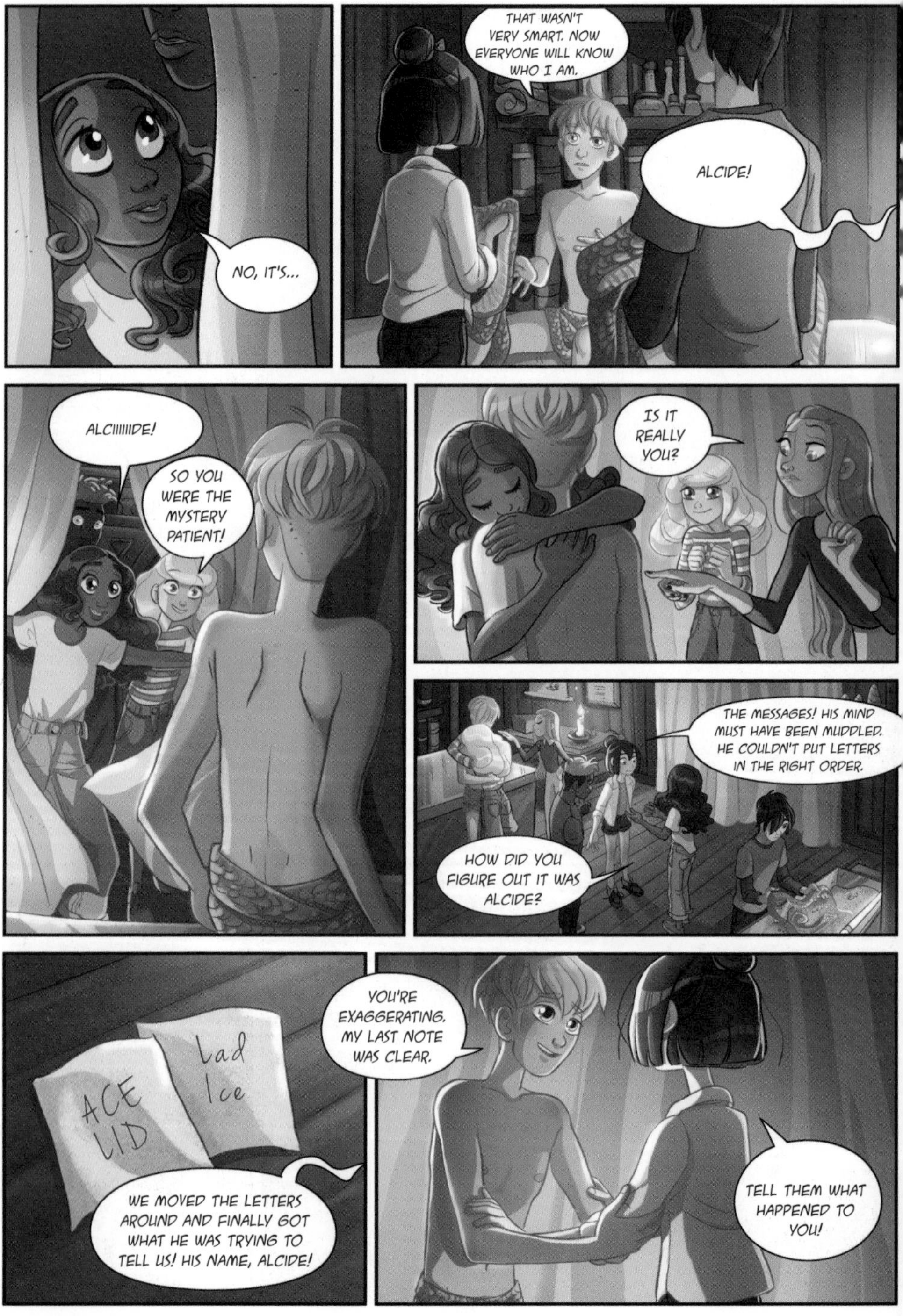
NO, IT'S...
THAT WASN'T VERY SMART. NOW EVERYONE WILL KNOW WHO I AM.
ALCIDE!
ALCIIIIIIDE!
SO YOU WERE THE MYSTERY PATIENT!
IS IT REALLY YOU?
THE MESSAGES! HIS MIND MUST HAVE BEEN MUDDLED. HE COULDN'T PUT LETTERS IN THE RIGHT ORDER.
HOW DID YOU FIGURE OUT IT WAS ALCIDE?
ACE LID
Lad Ice
WE MOVED THE LETTERS AROUND AND FINALLY GOT WHAT HE WAS TRYING TO TELL US! HIS NAME, ALCIDE!
YOU'RE EXAGGERATING. MY LAST NOTE WAS CLEAR.
TELL THEM WHAT HAPPENED TO YOU!

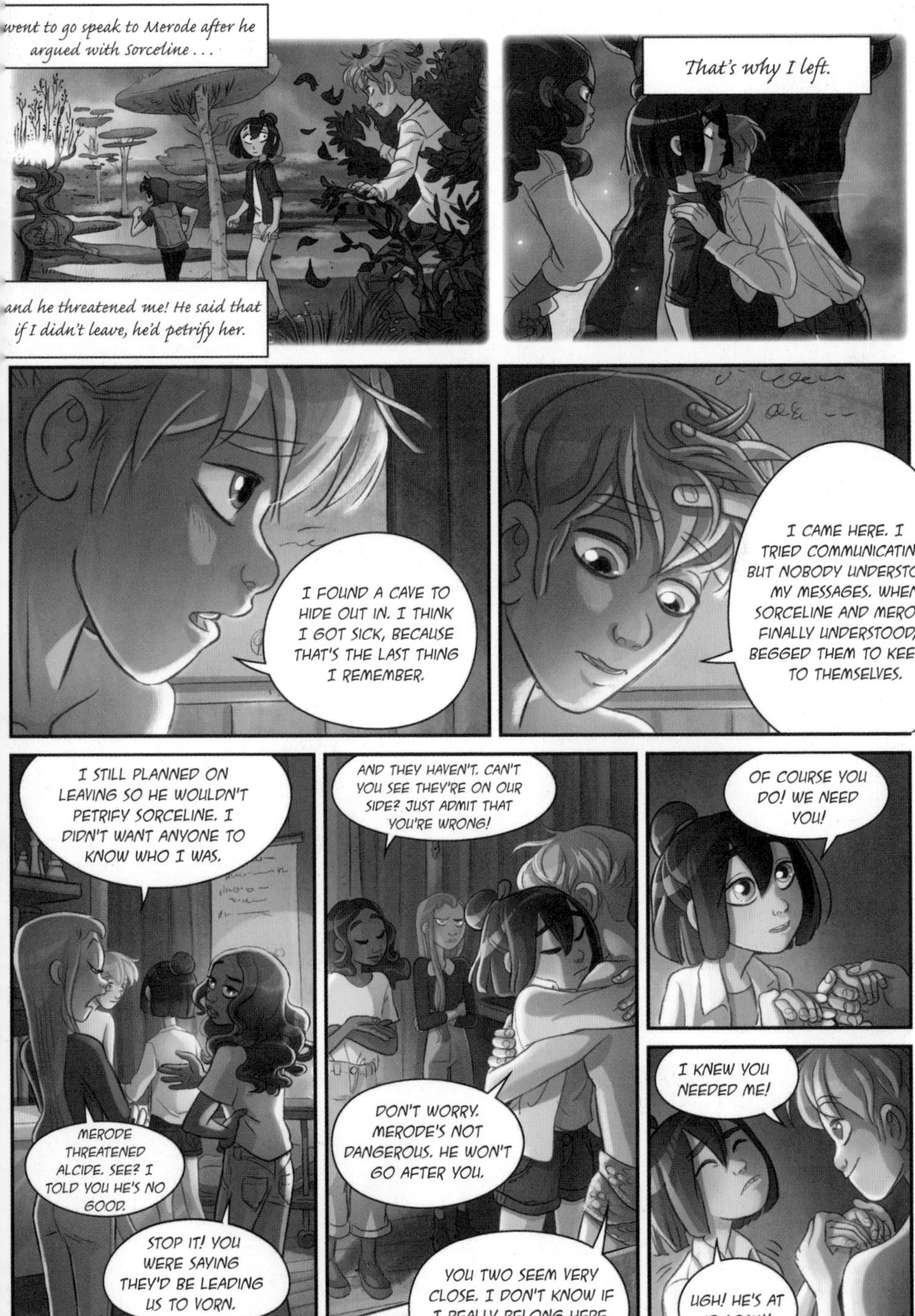
went to go speak to Merode after he argued with Sorceline . . .
and he threatened me! He said that if I didn't leave, he'd petrify her.
That's why I left.
I FOUND A CAVE TO HIDE OUT IN. I THINK I GOT SICK, BECAUSE THAT'S THE LAST THING I REMEMBER.
I CAME HERE. I TRIED COMMUNICATING, BUT NOBODY UNDERSTOOD MY MESSAGES. WHEN SORCELINE AND MERODE FINALLY UNDERSTOOD, I BEGGED THEM TO KEEP IT TO THEMSELVES.
I STILL PLANNED ON LEAVING SO HE WOULDN'T PETRIFY SORCELINE. I DIDN'T WANT ANYONE TO KNOW WHO I WAS.
MERODE THREATENED ALCIDE. SEE? I TOLD YOU HE'S NO GOOD.
STOP IT! YOU WERE SAYING THEY'D BE LEADING US TO VORN.
AND THEY HAVEN'T. CAN'T YOU SEE THEY'RE ON OUR SIDE? JUST ADMIT THAT YOU'RE WRONG!
DON'T WORRY. MERODE'S NOT DANGEROUS. HE WON'T GO AFTER YOU.
YOU TWO SEEM VERY CLOSE. I DON'T KNOW IF I REALLY BELONG HERE.
OF COURSE YOU DO! WE NEED YOU!
I KNEW YOU NEEDED ME!
UGH! HE'S AT IT AGAIN!

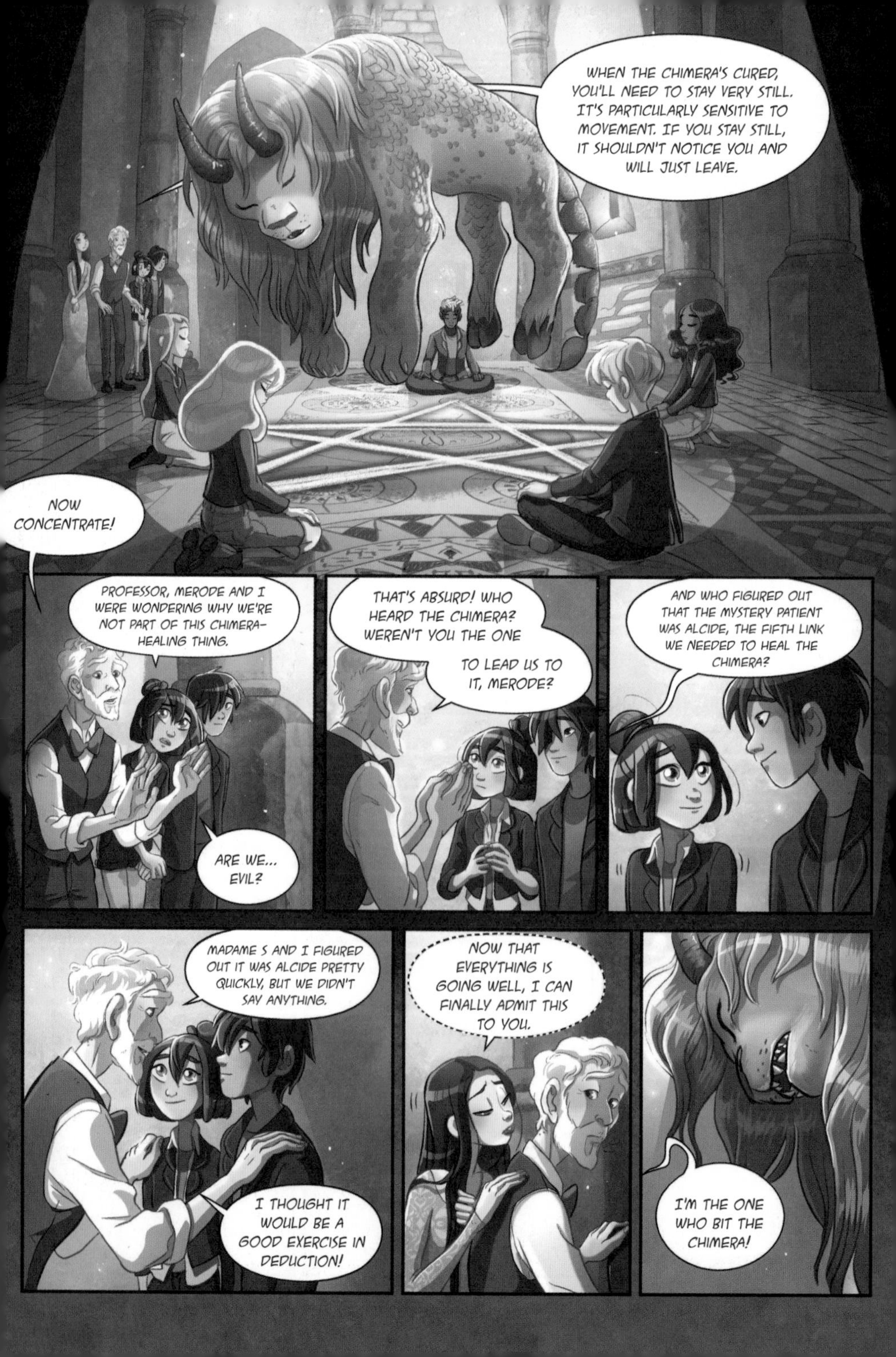

WHEN THE CHIMERA'S CURED, YOU'LL NEED TO STAY VERY STILL. IT'S PARTICULARLY SENSITIVE TO MOVEMENT. IF YOU STAY STILL, IT SHOULDN'T NOTICE YOU AND WILL JUST LEAVE.
NOW CONCENTRATE!
PROFESSOR, MERODE AND I WERE WONDERING WHY WE'RE NOT PART OF THIS CHIMERA-HEALING THING.
ARE WE... EVIL?
THAT'S ABSURD! WHO HEARD THE CHIMERA? WEREN'T YOU THE ONE
TO LEAD US TO IT, MERODE?
AND WHO FIGURED OUT THAT THE MYSTERY PATIENT WAS ALCIDE, THE FIFTH LINK WE NEEDED TO HEAL THE CHIMERA?
MADAME S AND I FIGURED OUT IT WAS ALCIDE PRETTY QUICKLY, BUT WE DIDN'T SAY ANYTHING.
I THOUGHT IT WOULD BE A GOOD EXERCISE IN DEDUCTION!
NOW THAT EVERYTHING IS GOING WELL, I CAN FINALLY ADMIT THIS TO YOU.
I'M THE ONE WHO BIT THE CHIMERA!

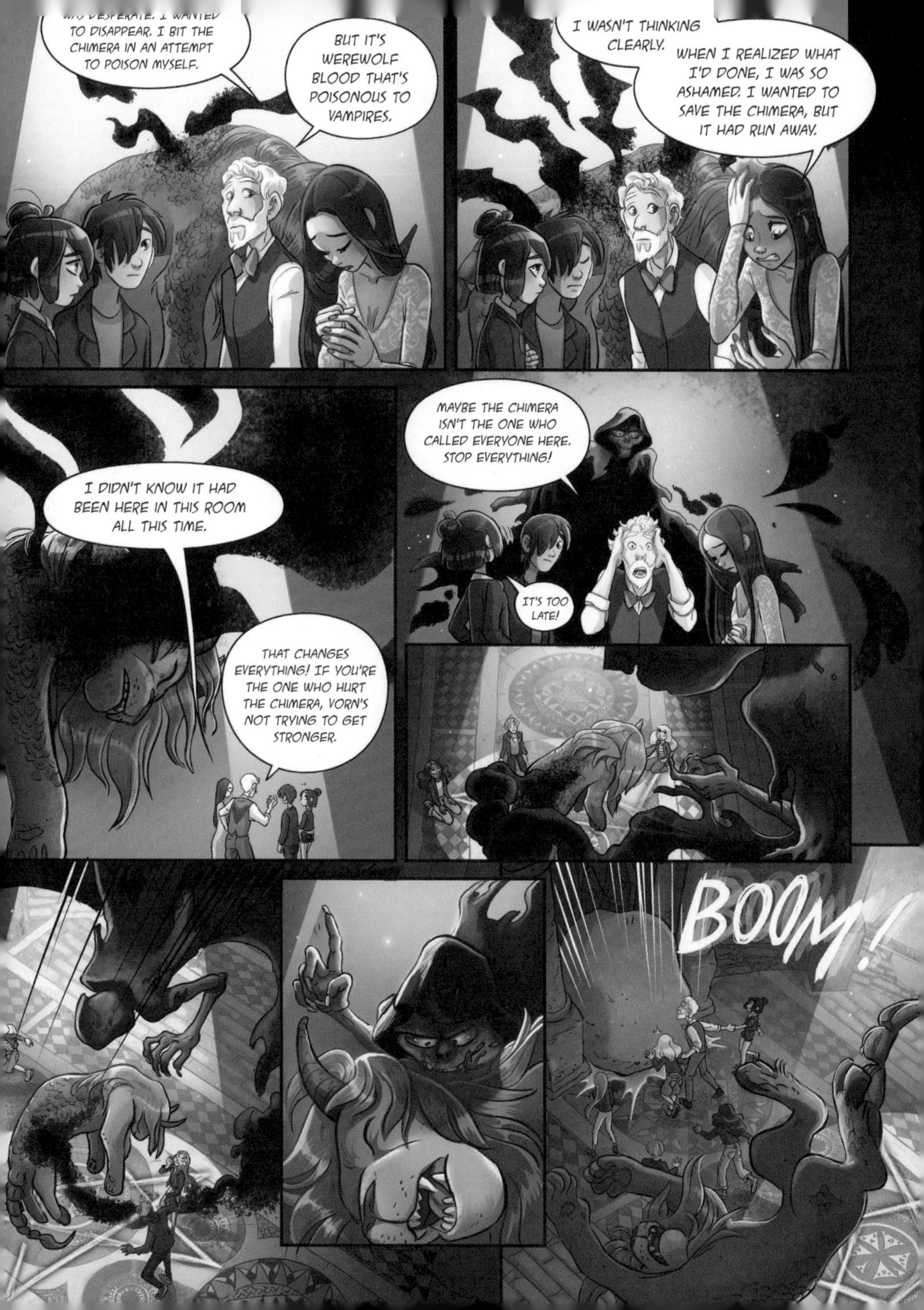
TO DISAPPEAR. I BIT THE CHIMERA IN AN ATTEMPT TO POISON MYSELF.
BUT IT'S WEREWOLF BLOOD THAT'S POISONOUS TO VAMPIRES.
I WASN'T THINKING CLEARLY.
WHEN I REALIZED WHAT I'D DONE, I WAS SO ASHAMED. I WANTED TO SAVE THE CHIMERA, BUT IT HAD RUN AWAY.
I DIDN'T KNOW IT HAD BEEN HERE IN THIS ROOM ALL THIS TIME.
THAT CHANGES EVERYTHING! IF YOU'RE THE ONE WHO HURT THE CHIMERA, VORN'S NOT TRYING TO GET STRONGER.
MAYBE THE CHIMERA ISN'T THE ONE WHO CALLED EVERYONE HERE. STOP EVERYTHING!
IT'S TOO LATE!
BOOM!

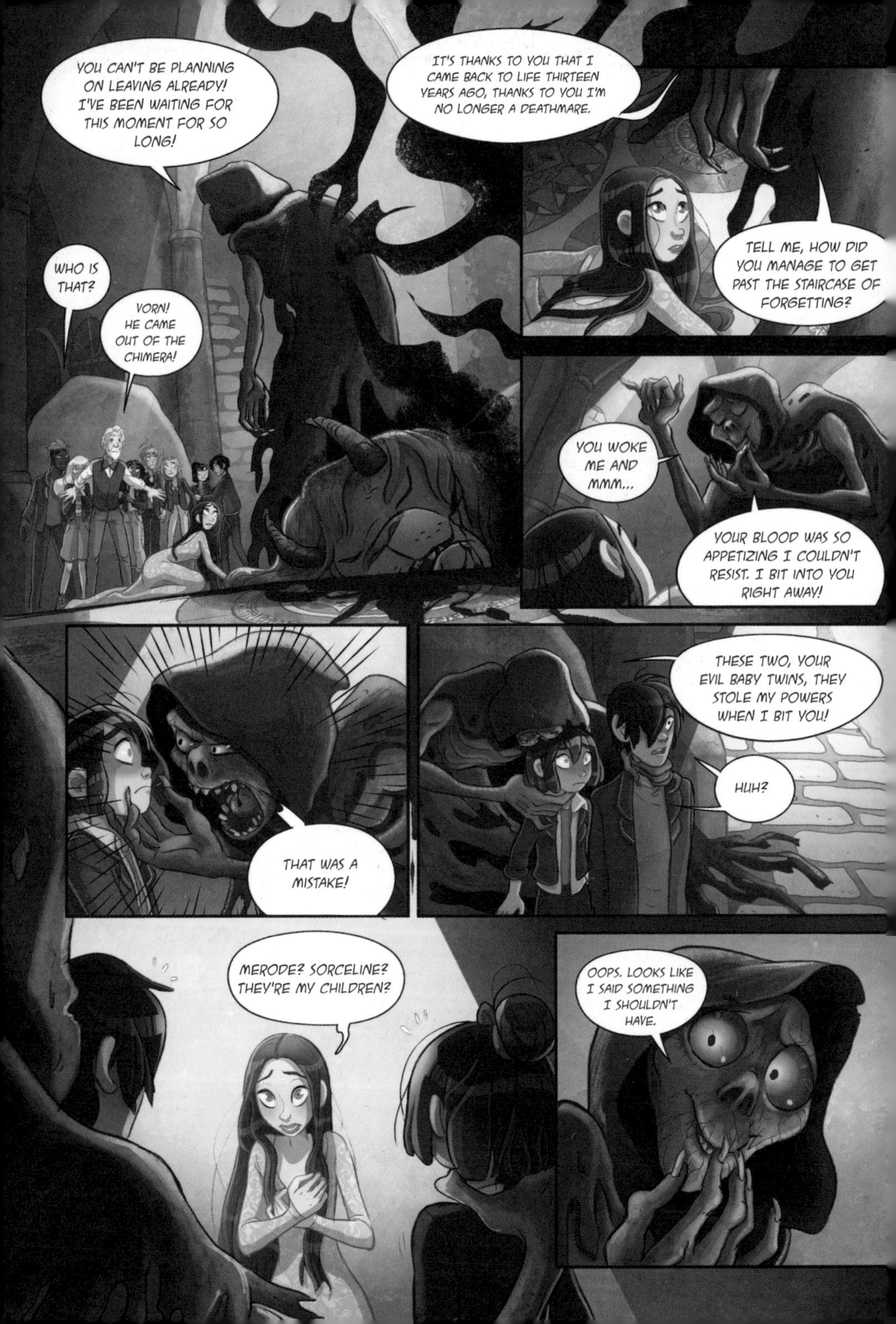
YOU CAN'T BE PLANNING ON LEAVING ALREADY! I'VE BEEN WAITING FOR THIS MOMENT FOR SO LONG!
IT'S THANKS TO YOU THAT I CAME BACK TO LIFE THIRTEEN YEARS AGO, THANKS TO YOU I'M NO LONGER A DEATHMARE.
TELL ME, HOW DID YOU MANAGE TO GET PAST THE STAIRCASE OF FORGETTING?
WHO IS THAT?
VORN! HE CAME OUT OF THE CHIMERA!
YOU WOKE ME AND MMM...
YOUR BLOOD WAS SO APPETIZING I COULDN'T RESIST. I BIT INTO YOU RIGHT AWAY!
THAT WAS A MISTAKE!
THESE TWO, YOUR EVIL BABY TWINS, THEY STOLE MY POWERS WHEN I BIT YOU!
HUH?
MERODE? SORCELINE? THEY'RE MY CHILDREN?
OOPS. LOOKS LIKE I SAID SOMETHING I SHOULDN'T HAVE.

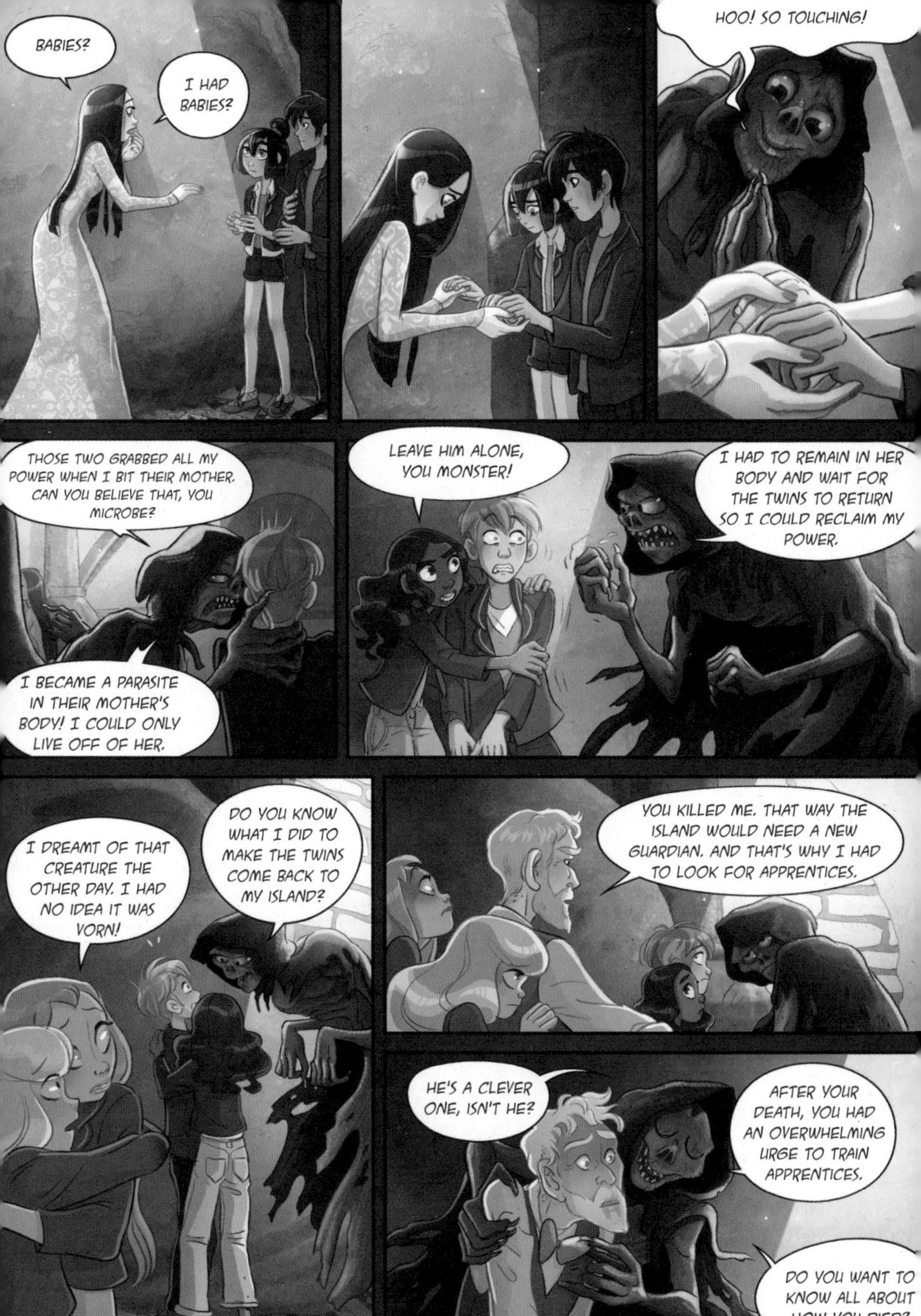
BABIES?
I HAD BABIES?
HOO! SO TOUCHING!
THOSE TWO GRABBED ALL MY POWER WHEN I BIT THEIR MOTHER. CAN YOU BELIEVE THAT, YOU MICROBE?
I BECAME A PARASITE IN THEIR MOTHER'S BODY! I COULD ONLY LIVE OFF OF HER.
LEAVE HIM ALONE, YOU MONSTER!
I HAD TO REMAIN IN HER BODY AND WAIT FOR THE TWINS TO RETURN SO I COULD RECLAIM MY POWER.
I DREAMT OF THAT CREATURE THE OTHER DAY. I HAD NO IDEA IT WAS VORN!
DO YOU KNOW WHAT I DID TO MAKE THE TWINS COME BACK TO MY ISLAND?
YOU KILLED ME. THAT WAY THE ISLAND WOULD NEED A NEW GUARDIAN. AND THAT'S WHY I HAD TO LOOK FOR APPRENTICES.
HE'S A CLEVER ONE, ISN'T HE?
AFTER YOUR DEATH, YOU HAD AN OVERWHELMING URGE TO TRAIN APPRENTICES.
DO YOU WANT TO KNOW ALL ABOUT HOW YOU DIED?

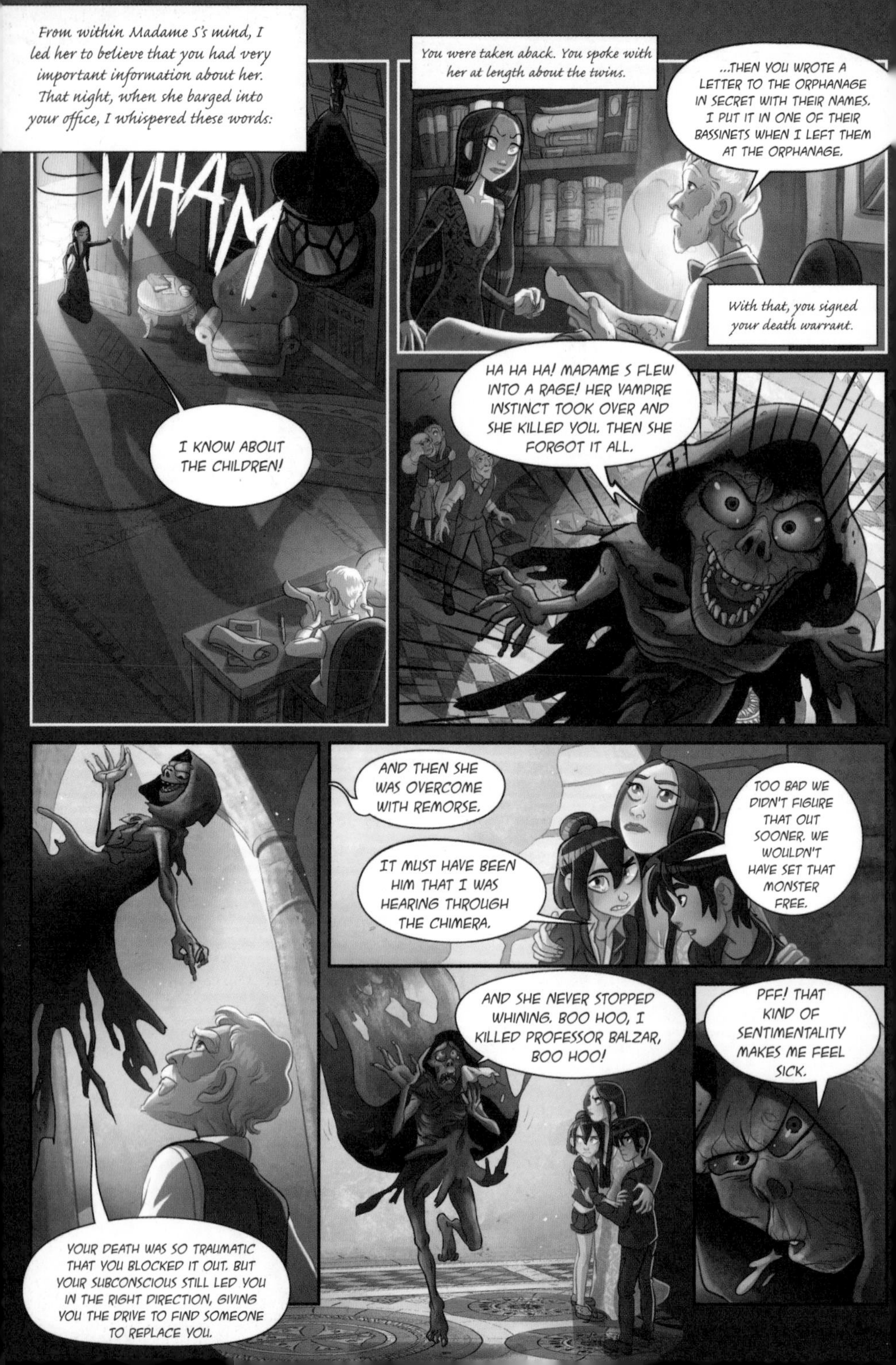
From within Madame S's mind, I led her to believe that you had very important information about her. That night, when she barged into your office, I whispered these words:
WHAM
I KNOW ABOUT THE CHILDREN!
You were taken aback. You spoke with her at length about the twins.
...THEN YOU WROTE A LETTER TO THE ORPHANAGE IN SECRET WITH THEIR NAMES. I PUT IT IN ONE OF THEIR BASSINETS WHEN I LEFT THEM AT THE ORPHANAGE.
With that, you signed your death warrant.
HA HA HA! MADAME S FLEW INTO A RAGE! HER VAMPIRE INSTINCT TOOK OVER AND SHE KILLED YOU. THEN SHE FORGOT IT ALL.
AND THEN SHE WAS OVERCOME WITH REMORSE.
IT MUST HAVE BEEN HIM THAT I WAS HEARING THROUGH THE CHIMERA.
TOO BAD WE DIDN'T FIGURE THAT OUT SOONER. WE WOULDN'T HAVE SET THAT MONSTER FREE.
YOUR DEATH WAS SO TRAUMATIC THAT YOU BLOCKED IT OUT. BUT YOUR SUBCONSCIOUS STILL LED YOU IN THE RIGHT DIRECTION, GIVING YOU THE DRIVE TO FIND SOMEONE TO REPLACE YOU.
AND SHE NEVER STOPPED WHINING. BOO HOO, I KILLED PROFESSOR BALZAR, BOO HOO!
PFF! THAT KIND OF SENTIMENTALITY MAKES ME FEEL SICK.

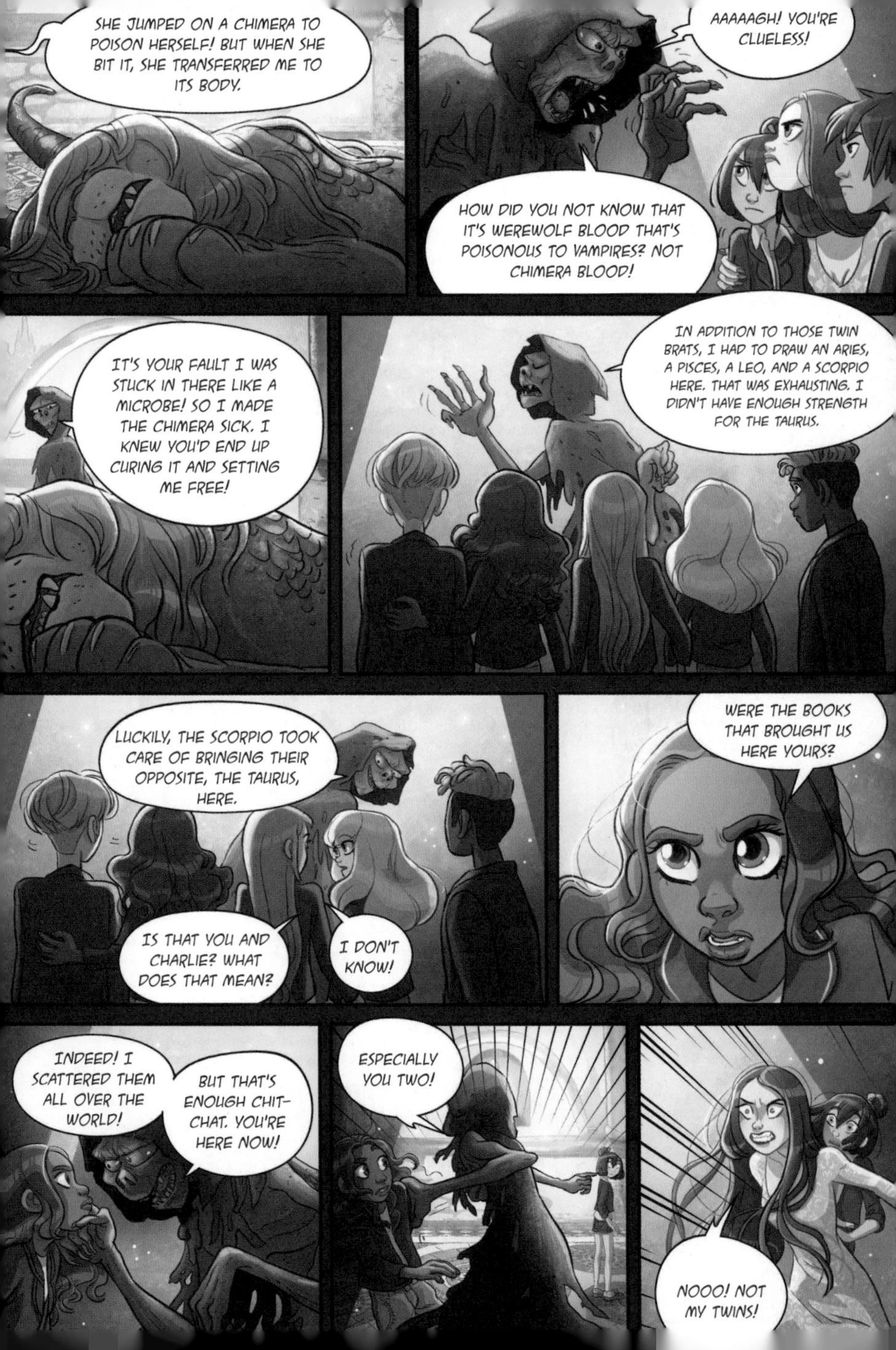
SHE JUMPED ON A CHIMERA TO POISON HERSELF! BUT WHEN SHE BIT IT, SHE TRANSFERRED ME TO ITS BODY.
AAAAAGH! YOU'RE CLUELESS!
HOW DID YOU NOT KNOW THAT IT'S WEREWOLF BLOOD THAT'S POISONOUS TO VAMPIRES? NOT CHIMERA BLOOD!
IT'S YOUR FAULT I WAS STUCK IN THERE LIKE A MICROBE! SO I MADE THE CHIMERA SICK. I KNEW YOU'D END UP CURING IT AND SETTING ME FREE!
IN ADDITION TO THOSE TWIN BRATS, I HAD TO DRAW AN ARIES, A PISCES, A LEO, AND A SCORPIO HERE. THAT WAS EXHAUSTING. I DIDN'T HAVE ENOUGH STRENGTH FOR THE TAURUS.
LUCKILY, THE SCORPIO TOOK CARE OF BRINGING THEIR OPPOSITE, THE TAURUS, HERE.
IS THAT YOU AND CHARLIE? WHAT DOES THAT MEAN?
I DON'T KNOW!
WERE THE BOOKS THAT BROUGHT US HERE YOURS?
INDEED! I SCATTERED THEM ALL OVER THE WORLD!
BUT THAT'S ENOUGH CHIT-CHAT. YOU'RE HERE NOW!
ESPECIALLY YOU TWO!
NOOO! NOT MY TWINS!

RAAARH!

YOU'LL NEVER TOUCH A SINGLE HAIR ON THEIR HEADS!

NEVER, YOU HEAR ME?

NEVER!

?

WHERE... WHERE ARE WE?

YOU'RE SAFE! AT HOME!

HUH?

WE COULD BE ANYWHERE—IN A CAVE, IN THE WOODS, IN THE MIDDLE OF A SWAMP...

VAMPIRES CAN TAKE US ANYWHERE USING THEIR MINDS, YOU KNOW.

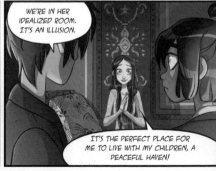

WE'RE IN HER IDEALIZED ROOM. IT'S AN ILLUSION.

IT'S THE PERFECT PLACE FOR ME TO LIVE WITH MY CHILDREN, A PEACEFUL HAVEN!

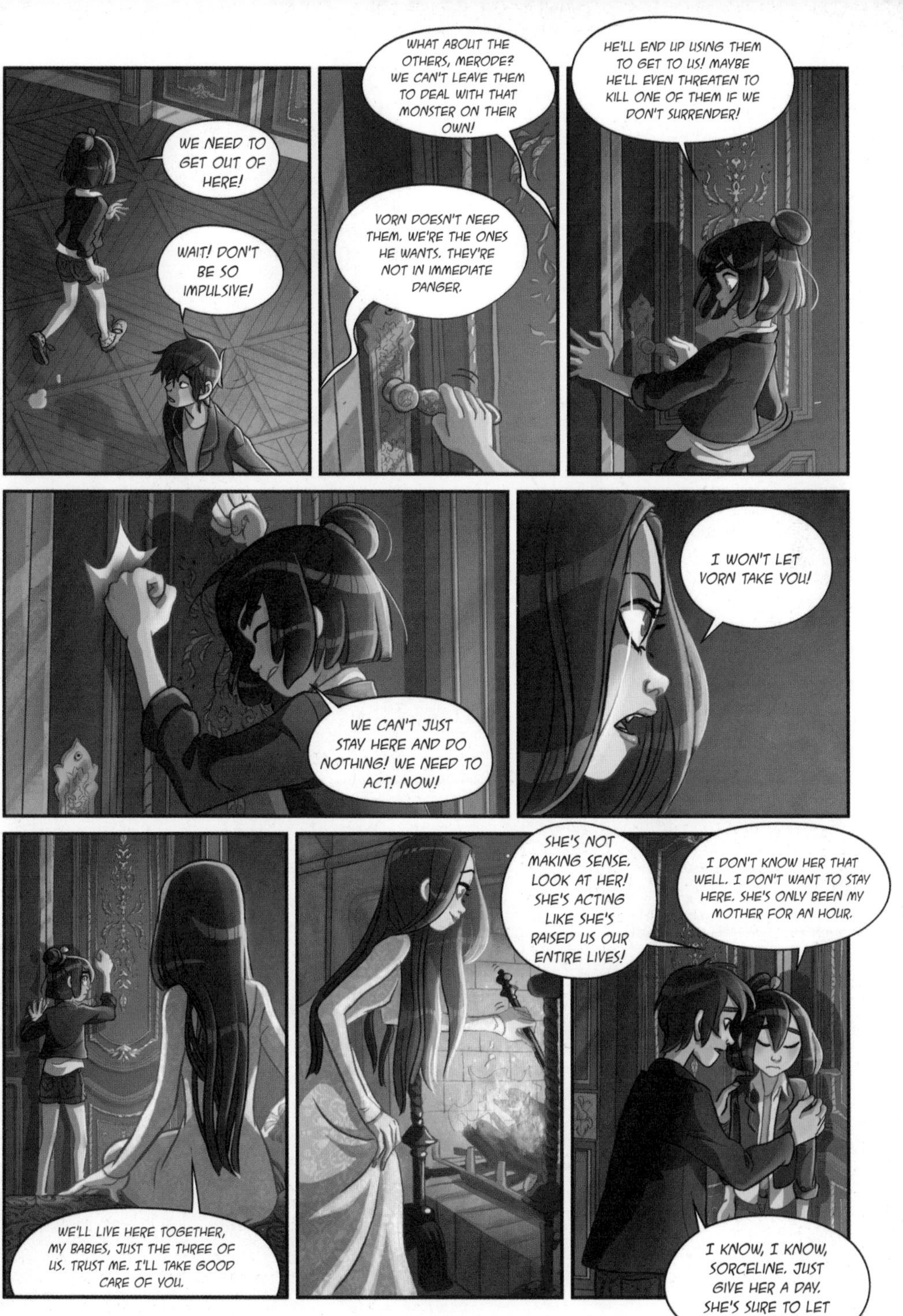
WE NEED TO GET OUT OF HERE!
WAIT! DON'T BE SO IMPULSIVE!
WHAT ABOUT THE OTHERS, MERODE? WE CAN'T LEAVE THEM TO DEAL WITH THAT MONSTER ON THEIR OWN!
VORN DOESN'T NEED THEM. WE'RE THE ONES HE WANTS. THEY'RE NOT IN IMMEDIATE DANGER.
HE'LL END UP USING THEM TO GET TO US! MAYBE HE'LL EVEN THREATEN TO KILL ONE OF THEM IF WE DON'T SURRENDER!
WE CAN'T JUST STAY HERE AND DO NOTHING! WE NEED TO ACT! NOW!
I WON'T LET VORN TAKE YOU!
WE'LL LIVE HERE TOGETHER, MY BABIES, JUST THE THREE OF US. TRUST ME. I'LL TAKE GOOD CARE OF YOU.
SHE'S NOT MAKING SENSE. LOOK AT HER! SHE'S ACTING LIKE SHE'S RAISED US OUR ENTIRE LIVES!
I DON'T KNOW HER THAT WELL. I DON'T WANT TO STAY HERE. SHE'S ONLY BEEN MY MOTHER FOR AN HOUR.
I KNOW, I KNOW, SORCELINE. JUST GIVE HER A DAY. SHE'S SURE TO LET US GO.

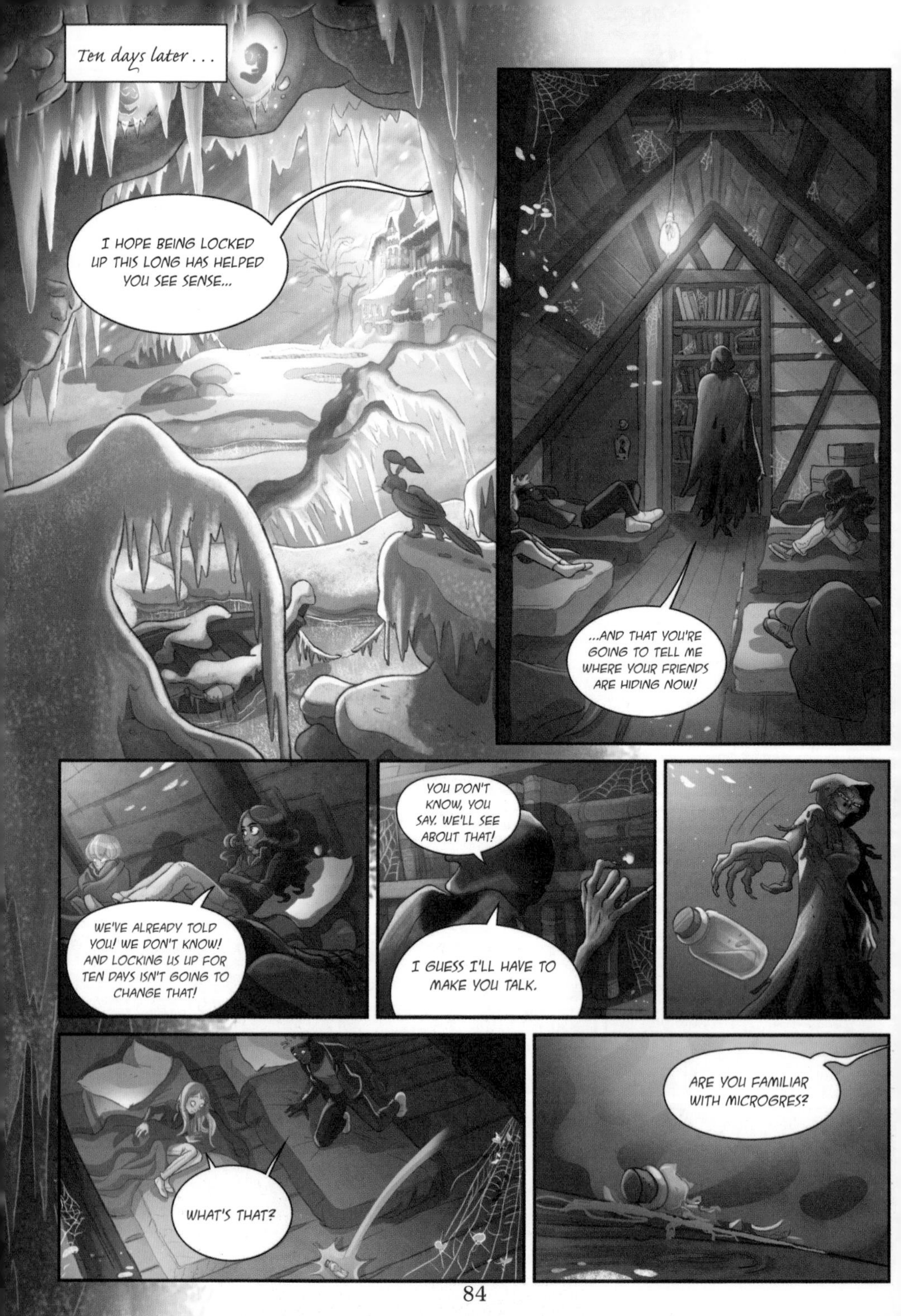
Ten days later . . .
I HOPE BEING LOCKED UP THIS LONG HAS HELPED YOU SEE SENSE...
...AND THAT YOU'RE GOING TO TELL ME WHERE YOUR FRIENDS ARE HIDING NOW!
WE'VE ALREADY TOLD YOU! WE DON'T KNOW! AND LOCKING US UP FOR TEN DAYS ISN'T GOING TO CHANGE THAT!
YOU DON'T KNOW, YOU SAY. WE'LL SEE ABOUT THAT!
I GUESS I'LL HAVE TO MAKE YOU TALK.
WHAT'S THAT?
ARE YOU FAMILIAR WITH MICROGRES?

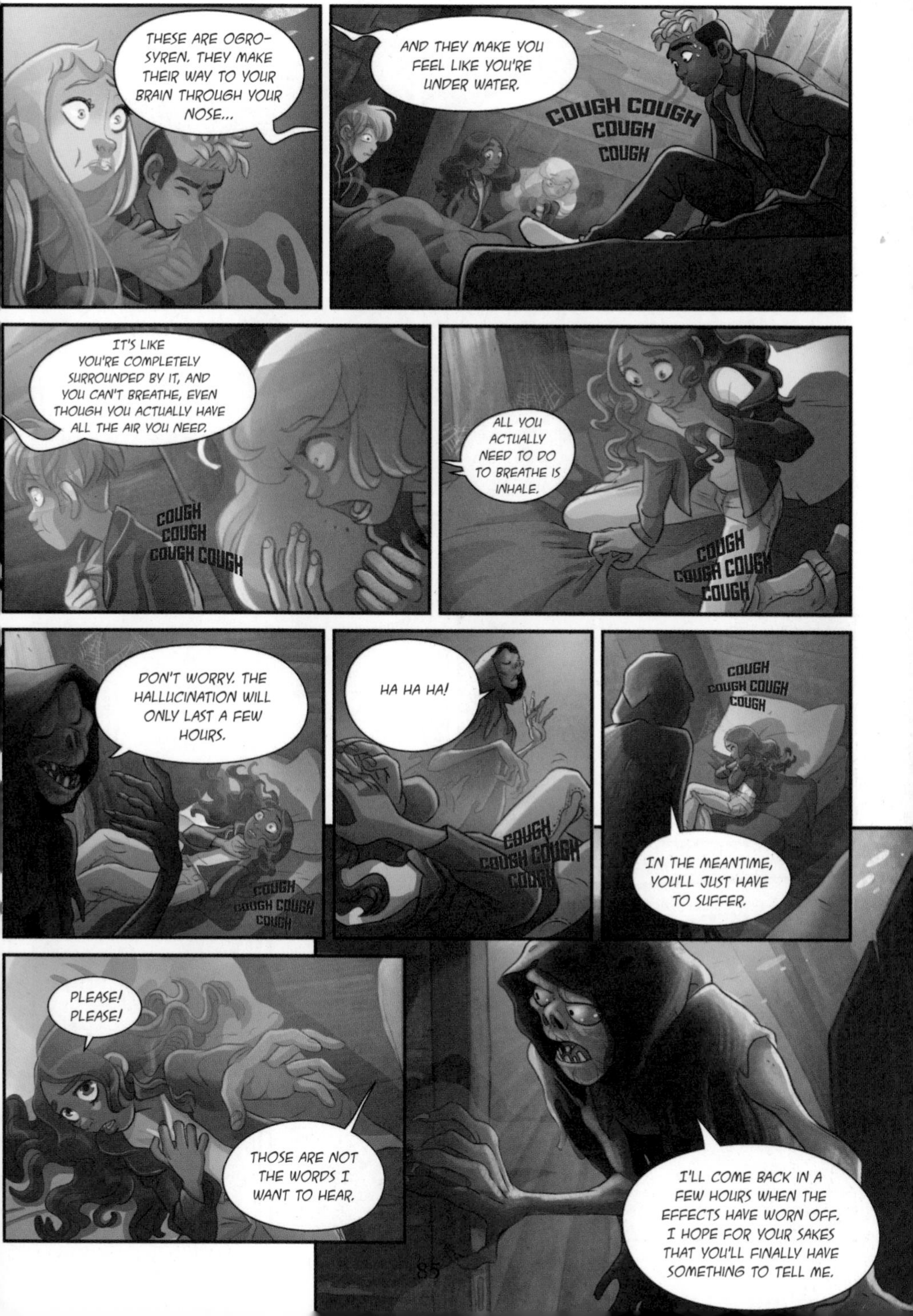
THESE ARE OGRO-SYREN. THEY MAKE THEIR WAY TO YOUR BRAIN THROUGH YOUR NOSE...
AND THEY MAKE YOU FEEL LIKE YOU'RE UNDER WATER.
COUGH COUGH COUGH COUGH
IT'S LIKE YOU'RE COMPLETELY SURROUNDED BY IT, AND YOU CAN'T BREATHE, EVEN THOUGH YOU ACTUALLY HAVE ALL THE AIR YOU NEED.
COUGH COUGH COUGH COUGH
ALL YOU ACTUALLY NEED TO DO TO BREATHE IS INHALE.
COUGH COUGH COUGH COUGH
DON'T WORRY. THE HALLUCINATION WILL ONLY LAST A FEW HOURS.
COUGH COUGH COUGH COUGH
HA HA HA!
COUGH COUGH COUGH COUGH
COUGH COUGH COUGH COUGH
IN THE MEANTIME, YOU'LL JUST HAVE TO SUFFER.
PLEASE! PLEASE!
THOSE ARE NOT THE WORDS I WANT TO HEAR.
I'LL COME BACK IN A FEW HOURS WHEN THE EFFECTS HAVE WORN OFF. I HOPE FOR YOUR SAKES THAT YOU'LL FINALLY HAVE SOMETHING TO TELL ME.

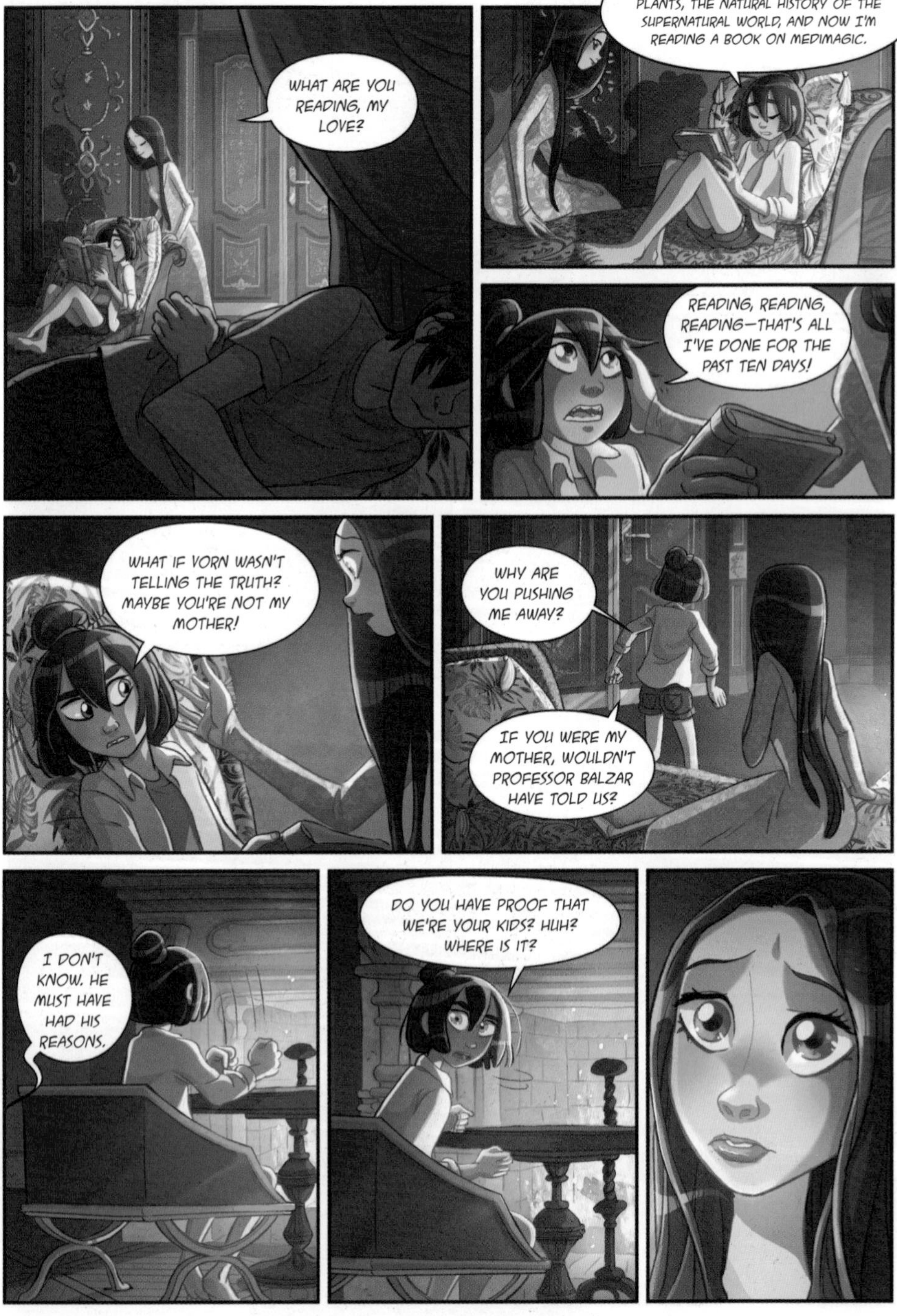
WHAT ARE YOU READING, MY LOVE?
I READ THE GUIDE TO AROMAGIC PLANTS, THE NATURAL HISTORY OF THE SUPERNATURAL WORLD, AND NOW I'M READING A BOOK ON MEDIMAGIC.
READING, READING, READING—THAT'S ALL I'VE DONE FOR THE PAST TEN DAYS!
WHAT IF VORN WASN'T TELLING THE TRUTH? MAYBE YOU'RE NOT MY MOTHER!
WHY ARE YOU PUSHING ME AWAY?
IF YOU WERE MY MOTHER, WOULDN'T PROFESSOR BALZAR HAVE TOLD US?
I DON'T KNOW. HE MUST HAVE HAD HIS REASONS.
DO YOU HAVE PROOF THAT WE'RE YOUR KIDS? HUH? WHERE IS IT?

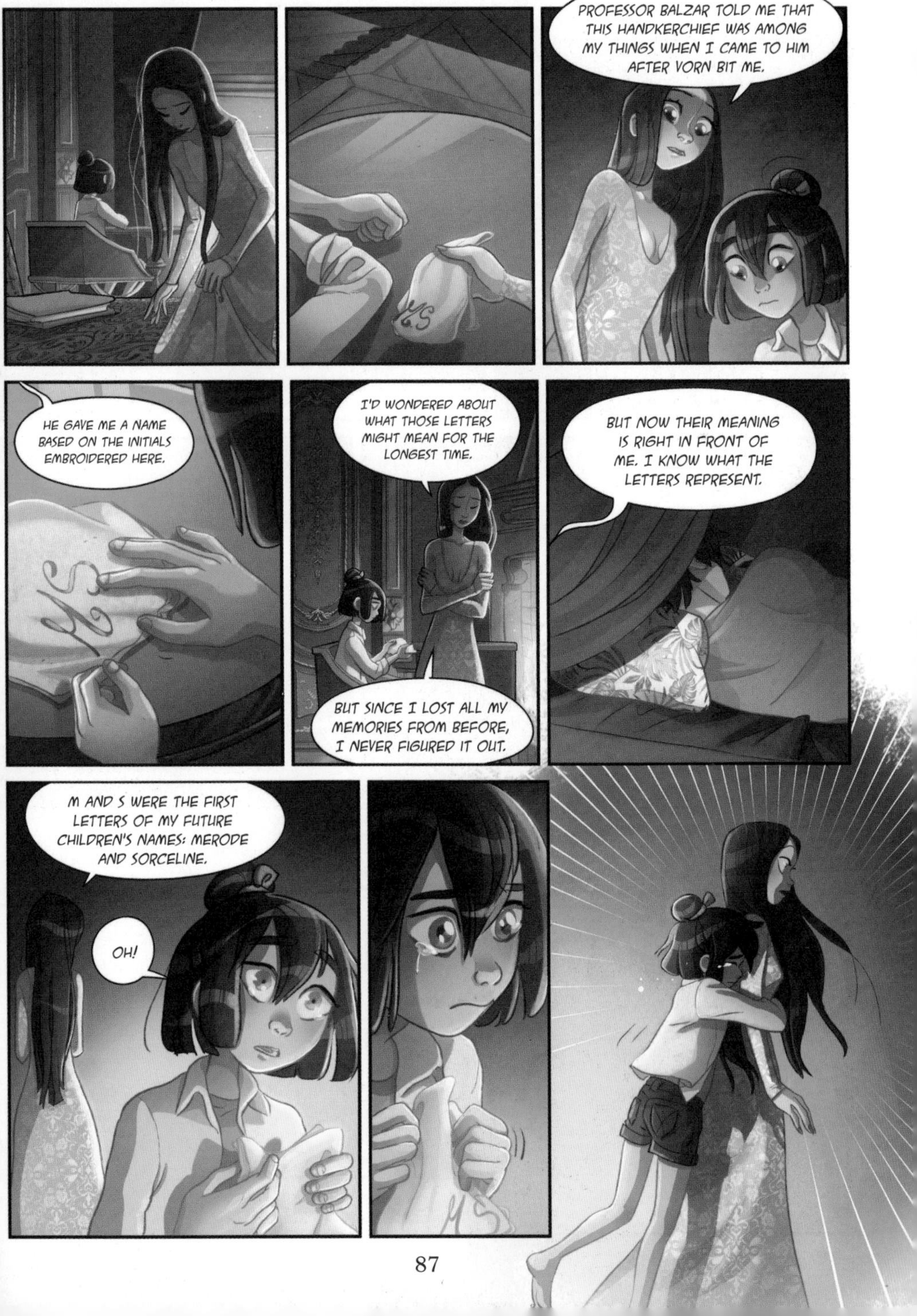
PROFESSOR BALZAR TOLD ME THAT THIS HANDKERCHIEF WAS AMONG MY THINGS WHEN I CAME TO HIM AFTER VORN BIT ME.
HE GAVE ME A NAME BASED ON THE INITIALS EMBROIDERED HERE.
I'D WONDERED ABOUT WHAT THOSE LETTERS MIGHT MEAN FOR THE LONGEST TIME.
BUT SINCE I LOST ALL MY MEMORIES FROM BEFORE, I NEVER FIGURED IT OUT.
BUT NOW THEIR MEANING IS RIGHT IN FRONT OF ME. I KNOW WHAT THE LETTERS REPRESENT.
M AND S WERE THE FIRST LETTERS OF MY FUTURE CHILDREN'S NAMES: MERODE AND SORCELINE.
OH!

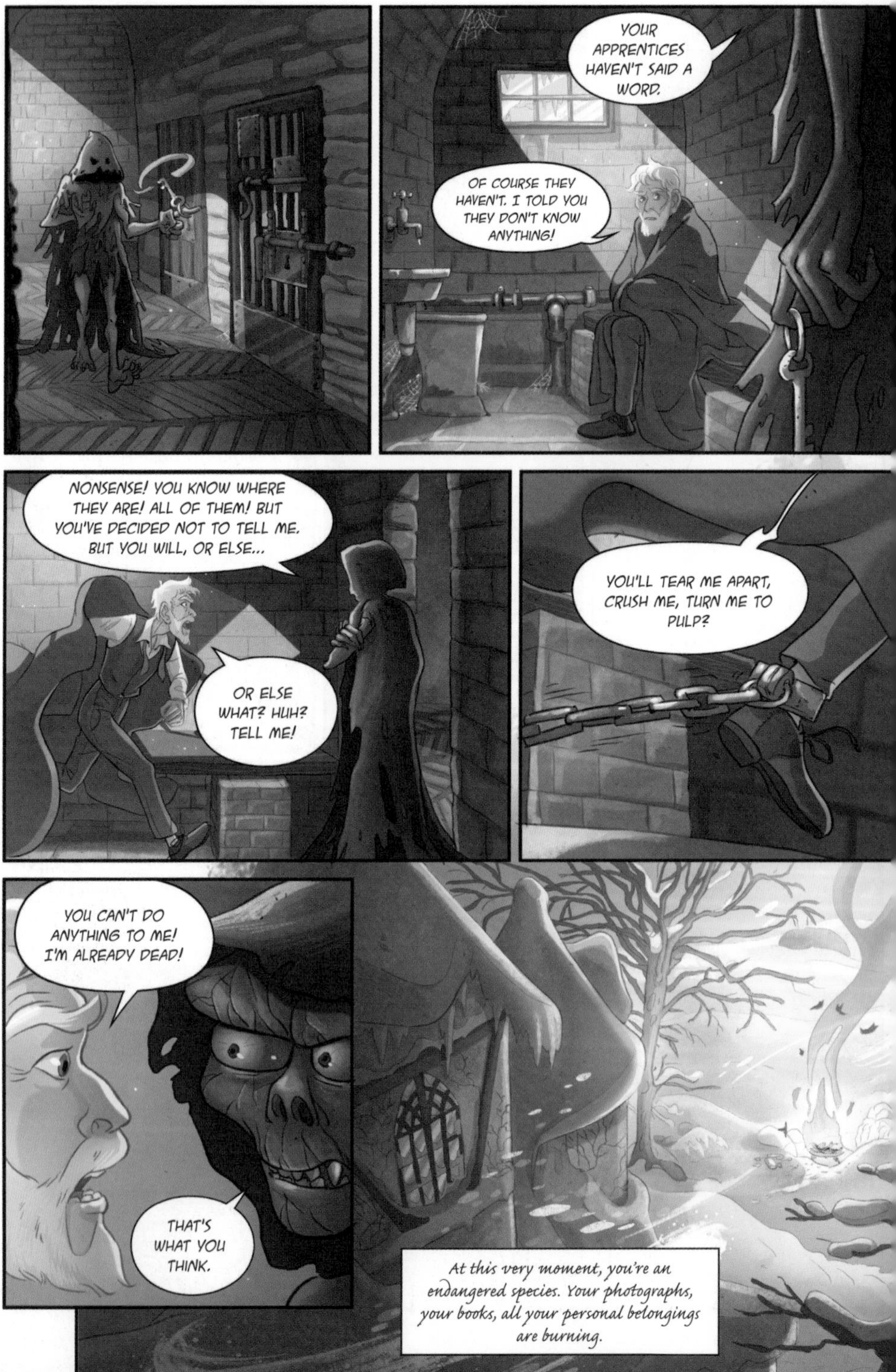
YOUR APPRENTICES HAVEN'T SAID A WORD.
OF COURSE THEY HAVEN'T. I TOLD YOU THEY DON'T KNOW ANYTHING!
NONSENSE! YOU KNOW WHERE THEY ARE! ALL OF THEM! BUT YOU'VE DECIDED NOT TO TELL ME. BUT YOU WILL, OR ELSE...
OR ELSE WHAT? HUH? TELL ME!
YOU'LL TEAR ME APART, CRUSH ME, TURN ME TO PULP?
YOU CAN'T DO ANYTHING TO ME! I'M ALREADY DEAD!
THAT'S WHAT YOU THINK.
At this very moment, you're an endangered species. Your photographs, your books, all your personal belongings are burning.

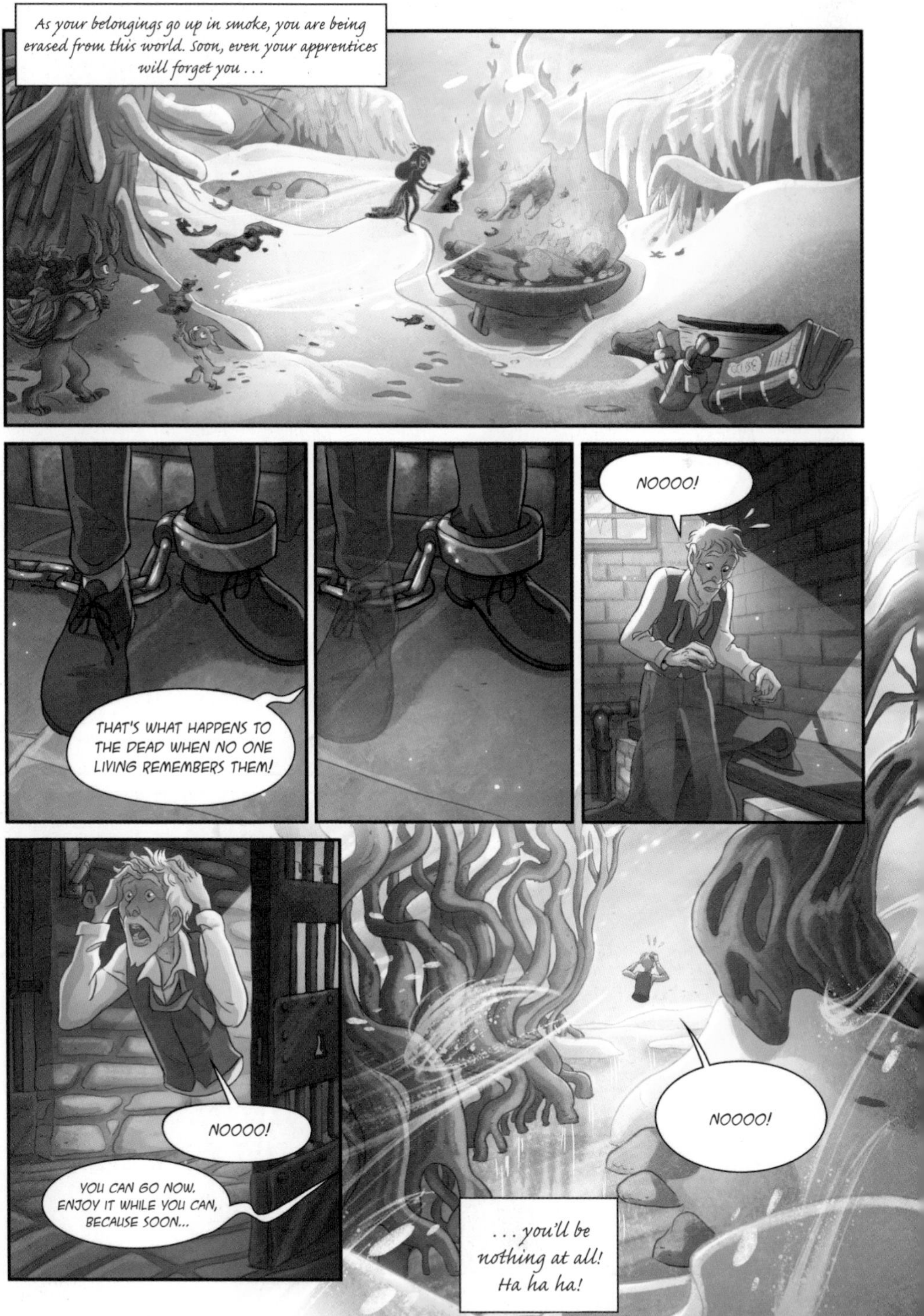
As your belongings go up in smoke, you are being erased from this world. Soon, even your apprentices will forget you . . .
THAT'S WHAT HAPPENS TO THE DEAD WHEN NO ONE LIVING REMEMBERS THEM!
NOOOO!
NOOOO!
YOU CAN GO NOW. ENJOY IT WHILE YOU CAN, BECAUSE SOON...
NOOOO!
. . . you'll be nothing at all! Ha ha ha!

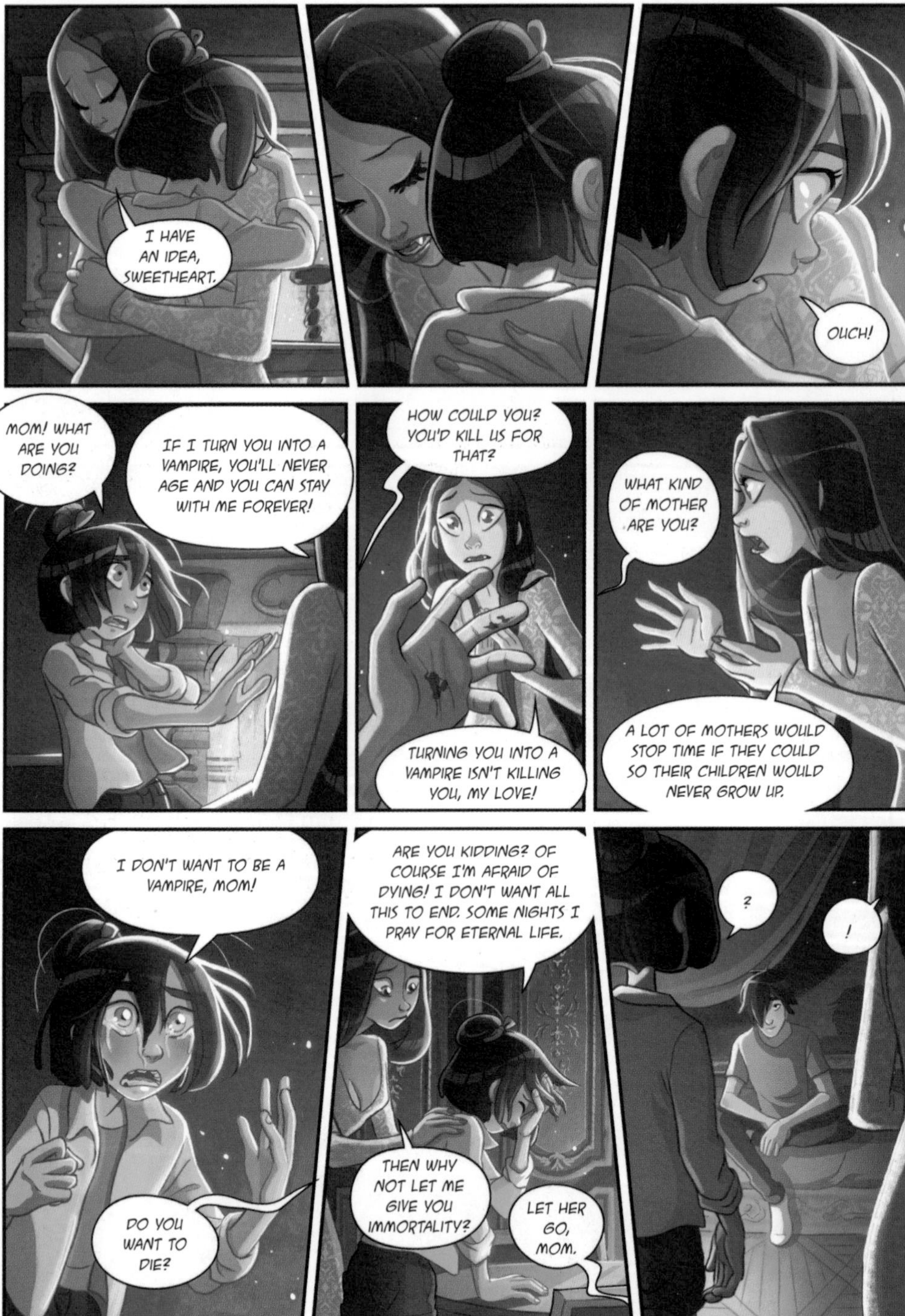

I HAVE AN IDEA, SWEETHEART.
OUCH!
MOM! WHAT ARE YOU DOING?
IF I TURN YOU INTO A VAMPIRE, YOU'LL NEVER AGE AND YOU CAN STAY WITH ME FOREVER!
HOW COULD YOU? YOU'D KILL US FOR THAT?
TURNING YOU INTO A VAMPIRE ISN'T KILLING YOU, MY LOVE!
WHAT KIND OF MOTHER ARE YOU?
A LOT OF MOTHERS WOULD STOP TIME IF THEY COULD SO THEIR CHILDREN WOULD NEVER GROW UP.
I DON'T WANT TO BE A VAMPIRE, MOM!
DO YOU WANT TO DIE?
ARE YOU KIDDING? OF COURSE I'M AFRAID OF DYING! I DON'T WANT ALL THIS TO END. SOME NIGHTS I PRAY FOR ETERNAL LIFE.
THEN WHY NOT LET ME GIVE YOU IMMORTALITY?
LET HER GO, MOM.
?
!

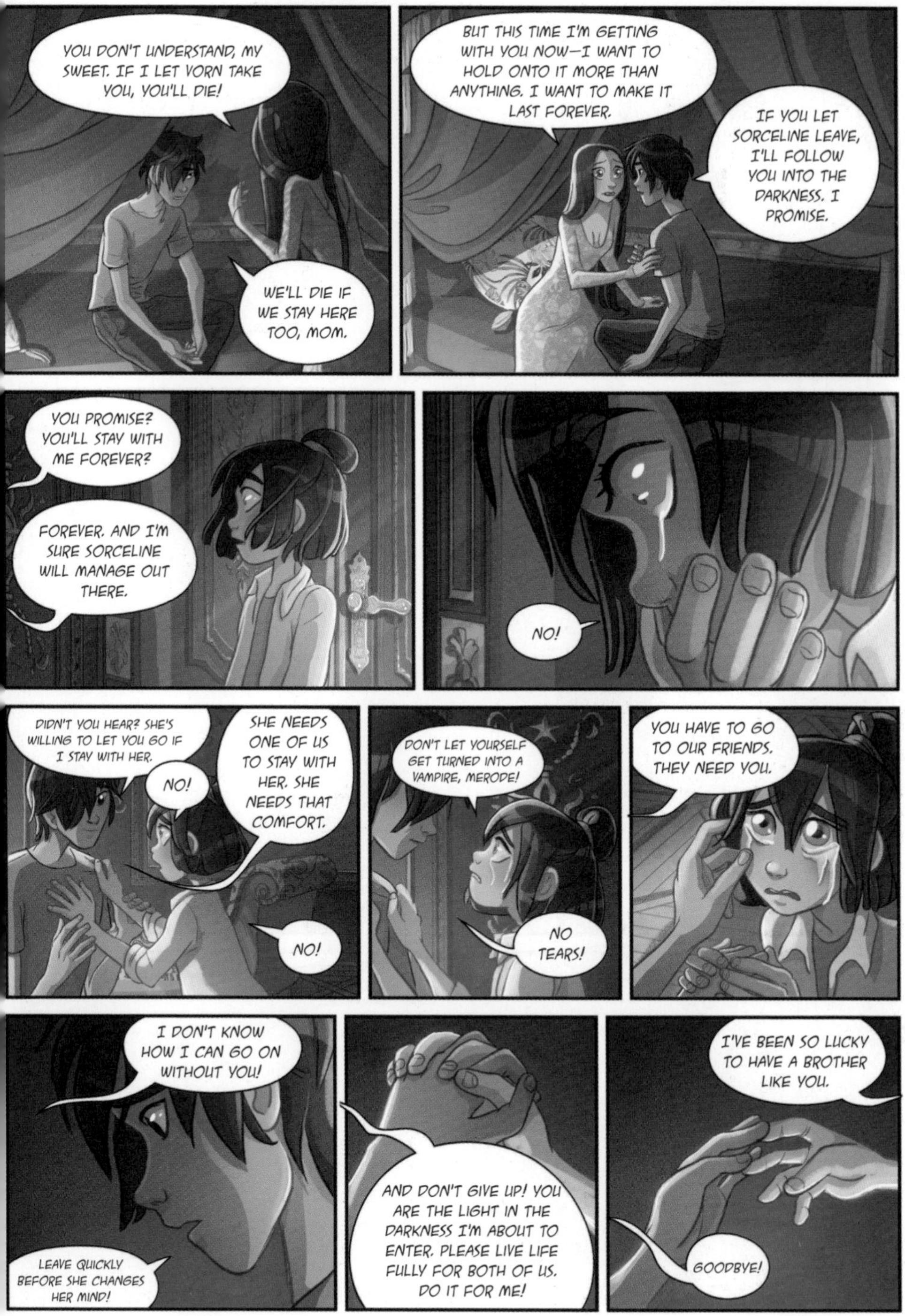
YOU DON'T UNDERSTAND, MY SWEET. IF I LET VORN TAKE YOU, YOU'LL DIE!
WE'LL DIE IF WE STAY HERE TOO, MOM.
BUT THIS TIME I'M GETTING WITH YOU NOW—I WANT TO HOLD ONTO IT MORE THAN ANYTHING. I WANT TO MAKE IT LAST FOREVER.
IF YOU LET SORCELINE LEAVE, I'LL FOLLOW YOU INTO THE DARKNESS. I PROMISE.
YOU PROMISE? YOU'LL STAY WITH ME FOREVER?
FOREVER. AND I'M SURE SORCELINE WILL MANAGE OUT THERE.
NO!
DIDN'T YOU HEAR? SHE'S WILLING TO LET YOU GO IF I STAY WITH HER.
NO!
SHE NEEDS ONE OF US TO STAY WITH HER. SHE NEEDS THAT COMFORT.
NO!
DON'T LET YOURSELF GET TURNED INTO A VAMPIRE, MERODE!
NO TEARS!
YOU HAVE TO GO TO OUR FRIENDS. THEY NEED YOU.
I DON'T KNOW HOW I CAN GO ON WITHOUT YOU!
LEAVE QUICKLY BEFORE SHE CHANGES HER MIND!
AND DON'T GIVE UP! YOU ARE THE LIGHT IN THE DARKNESS I'M ABOUT TO ENTER. PLEASE LIVE LIFE FULLY FOR BOTH OF US. DO IT FOR ME!
I'VE BEEN SO LUCKY TO HAVE A BROTHER LIKE YOU.
GOODBYE!

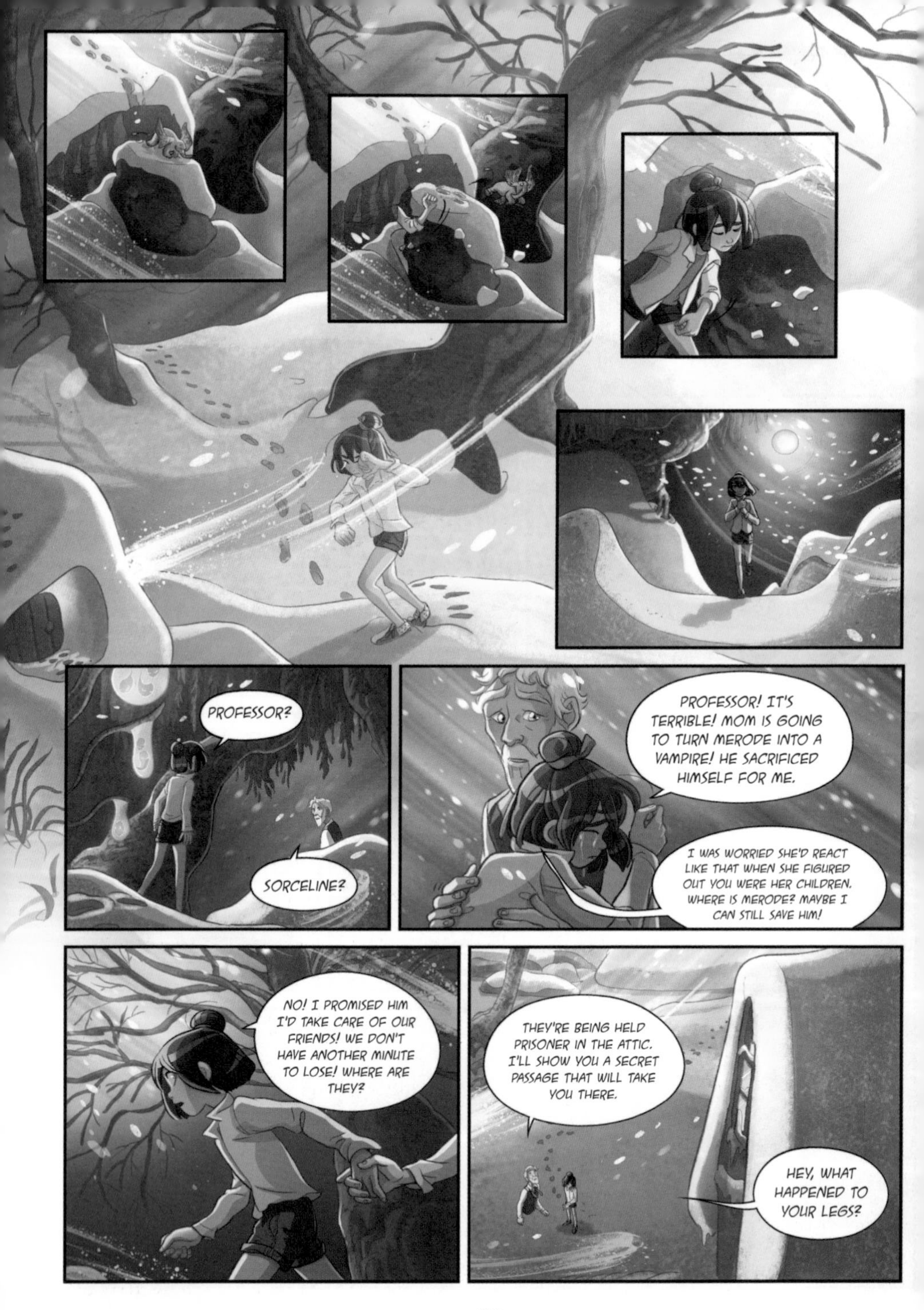
PROFESSOR?
SORCELINE?
PROFESSOR! IT'S TERRIBLE! MOM IS GOING TO TURN MERODE INTO A VAMPIRE! HE SACRIFICED HIMSELF FOR ME.
I WAS WORRIED SHE'D REACT LIKE THAT WHEN SHE FIGURED OUT YOU WERE HER CHILDREN. WHERE IS MERODE? MAYBE I CAN STILL SAVE HIM!
NO! I PROMISED HIM I'D TAKE CARE OF OUR FRIENDS! WE DON'T HAVE ANOTHER MINUTE TO LOSE! WHERE ARE THEY?
THEY'RE BEING HELD PRISONER IN THE ATTIC. I'LL SHOW YOU A SECRET PASSAGE THAT WILL TAKE YOU THERE.
HEY, WHAT HAPPENED TO YOUR LEGS?

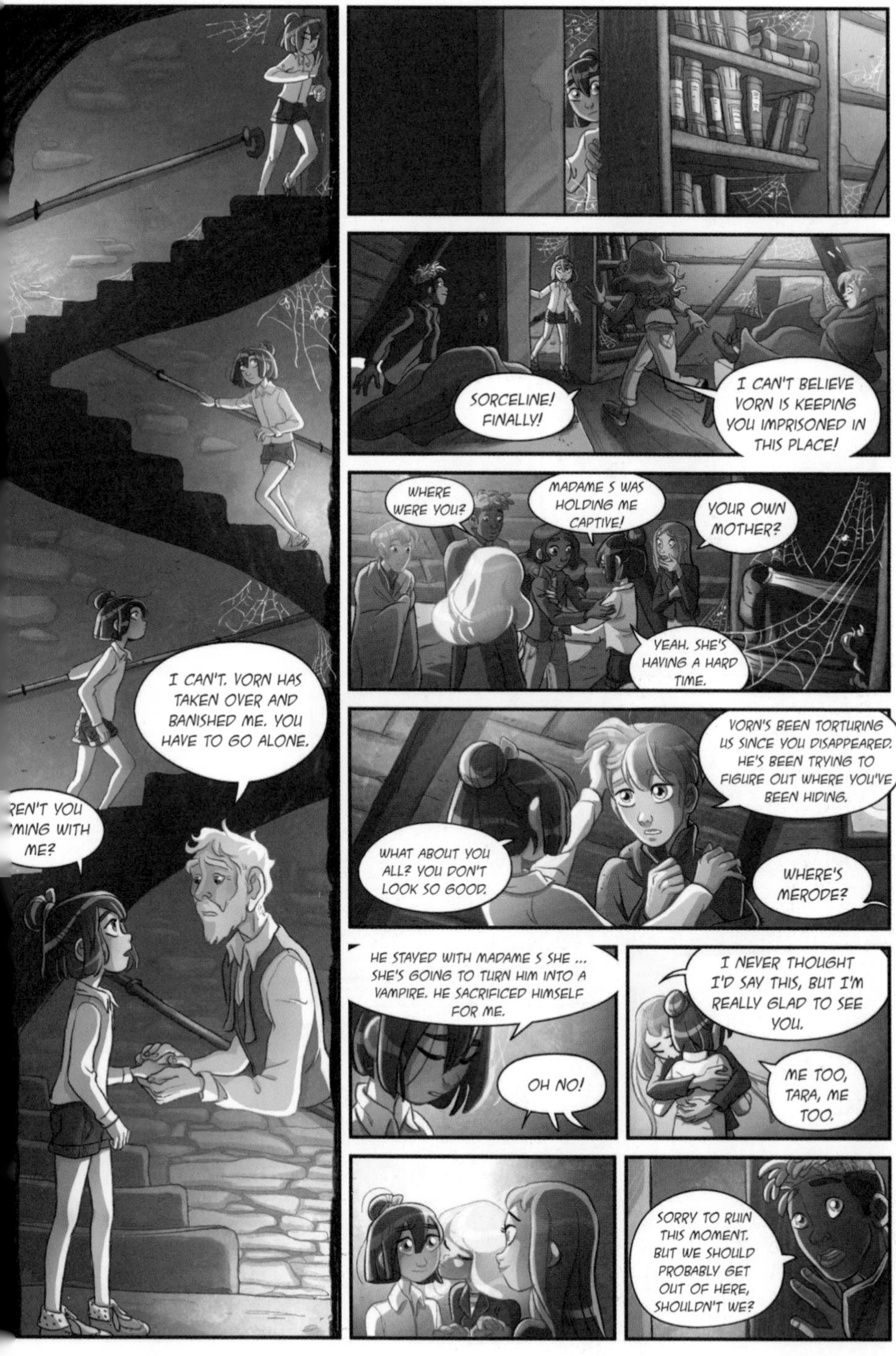
REN'T YOU MING WITH ME?
I CAN'T. VORN HAS TAKEN OVER AND BANISHED ME. YOU HAVE TO GO ALONE.
SORCELINE! FINALLY!
I CAN'T BELIEVE VORN IS KEEPING YOU IMPRISONED IN THIS PLACE!
WHERE WERE YOU?
MADAME S WAS HOLDING ME CAPTIVE!
YOUR OWN MOTHER?
YEAH. SHE'S HAVING A HARD TIME.
VORN'S BEEN TORTURING US SINCE YOU DISAPPEARED. HE'S BEEN TRYING TO FIGURE OUT WHERE YOU'VE BEEN HIDING.
WHAT ABOUT YOU ALL? YOU DON'T LOOK SO GOOD.
WHERE'S MERODE?
HE STAYED WITH MADAME S SHE ... SHE'S GOING TO TURN HIM INTO A VAMPIRE. HE SACRIFICED HIMSELF FOR ME.
OH NO!
I NEVER THOUGHT I'D SAY THIS, BUT I'M REALLY GLAD TO SEE YOU.
ME TOO, TARA, ME TOO.
SORRY TO RUIN THIS MOMENT. BUT WE SHOULD PROBABLY GET OUT OF HERE, SHOULDN'T WE?

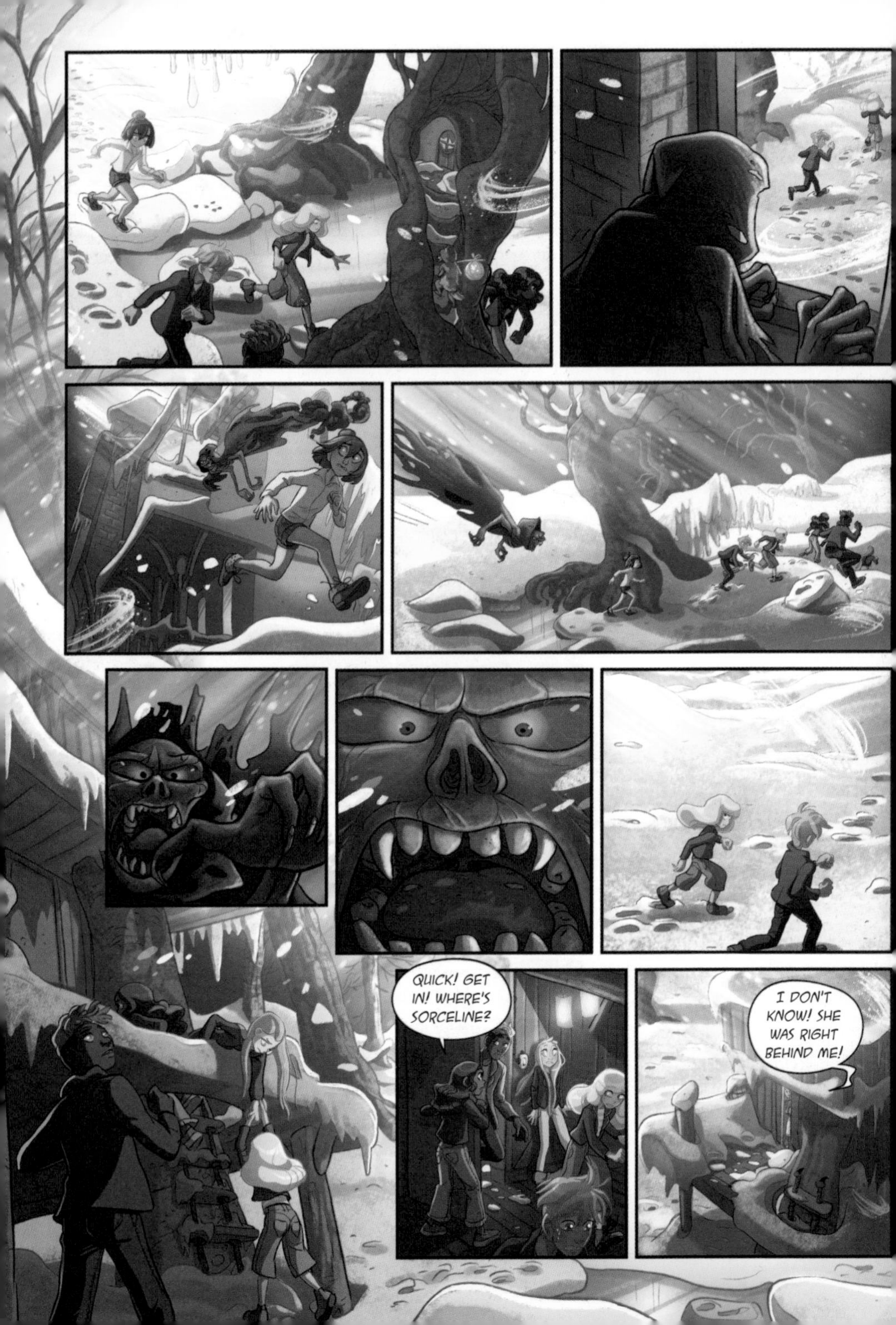
QUICK! GET IN! WHERE'S SORCELINE?
I DON'T KNOW! SHE WAS RIGHT BEHIND ME!

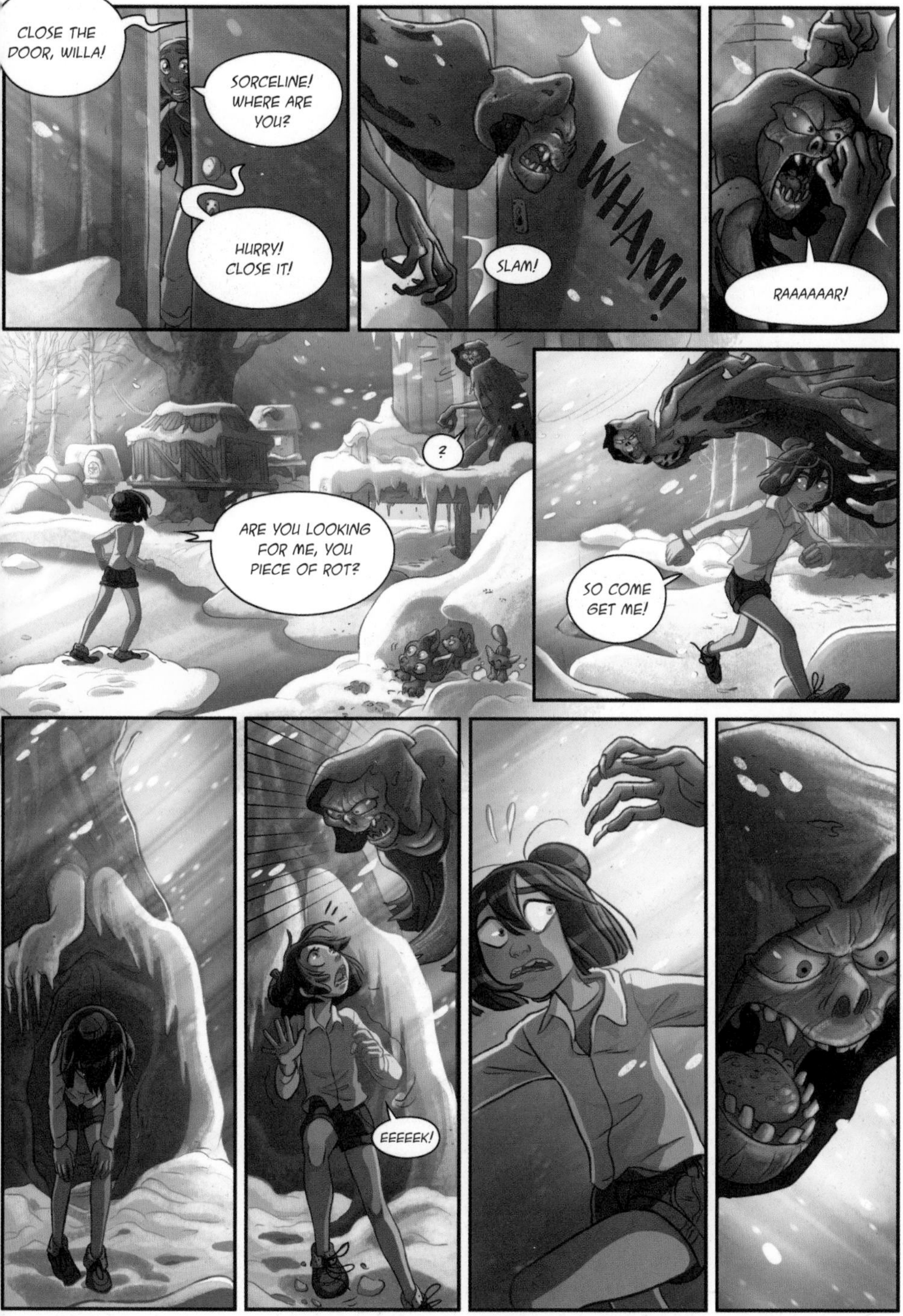

CLOSE THE DOOR, WILLA!
SORCELINE! WHERE ARE YOU?
HURRY! CLOSE IT!
WHAM!
SLAM!
RAAAAAAR!
?
ARE YOU LOOKING FOR ME, YOU PIECE OF ROT?
SO COME GET ME!
EEEEEK!

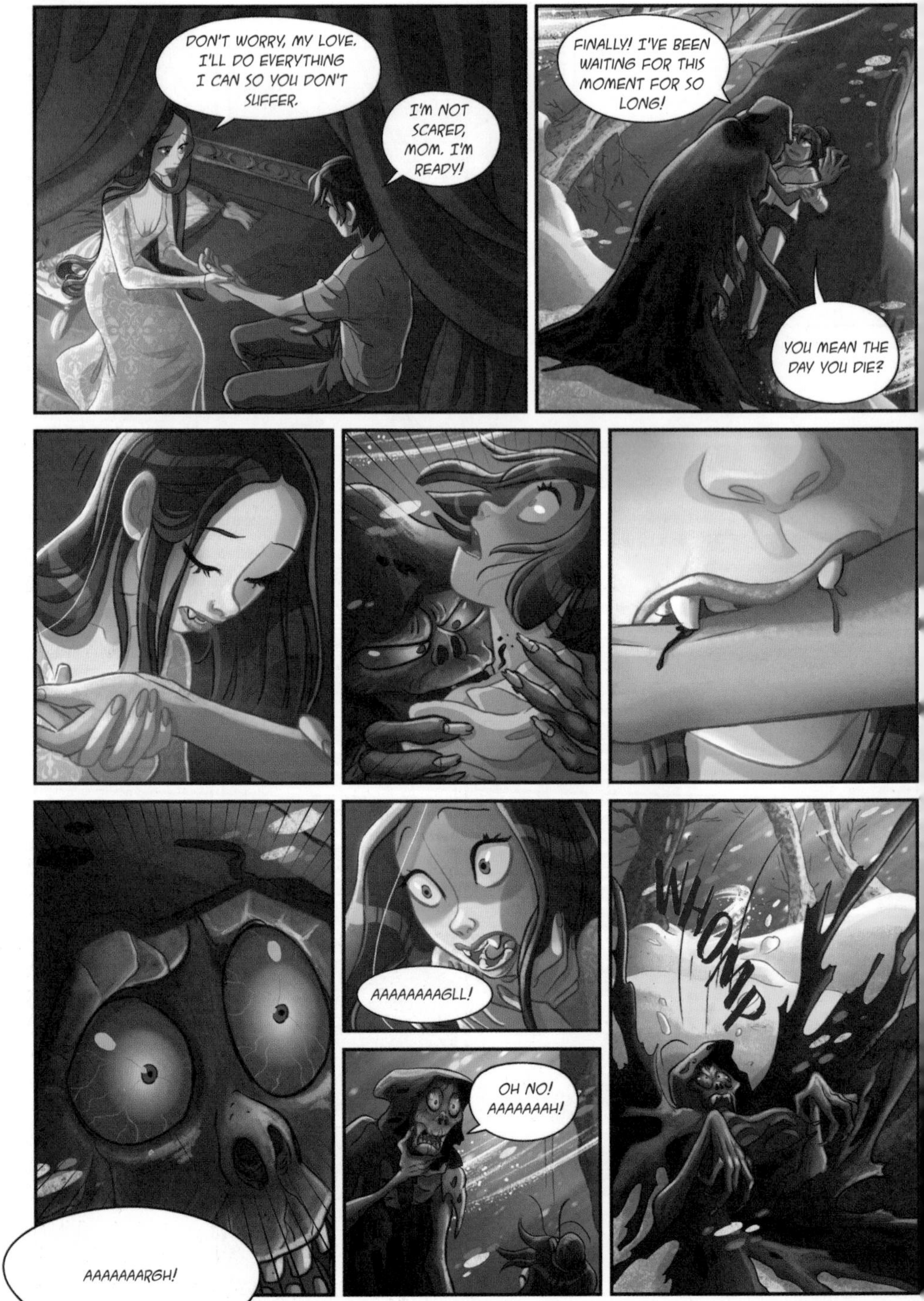
DON'T WORRY, MY LOVE. I'LL DO EVERYTHING I CAN SO YOU DON'T SUFFER.
I'M NOT SCARED, MOM. I'M READY!
FINALLY! I'VE BEEN WAITING FOR THIS MOMENT FOR SO LONG!
YOU MEAN THE DAY YOU DIE?
AAAAAAAARGH!
AAAAAAAAGLL!
OH NO! AAAAAAAH!
WHOMP

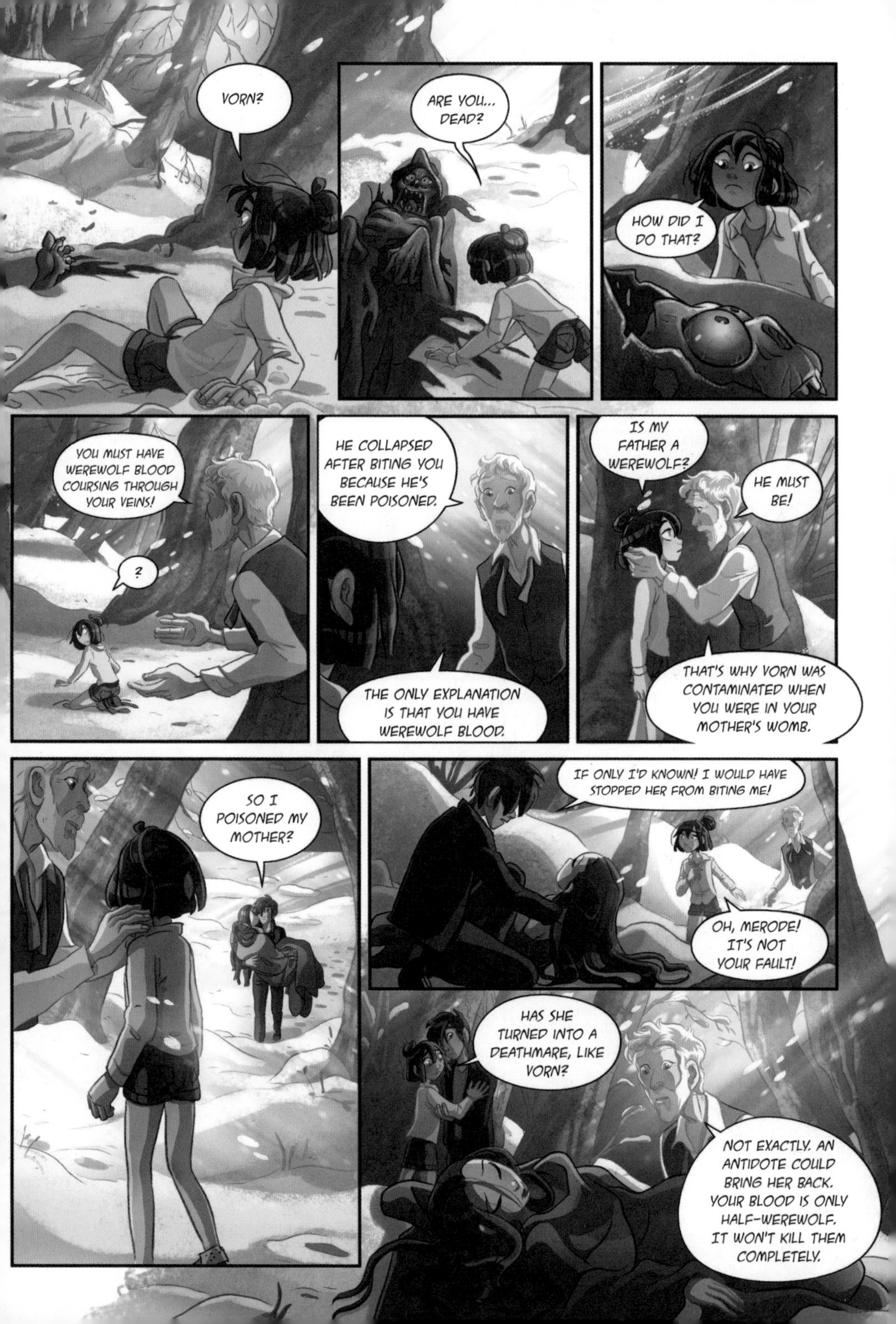
VORN?
ARE YOU... DEAD?
HOW DID I DO THAT?
YOU MUST HAVE WEREWOLF BLOOD COURSING THROUGH YOUR VEINS!
?
HE COLLAPSED AFTER BITING YOU BECAUSE HE'S BEEN POISONED.
THE ONLY EXPLANATION IS THAT YOU HAVE WEREWOLF BLOOD.
IS MY FATHER A WEREWOLF?
HE MUST BE!
THAT'S WHY VORN WAS CONTAMINATED WHEN YOU WERE IN YOUR MOTHER'S WOMB.
SO I POISONED MY MOTHER?
IF ONLY I'D KNOWN! I WOULD HAVE STOPPED HER FROM BITING ME!
OH, MERODE! IT'S NOT YOUR FAULT!
HAS SHE TURNED INTO A DEATHMARE, LIKE VORN?
NOT EXACTLY. AN ANTIDOTE COULD BRING HER BACK. YOUR BLOOD IS ONLY HALF-WEREWOLF. IT WON'T KILL THEM COMPLETELY.

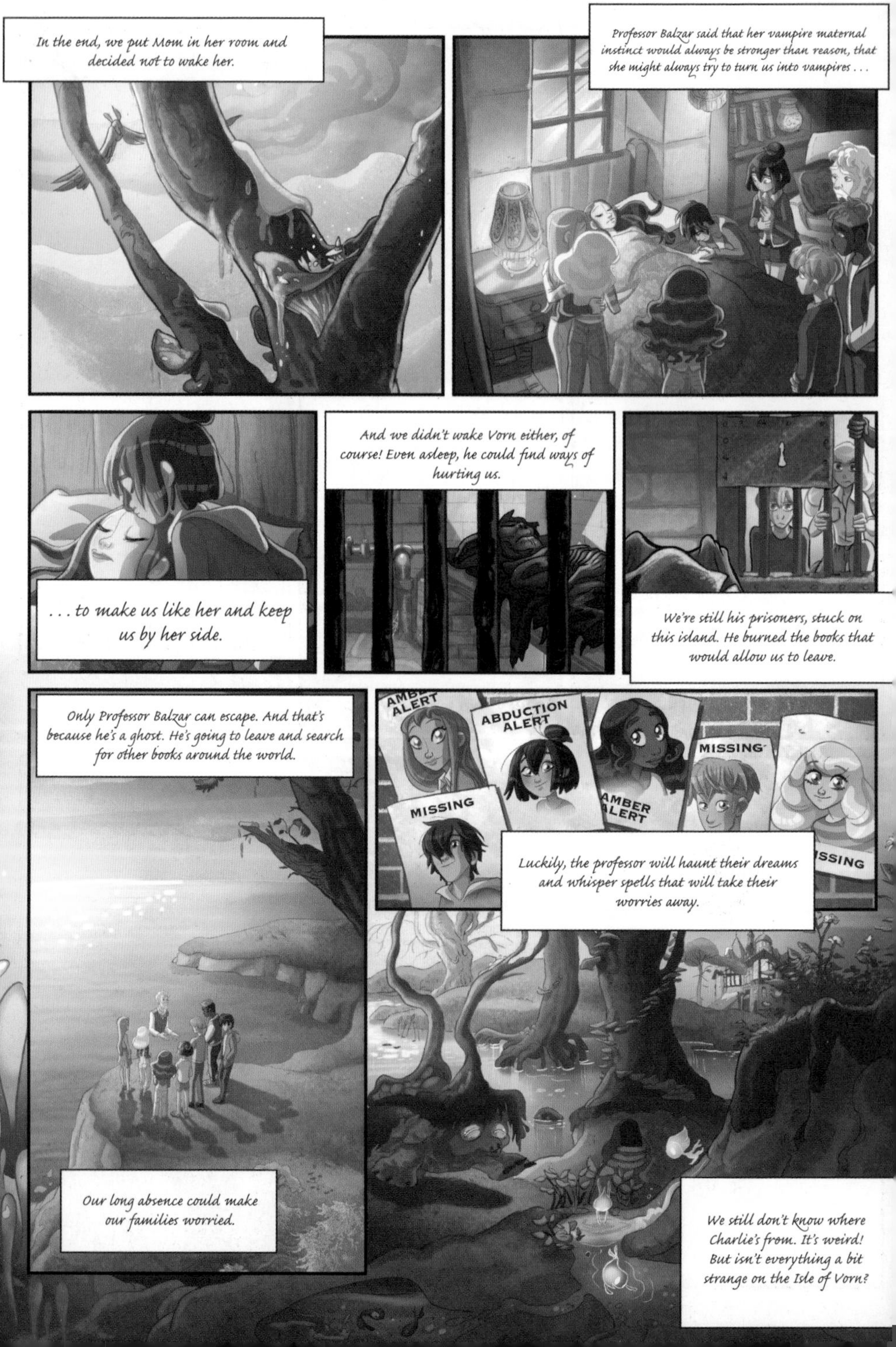

In the end, we put Mom in her room and decided not to wake her.
Professor Balzar said that her vampire maternal instinct would always be stronger than reason, that she might always try to turn us into vampires . . .
. . . to make us like her and keep us by her side.
And we didn't wake Vorn either, of course! Even asleep, he could find ways of hurting us.
We're still his prisoners, stuck on this island. He burned the books that would allow us to leave.
Only Professor Balzar can escape. And that's because he's a ghost. He's going to leave and search for other books around the world.
Our long absence could make our families worried.
AMBER ALERT
ABDUCTION ALERT
MISSING
AMBER ALERT
MISSING
MISSING
Luckily, the professor will haunt their dreams and whisper spells that will take their worries away.
We still don't know where Charlie's from. It's weird! But isn't everything a bit strange on the Isle of Vorn?

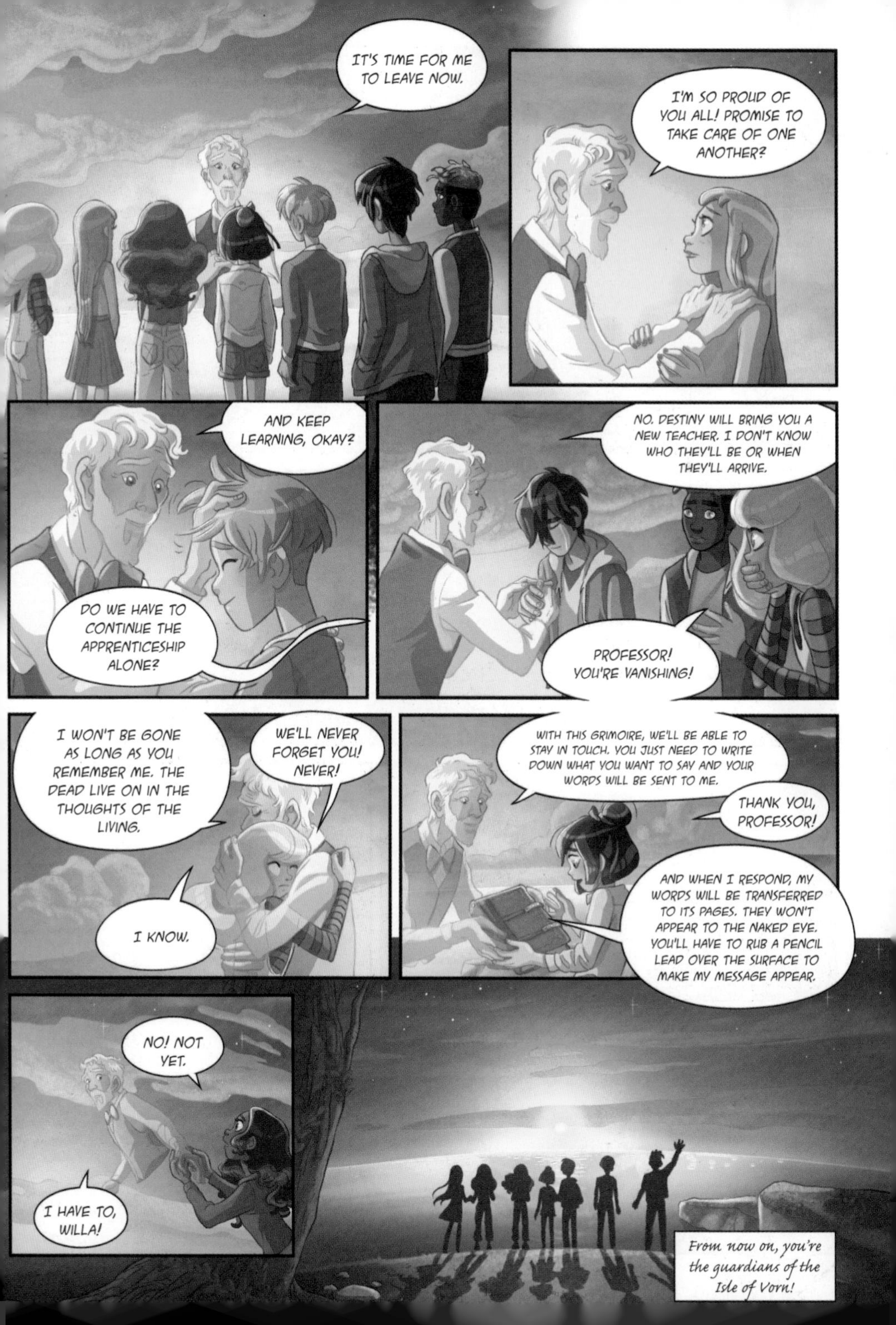
IT'S TIME FOR ME TO LEAVE NOW.
I'M SO PROUD OF YOU ALL! PROMISE TO TAKE CARE OF ONE ANOTHER?
AND KEEP LEARNING, OKAY?
DO WE HAVE TO CONTINUE THE APPRENTICESHIP ALONE?
NO. DESTINY WILL BRING YOU A NEW TEACHER. I DON'T KNOW WHO THEY'LL BE OR WHEN THEY'LL ARRIVE.
PROFESSOR! YOU'RE VANISHING!
I WON'T BE GONE AS LONG AS YOU REMEMBER ME. THE DEAD LIVE ON IN THE THOUGHTS OF THE LIVING.
WE'LL NEVER FORGET YOU! NEVER!
I KNOW.
WITH THIS GRIMOIRE, WE'LL BE ABLE TO STAY IN TOUCH. YOU JUST NEED TO WRITE DOWN WHAT YOU WANT TO SAY AND YOUR WORDS WILL BE SENT TO ME.
THANK YOU, PROFESSOR!
AND WHEN I RESPOND, MY WORDS WILL BE TRANSFERRED TO ITS PAGES. THEY WON'T APPEAR TO THE NAKED EYE. YOU'LL HAVE TO RUB A PENCIL LEAD OVER THE SURFACE TO MAKE MY MESSAGE APPEAR.
NO! NOT YET.
I HAVE TO, WILLA!
From now on, you're the guardians of the Isle of Vorn!

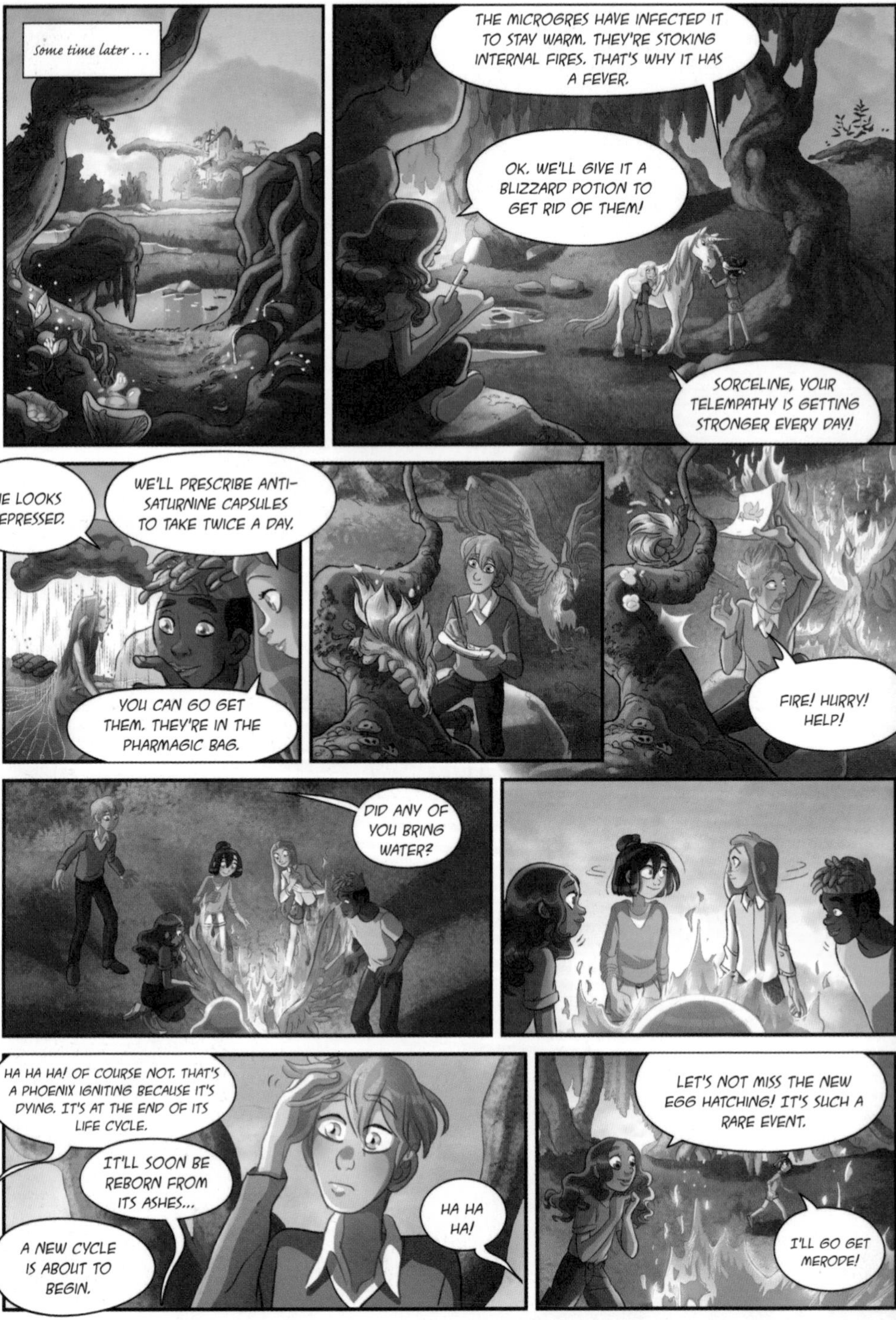

Some time later . . .
THE MICROGRES HAVE INFECTED IT TO STAY WARM. THEY'RE STOKING INTERNAL FIRES. THAT'S WHY IT HAS A FEVER.
OK. WE'LL GIVE IT A BLIZZARD POTION TO GET RID OF THEM!
SORCELINE, YOUR TELEMPATHY IS GETTING STRONGER EVERY DAY!
HE LOOKS DEPRESSED.
WE'LL PRESCRIBE ANTI-SATURNINE CAPSULES TO TAKE TWICE A DAY.
YOU CAN GO GET THEM. THEY'RE IN THE PHARMAGIC BAG.
FIRE! HURRY! HELP!
DID ANY OF YOU BRING WATER?
HA HA HA! OF COURSE NOT. THAT'S A PHOENIX IGNITING BECAUSE IT'S DYING. IT'S AT THE END OF ITS LIFE CYCLE.
IT'LL SOON BE REBORN FROM ITS ASHES...
A NEW CYCLE IS ABOUT TO BEGIN.
HA HA HA!
LET'S NOT MISS THE NEW EGG HATCHING! IT'S SUCH A RARE EVENT.
I'LL GO GET MERODE!

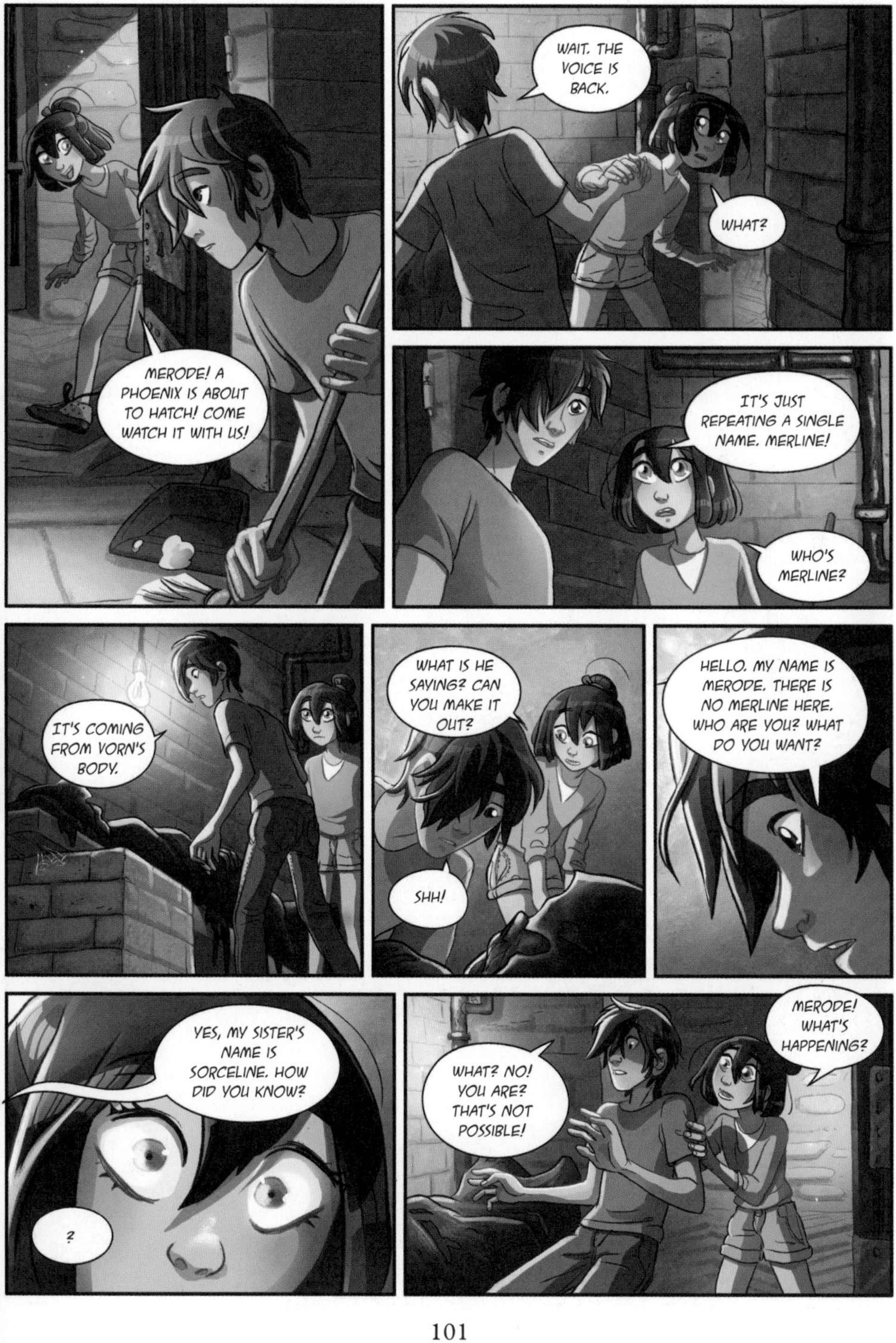
MERODE! A PHOENIX IS ABOUT TO HATCH! COME WATCH IT WITH US!
WAIT. THE VOICE IS BACK.
WHAT?
IT'S JUST REPEATING A SINGLE NAME. MERLINE!
WHO'S MERLINE?
IT'S COMING FROM VORN'S BODY.
WHAT IS HE SAYING? CAN YOU MAKE IT OUT?
SHH!
HELLO. MY NAME IS MERODE. THERE IS NO MERLINE HERE. WHO ARE YOU? WHAT DO YOU WANT?
YES, MY SISTER'S NAME IS SORCELINE. HOW DID YOU KNOW?
?
WHAT? NO! YOU ARE? THAT'S NOT POSSIBLE!
MERODE! WHAT'S HAPPENING?

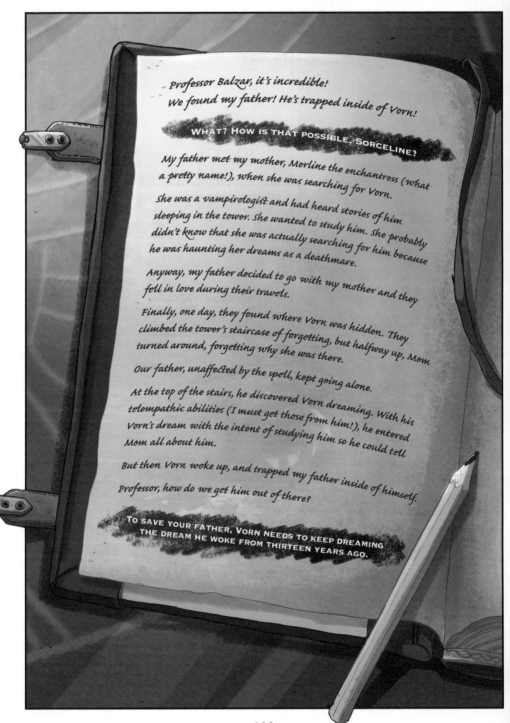

Professor Balzar, it's incredible!
We found my father! He's trapped inside of Vorn!

WHAT? HOW IS THAT POSSIBLE, SORCELINE?

My father met my mother, Merline the enchantress (what a pretty name!), when she was searching for Vorn.

She was a vampirologist and had heard stories of him sleeping in the tower. She wanted to study him. She probably didn't know that she was actually searching for him because he was haunting her dreams as a deathmare.

Anyway, my father decided to go with my mother and they fell in love during their travels.

Finally, one day, they found where Vorn was hidden. They climbed the tower's staircase of forgetting, but halfway up, Mom turned around, forgetting why she was there.

Our father, unaffected by the spell, kept going alone.

At the top of the stairs, he discovered Vorn dreaming. With his telempathic abilities (I must get those from him!), he entered Vorn's dream with the intent of studying him so he could tell Mom all about him.

But then Vorn woke up, and trapped my father inside of himself.

Professor, how do we get him out of there?

TO SAVE YOUR FATHER, VORN NEEDS TO KEEP DREAMING THE DREAM HE WOKE FROM THIRTEEN YEARS AGO.

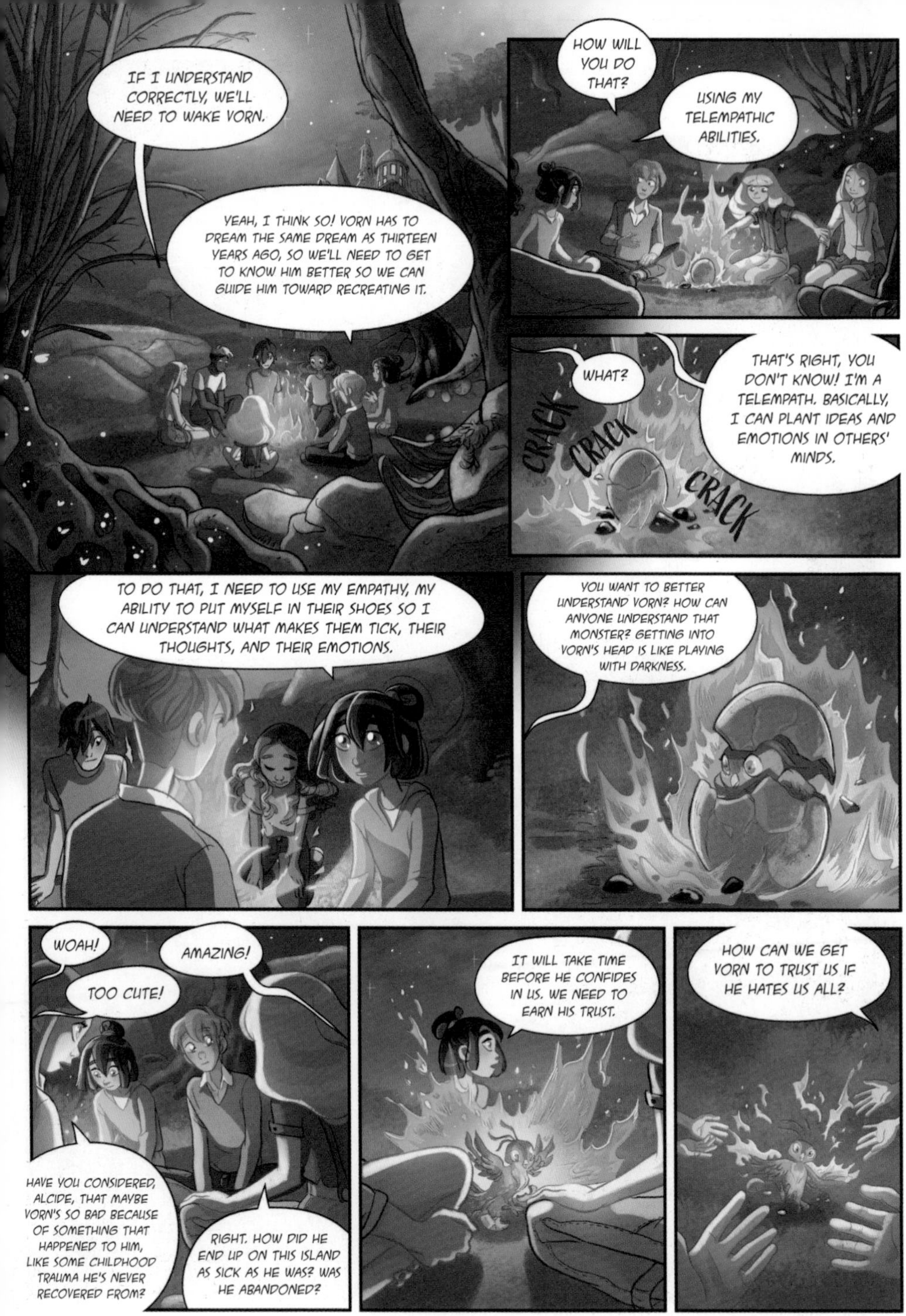
IF I UNDERSTAND CORRECTLY, WE'LL NEED TO WAKE VORN.
YEAH, I THINK SO! VORN HAS TO DREAM THE SAME DREAM AS THIRTEEN YEARS AGO, SO WE'LL NEED TO GET TO KNOW HIM BETTER SO WE CAN GUIDE HIM TOWARD RECREATING IT.
HOW WILL YOU DO THAT?
USING MY TELEMPATHIC ABILITIES.
WHAT?
THAT'S RIGHT, YOU DON'T KNOW! I'M A TELEMPATH. BASICALLY, I CAN PLANT IDEAS AND EMOTIONS IN OTHERS' MINDS.
CRACK
CRACK
CRACK
TO DO THAT, I NEED TO USE MY EMPATHY, MY ABILITY TO PUT MYSELF IN THEIR SHOES SO I CAN UNDERSTAND WHAT MAKES THEM TICK, THEIR THOUGHTS, AND THEIR EMOTIONS.
YOU WANT TO BETTER UNDERSTAND VORN? HOW CAN ANYONE UNDERSTAND THAT MONSTER? GETTING INTO VORN'S HEAD IS LIKE PLAYING WITH DARKNESS.
WOAH!
AMAZING!
TOO CUTE!
HAVE YOU CONSIDERED, ALCIDE, THAT MAYBE VORN'S SO BAD BECAUSE OF SOMETHING THAT HAPPENED TO HIM, LIKE SOME CHILDHOOD TRAUMA HE'S NEVER RECOVERED FROM?
RIGHT. HOW DID HE END UP ON THIS ISLAND AS SICK AS HE WAS? WAS HE ABANDONED?
IT WILL TAKE TIME BEFORE HE CONFIDES IN US. WE NEED TO EARN HIS TRUST.
HOW CAN WE GET VORN TO TRUST US IF HE HATES US ALL?

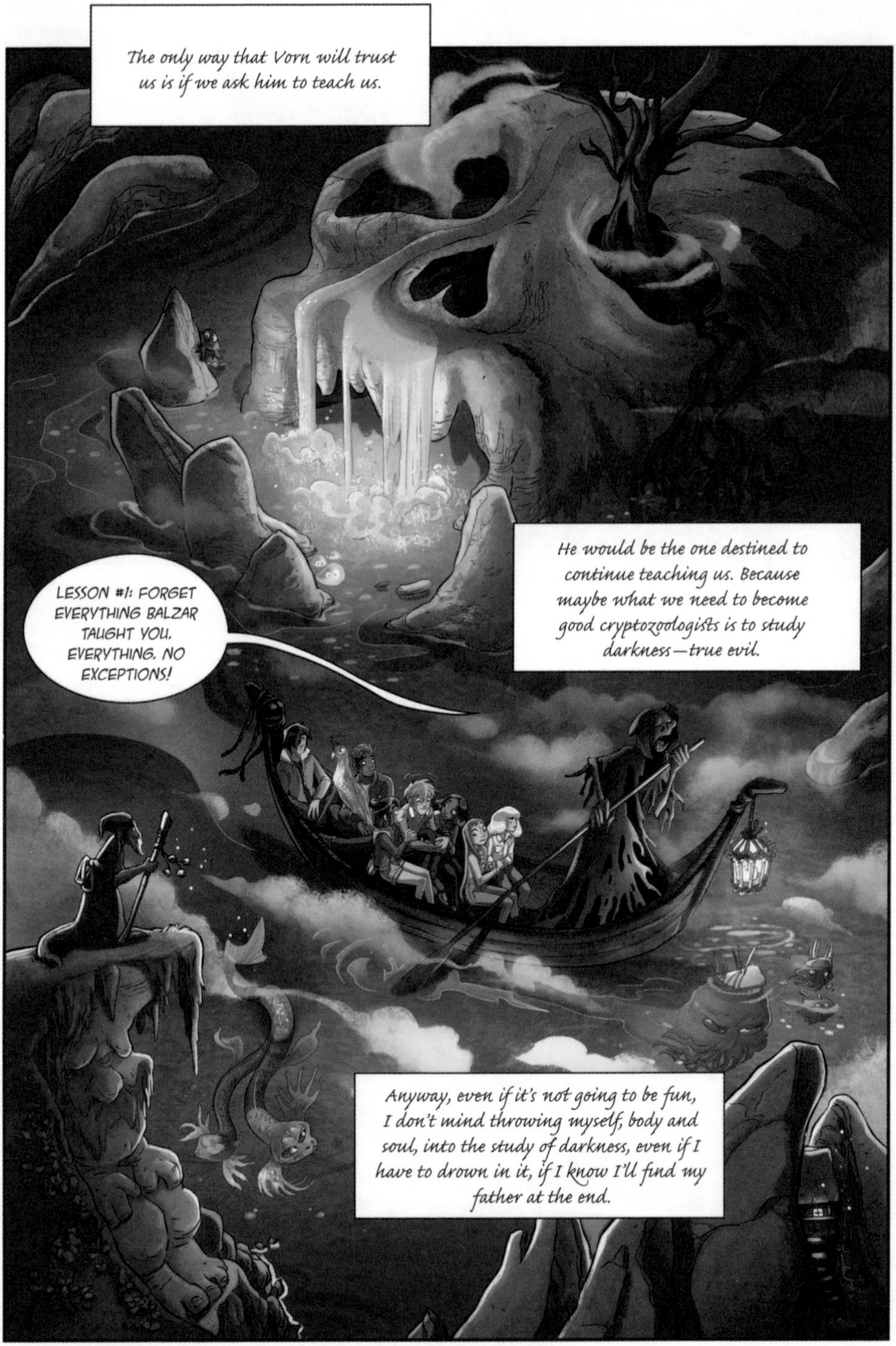
The only way that Vorn will trust us is if we ask him to teach us.
He would be the one destined to continue teaching us. Because maybe what we need to become good cryptozoologists is to study darkness—true evil.
LESSON #1: FORGET EVERYTHING BALZAR TAUGHT YOU. EVERYTHING. NO EXCEPTIONS!
Anyway, even if it's not going to be fun, I don't mind throwing myself, body and soul, into the study of darkness, even if I have to drown in it, if I know I'll find my father at the end.

THE END (FOR NOW!)

The Bestiary

Get to know some of the creatures on the Isle of Vorn!

The Owlet

Habitat:
Dark and swampy places

Special characteristics:
Its eyes can shoot
lightning bolts.

Life Span:
75 years

The Pegazeus

Habitat:
Clouds and fog

Special characteristics:
It controls the weather
and can start storms.

Life Span:
2,000 years

The Chrysanther

Habitat:
Forests and wooded
areas

Special characteristics:
It leaves no trace and
becomes invisible when
standing still.

Life Span:
150 years

The Rabbird

Habitat:
Meadows

Special characteristics:
Its legs are anchored
into the ground like a
plant for the first two
years of its life.

Life Span:
50 years

The Lumiole

Habitat:
Wherever there's fire

Special characteristics:
It travels along rainbows.

Life Span:
A few minutes

The Dracorn

Habitat:
Caves and grottoes

Special characteristics:
Each spring, it sheds its horns, which turn into dracorn trees.

Life Span:
999 years and 999 seconds

The Garganniihilator

Habitat:
Swampland

Special characteristics:
When it cries, everything in the water around it dissolves.

Life Span:
350 years

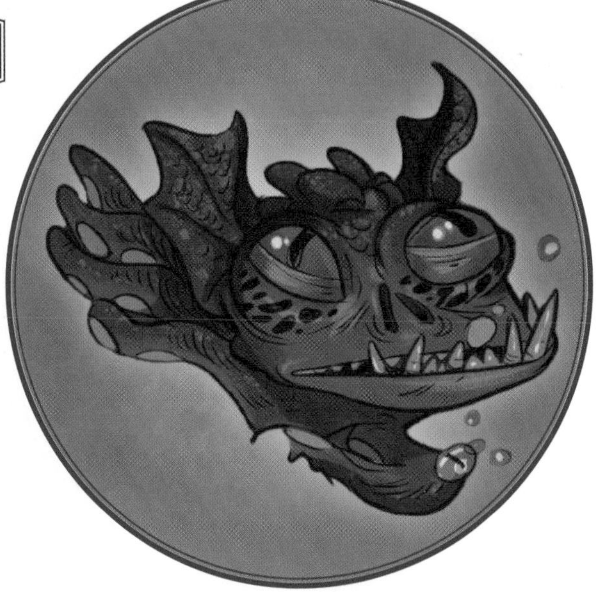

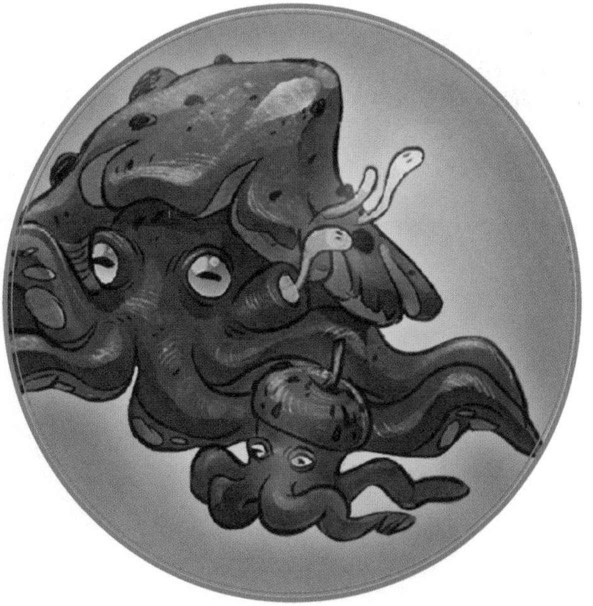

The Mudbeast

Habitat:
Anywhere there's mud

Special characteristics:
It announces the death of another creature with a scream.

Life Span:
Unknown

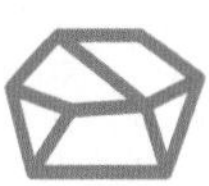

The Lullabis

Habitat:
Anywhere

Special characteristics:
It has the power to grant wishes.

Life Span:
3 years

The Manta-Nymph

Habitat:
Underground lakes

Special characteristics:
It hibernates during the summer and only comes out when it's really cold.

Life Span:
100 years

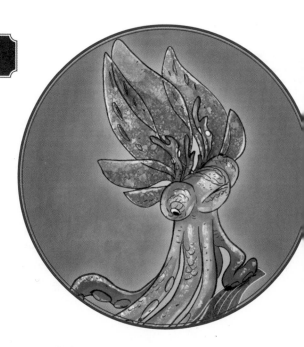